Praise for *A House Between E*

"Compulsively readable . . . *A House Between the Earth and the Moon* is a thought-provoking and absorbing read. By deftly combining the subjects of big tech and climate change, Scherm has created a world that fully embodies the anxiety and indignity of our times."

—Sandra Newman, *The New York Times Book Review*

"Riveting . . . Rebecca Scherm's *A House Between Earth and the Moon* grapples with a gaggle of red-hot current issues: income inequality, surveillance, capitalist overreach, AI, cyberbullying, gun control. She packs them all into the powerful rocket engine of climate disaster—the biggest, baddest issue of all—and launches the whole shebang into space. It's a rocking ride. The novel is propulsive, captivating, touching, funny—and utterly terrifying."   —L.A. Taggart, *San Francisco Chronicle*

"Part ensemble family drama, part coming-of-age story, part social novel, part cli-fi, [*A House Between Earth and the Moon* is] original and affecting not despite its overstuffed mélange of big ideas but because of how deftly Scherm weaves them together. . . . [The novel] primarily takes place in space, but it succeeds because of how richly Scherm depicts her characters' interior lives. This is the kind of book that practically begs for a sequel, one that dangles some tantalizingly loose ends. This is a house with more rooms to explore."   —Kate Knibbs, *Wired*

"Rebecca Scherm's *A House Between Earth and the Moon* returns us to the cautionary mode of futuristic fiction, taking place largely in a billionaire-funded space station called Parallaxis. On Earth, global warming has brought about hurricanes, drought, food shortages, stink bug infestations, and deadly heat waves. A tech juggernaut called Sensus has exploited the insecurity, manufacturing phone chips that are implanted beneath the skin and can, of course, capture endless amounts of personal data. Sensus is the mover behind Parallaxis, into which they have sent a team of scientists who are tasked with both constructing living quarters and perfecting their research innovations to provide food, water, and clean air. . . .

I like the point that luxury space residences, portrayed in films in spotless modular fashion, will more likely be depressing and unhygienic cubes."

—Sam Sacks, *The Wall Street Journal*

"This book had me sleepless and wild-eyed, obsessing over how I would live if I, like the characters in Scherm's novel, lived on a climate change-ravaged Earth, watching billionaires flee to their own private oasis in outer space. . . . Scherm's book will embed in your brain like a futuristic smartphone, in part because she wisely sets it just a couple of years in the future. Her characters may have technology we don't, but they share our collective sense of denial about the ramifications of climate devastation, and they share our hope." —Jenny Singer, *Glamour*

"Rebecca Scherm is a novelist gifted with both a visionary sense of invention and an unrelenting attention to fine-grained details. . . . Compellingly plotted and thoughtfully made, her novel speaks to what constrains each of us, as inhabitants and inheritors of this fraught world, as parents and caretakers, as people caught between good intentions and bad options. How we might move beyond those limits is the essential question at the heart of this eerie, deeply affecting book."

—*Los Angeles Review of Books*

"This dystopian novel will carry you far away, no matter where you are."

—*Good Housekeeping*

"Part sci-fi, part dreamy drama, *The House Between Earth and the Moon* follows the residents of Parallaxis (a luxury space station developed by tech giant Sensus) as they try to build a home for billionaires to escape Earth's increasing inhospitality. Meanwhile, the people they leave back home—particularly the family of Alex, a researcher seeking to create a carbon-guzzling algae—are struggling with both their present and futures."

—*Marie Claire*

"[*A House Between Earth and the Moon*] repeatedly engages with competing ideas about the most effective way to make the world a better place. . . . Scherm's characters seem unsatisfied with the ways they themselves answer such questions, an interpretive ambiguity that is one of the book's strengths. . . . *A House Between Earth and the Moon* does not offer prescriptive answers to the various problems it identifies, leaving the reader room to consider their own views. In doing so, the reader may learn something about themselves. In the end, what more can one ask of a book?"   —Eric P. S. Baumer, *Science Magazine*

"A surprisingly timely work of science fiction, Rebecca Scherm's *A House Between Earth and the Moon* follows Alex, a climate scientist, as he leaves the burning Earth behind for Parallaxis—a luxury space station owned by a tech titan, who has agreed to bankroll his latest research. Moving between Alex, his teen daughter living back on Earth, and the psychologist tasked with observing Alex and the other Parallaxis Pioneers, Scherm's novel explores humanity's fraught relationship with technology and innovation."   —*Bustle*

"Inventive and thrilling, *A House Between Earth and the Moon* dives into the near-future climate apocalypse with eerie prescience, startling humor, and, somehow, hope. I couldn't put it down."

—Brit Bennett, #1 *New York Times* bestselling
author of *The Vanishing Half*

"Rebecca Scherm is a treasure of a novelist: searching, inventive, her scope both everyday and expansive, her work marked by a tender but merciless psychological acuity. In *A House Between Earth and the Moon*, she has the near future—or the present—of perpetual emergency firmly within her grasp. It's a thrill to read this novel, which punctures, urgently and humanely, the technocrat fantasy that space might save us; it brilliantly vivifies the terrors of love and surveillance and ambition, the dream and impossibility of escape."

—Jia Tolentino, *New York Times* bestselling
author of *Trick Mirror*

"If *A House Between Earth and the Moon* wants us to ask what makes a house into a home, it wants us to know that family is the answer. . . . What *A House Between Earth and the Moon* suggests is that there is no solution but some kind of strange mix of hope and resignation, a wry kind of wonder."   —Bekah Waalkes, *Ploughshares*

"*A House Between Earth and the Moon* is a compelling, urgent book. I couldn't put it down. Rebecca Scherm brilliantly, and with such heart and tenderness, imagines a frightening future for our planet and our flawed, complicated species; and the worlds she imagines are so vivid, and feel so real I wondered if she owns a crystal ball. I loved these characters and their struggles and desires, and I rooted for them, and worried about them, and I can't stop thinking about them. This is a remarkable novel." —Edan Lepucki, *New York Times* bestselling author of *California*

"If you read just one novel about future billionaires funding scientists to try to save a select few from global warming by making it possible to live in outer space, definitely let it be *A House Between Earth and the Moon*."
—*Glamour*

"I loved *A House Between Earth and the Moon*—a smart, propulsive, sharply observed psychological novel set in a convincingly detailed near future, as well as an insightful examination of how rapid advances in communication technology can inadvertently render us indecipherable to each other." —Dexter Palmer, author of *Version Control*

"Addictive . . . Fast-paced . . . Scherm's character-driven science fiction story centers on individuals working against the clock to find a solution to climate change. . . . Scherm beautifully captures emotion in her writing as she shows how important connection is to our shared humanity."
—*Booklist*

"A high-concept domestic novel that merges science fiction and eco-fiction tropes . . . Scherm [gives] the climate change novel a wider yet still realistic scope and . . . nuanced characters in Alex and Mary Agnes, who are both eager to do the right thing but are undone by humanity, its fickle nature, and its allegedly liberating but often self-imprisoning technologies."
—*Kirkus Reviews*

PENGUIN BOOKS

A HOUSE BETWEEN EARTH
AND THE MOON

Rebecca Scherm is the author of *Unbecoming*. She lives in California with her family.

Penguin Reading Group Discussion Guide available
online at penguinrandomhouse.com

ALSO BY REBECCA SCHERM

Unbecoming

A House
Between
Earth
and
the
Moon

Rebecca Scherm

PENGUIN BOOKS

PENGUIN BOOKS
An imprint of Penguin Random House LLC
penguinrandomhouse.com

First published in the United States of America by Viking,
an imprint of Penguin Random House LLC, 2022
Published in Penguin Books 2023

ISBN 9781101980125 (paperback)

THE LIBRARY OF CONGRESS HAS CATALOGED THE HARDCOVER EDITION AS FOLLOWS:
Names: Scherm, Rebecca, author.
Title: A house between Earth and the moon : a novel / Rebecca Scherm.
Description: New York City : Viking, [2022]
Identifiers: LCCN 2021032894 (print) | LCCN 2021032895 (ebook) |
ISBN 9781101980101 (hardcover) | ISBN 9781101980118 (ebook)
Classification: LCC PS3619.C3496 H68 2022 (print) | LCC PS3619.C3496 (ebook) |
DDC 813/.6—dc23
LC record available at https://lccn.loc.gov/2021032894
LC ebook record available at https://lccn.loc.gov/2021032895

Printed in the United States of America
1st Printing

BOOK DESIGN BY LUCIA BERNARD

For the Comet and the Bear

Lift Off

1.

Alex had been in space for only six days when Carl Bouchet, who was a real astronaut, told him to put on his suit and go outside.

To "go outside" the station was a procedure that Alex had practiced just twice during his summer of training, and that had been in a zero-gravity simulation chamber. Not the same at all. Carl had assured him then that this was emergency training, to be used only in the unlikely event that he needed their assistance. Maybe the others had been disappointed to hear that, but Alex had taken a deep, quiet breath of relief. He hadn't minded Carl's arrogance, in this context. It made him feel safe.

"Me?" he asked Carl now. "What about Irma? Malik? They're probably more—"

"They're coming, too. Battery refresh." Carl turned away, and when Alex hesitated, Carl turned back, right hand on his belt, where he wore two spools of retractable cording with clips at the end. He started to pull out a line and offered the end to Alex.

"You want a tow?" he asked.

"No, no," Alex said, and he pushed off the wall behind him to follow, pulling up Carl's training sessions in his phone's archive: *training, Ground, space walk, "unlikely event."* He was certain he remembered nothing. When he found it, he sped up the footage to 4x with captions. Two Carls, now: Carl-of-the-past instructed him, the footage like stained glass over the Carl who floated in front of him. That Carl slid open the door to the suit room. He turned around just as Alex shook his head to stop the video.

"You'll be fine," Carl said.

Inside, their pale, pearly space suits were lined up along the wall. Malik and Irma were already getting dressed, and when they looked up to greet Alex, they did not look afraid, and they did not look like they were reviewing training footage at 4x.

"It's *happening*," Irma sang.

Alex laughed uncertainly, the only way he laughed lately, and floated toward his own suit. On the wall next to it were three numbered packets of underlayers. Malik and Irma were into their second layers already, full-body leotards that covered them from the tips of their fingers and toes up to the tops of their necks. Alex pushed his limbs into the tight tubes and tried to catch up.

"Don't rush it," Carl reminded him. "That only makes it harder."

A space walk on day six was surely rushing it.

When all four of them were in their complete underlayers, they carefully opened the seals that made their three-piece space suits into one body. Now each suit was a boot-pant piece, a torso-to-glove piece, and a helmet. "Remember," Carl said. "The suit stays put, and you move into it. Legs first."

Alex pulled himself up along the ridged wall until he was just above his target, the open waist of his pants. He slid his legs inside, and the pants crunched down with his knees. Carl had to come pull them up for him. But when it was time to put on his top half, Alex had no trouble at all. Malik struggled with his seals, and Irma got her gloves twisted, but Alex slid into his floating empty astronaut body with ease.

He was nine-tenths astronaut now. The last tenth required opening the hatch.

WHAT WAS ALEX DOING UP HERE, if he was not a real astronaut? For the last twenty years, Alex Welch-Peters had been manipulating algae in hopes of creating a new species that captured more carbon dioxide than naturally occurring species did, resulting—if he cracked it—in less CO_2 and more oxygen in the atmosphere: a slowing of global warming. Scaled up, it might begin to reverse the damage of his own species. It was not a question of whether it could be done, because Alex had done it—once, a little less than a year ago. Tray 182. Alex believed with all his brain that he could replicate that result here, and he believed with all his heart that he must, but that was a little different.

Alex had been offered three years of support and a completely controlled environment to create a means for carbon capture on this private space station. The owners of Parallaxis I wanted frontier scientists, unconstrained by the pressures of home, to show off to their billionaire clientele, and those billionaires would need air to breathe. Alex had been a lousy husband and father for the last several years while he tried and failed to save the world, and he had lost his marriage because of it. The offer had come at the right time. If he succeeded here, his children could carry with them the knowledge that their father's absence had not been in vain. That his work was for them, and that it had been worth it.

EXCEPT FOR HIS HELMET, which, tethered to his neckline, floated at his shoulders like a second head, Alex was fully suited now. While Carl slipped easily into his own suit, Alex, Malik, and Irma looked one another over, experimenting with their new exoskeletons. It was helpful to think of the space suit that way: *not* a costume but a protective shell, evolved ideally for his survival.

"Nervous?" Irma asked him. Her dark cloud of curls floated around her face like cotton candy. She tried to look sympathetic, but her cheeks looked ready to pop.

"A bit," said Alex.

"Ginger chew?"

He nodded and, with some difficulty, took the little lump from her outstretched glove, where it slipped right through his fingers and he had to catch it in the air like a fat, slow fly. In his mouth the ginger chew was squishy, spicy, and familiar. Meg had gone through a dozen a day when she was pregnant with Shane. He didn't think he'd had one since.

"Finish up quick," said Carl.

Alex imagined suits for his family hitched to the wall—for Meg, for Mary Agnes, and a tiny one for Shane. His was the one that punctured the fantasy. No one was making space suits for six-year-olds.

Alex was one of eight newcomers to Parallaxis: three research scientists, including himself, a robotics engineer, two doctors, a 3D fabricator, and Carl the Astronaut. Irma Garcia, one of the other research scientists, called herself a space gardener. She would grow food so that they would not have to live on reconstituted mushes and go-gels alone. The other was Malik Cobb, who had created Parallaxis's water supply by designing mechanisms by which ice was mined from the atmosphere's noctilucent clouds. Alex did not exactly understand it. What he understood was that Irma and Malik were brilliant and proven. They knew that they belonged here.

Carl knocked on the inside of the doorframe for good luck and led them out of the suit room and up to the airlock. Alex's ginger chew was gone, but the spice was still hot in his throat, a little too much like fear.

"Hey, you all right?" Malik floated up next to him.

Alex swallowed. "I am all right, yes, but also, I think some nervousness is a pretty rational, warranted response to an unexpected space walk?"

"Yeah, for sure," said Malik. "But you look—"

"I'm fine," said Alex.

"We all had training, the exact same training," he said. "It's the same motions, just different scenery."

Alex turned to see if Malik really believed this.

Malik coughed. "What I'm saying is, since you're no better or worse prepared than I am, all this sweat on your face is stressing me out."

"The suit is hot," Alex said.

"The suit *is* hot," said Malik. "We'll go with that."

PARALLAXIS I, 220 miles from Earth, was shaped like a ring, or a tire. In a few months, it would begin to rotate around a central axis, as a wheel does. Like a Tilt-A-Whirl, this spinning would draw everything and everyone floating in the ring outward until they were flat against the outermost wall. Not stuck, though—once they had their strength back, they would be able to stand, walk, set down a cup of coffee and have it stay put. They would be able to walk all the way around the ring and end up right back where they started. Parallaxis I was a big station by historical standards and small by fantasy ones: to walk a lap would be like walking around four city blocks in Chicago or Melbourne or the perimeter of four Wrigley Fields that shared the same home plate. There would be a gracious central promenade with ambient lighting that changed to evoke the hour of the day, and dozens of precisely designed pods—labs, homes, closed storage, staff areas, and exquisite recreational spaces—on either side of it, a few entered by intimate corridors that would function like private driveways. These would be for the billionaires who would start moving in later this year, once Alex and his colleagues had built all of this.

For now, the ring was mostly empty, except for the simulated Sky and the slapdash barracks that housed Alex and his colleagues: four walls zip-tied together and seven cots mounted upon them, with seven fleece sleeping bags and stretchy straps to keep them tucked in. Not comfortable by any stretch, but they would rather sleep together in their barracks than in the Helper station, which was tiny, old, and smelly. Docked to the inside of the ring, the Helper was a kind of baby station inhabited for the last eight years by the rotating cast of astronauts and former marines who had built Parallaxis I. The only remaining inhabitant of the Helper was Josef Mozgov, their captain. He had been up for all eight years.

Alex hadn't seen Mozgov since their first day. When their shuttle had docked to the Helper, it had been Mozgov who opened the airlock for the seven frightened newcomers, all gray-faced with nausea.

"Welcome," he'd said.

His remaining crew, two exhausted astronauts trying to make it just one more day before they were sent back home to Earth, had released them from their confinement in the shuttle. The newcomers had been instructed to hold hands, and in this fashion they were pulled slowly through the airlock into the packed and grimy Helper, through the second airlock, and finally into the cavernous donut that was Parallaxis I. The crew had let go of their charges' hands and tried to demonstrate that it was safe to move around. They'd waved their arms and shaken their hair, which floated off their heads in greasy ropes, like seaweed. One had managed enough enthusiasm for a slow flip. They would be gone the next day.

The newcomers floated together like a school of fish. Alex saw no doors, no floor, only the expanse of moonlit night sky that stretched out right in front of them, threatening to pull him out into it.

"The Sky is a screen, just a screen," Mozgov said.

Right. He knew that.

"It will help if you orient yourselves this way," Mozgov said. He rotated himself ninety degrees so that the night sky was overhead, and raised his index finger. "That's 'up.'"

The floating huddle broke up. Alex wiggled around to get the Sky overhead, where he didn't have to look right at it. Its depth and darkness looked too real. How could you face the deep night sky without your feet on any ground?

"They could have set it to morning," Malik whispered to him. "Might have been more welcoming."

Mozgov and his crew unfurled a long cord and had the newcomers hold on to it in a line, like preschoolers on a field trip, and led them around the ring on a tour of their new home. Alex was in the middle of the pack, behind Macy Slivens, the doctor, who twitched her head from side to side like a watchful bird, and Malik, whose quiet sighs were unsettling at best.

The station was not nearly as complete as they had been told. To Alex, it appeared that just enough had been done so that they wouldn't need their space suits inside, and nothing more. Certainly no luxury apartments or viewing lounges. He hoped they'd double-checked all the joints so that no one would be sucked out through a hole if a piece of wall fell off. The heating and electrical systems were working, but that was about it.

Mozgov pulled open a panel to reveal the mechanicals running beneath the ground, or what would be "beneath" and "the ground," someday. He showed them the lots for the client homes, not yet built, and their own lab pods and home pods: all blank space.

"Raw possibility," said Irma, her voice light, almost bouncing. She was first among them to master the backflip.

"LINE UP," Carl told them now. "Tether together."

He and Irma would be first and last, and they would clip to the exterior of the station. They would be the ones refreshing the batteries, with Malik and Alex between them in supporting roles. Mozgov would supervise from Control in the Helper. "The people before us did this repair without a hitch," Carl said. He said nearly everything as though he'd told them already and didn't trust them to remember, which Alex appreciated, though he could tell Malik did not. "We expect no problems."

They entered the airlock, and the door to the station slid shut. "Ready?"

Helmets, down. Seals checked, double-checked, triple-checked. One, two, three, four human beings, clipped into formation, ready to face the dark unknown.

"Ready?" Carl asked.

"Cobb ready."

"Garcia ready."

"Welch-Peters ready."

"All ready," said Carl.

The hatch slid open, and outside, there was nothing.

THE EDGELESS DARKNESS, the thinness of it—it didn't matter that Alex had already seen it through glass. The darkness filled his eyes first and drew the breath right out of him. And then, looming behind him was Earth, huge and round and real. White streaks wrapped the blue and green marble like cotton, protecting it. The sight was hard to reconcile with the ground he lived on—had lived on, until a week ago. In his country alone, California was on fire nine months a year, half of Texas was flooded with mud, and the hurricanes that turned coastal towns into mulch no longer kept to any calendar, but from up here, you would think the whole planet lived in verdant spring bloom.

Then he noticed the silence, one he had never heard before. At home silence meant that he had erected a thick barrier between his brain and the ceaseless noise around it. This silence was the opposite: empty. He could not hear the bodies moving next to his. He watched Carl pulling himself along the gray exterior of the station, hand over hand toward the solar panels, and his mind expected bumps, crunches, and squeaks, but he didn't hear anything at all.

"Alex." Carl's voice was as clear and close as if they were still inside together. "Do you have the hiccups?"

"Yeah, I do," said Alex. "Is that okay?"

"They won't kill you."

Alex faced the solar array, a grid of blessedly familiar rectangles and flat surfaces. If he looked down, up, or sideways, it was there: space. He looked at Irma, half dreading her jubilance, because if she wasn't at least a little scared now? He knew she could be reckless—all her stories were adrenaline safaris. But Irma was focused on the battery compartment before her, her gloved fingers slowly working through the latches. She did not ask him for support.

Alex raised his eyes past the solar panels, blinking at the stars and the light they seemed to smear around them, at the giant Earth again. He was staring straight at the Great Lakes, tracing southward from Lake Michigan, and while Michigan was, as usual, obscured by clouds, he knew he was looking at home. He didn't know what his children and Meg were doing right now, but he wished they could know that he was outside, right this minute, looking for them.

His hiccups were gone.

Twenty-seven minutes later, they finished, and moved tidily back toward the airlock. When they were back inside, Alex's legs were jelly trembling in the air. He was not the only one overcome—Irma was flushed behind her freckles, and Malik was smiling insanely with only half his mouth.

Even Carl broke, just a little. "Well done," he said. "It's good to know you can do that, isn't it?"

THOUGH THE SON SISTERS had hired him to make clean air for Parallaxis, helping the wealthy to self-isolate in outer space had never been Alex's ambition. He wanted to save his planet, and with each disastrous year, his work became more necessary and less possible. So often, he had caught himself—in the mirror, say, brushing his teeth, foamy around the mouth—and shrunk from the sight of his meager human-scale abilities in the face of screaming catastrophe. What helped was to remind himself that thousands of scientists in every field were working against the same fate, and at least thirteen other biochemistry labs were working on it the same way he was, through algae-aided carbon capture. Only one of them had to crack it, and they'd all gotten close, at times. It didn't matter who solved it, but they all had to keep trying.

"Are you *sure* it doesn't matter who solves it?" Meg had asked him with withering calmness shortly before the split.

"Are you serious?" Alex answered her. "I would love someone else to solve it. Anyone."

"I think you're about sixty percent serious, when you say that," said Meg. She paused for a long moment, and Alex was so angry he wanted to laugh. "But the rest wants it to be you, your lab."

He didn't laugh. This conversation had occurred on Christmas Eve, while Alex was putting on his snow boots to head back into the lab. He had done family dinner, the ritual pajama exchange, he had *been there*. Meg said it didn't count, not at all, if he was working on his phone the whole time. Maybe they couldn't see what he was doing but they could tell— Meg, Mary Agnes, even Shane could tell—that he didn't hear anything they were saying. Shane, Meg had pointed out, never said only "Dad." Instead, he said "Dad—Dad?" as if Alex's presence were always a question.

Alex stood in his muddy snow boots at the edge of the kitchen door. If she weren't starting an argument right now he'd be out the door, sooner into the lab and sooner home again. Instead, she started peeling an orange, no hurry at all.

"It would be easier," she said, "if you just admitted you wanted to be the hero." She dropped a section of peel and started on another without looking at him. "I mean, I can admit that. In my work, I wanted to be the hero to those girls. I wanted to be the one to help."

She had given up her own career as an aid for pregnant teenagers when Shane was born, in part so Alex could continue his. Now she was a remote-floater high school guidance counselor for their well-funded district, which meant she mostly wrote college recommendations. She hated it, but somebody had to be in charge at home, and Alex had always made sure it wasn't him.

"I'll be back by morning. They won't know I was gone." But as soon as he'd shut the back door, Mary Agnes messaged him from her bedroom. *Can I help tonight? Or just come and watch?*

He missed the old days, before Sensus phones, when you could say you'd left your phone at home or that you hadn't felt the buzz through your heavy coat. There was no forgetting your phone anymore, and with each message scrolling right into your vision, there was no way to pretend you'd missed it.

Not tonight. Cover for me, if your brother wakes up?

Will do, she said. When he pulled the car out of the driveway, headlights off, she waved at him from her bedroom window.

ALEX'S PLAN WAS THIS: Human beings, the invasive species to end them all, would never change their ways, not with money, power, and convenience at stake. A new invasive species, however, might begin to counteract the ill effects of humanity. Green algae had been around for at least one billion years to *Homo sapiens'* piddly two hundred thousand, and it was algae, Alex was certain, that would save them from themselves. Algae cleaned the air, cleaned waste, fed plants and animals. It could provide a thermal control in waters with rising temperatures. What the planet needed was superalgae, super-efficient and super-hardy cyanobacteria with dramatically increased carbon capture properties, that could grow in the open ocean or anywhere else it was needed, gobbling up carbon and scoffing at the temperature swings that slowed its nonmodified cousins.

Alex had been working on this problem since his second year of graduate school, and he'd gotten close when he was twenty-six, a postdoc glowing with promise and rich in grants. But he didn't crack it then, and by the time Shane was born, his funding streams were mere trickles—not because his project had lost its luster, but because he had. He was thirty-four then, and the amount of CO_2 in the Earth's atmosphere had hit 450 parts per million ahead of even dire predictions, and he had brought two more humans into this world, back when he had been slightly more optimistic about the future of algae-aided carbon capture.

More like delusional, he'd thought when Shane was born early, small, and allergic, it seemed, to everything outside, like someone who should have been born hundreds of years in the future, when people would be smaller and didn't go outside anymore.

Alex had been, for several years, in a dark place. His dread of the planet's death was perhaps more visceral than that of most people outside his field, not only because he had made climate catastrophe his life's work but because funding that work required that he often describe, in vivid detail, the utter nightmare that life on Earth would soon become for all but the very, very rich, if humankind did not find a way to reverse some of the damage done. That was how he got all those grants, by first detailing his data-driven nightmares and then by revealing his solution, always just around the corner. But by his fortieth birthday, his doomsday ravings were all he really had to show for himself. He imagined quitting with a final paper. Abstract: Editing genes to increase the efficiency of marine plants has proved intractable; ergo, we are fucked.

"Maybe you can join your lab to another, do something more collaborative," Meg had said on Christmas night. They'd paused the argument for the day, and now that they were alone again, Meg picked it up. She sat on the edge of their bed, braiding her hair. "We'll move! It's not that I want you to give up."

She sounded more optimistic than she had the night before, he thought, less accusing.

"I would never ask that of you," she said quietly. "But something has to change."

"I have a new grad student coming on this spring," he said.

Meg pressed her lips together and dropped the heavy braid unfastened on her shoulder.

"That's not what I meant," she said. "You just pass right through us. I've gotten used to it, and that might be the worst part." She balled her hands into fists at her sides. "The kids are used to it, you floating in and out when it's convenient—oh, don't get all puffed up, you know what I mean. You've trained them not to expect you." She opened her hands and stretched out her fingers, and Alex found himself watching them so he wouldn't have to see her face for whatever she said next.

"Something has to change—now," she said. Meaning that if he didn't change anything, she would make a change without him. She'd gotten used to making decisions alone. They separated two months later.

HE HAD MADE *one* change, just not the one that mattered to Meg. Alex had spliced cyanobacteria DNA with that of many different plants over the years, but hydrilla, an Asian water weed, was new to his lab. Hydrilla had been popular in American aquariums in the 1950s and, since its disposal into the freshwater supply, had wrecked Florida's freshwater. Now it had adapted itself to saltwater environments as well. Hydrilla could grow in the deepest, darkest waters where little else could, each spiky tendril advancing an inch each day.

Hydrilla was a monster. Hydrilla was the answer. Alex's algae-hydrilla hybrid flourished in Tray 182 with a 130 percent increase in photosynthetic efficiency compared to his nonmodified algae.

None of the others. Just 182.

Meg had already left him. She was still the first person he called.

One of the undergrads who worked in his lab blabbed to a friend, and before Alex understood how Tray 182 had happened, the media descended. It did not matter how Alex hedged and qualified, Tray 182 was declared a hero and shared over forty million times, with worse and worse information attached to it. *One cool trick to save the planet.* Quickly, the insistence of intrusive strangers that he had achieved the impossible mingled with a niggling doubt: he did not know *why* Tray 182 had succeeded where trays 1–181 and 183–200 had failed, and how could he concentrate with all these people shrieking at him with their premature euphoria?

He was in the lab at all hours, terrified that the environmental chamber would crash, that something would happen to Tray 182 before he knew its secrets. Twice a day he did cell counts, checked chlorophyll-a fluorescence, and measured the cells' health with PAM fluorometry. He didn't understand why Tray 182 was working, but at least he knew it was happy and healthy. But nine days into Tray 182's life, the PAM fluorometry measurement plunged from its solid 0.8 to 0.6, which meant that the cells were stressed.

By the next morning, the measurement was 0.5 and the vibrant green culture had turned a sickly yellow. He transferred samples from Tray 182 into six other cuvettes, trying to save them, and the measurements of all plummeted to 0.3 and 0.2. Two days later, Tray 182 was bleached white and dead. He didn't know why it had come into the world, and now he didn't know why it had gone.

Over the next two months, his lab failed to replicate Tray 182, and Alex wanted to crawl into a hole in the ground. The best thing he did during those months was spend more time with his children, who saw his weaknesses and somehow loved him anyway.

THEN RACHEL SON HAD CALLED. Would Alex like to pursue his research on Parallaxis I, the first private luxury space station intended for long-term habitation? He would advance his superalgae in space, where it would clean the air that the space colonists breathed.

"Algae can do even more than that," Alex said. "It will revitalize your air, it will provide biomass for crops, it can remediate waste streams— both fecal and urine—and provide thermal control. I don't know if you're planning on raising fish or mollusks, but algae can be their foodstock—"

"Exactly," she said. "We want you and your superalgae."

He would have a controlled environment complete with simulated gravity, unlimited research funds, and *no media* whatsoever. His lab would not get shut down without warning every few weeks because of tornadoes, ice storms, heat waves, plague, or dried-up funding: stability. Five hundred thousand dollars a year with a three-year contract, comprehensive health insurance from signing for a period of ten years, to ensure care for any re-entry issues. All research, travel, and living expenses paid, obviously.

"And Sensus would own my research," Alex said.

"Parallaxis would own the rights to any *new* findings," she said. "But the university owns you now, right? And when you figure out how to save the world, we will have the reach to help you do it." She laughed in a friendly way. "We want to boast about our role in your success."

"Oh, wow," he'd finally said. "This is a lot."

He would have to think about it.

He had his family to consider. His children.

He had no training in astrophysics, engineering, anything remotely related to—

"Doesn't matter," Rachel had said. "You won't be expected to be an astronaut—or anyone but who you are. We *need* you with us." She had known just what he needed to hear.

AFTER THEY'D HUNG UP their suits, all Alex wanted to do was strap himself to his cot in their barracks and close his eyes, but Malik and Irma rushed to tell the others, following the sounds of crinkling plastic and cracking joints that bounced around the station. As they drew closer to the huddle, Alex heard Macy giving someone instructions, and he winced, anticipating her jealousy. She was a marathoner, and ex-military, without a wavering nerve in sight. Carl should have asked her to do a space walk, not him.

Macy didn't say that, not outright. She sucked down a go-gel. "Next time, I'm going," she said.

But what next time? There shouldn't be a next time. "Carl didn't need three of us to help him refresh two batteries," he said quietly, so that only Irma would hear. "He probably didn't need any of us."

"I guess he wanted us to know we could do it," Irma said.

"But why?" asked Alex. Macy was watching, listening now. "Our whole training, he told us what we can't do. And then six days up here, he shoves us out the door? Me?"

"Boot camp structure," Macy said. "You tell the new guys they can't do shit to make sure they pay attention, and then you give them a common enemy and show them what they can do, if they have to." She curled her lip. "It works."

"What enemy?" Alex asked. "I'm not military. If you tell me I can't do something, I believe you."

"You've been chasing superalgae for twenty years," Malik said. "So that better not be true."

Alex laughed only because he had to. He didn't have a lab yet, not even four walls and a tank. There was no reason to worry. He had time.

2.

As soon as the bell rang, Mr. Fonseca told them to pair up for rejoinders. Freshman year, Mary Agnes had done rejoinders with Ivy, but Ivy sat with Mercedes now, and the seats on either side of Mary Agnes were empty. She tried to look around for a partner inconspicuously, but it didn't matter, because everyone else was paired up already, with one group of three in the way back.

Mr. Fonseca pulled an empty chair to the other side of her desk, and it screeched against the linoleum so that if anyone hadn't yet noticed that Mary Agnes was left to partner with the teacher, they would now.

He set down his thermos. "Maria Agnese, cómo estás?" he began, and his face shield fogged all the way up to his eyes. He waved some fresher air up under it.

"Me quiero morir," she said.

He cocked his head, arched an eyebrow.

"Don't report me," she said, groaning. "I didn't mean it, I'm not at risk. Just a stupid day."

"Already?" he said. "In that case, you just want 'quiero morir,' you don't need the *me*."

"Quiero morir," she repeated.

"Perfecto," he said. "Have you heard from your dad?"

"He's been in training all summer," she said, wincing at the fine spray of spittle that had escaped her mouth onto her face shield. She tried to avoid the letter *s* or at least really concentrate on drying out her mouth first. If she'd been speaking Spanish, she would have said *verano* and this would not have happened.

"Wow," he said. "So crazy, right? I wonder if he could video into class, once he's up there? He has to be way too busy, though."

"Yeah," she said. "I think the algae is really the main thing."

"Your dad's saving the world." Mr. Fonseca smiled at her like he wanted to be joking but knew he wasn't pulling it off.

"Well, he hasn't done it *yet*," she said. "But he will."

A LOT OF PEOPLE had heard of Parallaxis, even if it wasn't that clear what exactly Parallaxis was. The Son sisters were building a space station (space palace?) with their Sensus money. There were two private space stations for rich tourists already, but this was the first station built just to live on. It was that nice. That was all Mary Agnes had known about it, until Rachel Son *herself* had called her dad at work.

Her dad.

Mary Agnes had always known that her dad was a genius, but now other people knew, too. The whole world knew. He'd been working on the algae her entire life, longer than that, and then Tray 182 happened out of nowhere. That it happened *after* the separation, after he had moved out of their family's house, meant that her mother was right about something: their family was a distraction that her father didn't need, not while he was trying to save the world.

He had left their house in February. He shouldn't have been the one to move out, she was sure, because the separation was definitely her mother's decision. Every controversial decision in their house was her mother's doing. Her dad just went along and didn't bother anybody.

The day he'd left for training, hours after he had hugged them goodbye, she was halfway down the stairs when a message bubbled across her dash.

Just realized I didn't set you up with more snails for the pea puffers

Mary Agnes shook her head to pause the show she'd been watching. No, he hadn't set her up with snails for the fish before he'd moved out; he hadn't needed to. She knew what to do.

Their teeth will be way overgrown now, said the next message. *You have to trim them or they'll starve*

Like she hadn't watched him trim the puffers' teeth, hadn't *helped* to do it—

It's a little yikes-y but you can handle it. You need to get clippers, a big bowl of clean water, and the clove oil

Stop, Mary Agnes sent back. Just like her mother said: he didn't hold on to anything about their life at home, it all slipped through his mind. Like it wasn't worth keeping. A disloyal thought. She kicked it away. *I've got a new colony of red ramshorns going. Teeth are tidy. Where are you now?*

In the helicopter, almost there. Training's going to be totally sealed, no contact. I miss you guys so much already.

She tried to think of something to say that would mean everything—

I love you more than you could ever know, he said.

You too, Dad, she said. *Do you know your launch date yet?*

The thinking cloud inflated and deflated a few rounds, and then it disappeared.

Well, have a good training, she said. *Say hi to your scum for me.*

No answer. His quarantine had begun, and he was gone.

MARY AGNES WAS walking to school the second week of her sophomore year when she saw Ivy come out her front door and freeze.

They had used to walk to school together. Mary Agnes raised her hand without meaning to, without wanting to, and waved. Ivy did the same, but then she went back inside like she'd forgotten something. Mary Agnes waited.

You're going to be late, her phone said. *Let's keep moving.*

Ivy was waiting for her to pass. Oh.

Mary Agnes went on, her face burning. She'd felt Ivy drifting away, pulling really, before school let out for the summer, as soon as Dani moved to Vancouver. Their small alliance of three had fallen apart, and then Ivy had decided to become cool. Over the summer she'd made a clean break. Mary Agnes didn't know how she'd done it, because Ivy had drawn a thick curtain between her old self and her new one, and when Mary Agnes watched her cavorting with Mercedes Mills, et cetera, Ivy was a totally different person. Online she acted both bored and embarrassed about everything, like *uhhh no*. At school, she'd started puffing out her top lip in a weird way when she smiled, and she didn't lift her voice when she asked questions, kept it totally flat. Didn't her new friends find that weird and suspicious? Mary Agnes was functionally friendless now, alone at lunch, working on her phone stuff and playing *Outlander* and *Quixotix* when she got frustrated and needed a break. There were a lot of people without IRL friends, she knew. It wasn't a big deal. It would have been easier if her dad were still around, though.

She didn't see Ivy until third-period Spanish, and she was careful not to look at her. At anyone.

Ellis Evans, who sat directly behind her, on the other side of Mercedes and Ivy, and on whom Mary Agnes had had a pointless crush since she was twelve, leaned forward in his seat and asked, "Did your dad leave yet?"

"What?" Mary Agnes said, sounding as startled as someone who had never before been spoken to.

"Did he go up yet? To Parallaxis?"

She turned around. His icy blue eyes were pinned right on her, and she squirmed. She had liked Ellis from a distance, from the side, or sitting near him, for so long that it was hard to look at him up close like this. "Oh, um, yeah," she said. "We watched the launch, but we haven't gotten to talk to him. They told us he made it up okay, but, like, the quarantine."

"It has to be totally blackout," he said, his knee bobbing. And then he switched to phone. *Did he get privatized?*

Oh yeah, she said, relieved that she didn't have to think about her voice, the way her mouth moved awkwardly around familiar words. *Z-level.* Not only did Z-level mean no scraping your data for sale, it meant no tracking of any kind. No shopping filters that hid competing goods or information that might scuttle the impending transaction. No personal ratings or encounter reviews following you around. No trading your social media keys just to check the weather.

Holy shit, said Ellis. *That's what I want to do, with my money.*

Get privatized?

Yeah, all the way. Someday. I've been at J for a year and really want to be making enough for L or M by next summer.

You're at J now? Isn't that, like, a hundred grand a year?

Give or take.

Ellis Evans had made all his money by unhitching Shepherd and the other parental-spying extensions from everybody's phones. He'd done half their high school, it seemed like, but he probably did tons of phones remotely.

What are you charging now? she asked him. She already knew the answer. Mr. Fonseca was going to start talking any moment and break the spell (break the spell? What was she, five?) and—

"Buenos días!" shouted Mr. Fonseca.

Three hundred a pop, Ellis said. *I haven't done yours, have I?*

Mary Agnes had turned forward to face Mr. Fonseca, her eyes wide in fake attention, the back of her neck glowing warm and pink in anticipation of the answer she was about to give to Ellis.

I did my own, she told him.

Nice, he said, and Mary Agnes grinned, she couldn't help it. Mr. Fonseca smiled back at her with cheerful sarcasm.

"En grupos de cuatro!" he said, clapping twice.

Mary Agnes's smile fell. Oh, how she hated this part. She heard the chairs scraping against the floor, the murmuring of other people so easily organizing themselves.

"Mary Agnes," Ellis said. When she turned around, he and Mercedes Mills were looking at her like, *Yes, obviously you are in our group, you sit right in front of us.* Ivy didn't look at her at all.

Their conversation was supposed to be about ordering lunch in a restaurant, but instead they talked about Mary Agnes's dad, in space. The Son sisters, had he met them? Had they been following his career for a long time, or did they find out about him with everybody else? How long would he be there? She hardly knew any of the answers. Was she going to go up, too?

Mary Agnes swallowed. "Sí, tal vez," she said. "Voy a ir."

"Ugh," said Mercedes. "That's wild, I can't stand it. Would you be the youngest person to go to space, ever?"

"No," said Ellis. "There was a thirteen-year-old who went on a trip with his parents."

"Yeah, for, like, a minute," Mercedes said. Mr. Fonseca passed behind them. "Por un momento," she said loudly.

Ivy was pointedly not asking any questions about Mary Agnes's dad, who was just Alex to her, as he had been for years. She was not talking to Mary Agnes at all, really, as though to speak even one unnecessary word to her would undo all her separation work.

You'd be the youngest to live in space, though, said Ellis, watching her.

"Rude!" said Mercedes. "Include us, please!"

Mary Agnes blushed, and Ivy saw it, Mary Agnes was sure she did, because she saw Ivy smile to herself. Ivy knew that Mary Agnes had had a crush on Ellis Evans practically forever, and Mary Agnes really wished she didn't know that anymore.

"You have to tell us about it," Ellis said, picking at a small white crease in his face shield. "I mean, you'll be in touch, right? Or, like, when you start your training prep, you have to tell us about it."

"It wouldn't be until the summer," Mary Agnes said. "If I get to go, I mean."

"I'm so jealous," said Ellis.

"Me, too," said Mercedes. "I want to leave Michigan and move to space." She chewed on the end of her pinky nail. "Mary Agnes is such a *mouthful*," she said. "We should call you Magnes."

"Magnes in space," said Ellis, and Magnes smiled.

"HELLO!" HER MOTHER SANG OUT, setting her net bags of groceries on the counter. They were the only people on the block who didn't get their groceries delivered. When her mother saw Mary Agnes slumped over the counter in a heap, her smile fell off. "What?" she asked. "What's wrong?"

"I want to go to space," Mary Agnes mumbled.

"Oh, that," said her mother. She took off her face shield and tossed it in the kitchen sink.

Her little brother trailed in after her, still in his bug suit. It was bright white, so anything clinging to the fabric could easily be seen, with a sheer oval over his face so he could see and talk.

Shane planted himself in front of their mother. "You forgot to unsnap me," he said.

"Sorry, honey." She pulled the snap at the top of the hidden zipper and followed him into the mudroom, where he emerged, unstung and unbitten, from the gear that protected him during the walk from the doors of his school to the car and from the car to the house. Shane was deathly allergic to beestings, which was common enough, but also many other insects, pollens, saps, and seeds, and, most problematically for where they lived, the secretions of stinkbugs, which were absolutely everywhere and always trying to get inside.

When her mother came back into the kitchen with more groceries, Mary Agnes was ready with her argument. She cleared her throat and spoke calmly, with composure and authority, just like her mother had taught her.

"I know that *you* don't want to live in space, and I know that you think it's not safe for Shane," she began. "But *I* could go, and when the family option opens, I want to." She climbed off the counter stool and began sorting out the dry goods, just how her mother liked. "I'll research homeschooling materials, to be vetted and approved by you, and preplan with a college counselor." She smiled and clasped her hands.

Her mother shook her head. How could she just shake her head like that, without taking even a minute to think about what Mary Agnes had said? "We're not going to live in space," her mother said. "*You're* not going to live in space."

Mary Agnes's mask of poise had fallen off. "Because you and Dad split up."

"No," her mother said with a gentle exasperation that drained all of Mary Agnes's remaining composure. "Because we don't know what it will do to your body, or your mind, and as much as they pretend they know everything and can predict every outcome, their predictions are self-interested ones."

"And it's not self-interested for you to keep me here, without my dad?"

That was a sharp one, probably too sharp, but Mary Agnes *tried* to say it as though this were a casual conversation between two reasonable people, as opposed to herself and her mother, a paranoid Luddite who would have been happier living off the grid like Uncle Anthony. "You could think of it like joint custody!" she said brightly. "All I'm asking for is joint custody."

Her mother gathered her mass of red hair up in a knot, the wavy gray streaks at her temples suddenly taut. She put her hands on her hips and looked down at the floor, breathing slowly.

"Okay," she said. "Listen. I do not think your dad should have done this, but he is an adult and he does what he wants." She did not look up at Mary Agnes. "When you are an adult, you can do what you want, even if it is unsafe, unwise, and subjects you to unknown and unending consequences. But until then, it's my job to keep you safe from harm, or as safe as I can in the fucked-up world we live in." Now it was her turn to offer the ironic smile.

"That's what this is really about," Mary Agnes grumbled. The Parallaxis project was owned by the Son sisters and paid for with Sensus billions, and there was no resentment that her mother could not trace back to Sensus phones and her hatred of them. "If you think the world is so fucked-up"—her mother couldn't get mad, she'd said it first—"why don't you just go OTG and live with Uncle Anthony? No phones, just house projects and yard projects, forever. And no Dad. You'd be so happy."

Shane came back into the kitchen then, clutching a packet of crackers.

"You know why," her mother said quietly.

"This probably isn't okay, is it?" Shane asked. "It's from Bernie's birthday, but I think it has seeds in it."

"Yeah, sorry, bub," her mother said, taking the crackers. "Not for us. How about some cheese and apples?"

Shane shrugged. He had never even been to visit Uncle Anthony's settlement. Too dangerous, even with the suit. Their cousins kept little cages of bugs as pets, *in the house.* They said her fish weren't that different, but her fish couldn't crawl themselves out while she cleaned the tank.

"I just miss him," Mary Agnes said.

"I do, too," her mother answered.

THAT NIGHT, curled in bed like a shrimp, Mary Agnes pulled her blankets up around her chin and watched the Parallaxis tour again. Her dad had sent her the video from the retreat at the Son sisters' compound in Ticaboo, Utah, where he had met the other scientists. The tour was the only part of the weekend he could send to her; everything else was private.

The video started in darkness, as dark as if you had your eyes closed.

"Our name comes from Greek astronomy: *parallelos* and *axis*, a pivot or axle in the earth or sky," said the voice. "It means 'alternation.' A simple word for another world."

Mary Agnes knew the words by heart, just as she knew Rachel Son's voice anywhere, even if she couldn't see her. Hers was the voice in her head, the voice in the phones: the most familiar voice in the world.

"We imagine Parallaxis as a pivot in the direction of humanity," Rachel Son said, "a chance to reject our crowded, noisy, well-trodden lives, and become a pioneer in the new world."

Stars begin to pierce the darkness, and a silvery ring turned softly in the distance. "Parallaxis is a modular city in the making," she said as three more rings docked to the first, one on top of another, with a gentle click. The stack of rings turned together. "There will be a Parallaxis II, and III, and IV, but you are the extraordinary first citizens of Parallaxis I. This place is yours to create."

The promise hung in the air as the first ring broke open to reveal the life inside. Built along the ring's outer rim was a little town, turning slowly. Tiny people walked along a path past the buildings clustered along the sides. The buildings were warm white and rounded, both concave and convex. From this distance they looked like teeth, if they went all the way around a mouth.

"Let's go inside," Rachel said.

The first stop on the tour was an airy lounge, warm and light. "The interior of Parallaxis is inspired by honeycombs, seashells, the lamination of a perfect croissant, and the Hourglass Nebula." The walls inside the lounge had the soft, baked color of balsa wood. They were deeply ribbed, and the thin lines of shadow seemed to ripple and breathe. Usually Mary Agnes was entranced by this part of the tour, the tightly organized beauty of the lounge's walls, the tessellating patterns on the floor. But this time, it all looked too pristine, and Mary Agnes felt a lump rising in her throat.

She tried to imagine her dad—the same one who wrote WASH ME in the algae inside of the puffer tank when they'd gone too long without cleaning it, who referred to the horrible people at her school as "the gnats," who had messy dust-colored hair and crumb-sprinkled clothes—living on a space station that looked like Parallaxis, and she could not do it, not without changing him, too. Her mother had kicked him out (and why call it anything else?) for the very qualities that Mary Agnes herself so loved and needed—his kind whatever-ness, his sloppy and distracted Dad-ness—and so he had gone somewhere he was wanted. His algae would make him a hero, she knew, but she feared that Parallaxis would do something else. That silvery ring of systematized living would iron out every wrinkle. What if he came back in three years totally different, and she didn't know him anymore? What if he didn't know her? What if he didn't *like* her anymore?

She rolled over in bed and stared at the glowing puffer tank on her dresser. They used to keep the tank in the living room, but he had helped her move it up to her room when he left.

It's getting late, and you're pretty wound up, said the voice of Rachel Son in her head. *You have a Spanish quiz tomorrow. Should we do a vocabulary review at seventy-five percent playback speed, as usual?*

"Dad?" she murmured. "Dad, are you there?" She knew he couldn't answer, that his old phone was a dead end. She hadn't spoken to him in three months. Now it was just her and the three tiny pea puffers who would all be dead before he got back. Three years. Forever, to a fish.

3.

Tess got her first Sensus phone, a second generation, in 2024, when she was seventeen. Her mother had taken a job at Stanford, and they'd just moved across the country. In Palo Alto, all the kids had Sensus phones. Back in St. Paul, only a few had—the rich kids, or the ones Tess had learned from her parents to call "rich kids." Her mother was a lefty economics professor and her father wrote TV shows for the internet. She thought they made more money than they let on because they so harshly judged others' extravagance, but they never lacked anything themselves. Tess's parents had phones already, but her father insisted, embarrassingly, that Tess's phone insertion be done by a pediatrician. He said he wanted someone to sue if it went wrong—there were stories, though they didn't know anyone who'd had a serious problem. Dr. Suresh instructed Tess to hold very still while she popped the phone into her ear, and then Tess felt the proboscis slide inside. Dr. Suresh told Tess not to stand or walk by herself for a full hour while she got used to it. "I haven't seen any physical problems from them yet," she assured Tess's father. "But, you know—insertion isn't the risky part. It's best to talk about it together, what she sees and how it affects her experience, your experience. And take them out sometimes, for a long weekend, to remember what the world looks like without a screen over it." But they never took them out.

Layered over Tess's vision was a screen, a kind of dashboard that curved around the perimeter. *Let's start with body language,* said a voice, at once familiar and yet unidentifiable. *Nod for yes and shake for no, flick up for more, slow nod to end.* She'd seen her classmates doing these gestures and hurried through the tutorial. *Let's practice. What do you want to know?*

Was it true that Mr. Georgiou had married a former student? Where did her scores put her in relation to this year's freshman class at Stanford? What did people say about her at her old school?

"Tess," her dad was saying. He waved his hand in front of her face. "Hello, Tess."

"Sorry, what, yes?"

"Don't forget to blink," Dr. Suresh said, and then, to her father: "Maybe get some eye drops, the gel kind. You look like you could use them, too."

At school the next day, the other kids immediately noticed the fresh tab in her ear, and then they paid attention to her, clustered around to trade insertion stories while all their phones grabbed on to Tess's. They treated her as if she were suddenly alive, as though before, she had been a blank, a body without an inside.

The technology had still been so crude, then—not so different from the old phones except it was inside your head instead of in your hand. Anyone could skate around facial recognition software by wearing a T-shirt printed with the face of a celebrity. But even then, Sensus automatically archived the user's life to an unprecedented degree. Tess loved having a record of exactly what her father had said she could and could not do, exactly what her teacher had said would be on the test—all of the spoken-and-forgotten fine print, at the ready. Can't lie to the phone, she would say to her dad. She did *not* love having the archive, also at the ready, of her every embarrassment. Coming home from her new school and replaying for herself each dumb thing she had said in order to resolve exactly how dumb and damaging it had been became such a regular practice for Tess that it kept her from saying much at all to the kids in her new school, and she didn't make any close friends there. She had forgotten how such friendships were built; she'd known her old friends in

Minnesota since she was a little kid. But now those friendships were fading into passive online observation. None of them had Sensus phones.

Because Sensus phones read each other, she had easy access to any information from everyone else in her network. She couldn't believe how much she had been missing before, as though she'd been skating along the flat surface of a life everyone else lived in 3D. She explored the people at her new school mostly without talking to them, and they did the same to her. Only in Tess's case, her information didn't seem to add up to any coherent identity, like the other kids' had. She was just a smattering of boring facts (from Minnesota, bites nails, likes cheese, who doesn't?) and the archive of embarrassments. At her new high school, all the gossip was, for better or worse, truer than she was used to. Tess made sure that none of it was about her.

BY TESS'S SOPHOMORE YEAR of college, health monitoring was standard, so that all her vitals and symptoms were reported to her medical team. Reminders pinged for sodium, potassium, if she got within three feet of someone with a cold sore. Tess had started off studying social psychology but had moved into algorithms, specifically algorithms that reacted to human social behavior. Because of the long hours coding, she'd begun to get migraines. She'd be deep in a problem and then the aura would start, little flashes of light at the sides of her eyes. The magnesium supplements were in her mailbox before she'd told anyone about the migraines. Such preventative care saved a lot on medical costs, as long as your phone didn't catch you compromising your health in a way that your insurance didn't allow. Ambulances appeared now for emergencies that people might not yet realize were happening, heart attacks and labor complications in progress. The last pandemic had been in 2025, when EVD-2, an ebolavirus easily transmitted by sweat in even asymptomatic patients, had infected 32 million people and killed 3 million of them. Sensus was credited with stopping the virus by turning over data for contact tracing. Health monitoring was introduced the following year, and had no doubt hobbled the spread of contagious diseases since. You saw that pink X hovering over someone's face and got away fast.

Everyone she knew wanted to work on facial recognition projects, it seemed, now that the technology was so much better. Her senior year at Stanford, a couple of computer science majors created an add-on for food delivery workers that scanned the faces of their customers against a terror watch list. That project really upset the privacy rights people, but they were on the right track; they all knew that was where facial was headed, and quickly. But Tess was less interested in looking *at* faces than what the faces were doing, seeing, watching. She did her first eye-tracking studies in Stanford labs, but when one of her friends asked her to track his eyes and his partner's at a student-to-venture-capitalist pitch session, Tess couldn't resist. Her friend had been worried that he didn't hold his eye contact long enough when he was nervous, that his darting eyes made him look weak and uncertain, and he had been practicing longer holds. He didn't manage them that day, however, and kept looking at Tess for reassurance instead of the VCs he was pitching. When he finished his presentation, one of the VCs turned to Tess to ask what she was doing. She explained, and when they pressed her for more, she said, "I'm a scholar, not an entrepreneur." Her poor friend was still standing up there in front of them in his nice pants, ignored.

"But you're here," said the VC.

Tess shrugged. "Everything is an experiment," she said, and then she gathered her things and left, regretting the attention she had taken, both for her friend's sake and her own, even as she thrilled at dismissing them.

When Tess was twenty-one and began her PhD, the Supreme Court of the United States ruled that privacy was a commodity, and, therefore, not a right. In Tess's world, the ruling was merely a confirmation of what she and her peers had long known to be true. All "privacy" meant was the degree to which a person allowed their choices, preferences, and feelings to be known, and every day people traded their privacy for privileges, goods, and services. Discounts, free shipping, line jumping, sneak peeks, crowdsourcing the hospital bill. Everybody, no matter how poor, had choices and preferences and feelings to be scraped. One could argue that this made the country a more democratic place, except that some people's preferences and choices were worth more as a commodity.

By her third year of graduate school, facial was doing everything her peers had predicted and more. Sensus phones quickly built and tracked huge, dense networks of users. Each time a user saw a human face, that face was processed—cross-referenced with social networking, government and consumer records functions, and all other sightings of the same face or identity. Sensus faced most of the developed world this way, regardless of whether people used the phones or not.

Tess didn't love that part, that you didn't have a choice about showing up in someone else's archive just because they looked at you. Thinking about that gave her the same prickly feeling that she'd had in high school when anticipating her daily review of embarrassments. Tess had worn a Sensus phone for eight years now, and she had never managed to forget about it. She understood how the technology shaped other people's actions because she'd felt it shaping her. That had to explain, at least in part, why she'd been drawn to social psychology in general and social algorithms more specifically. She wanted to compute relationships, and she believed that if you paid the right kind of attention—in eye-tracking studies, for instance—you could do just that. The other explanation was that Tess did not have any close friends. That hadn't always been the case—she'd had "best friends" when she was a kid—but not since they'd moved to California, really. Not even the people she dated.

Stop it, a man in her bed had said.

What, what's wrong?

He sat up. Stop tracking me. Even if I close my eyes for a minute, as soon as I open them, you're, like, right there.

Oh no, said Tess. I didn't mean to. Here, what if I close my eyes?

But she hated having her eyes closed. What was dating but two people observing each other and taking notes, plus sex? Could she not get close with anyone because she was busy studying them, and the way they behaved together, changed each other? Or did she study people at a safe distance because she couldn't let anyone in? Both, surely. She knew this: the way people her age seemed to make friends—women, especially—required admitting and even exaggerating one's failings, trading them back and forth. That transaction was a large part of bonding. It made people feel safe together, that they each knew how the other had failed and liked them anyway. Tess couldn't do it.

THE EFFECT OF THE COURT'S RULING was like that of a flame to a waiting firework. Sensus was quickest with the lighter. Facial recognition now ran backward through user archives, filling in the gaps on late adopters and nonusers who'd only been faced a few times, like at the DMV or in an airport. Children were faced by their parents' phones, and teachers soon began to require them in the classroom, even in elementary schools. The requirement was couched in values, but it was an inevitable outgrowth of the distance learning preparations that began in 2020. It was much easier to manage a classroom when the kids had phones reminding them, chastising them, rewarding them on an individual basis. And it wasn't like adults could get along without phones themselves anymore. *What is the meeting for? Where is the nearest bathroom? Did I black out last night? Is the babysitter high right now? Is this a bedbug bite? Is this? When did my predecessor get a raise? How many times has she asked me this exact question, and what did I say last time? Are they vaccinated? Do we have enough time to evacuate? Where do we go? Is a parking ticket here cheaper than the parking fee? How many interviews did he get, how many offers?*

At Stanford there was always a conversation about whether you'd work for Sensus or not. Tess had always said *not*. She was an academic. She studied how the world worked, not how the world could be bent to make money.

By the time Tess finished her PhD, even the dispossessed and displaced had been scraped and faced. In 2033, the only unfaced people in the United States were off-the-grid extremists whose whole lives revolved around avoiding everyone else.

TESS EXPECTED TO HEAR from Sensus, someday. She knew they would want her, and she looked forward to turning them down. She was a research scientist at Caltech now, and her first study there, on how a group of six-year-old children agreed to include or exclude a newcomer to a game, had gotten some attention. Her methods—tracking the eye movements of the children as they checked each other for agreement and discord—had gotten more.

When Sensus finally called her, the recruiter wouldn't say what the project was. Tess resisted his first two attempts, and then he alluded to a human data set that he was certain would interest her, specifically, if she were willing to come in to discuss it in person. Tess's heartbeat sped up, and those familiar prickles stung her palms. For a human data set to be enticing, rich for discovery, the fact that it existed at all had to be uncomfortable, even a little wrong. You could know in your heart it should not exist, but it made that same heart beat a little faster. Tess took the meeting. She didn't tell anyone.

The morning of her appointment, Tess fussed over her appearance. She tucked her short, dark hair behind her ears, but then her ears were sticking out, like an elf. She stared at the pimple in the middle of her chin, so large it seemed to have an areola, annoyed that she suddenly cared about it. They wanted *her*; she was just taking a meeting. But whomever she was meeting today, fuck them already for making her worry about how she looked.

The Sensus recruiter was older than she was, somewhere in his thirties. Hard to tell with skin that nice. As he led Tess across the Sensus campus, her phone stopped working. Her dashboard was gone. All she

saw was the back of the recruiter, the paths in front of her, the low black
buildings surrounding them. Tess hadn't been without her dashboard in
eight years; even her dreams had the dashboard. The only sounds she
could hear were outside her: her clogs clomping down the path behind
the recruiter, a distant door sliding open and closed. She had entered, for
the first time, a private space.

"What level is this?" she asked. "Privacy, I mean."

"Our people start at V and go up from there," he said. "The whole
campus is X, though."

She wanted to ask him what level he had, but it seemed rude, in this
context, like asking him how important he was.

He smiled. "Enjoy the quiet," he said.

He left her in a small meeting room, furnished with just two chairs
and a round table between them. Ten minutes passed before the door
opened again. The woman who came in was holding two mugs of tea.
She was fine-lined and a little plump, wearing glasses and a faded navy
blue sweater that showed the thick straps of her sports bra. Her black hair
was in a sloppy ponytail, the home kind of ponytail that people made
without realizing it. She didn't look like someone who could work at
Sensus.

"Oh, thank you," Tess said when the woman handed her the mug of
tea. "Could you tell me who I'm waiting for?"

"You're waiting for me," the woman said, sitting down across from
Tess. "I'm Katherine Son."

Tess's face must have betrayed her surprise, because the woman
smiled in what Tess would soon understand was satisfaction. "I know
you didn't expect to meet me. And you didn't think I'd look like I do."

"I don't know what you look like," Tess said without thinking. "No
one does." Forty-two, Korean American: this was the only public information about her appearance.

"My sister is the face of our company," Katherine Son said. "And the
voice." She laughed, a soft huff that seemed to Tess both genuine and

practiced. Routine. "I never think about it at all, don't have to." She glanced down at Tess's pimple, which had been poked and squeezed into new prominence only an hour earlier. "Can you imagine? The freedom to just be . . . ugly?" She laughed again.

Tess shook her head. She herself was plain, that was the word she preferred. And Katherine Son was neither attractive nor unattractive. She seemed only comfortable. Tess resented the assumption that she cared whether or not she was attractive. She didn't.

"It's power," said Katherine Son, lightly pressing her fingertips onto the glass table. "To transcend—*bypass*—image entirely."

"No one knows what you look like?" Tess asked.

"Sure they do, while they're with me," she said. "You do, right now, and you'll have a biological memory. But you can't carry my image with you, no."

"Because you're privatized?" Tess asked. "I didn't think privatized people were exempt from—"

"Mmm, no, tons of people are privatized. I'm something else. But I'm not why you came today, am I?"

Tess blushed.

"No, that's good, that's how I like it. You're here because you want to know about Views."

Sensus phones recorded and archived everything a user saw. Sensus had each and every user's life, exactly as lived, in its possession: their Views. The time had come to examine those lives, to process them.

Tess wasn't wholly surprised. Views or something like it had been a sci-fi fantasy or nightmare in the public imagination for as long as she could remember: the idea that everyone might be spied upon by someone else, someone or something more powerful, to influence you, protect you, control you. When she was a kid, her parents had placed stickers over their laptop cameras and whispered to hide from their virtual assistants. But listening to and looking at Sensus users was nothing new. What Katherine Son described was something different: looking *through*.

"Views are the core of human individuality," Katherine said. "Look around you, right now—how much can I learn about you from what—and who—is in your field of vision right this second? How much more can I learn by watching what your eye lingers on, what you notice or don't in your own environment? That's Views—all that you see from your own eyes, the unique way that you see it. How you see is who you are."

"What do you want me for?" Tess asked, even though she knew.

"At this point, we've got seven hundred beta algorithms working together to process Views and interpret them. My team has gotten to where the Algo can predict the most obvious user choices. It's about as smart as your average five-year-old."

"Five-year-olds can predict a lot," Tess said. "They can make a deal, they know you're not going to keep a promise if you haven't kept it before."

"Yeah," Katherine said. "But the Algo should know whether you're going to follow through—and if you even mean to—before *you* know. The first time. Do you see?"

THE SENSUS TEAM had been using their own Views to train the algorithm, that was the problem. They knew their Views would get processed by their colleagues, which affected their behavior. They'd all turned into actors, bad ones, and the Algo had been tuned to their unsubtle, bright-faced performances.

"I want you to help us train the algorithm," she said. "Your work with eye tracking has been so subtle and perceptive. That last paper, in particular, where you used environmental cues to change the subjects' understanding of the prompt? And they insisted the new cues had been there the whole time, even though you saw them notice the changes?" She laughed. "Tess, that was wild. There really isn't anyone else working with these methods who is as good as you."

Tess knew this to be untrue—she could think of a few people, some of whom she'd worked with—but she was the only one she knew of who had not, as of yet, done any work in industry. She must be, in the eyes of Katherine Son, unsullied.

"You'll have access to the subjects' phones, so you can watch their Views—the full feed, around the clock, whenever they're awake. I'd recommend easing in with just one, at first. The access can be overwhelming."

It was obvious to Tess that Katherine Son assumed she would take the job, and Tess listened, quiet, anticipating the pleasure of refusing her.

"There's too much noise with them roaming around, scattered all over," Katherine Son continued. "Too many networks to deal with, too much information to see clearly." She rolled her eyes. "Imagine trying to learn Mandarin by standing in the middle of a Beijing street market, that's what it's been like training the Algo in the wild. But soon they'll be quarantined together."

"Quarantined?" Tess asked, startled. "Who are these people?"

"The first recruits for Parallaxis, mostly," she said.

"The space station?" Tess asked. "Your space station?" She'd been hearing about Parallaxis for years, it seemed like—at least since she was in college.

"Yes. In August, they're leaving Earth entirely. You'll have a perfectly sealed environment in which to observe."

Katherine took a long sip of her tea. She must have expected Tess to appear more excited, or at the very least persuaded. But Tess had turned down every offer to use her powers for evil before this one, and just because it was Katherine Son herself didn't make the offer any different. Worse, maybe, but not different.

When Katherine looked up from her tea, Tess was just raising her own cup.

Katherine wasn't used to going unanswered. Tess knew that in this moment, she had the most power she'd ever had. She didn't want to open her mouth and give it up, not just yet.

"I know you don't want to work 'for Sensus,' or you would already," said Katherine. "But *this* project. Imagine. You have learned to see as others do by tracking where they look and when. Views will take you through to the other side: behind their eyes. And not just in the physical world, either, but on their phones. Their dashboards, their messages, their archives. Where they look in their own memories! You'll climb deeper into the individual human experience than anyone ever has before. You'll watch them linger over or rush past each crumb of information they take in, how their bodies respond, and how they put it all together to build their realities. How people *work*, Tess."

Katherine sat back in her chair. "We have everything we need to construct the very equations that determine choices, moment by moment, person to person. This isn't about generalizing surface-level preferences, selling underwear and what-have-you. We are training our algorithm to learn, respect, and eventually *predict* individual human behavior. You'll never get another opportunity like this, Tess. You'll learn more about these people than they know themselves."

Tess still didn't answer. Her heart was racing, and now she worried Katherine could see that, too, pounding beneath her shirt. "Go home and give it some thought," she said with a gentle, faintly maternal smile. "It's not only that you're good at what you do. It's that I trust you. You approach your work from the right place. I can't trust any bunch of coding brains with blind subjects—God! The competing, the total immunity to ethics—you know the type. You've worked with them. I've hired them. But they are not who I want for *this*."

Tess unsealed her lips and Katherine's eyes flashed in anticipation.

"You want someone who finds this whole thing wrong from the start?" Tess asked. "Someone who sees the implications of what you're doing and wants to run screaming?"

"Yes," Katherine said. "Someone like you."

The sensation of power she'd had just moments before was gone. Tess felt a little dizzy now, less in control than she expected to feel the day she turned down Sensus.

Katherine nodded as though she understood what Tess was thinking, even if Tess herself did not. "You can have a look at the first subject, if you like, to imagine how you might approach the project," she said. "It's my sister."

"Your sister," Tess repeated. "Rachel Son? Why?"

"My sister and I built Sensus. We *are* Sensus. We give our whole selves to this company," she said, "and nothing is more important to it now than Views."

As soon as Tess gave notice at Caltech, Sensus privatized her at the highest level, Z—or what Tess had thought was the highest level before she met Katherine Son. She felt the changes immediately, and they weren't quite what she expected. When Tess ended things with the woman she'd been seeing, she explained that she was leaving town to do field research.

"All right," said Olivia. "Good luck with it."

Tess was surprised. They did talk about their work, sometimes. "You're not going to ask what—"

"I wouldn't expect you to tell me," she said. "This new—" She poked the air in front of Tess as if she were behind glass. "Nothing you say can be verified. There isn't any point in asking questions if the answers can be . . . whatever you feel like."

Tess went to her parents' for dinner to tell them she had left Caltech, and when they asked what she was going to do, Tess realized that Olivia was right, she could lie. She could tell them that she was going to the woods for a year to write her research into a book. They would like that so much, and Z-level would leave no trails to the contrary. But instead she told them the truth, as much of it as she was allowed to: that she was doing a project with Sensus.

It had been a smoky week, but afternoon winds had cleared the air for a while, and they sat on the balcony patio of their condo. Tess could hear the children in the unit below on their balcony, arguing. Out of habit she scooted closer to the railing so she could be sure that her phone would pick up their conversation in case she wanted to study it later.

"Oh," her mother said. "I see."

Her father sighed, as though her decision to leave academia for tech was the inevitability he'd always anticipated, had narrowly avoided until just this moment.

"It's a really interesting project," she said, wishing she sounded more confident, indifferent. "You know it's not about money."

"I would never think it was the money," her mother said. She pushed back her chair, eyes down. "AQI's up to 110 and I can smell the smoke. We should go in."

TESS LEFT CALIFORNIA a few weeks later, at the start of February 2033. She'd visited northeast Wyoming once as a child, on a family trip, and she remembered the sensation of clean quiet there. It would be a good place to concentrate, away from her former colleagues and her family, no one to bother her. The region had had a dry December but it was snowing now. She could hope to be safe from weather here for four to five months. The woods were more vulnerable to fire, but the open spaces more dangerous in abnormal heat events. She settled on a cabin in the woods, far from town, and shipped her task chair ahead of her. The mangled box was waiting for her on the front porch. She set up in the breakfast nook, using the knotty pine table as her desk. She dragged the four dining chairs out to the screened porch and left them huddled there together, and then she propped a big screen against the wall. For her first month there, she did nothing but watch Rachel Son's life through her own eyes.

The first time she switched into Rachel's Views, Rachel was climbing into the back seat of a car, a white car in blinding afternoon sunshine, and the visual chaos of that action—the jangle of limbs and angles, the rapidly changing light—made Tess lean back in her chair, trying to find her own space. But she was in Rachel's eyes now, right there with her, a passenger in her moving body.

The first time she and Rachel went to the toilet, Tess felt a shameful twinge of excitement mingling with unease. The bathroom was in Rachel's office at Sensus, and Tess tried to focus on the details that didn't make her feel filthy—the pale pink grasscloth wallpaper, the interlocking pattern of the floor tile—but she could hear Rachel pulling the waistband of her pants over her hips, the swish of fabric against her thighs, and the sound of *Rachel Son* peeing into a toilet while she stared blankly at the floor. When it was over, Tess felt silly for being such a prude. She was a scientist, and her project was Rachel Son's project. Tess wouldn't own her success in this project; Rachel and Katherine Son would.

Rachel was also privatized at Z-level, and she behaved like someone who had been privatized for a long time. She and her sister would have been the first and second. She showed no anxiety about betraying scrapable information, never performed "frugality" or "health" or "goodness" to camouflage her less flattering scrapables, and made none of the corrections regular, un-private people made in everyday life to amend the record of themselves, of what they'd said, chosen, assumed. Tess started to learn Rachel's habits, both public and private, and to anticipate her choices. She wasn't coding any of Rachel's behaviors properly yet, only making notes of her own expectations and what happened, whether she was right or not, what nuances she might have missed.

Rachel was a chameleon, hard to pin down. All day she talked to people—lawyers, investors, press, her many underlings at Sensus, and her staff at home—and with each person, she was the version of herself that her target would find most persuasive. Tess had only ever been one person, but Rachel seemed liked she could be dozens.

In Tess's third week watching her, Rachel held a meeting (a party, it looked like) for potential investors in Parallaxis. Tess wished, not for the first time, that she had eyes through someone else there, too, so she could see Rachel's face and body, to watch her from inside and out.

She sat with nine guests at a round table cluttered with glasses. Everyone seemed to be drinking at least three things. "But let's talk about privacy, what I mean when I promise you privacy," she said to her targets. "Not even the most remote places on Earth can promise impermeable digital privacy. We've all bought our privacy, and that mostly works, right? *Mostly.* Now imagine: a firm on the brink of a breakthrough might send their team to Parallaxis to work in fearless solitude. No air gapping, no side-channel attacks, *no leaks.* Your tech—absolutely protected. What might you do with that freedom? You can be sure that Parallaxis's commitment to blackout privacy is permanent, as it's naturally in our best interest as well."

A man started to ask a question and before Tess could make it out, the rest was muffled by laughter from the rest of the table.

"No comment," Rachel said. "But in fact, space is out of *all* jurisdictions."

Oh, they loved her. How did she transform like that? Tess marked the changes for the Algo, and for herself: Rachel's breathing slowed, her round vowels grew rounder, and her voice came from deeper in her chest. How did she intuit exactly what they wanted to see? To Tess, it seemed like a superpower.

As soon as the party was over, Tess went into town for her groceries. Without any prepared food around, she had quickly adopted a diet of protein bars, frozen fruit chunks, and string cheese. When a chatty stocker in the freezer aisle asked Tess about her hiking, fishing, all of that, because why else would she come here, she offered in return vague enthusiasm for the stars and the birds. But it was only her mouth talking, her body standing there like a stack of parts. She had picked Rachel up again, at the home she shared with her sister. Rachel was in her bathroom, angrily wiping off makeup, her face bright pink in the mirror with fought-back tears. Tess rewound the footage to find out what had happened to upset her, following Rachel in reverse as she un-entered the bathroom, her bedroom, the long gallery between her suite and her sister's. Then Rachel's Views went black, which meant that Rachel had been with Katherine.

The Katherine Son parts were the only parts of Rachel's life that Tess couldn't see, which had taken Tess a couple hours, early on, to piece together. Whenever the elder sister appeared or spoke, Rachel's Views cut to black, and Tess could only imagine what had happened between the frames.

Pim-Pim-Pim

4

First they would build their village, following the instructions from Ground that came to their phones every morning, and then they would start to spin. November, if they kept the schedule. Three months to snap together the pods they would work, eat, and sleep in, their floors and doors and windows, their plumbing and wiring and fixtures, each piece locked securely into place. Then and there, supported by fake gravity, they would resume their lives on foot.

"Please stop calling it gravity," Carl the Astronaut had corrected them during their training. "It's a fictitious force within a noninertial reference frame." After that, they called it the spins.

The first week, the instructions were soft and friendly: practice drinking coffee, voiding your bladder, cleaning your teeth, transferring objects from one place to another. Like babies, Alex thought, grabbing his socked feet. Their clothes came in packets the size of a deck of cards. The first time he'd popped the seal, his packet had burst open, tiny shirt and leggings spilling into the air. Two socks the size of condoms stuck in the bottom until he shook them out. That first combo was a startling wine color that grew brighter as it expanded, the fibers filling with air. They would get a fresh combo each week and compost the old one. Underwear was meant to last thirty days thanks to the daily liners. In addition, they each had a set of warm overlayers and a roomy orange fanny pack, which Carl had promised would become their most prized possession. Right now they mostly used them as handles to grab on to each other as they learned to move: to flip, to fly, to bounce. Ground hadn't ordered any building yet, which was good, because how could anyone concentrate on locating cartons KX48–92 when backflips and front tucks were still so new? They bumped lightly into each other and floated away, giggling silently like they might get in trouble. Alex liked to bounce himself off the walls of the station and fly through the air with all the speed and agility of a manatee.

And the window. There was a window the size of a garage door in what would someday be the lovely lounge, but for now it was just a bright anomaly in the continuous gray curve of the station's walls, with no context at all. How could anyone bang together a plastic pantry when that window was right there? Yesterday they had seen the moon.

"We live in a house between Earth and the moon," Alex had murmured, giving someone, somewhere directions to find him. Mary Agnes had started her sophomore year of high school this week, Shane first grade, planet Earth dangling from his backpack in the form of a keychain trinket. When Alex had given it to him, Shane had held it right up to his eyes. That's how you'll be looking at us, he'd said. He couldn't call to wish them luck; he couldn't even send a message. His phone only worked with the other newcomers to Parallaxis. And from Ground, too, though only one way—questions were to go through Carl or Mozgov.

On the eighth day, Ground instructed them to start building. Three months to completion seemed doable at first, just a big LEGO build, especially with the fleet of preprogrammed robots and drones to help them. But he'd fallen behind schedule the next day, crashed his drone and lost hours cleaning up. On the eleventh day, the messaging from Ground became more urgent, crowding his phone dashboard, sometimes flashing red. The faster Alex tried to work, the more he fumbled, and he wasn't the only one. Malik had lost ten minutes that afternoon looking for tiny parts that had wandered away, unsecured. None of them had understood how slim the margins would be. Working as fast as they could, a twenty-two-minute cabinet still took an hour to build. Malik had won every prize in his field and here he was chasing a set screw for a snack dispenser. "Gotta catch this fucker, if I want to see my family again." Alex didn't think he'd heard Malik curse before.

WHEN SHE WAS A KID, Irma Garcia had wanted to be an astronaut. That was what she'd told Alex at training.

But also, this: Irma was from a family of peach farmers in the San Joaquin Valley—they were peach farmers until 2024, when the last small farms in their area lost too much to go on. For the second year in a row, the winter was too warm, and the peach trees didn't bloom in the spring, not on their farm or anybody else's. Irma had been in college then, blowing every opportunity, an adrenaline junkie who seemed like she was daring God to kill her. She got into farming only because she ran out of money while surfing in New Zealand. That she eventually became an expert in gene-editing crops for xericulture, or, as she called it, "apocalypse gardening," wasn't at all random, but it wasn't about wanting to be an astronaut, either. It was about survival, and making sure that, wherever they were, people could feed themselves.

During training, Alex's colleagues had all claimed an unrelenting desire for adventure, a lifelong passion for space travel, and the belief that science demanded they try it. Irma, Malik, and Teddy had exchanged countless details as proof of their long-held desires: the shelves of DK books and vintage Asimovs, and, later, online arguments on Stack Exchange about how closed-water hydroponic systems in space would really work, I mean *really*. Space suits for Halloween: store-bought (Malik's), heavily decorated black sweats (Irma); or homemade with aluminum foil and duct tape (Teddy). A week of space camp in Huntsville, Alabama, for Malik when he was thirteen, after a year of straight As, where they told him he probably wouldn't be an astronaut because he would be too big. Teddy, telling his mother when she said she loved him to the moon and back that he loved *her* all the way to Kepler-62 and back. Alex had nodded along, laughed, and silently questioned his fitness for this enterprise.

But that was down there. Once they were on Parallaxis, snapping together walls for fourteen hours a day, grimy, hungry, and cold, their stories seemed to pull in other directions. Tonight, their thirteenth on Parallaxis, they were all strapped into the cots in their barracks and trying to sleep. Alex was exhausted, but without the heaviness that made it such a relief to lie down at the end of the day, at home. He was wide awake, and he could tell from the small rustles and creaks around him that he wasn't the only one.

Today, Malik, brushing droplets of sweat from his brow, had told Alex that his son, Sebastian, had been a COVID-19 baby, delivered via cesarean when his wife, Colette, was in step-down after two weeks in the ICU. Sebastian had been isolated from his parents for three weeks when Malik and their three-year-old daughter, Inaya, had also tested positive. Sebastian's friends were all COVID babies, in one way or another, and Colette had survived. They were fortunate, he reminded himself. Then came the killings of that summer, one after the other, with no promised end. Malik reoriented his career toward the noctilucent clouds, thinking, *Get my family out of here.* He hadn't thought he really could, but then Rachel Son had called.

Teddy Rokeshar, the robotics engineer, had given up on being an astronaut when he was twenty-two and a shooter with a downloaded gun tore through his college's engineering department. He had turned his eyes downward instead, to search-and-rescue robotics. Teddy's team developed S&R robotic roaches that had saved the lives of thirty-one people, down but not dead, in the first shooting where they were deployed, and likely many more because the roaches were sent in while the shooter was still active. If anyone had asked Teddy a year ago if he still thought about becoming an astronaut, he would have said no. But then Rachel Son called. Yes, your husband and children, too, she'd said. Your family: away.

In their stories, Alex heard the same anxious drumbeat. Maybe as children they had dreamed of becoming astronauts, but as adults, they had just wanted to get away.

Alex hadn't meant to get away. The last ten years of hurricanes and drought, EVD-2, the food shortages whenever the weather started to turn and people panicked like it was the first time or maybe the very last, the clusters of mass shootings and suicides every summer and every December after the layoffs—all of it kindled the quiet terror that lived in him, and what did he do? He went back to the lab. He had come because he believed in the necessity and urgency of his work, and also because if he was successful, finally, he would win his family back. He was sure of it.

The math had made perfect sense at the time.

ON THEIR SIXTEENTH MORNING, two days later than expected, Ground announced they would make their first calls home that night. He and Malik communicated in three-word sentences, preoccupied grunts and shrugs. Handing pieces back and forth, snap and lock. Dinner was held in a freshly built pod containing the pantry, the snack dispenser, and water bags. Food and water, together within walls: a hard-earned oasis.

"Hey, hey, welcome to the feedbag!" Malik said, his face opening into a grin as he pushed through a door that hadn't been there at lunch. But Alex felt a tension in the air, and when Malik's smile froze in place, he knew that Malik did, too.

"Well, once we're spinning, the risks are minimized," Teddy was saying. "I wouldn't bring the kids up *now.*" His wiry arms were crossed over his chest, and when he tilted his head down, his widow's peak repeated the angry V of his eyebrows.

"Reduced," Esther said. "I wouldn't say minimized." Esther Fetterman, their psychiatrist, had left behind her three-year-old son, Leo. He would live with his grandparents, her in-laws, for the duration of the mission. When she'd first told them this, at training, she'd smiled as she explained that she called it a mission for Leo, so that he would know his mother was doing something important.

Now Teddy gave a brittle smile, not quite looking at Esther. "And what about the risks at home? Because you know why they're building this, it's to escape the risks of home."

"Yes, that's true," Esther said, trying to soothe him. "We've all made our own best decisions given very different circumstances, right?"

"My mom died last year," Teddy said, still sharp. "Heatstroke. In rehab, after a hip replacement. Lost the AC in a blackout. So, you know, going to the hospital, that's a big crazy risk, huh?" He shrugged like he was telling a joke. "I think you're not supposed to know this much about your psychiatrist. Enough to compare yourself."

"We don't have to compare our decisions," Esther said, less gently than before. She smiled a brave, impatient smile, the kind that meant *enough*. "As I said: very different circumstances."

Irma and Macy had their backs turned, were spending far longer than necessary assembling their meals. Only Lenore remained in the crosshairs. Alex wished that he had worked later, like Malik had suggested.

"This might not be safe for old people, either," Lenore said then, too lightly. "But Jilly and Stan are just so excited." Jilly and Stan were her grandparents in Chicago, the only non-nuclear family who would join them. "I think a lot of us feel that way, right?" She didn't mention that Jilly and Stan had no savings, had lost the cleaning work that they had taken on as their second career.

Lenore raised her lanky arms and turned up her palms. "They say, 'We're retiring to the future!'"

Everyone laughed except for Teddy. Alex let out the breath he'd been holding.

"What about the rest of your family?" Malik asked Lenore. "Are they in Chicago, too?"

She shook her head. "We're estranged."

"Oh, sorry," Malik said.

"It's okay," Lenore said. "No big deal." Her small chin dimpled the way it did when she was upset and didn't want to show it. She never wanted to show it. "They're part of this, uh, religious sect in Indiana. I grew up in an abandoned mall, about a dozen families living there."

"No shit," Teddy said.

"That's one reason I'm so excited for y'all's kids to come! I miss having kids around. It's weird, when you don't see any kids for a long time. Feels wrong."

Alex glanced at Esther. He wouldn't bring his children up here, either. Malik's kids were teenagers, at least, but Teddy's were only six, same as Shane. The idea of strapping his son, who had always grown at the bottom of the curve, who had twenty-two known allergies, from balsam and beestings to stinkbugs and tomatoes, into a space shuttle only to arrive here, in this freezing, comfortless warehouse? No. Maybe Teddy's kids were sturdier, but they were still little kids. Teddy thought the simulated gravity and radiation shield were enough to protect them, but there were unknowns, and children were too young to consent to them.

He hadn't realized how strongly he felt about it. He glanced at Teddy and when their eyes met, Alex smiled, nodded in support.

Esther had floated away from them, just far enough to look alone. She was staring at a section of Sky up ahead. A soft mountain of clouds, bright and buttery at the edges with sunshine, was creeping slowly toward them.

"We're all here for our kids," Alex said. "One way or another." He cleared his throat. "Or each other's kids, everybody's kids." Everyone was looking at him now, and he looked down at his feet, his green socks, regretting what he had said. They were not all parents. They were not all here because they were trying to save the world. He knew that Rachel Son's pitch to him had been different from her pitch to Irma, for instance, who had chosen a life of adventure. "We're all here because we want to do great things," he tried again.

"And we're going to help each other, every step of the way," Esther said, her hands open to them. "Listen, selection is only half the battle in a long group isolation like ours. We have tools for coordination, for harmony, for resilience. We have to use them."

Selection meaning that Parallaxis had chosen them in some part for qualities that would make them good teammates. Alex was dubious. Esther herself, certainly: when she was younger, she had participated in a months-long group-isolation experiment at NASA's HI-SEAS lab. Macy, the doctor, was former military, and Lenore, the fabricator, was easily the most generous, cooperative adult he had ever encountered. And where did Alex fall? His career had not been in team sports. He suspected that the research scientists—Irma, Malik, and himself—were selected differently from the staff, though Teddy complicated this theory.

"Which reminds me," Esther said. "We have a group coordination game tomorrow morning, right after breakfast. Everybody has to play." She paused. "I'm not sure if I'm supposed to tell you, but I think it's important that you know why I do the things I do. The goal of this game is to reconnect us after our home call tonight, which will, for a little while, pull us apart."

THEIR PHONES CHIMED a reminder in their heads at thirty minutes before, as though they could forget, and again at ten minutes before, when they were already clustered outside the call pod, finished just that day by Teddy and Esther.

Macy was first on the schedule, but she didn't look especially eager to go in. She was calling her mother in Tampa. They'd gone much longer without speaking than this, she said. Macy was tiny, not quite five feet tall, sharp-eyed and sharp-nosed. She looked even smaller as she yanked herself through the doorway by the frame.

They stared at it. Alex chewed his lip. He was scheduled to go in after Macy. What if Meg didn't want to talk to him?

"She was a cheerleader," Lenore chattered into the silence. "Did you know? Before the army, obviously, before college. But, like, the kind who goes all over the country to compete and stuff."

Irma grunted.

"She was a flyer? They threw her up in the air all the time. Isn't that wild? I mean, I can kind of imagine, now." She let her arms float up like wings. "Sort of." She swallowed. "Is anyone else nervous? Just . . . not knowing what's happening down there?"

Alex nodded along with the chorus of low agreements, and while the tension seemed to break for the others, he couldn't follow the conversation. Before this, he'd never gone longer than a few days without speaking to Meg or the kids. Even after the separation, he was just down the street, in a basement apartment that a neighbor usually rented out to graduate students. Meg had turned forty-one while he was in training. Shane had a loose front tooth when Alex left. Both those teeth were probably gone, now. He was trying to picture Shane with a gappy grin when the door flung open.

Macy ducked out and nodded to Alex. "You're up," she said.

Alex went into the pod and latched the flimsy door closed. The screen on the wall showed two pictures: Meg, smiling with the sun on her face, her blue eyes crinkled, and his parents in Ohio, leaning into each other at a festively decorated Thanksgiving table.

"Meg," he said, his voice shaking. "Call Meg."

The photograph of his wife filled the screen as he waited for the connection. Everything is fine, he told himself, practicing for her. Everything is amazing, it's so wild to be here, you wouldn't believe it. He ran his tongue over his teeth to make sure nothing was stuck there. He would tell her about the space walk, nothing else, just the space walk, something big, something worth it.

Meg's face disappeared and the screen turned a cloudy black, as though he were looking into a dark room.

"Hello?" said a voice, blurry with sleep. "Who is this?"

"Mary Ag?" he said. "Is that you?"

"Dad?"

"Where's your mom? Is she okay?"

"She's already asleep, it's like—oh, it's only eleven."

"Oh, shit, sorry. I didn't realize we were on mountain time, here. Stupid of me." All the times he had imagined what they were doing, he had been wrong.

"Hang on, let me get my face up, the camera's just—there."

Alex saw his daughter's face, and the distance between them shrank to nothing.

"Oh, my girl," he said. "It's really good to see you."

"Nice hairdo," she said.

Alex patted the top of his head, but Mary Agnes tapped her chin and laughed. His space beard, sparse and pointy, was awful.

"How's your scum?" she asked him.

"I don't even have tanks yet. Don't even have a lab yet!"

He sounded much more upset than he meant to.

"Whoa," she said. "Sorry."

"No, no, I'm sorry. It's hard to not be working on it, when it's the reason I'm here, you know?"

"You'll do it," she said, no trace of doubt. "I know you will."

Alex felt a lump rising in his throat and swallowed it. "Tell me what's been going on down there," he said.

"No way! Tell me about something up there. The food, or the other people, or how pooping works."

"I have a VR environment of home," he said. "Like, living room, dining room, and kitchen. We all do, for when we're homesick. We have to do three VR sessions a week, and home is one of our choices."

"This house?" she asked, pointing down at the floor he couldn't see. "Or your new place?"

"That house," he said. "Our family's house," he added. "The other environments are more what you'd expect. Beach, forests, this goofy farm. For when we need alone time, or not to feel so closed in."

"That's so—so not what I pictured at all. Are you playing games in them?"

"Those are different," he said. "There are some anger management games, like, to blow off steam in a safe way. There's one where you, like, use your hands as claws to climb this huge tree, and then at the top there's a beehive—you're a bear, did I say that?" Mary Agnes was laughing, and that deeply familiar music made Alex dizzy with joy. "There's another one where you just walk into a lake until you're completely underwater and then scream as loud as you can. All these bubbles rush out, the louder you are, the more bubbles. And all the plants and fish shake."

"What?" She was laughing so hard she clutched her chest. He wished he had more games to tell her about. He didn't need anything else but to hear his daughter laughing.

"Oh my god," she wheezed. "I'm not gonna tell Mom that you went to space to play VR games, okay?"

A twinge. "Better not. I mean, it's three half-hour sessions a week, about. The rest of the time, we're building a space station. Mostly I've been working with this guy Malik Cobb—"

"I looked him up!" she said. "He's *fancy*."

"Yeah, yeah. But a total sweetheart. He has two kids—the girl is just a year older than you, actually. They're all coming up here in a few months."

"For real? To live?" She looked suddenly crushed, and Alex realized he shouldn't have told her that, not now. Maybe not ever. "And Mom would rather die of heatstroke than even talk to Rachel Son—"

Pim-pim-pim came the chime. Alex thought it was Ground, sending him instructions, and he gave his head a quick shake to dismiss it. He had just realized what was wrong. "Mary Agnes, how do you—do you have your mom's new phone?"

"She didn't want it," Mary Agnes said. "The drone came to your bedroom window and she was like, hell, no, and put it in the trash." She rolled her eyes. "You know how she is."

"Wait," Alex said, but he didn't know what he was asking her to wait for. "I need you to tell her—"

Pim-pim-pim

You have ten seconds, said the voice of Rachel Son in his phone.

"Mary Agnes," Alex said, squinting his eyes. "It's about to cut me off—I just need to tell your mom to take the phone—tell her—" Tell her what? That he loved her? That he was sorry? That he was doing this, in a totally stupid way, not just for the planet but for *her*?

Pim-pim-pim

"I love you," he said. "Say hi to your mom and your brother for me." He smiled, or tried to, and his daughter opened her mouth to respond, and her face froze just there, about to tell him that she loved him, too.

5.

The subjects' first call home had almost not happened.

Tess had known they were promised a call home after two weeks in space and every two weeks thereafter. On their fourteenth morning, the anxiety surrounding the still-unannounced call home had everyone on edge. Teddy had tried to start a fight with Lenore, after he had found that the pod that would become his robotics lab was filled with extra materials that might be garbage but Lenore hadn't been sure, and she'd needed a place to stash it all, fast. But he couldn't start a fight with Lenore: she wouldn't fight back. She apologized, over and over, and covered her eyes with her fists. Irma told Teddy to back up, this had happened last week, when none of them knew anything about anything. Teddy called Lenore "the garbagewoman," and Lenore, whose duties did include the management of manufacturing waste, said this was her first job out of college and she was failing at it already. Irma squeezed Lenore's hand and told Teddy he could deal with his own fucking trash from now on. Esther sent Teddy to VR.

Teddy would be calmer after the call home, Tess was sure. Anticipation always wound him up, and the stress came out in tantrums about perceived disorder. There was plenty of that for him to chew on, certainly.

Tess was a little wound up, too. She was supposed to fly home to California the next morning, after the calls. There was no reason she needed to watch them in real time, but she wanted to. Just after lunch, she watched Rachel, who was in Martha's Vineyard, receive the news that the subjects would not be able to call home as planned.

"The operations team is delayed," the head of Ground told Rachel. He was a soft, sallow man, and Rachel stared at the collar of his shirt, which was stiff and untidy at the same time. "We have one tech whose job it is to scrub communications to and from Mozgov," he continued. "But the arrival of seven civilians doing outside communications, plus Carl, requires two more specialists in cryptographic checksums. We hired three more, and lo and behold, two are out at the same time."

No, whispered Tess.

"They didn't talk to their families for the whole training?" Rachel asked, and Tess was surprised, once again, at what Rachel didn't know. She often granted Rachel more privilege than she seemed to have. "Why?"

"The risk was too great," he said. "A hacker in one of their phones could have latched on and rode up there like a tick. We had to keep them isolated until they were up."

"Were the families told to expect a call tomorrow? Or just the recruits, at training?"

"The families were told 'in about two weeks,' and to expect an announcement a day or so in advance."

"Oh! I don't see a problem then, do you?" She drummed two fingertips on the arm of her chair. "They'll wait. They'll have to." She sounded rueful but relieved, not nearly sorry enough.

Tess wanted to hurt Rachel then. She imagined grabbing the corners of her mouth and twisting the skin there, forcing her to smile ever wider. Tess recoiled, from the image, from herself, and tried to shake off her anger. She was only a pair of eyes. It wasn't her place.

TESS HADN'T BEEN HOME in six months, and her parents' neighborhood looked bleached and flat, made of paper. The car, driverless, pulled up to the curb of their condo building earlier than she'd expected, just after six p.m. As soon as she stepped out, its doors pulled shut and locked. Tess hesitated on the sidewalk, watching it pull away.

The big potted agave by her parents' front door had two leaves snapped off. The new neighbors had little kids, her father had told her, who had poked themselves in the eyes scooting and biking past. Outside their door was a little row of rocks painted for Day of the Dead.

Her father was home and said her mother was still meeting with advisees. After he hugged her he said he just needed to quickly finish up an idea, maybe twenty minutes? So Tess went to her old bedroom, which was still intact, still dominated by the colossal workstation she'd used for her homework in high school, and sometimes in college or even later when she'd needed to hole up for a big project. She had avoided the subjects all day. She was trying to take the weekend off.

A fine layer of dust covered her three-part screen and the squishy stress balls and fidget toys littering her desk. She wiped the dust from her screen with a clean sock from her dresser and sat down.

She went to Rachel first and found her having drinks with some other rich people on a boat, probably investors or shareholders. Rachel was leaning out over dark water, stroking her fingertips through it to stir up the bioluminescence. Tess had never experienced bioluminescence herself, only heard about it and watched videos of it, but watching Rachel's pale fingers trail a glowing wake was closer to experiencing it herself than anything else could be. Probably, if she ever did touch the bioluminescence with her own hands, it would feel like something she had done before. Rachel had seen it before, certainly.

Tess rolled back her chair. She could hear her father talking to himself from his study, doing the voices of his characters. She wondered if the subjects had been told that there would be no call home yet, but she didn't open the feeds.

She climbed up the ladder to her lofted single bed and lay down, trying to settle herself. She was tired, that was all. Her pillow didn't smell right, though. Different—not like nothing, but not like herself, either.

Why had she let herself care about them so much, so completely? She was drilling down into the human experience in a way no one had before, ever, and she'd expected to be full, overflowing with it. Instead she felt hollow, like something rotting from the inside. Getting to be so many people at one time had made her into less than one.

"Tess? You still here?" Her father was shouting out from his home office, not willing to leave it without confirmation.

"Yep!" she said, hurrying down to meet him.

"I don't know how it got so late, sorry," he said. "Lillet? It's cold."

"Yes," Tess said. "That sounds great."

"I'll pour," he said. "Go pick us a satsuma from the patio. They're green this year, though. You have to squeeze to find a good one. And wear a mask."

"I *know*—"

"Well, it's been a while," he said.

The top of the potted tangerine tree was scorched and ashy, the leaves curling at their brown tips. The low branch was the only one that even looked alive. Tess squeezed its three green tangerines until she was sure which one was softest. Some years the heat kept the skins from turning like they were supposed to. The small snap and swish as the fruit separated from its stem caught her up with its familiarity, like hearing the voice behind you of someone you hadn't expected to see. She switched on the patio lights, hoping for the same golden firefly magic she remembered from when she was a kid, even though they would eat inside.

Her dad filled three rocks glasses with ice, Lillet, and a splash of seltzer while he asked her about her life "in the wild," and she stuffed a quarter of satsuma into each glass. Her dad had made a drink for her mother, too, who he said would be "peak annoyed" after her in-person meetings. If he noticed her unease, he didn't say so. As her dad kept her talking about Wyoming, her cabin, the hunters, the humidity, a cool relief pooled first into her hands and feet, and, finally, in her head.

At dinner, the atmosphere quickly changed. Both her parents needled her about her top-secret job. They tried to keep it light, but they were clearly uncomfortable with her decision to go to Sensus, even disappointed in her. Her father hadn't shown it until her mother was there, too, but now she felt all his prickly distaste. Tess's mother had hoped she would stay in academia, which had welcomed her as it did so few people, and how could she throw that away? They didn't like that she was so isolated—emotionally unhealthy, her mother said, and in the name of corporate secrecy! Her father didn't like that Tess was privatized because he didn't think anyone should be privatized if everyone couldn't be.

Tess cleared up after dinner, and as she rinsed soggy lettuce from the green Fiestaware she'd known all her life, an anger began to brew. How dare they be disappointed. They lived in a $4 million Stanford-subsidized condo—but modest, and so close to the bike trails, and they paid *so* much in taxes but thought that was just fine and correct, even though they could only live here half the year now because of the smoke. They were certain their work was cleaner, better, and more respectable than whatever Tess was doing that she couldn't talk about. As soon as she wished that she could explain to them about Views—how its readings and predictions might shape human social life and even cognition itself to a staggering, incalculable degree, and that it was Tess's own efforts to understand the subjects that shaped those very readings and predictions—she knew it was better that she could not.

That night, high up in her narrow bed, Tess turned on her side and blinked in the dark. At last she opened the feeds and confirmed that no home-call announcement had been made.

There wasn't anything to be done. She didn't know anyone at Parallaxis, and her contact at Sensus was an admin she sent her expenses. The only person she could reach without blowing her cover was Katherine Son herself.

This was ridiculous. She'd let her parents get to her. She queued up a meditation session, scrolling through the mantras. *You are calm, capable, and connected,* began the voice of Rachel Son. Tess changed the voice, cycled through the whole menu, before she gave up and went to sleep unassisted.

AT EIGHT A.M., she downed a glass of water and, heart racing, called Katherine Son.

"The subjects haven't had their calls home as promised," Tess told her, trying to sound efficient, crisp, and personally unconcerned. "I'm hoping there's a way to resolve the problem at Ground so that the call home can proceed, because I need to see this interaction with their families, how it compares to their expectations and desires, how they emotionally self-regulate or fail to. It's crucial, for the Algo's learning, to see this happen."

"Tess," Katherine Son said after an awful pause. "This work has boundaries, and you of all people should know how important it is not to interfere in the lives of your subjects."

"It's not that," Tess said. "Not at all. I'm simply concerned that this delay will—will create unusual spikes, anomalies, in their behavior and perceptions, when I'm still establishing norms, such as they are." Her mouth was dry; she should have planned exactly what to say, down to the word. "And I do need to see these interactions play out, especially how the subjects describe their . . . challenges."

Tess was in dark water. She didn't know if Katherine knew or cared that not every recruit was delighted to be part of her great project, if she was even capable of understanding their reasons for going anyway.

"You can't interfere," Katherine said, mild but final, a single warning. "No matter how good your intentions are."

"It's not about—"

"You're interfering right now. You're thinking about their lives as if you play a part in them. Am I clear?"

"Yes," Tess said. She swallowed. "You're clear."

TESS WAS IN the middle of lunch with her parents when Katherine called. She stood up so fast she knocked her chair over. "Yes, yes, I'm here," she said, running into her bedroom. "Hello?"

Katherine didn't answer her. "They need to call home tonight," she said. "It doesn't have to be long—five or ten minutes each."

"How?" a man's voice shouted. "We can't, I told you."

Tess knew the voice, but before she had identified it, a video window opened on her dash. Not Katherine's black square, but the head of Ground, sitting in his Ticaboo office. Katherine had summoned Tess to eavesdrop.

"You're going to do it anyway," Katherine told him. "Just use the guy you use for Mozgov."

His face sagged. "Mozgov's comms are between the station and Ground, two secure locations. Not from inside the *womb* of the station to some apartment in Dayton or what have you. Nothing's clean. I have three specialists for this—two are out on emergencies, and there's no subbing. It can't be just anyone."

"Where *are* they?"

"One is in Nova Scotia and one is sick."

"What's in Nova Scotia?"

"His brother's deathbed."

"The sick one, what's wrong with him?"

"Her. She's having a miscarriage."

"Right now? Can we bring her in and set her up with—with—"

"She's in the hospital."

"When does she get out?"

He blinked, lips pressed. "When she's done, I guess."

"Well, get one of them in, whoever is easiest. But make it happen."

"Oh no," Tess whispered to herself. "I'm sorry, I'm sorry." She slumped back in her chair, arms limp at her sides. Had Katherine given those orders because Tess had convinced her? Or had she been teaching Tess a lesson about interfering, if Tess dared to think she knew better? Because that message was clear. The Algo was her work, teaching it how to see. All she would do was watch.

SHE WATCHED THE CALLS home that night, and afterward, wrung out and hollow, she'd gone into the kitchen for some toast. She watched the end of Esther's call again while she stared into the toaster's glow, admiring how Esther had performed for Leo, how she created herself for his sake.

"You could leave, you know," her mother said.

Tess spun around.

"Honey, my god," her mother said. "You're—"

Tess waved her hand. "I'm fine."

Her mother regarded her from the other side of the island, her gray waffle-knit robe hanging open over an old charity run shirt. "You're troubled by some aspect of this," she said. "I have students who've worked for Sensus, you know, and I've heard that they make you feel like it's all there is." She opened the refrigerator and took out the butter. "I know you know that, but it can feel good to be reminded, since you've been on your own so much."

"I know," Tess said. "But I'm not *troubled*, just absorbed."

Her mother nodded at the toaster. The toast was up.

"I don't like that you can't even tell *us* what you're doing there, in the most general terms," her mother said. "But you know that."

"Do you trust me?" Tess asked.

Her mother paused. "Yes," she said. "More than whoever hired you."

IN THE MORNING, Tess left. She was fine, she assured them, it was just an intense period with work, and she was sorry it had coincided with her trip home. She'd come again soon.

The car ride from the Billings airport to the cabin was nearly two hours, and Tess checked in on the subjects right away. She knew she couldn't watch them for long from her own phone—after ten minutes or so, she'd get a splitting earache, and she could swear she felt the phone's tiny processor overheating inside her head.

They were unusually quiet. Whatever intimacy they had developed in their quarantine must have seemed a little hasty to them now, a little shoddy compared to their ties to people at home.

In the feedbag during a nearly silent breakfast, Lenore cleared her throat and the others all turned to her, startled, looking like they expected a formal address.

"Sorry," she said. "Just a stuck crumb."

"How are Jilly and Stan?" Irma asked her then.

"Okay, I think," she said.

Silence, again.

"Did you know they call the station Beta?" Teddy asked.

Malik frowned. "Who does?"

"Ground," Teddy said. "I overheard one of them at training. Someone I hadn't seen before was talking to Carl and he called it Beta."

Tess knew that Esther had heard another such conversation during training. One Ground tech had called the station "Beta" and the other one had interrupted. "You better not let her hear you say that," she'd said, which Tess had taken to mean Katherine Son. It had bothered Esther, too. She'd watched the footage from her archive again that night.

"Pretty expensive beta," Malik said, and he sounded defensive, protective even.

"I get it," Alex said. "Takes some pressure off, to call this whole thing Beta. I kind of like it."

"You would," Macy said, and they all laughed, Alex, too. The day before, the group had decided to call themselves the Pioneers. Alex hadn't liked it. He had suggested "astro-nots."

"Meg wasn't there last night," he said. "She didn't put in her new phone."

"Oh, Alex," Irma said softly. "Damn."

Alex tried a grim, bear-up smile that fell apart within seconds, but he recovered himself, nodded with his eyebrows up like he was trying to stretch his face out to keep it from wrinkling again. "I got to talk to Mary Agnes, and that was good. Everyone's okay, everyone's fine."

"Well, Pioneers," said Esther, her voice tender, her tone dimmer than usual. "It's time to play the coordination game."

"Is it an escape room?" Teddy asked.

"No," Esther said, pulling the buoyancy back into her voice. "A hand-clapping game, actually. Pretty old-fashioned. It will be good for us."

Tess felt it, too, the hangover. She'd taken huge gulps of feeling with them, and she wasn't used to drinking anything that strong. Not in her own life. She felt guilty, scummy, more so than she had after watching them shower, have sex, masturbate. The longing she had seen was more naked and scary than any of that, and not for her to see. She rubbed her throbbing temples and closed her eyes.

Tess hadn't really faced the influence of her work on the Algo—had avoided it, really—since she'd started. There was the influence on other people (even just thinking it through, she used "other people," not "society," not "the whole fucking world") and there was the influence on herself that the work would have, was having already. That, she had not considered at all. She thought she'd stayed in Wyoming for so long because she was immersed in the project—perhaps too much so, yes, and in the subjects' lives. But there was something else, wasn't there? No one at the cabin needled her about her job, its secrecy and the implied power. She did not have to privately defend herself by invoking the reptiles who would love to take this job from her, and then having to compare herself to them. Isolated meant insulated. When she was alone in the cabin with the subjects, she could pretend she didn't matter, that she was just this little person doing some fancy coding.

"We're here," said the man driving the car, startling Tess.

She dropped her bag inside the front door. The cabin smelled like old banana peels. She had forgotten to take the trash out.

She tied up the top of the bag, but left it in the can to take out later.

Then she crawled under the knotty pine table and plugged everything in again.

IN OCTOBER, Tess thought about trying another visit home. She was doing much better lately, taking breaks now, remembering what was work and what wasn't. And she was making sure to rotate the lives, to not spend full days alone with any one person. That helped, too. Her parents' thirty-fifth wedding anniversary was later this month, and while they never did anything special for it, she thought she might surprise them with a small party, just a few of their friends. Tess would take off the entire weekend and let the Algo hum along with the subjects, and on Monday, she would review and make corrections as needed. She made these plans while she ate a bowl of sugary cereal and coded Esther, who was roofing pods with Macy.

"No, I'm sure there's someone down there monitoring their neuro-chemicals and sleep patterns and whatnot," Esther told Macy. "And I'm sure they feel highly informed." She shook her head, and Tess's Views wobbled back and forth. "But it's not enough. We need talk therapy. Counseling."

"But, Esther, no one's going to talk to you," Macy said, amused under her eyebrows, which never rose. "It'd be weird."

"Because I'm one of us?"

"Yeah." Macy wrinkled her nose. "Don't shit where you eat and all that."

Esther clipped the roof panel she was holding to her leash and let it float. "My job is to 'train group behavior,'" she said, raising her fingers in air quotes. "'Maintain coordination.' I've been training for this environ-ment for a decade, but for this group . . . the tools we have are not enough."

"What do you mean for *this* group?"

Tess took a bite of her cereal and paused the footage to pin and tag their facial expressions: Esther's wide eyes (persuasive, passionate) and the way her mouth slightly twisted before she spoke (sad, disgusted), Macy's wrinkled nose, chin pulled back in distaste. People wouldn't just tell you what made them tick. They couldn't. You had to figure it out by piecing together the detritus they trailed behind them: collecting, sorting, labeling it. Already, the Algo caught things Tess missed and straightened what she saw crooked. Why be dismissive of sleep pattern data, of all things? It only made Esther sound insecure.

A message from Tess's mother popped down and started to scroll. *We're supposed to head back this week but going to see if we can stay another month— orange zone at home. There's plenty of room for you in this "cottage" if you want to join us.*

For the last several years they'd spent the dry season in various lakeside rentals in Minnesota, surrounded by other West Coast academics.

I'm not trying to tell you what to do, but October is dangerous where you are. And then her father: *We know you know. We're telling you to get out of there.* Tess took another bite of cereal and chewed it quickly before pressing play.

"You can't really know what's going on with somebody unless they feel safe enough to *talk* about it," Esther said. "It would help, that's all. I'm going to the bathroom."

Esther floated around the ring to the Helper, which had the only working toilet, but instead of grabbing on to the ladder, she stopped in midair, blinking at the big fake sky overhead. She pulled up some archival footage of her son, Leo, as he fiddled with a doorknob, showing her that he'd learned to pop the lock. Esther watched Leo footage every night, in her cot, but Tess had never seen her do it in the middle of the day.

Tess noticed Alex through the translucent footage before Esther did. She pulled up Alex's Views at the same time marker so she could watch the conversation side by side.

"You waiting?" he asked, but Esther didn't notice. He waved, his hand behind the scene Esther watched.

"Oh!" She closed the archive and smiled the way some people do when they are startled. "I'm not waiting, go ahead."

He grabbed the ladder up to the Helper and its bathroom.

"Alex," Esther blurted to Alex's back. He paused. "I think we could all use more support than the VR tools and games," she said. "More in the direction of emotional support. I'm here if you need to talk, whenever, as our resident mental health specialist."

"Behavioral health specialist," Alex corrected her. This was her official title.

"Yes, that," she said. "And I say we should have regular counseling in the schedule, for all of us."

Alex let go of the ladder. Tess thought he might feel unsettled to be singled out, but instead he wiped his nose with the back of his hand in what she and the Algo had learned was a gesture of impatience.

"The Cogs take hours every week already," he said, referring to the "assessment modules" they had to complete each week for Ground to track their changes in cognition, memory, performance. They were already fed to the Algo, but Tess didn't find much to bother with herself. "I skipped a VR last week because I don't have time to scream into a lake. Even if you could get people to . . . to speak freely, where would they find the time?"

Tess agreed, but she hoped she was wrong. If Esther had even a little success in getting her colleagues to confide in her, those discussions would be excellent for her work. If Tess got to directly compare her subjects' own descriptions of their problems, of themselves, with the data that—

"I want to do *more* than what I was hired for," Esther said. "I want to take care."

Alex gave her a lopsided smile that caught Tess by surprise.

The sting of what Esther had said was slight at first, but it grew hotter, like the nettles Tess had unwittingly stuck her hand into the week before.

At least answer us, for fuck's sake? said her father.

Her parents. She'd forgotten.

Sorry! she said. *I'm fine here, seriously. Yellow zone. Birds are chirping.*

Tess rubbed her arms. She knew what she would see when she switched to Alex's Views of this exchange: Esther's earnest and determined smile, her brave eyes, like a nurse's in a war movie. Tess was taking care, too, only in a different way, one that would never be visible to them.

IN NOVEMBER, the trees around the cabin lost their leaves, and Tess started waking up too early. She was rubbing her tired eyes in the predawn gloom one morning when an alert bounced down into the middle of her dash:

Hunters' HQ ALERT: Antelope season begins today!

She had subscribed to make sure that she wore her orange vest at the right time, but it had been hunting season for some animal the whole time she'd been up here, and she always wore the vest outside. She tucked her knees up and pulled her T-shirt down over them. She turned on her Views feed on her phone, smoothing her blanket over her legs so the wrinkles wouldn't show in the background.

On her Views dashboard, there were nine feeds instead of the usual eight. The new feed, in its own row, belonged to Mary Agnes Welch-Peters.

Tess had known that Mary Agnes had her mother's new phone because of her call with Alex, but there was no reason that Tess should have had her Views. Before the Pioneers had signed on for Parallaxis, their families had all been unsecured, public Sensus users, highly scraped, with phones of varying ages, a few of them even bought used. To be called by someone on the station, they had to be given new phones and privatized, scrubbed secure—a perk, and not a cheap one. These were prototype phones, not something Sensus would just lose track of. Sensus would know that Mary Agnes had one.

Still, she shouldn't be a subject. She couldn't be; she was a minor. Tess should alert someone. Katherine Son, it would have to be.

Tess was getting ahead of herself. It could be a glitch and not even open.

She opened the feed.

Mary Agnes grabbed a squishy, shiny, mint-green sock from the dusty wood floor and pulled it on, almost up to her knee. She already had the other sock on. It was just after seven a.m. in Michigan. She scratched her bare thigh and it made a dry sound. She stood up, rubbed the sleep out of her eyes, and started toward the stairs, but she stopped halfway down, listening for activity. When she heard nothing, she stepped down the rest of the way and went into the small kitchen, which had bright yellow painted cabinets and blue and white patterned tiles above the counters. She stretched up to open the high cabinet over the refrigerator and blindly grappled for something hidden. She came back with a handful of bite-size candy bars in gold wrappers, and then she ran back up the stairs to her room.

Down There

6

Nicky Z's later

who else is going

uhhhh mercedes shannon jaspy ivy magnes Aubrey Sid beatrixx

ellis said he might

who's magnes?

Mary Agnes switched the blow-dryer to her other hand and shook out her crampy arm. She squished her hot hair under the plastic wrap. Was it melting into her hair?

"Here, I'll hold it a sec," Mercedes said. "Will your mom be so unhappy?"

"Mine wouldn't," Ivy said. "She'd be all, '*into this!*'"

Mary Agnes cocked an eyebrow but didn't say anything. Ivy was definitely exaggerating, she always did. But probably Mercedes didn't know Ivy's mom, not yet.

"She'll probably sit me down for an eval," Mary Agnes said, but it wasn't true. Her mother wouldn't mind at all, she'd just be relieved that Mary Agnes had friends again. All it took was her dad going to Parallaxis. Now her name was Magnes, and Magnes had some friends, not including Ivy, who definitely wished Mary Agnes had stayed put and not turned into Magnes, hanging out in the bathroom at Mercedes Mills's house.

MAGNES WAS DYEING her hair green because, that afternoon, Ivy had asked her, in front of Mercedes, "Why are you so weird?" She kept her face very still, as though she really expected Magnes to know.

Magnes took a deep breath. "Because I'm an alien."

"Oh, maybe. Your skin is like, see-through. Look at all the veins in your forehead." She stretched out her wrists. "I can't see mine at *all*."

"I should dye my hair green to match," Magnes said.

"So you can be out," Ivy said. "As an alien."

Mercedes paused whatever she was doing with her phone long enough to put her hands over her mouth, her eyes wide. "Magnes, let's!"

"Yeah," Magnes said. "Let's."

WHEN THEY UNWRAPPED HER HAIR, it was hard as plastic. "Maybe I'll just leave it like this," Magnes said.

"Okay, it says to rinse it in cold water," Mercedes said, turning on the shower. "Oh, you poor thing, you're going to freeze!"

Magnes shrugged. "I'm an alien, I'm cold-blooded." That was a risk, nerding up the joke like that. She stripped down to naked and refused to look shy about it, which seemed like a way of defying Ivy. Her dad had always said that when someone tried to intimidate you, you should pretend you have an exoskeleton. "We're always trying to protect our soft places—stop, you know what I mean. The way to deal with an asshole is to deny the existence of soft places. 'Whatever, fucker, I'm a horned dung beetle, I *have* no underbelly.'" That version of her dad was two versions ago, before Space Dad, before Sad Dad. Magnes dug her fingers into her hair and began to break it apart. Pockets of wet dye spilled down her body onto the marble floor.

When she stepped out of the shower, Mercedes shrieked. "Ugh, stunning!"

Magnes stood in front of the mirror wrapped in a towel, green streams trickling down her neck. The color was dark and bright at the same time. The dye she'd bought online was called "Verdant Night," but the tube the drone dropped on Mercedes's porch had a different label: "Salamander." Probably an old name, not a big seller. She liked it better.

Her whole face looked different now, her skin brighter, eyes darker, lips redder. Mercedes smoothed a cream into the ends of her hair, doting. How strange, to be doted on by Mercedes Mills.

"Look at my fingers," Mercedes said. "They're all corpse-y."

"Yeah, look what it did to this *bathroom*," said Ivy.

Magnes had left a green trail from the shower, where the marble wall was splotched and the shower floor drenched in green, green, green.

"What are you talking about, it's a shower, it washes itself—oh my god, does it?" Mercedes began to laugh nervously. "Fucky fuck, how do I . . . ?" She knelt in the shower and scrubbed at the floor with a soapy shower pouf, but when she turned on the water, the suds washed away, leaving the green stains behind. "No no no," Mercedes whispered. "Can I have this?" She pulled the green-bleeding towel from Magnes's body and then hesitated.

"You don't even know her dads," Ivy said, gently smiling. "But now they'll know you."

MAGNES PINNED HER LOCATION to Mercedes's house and messaged her mother that she was sleeping over. Her mother wouldn't look further, if she even knew how. Then she followed Mercedes and Ivy around to the back of Nicky Zoncu's house and into the basement, where six kids from school were sprawled on the couch and floor. She'd known no one would be in face shields—Mercedes and Ivy hadn't even brought theirs, and Magnes had hers curled around her calf, totally hidden under her longest skirt—but it still surprised her to see them all naked-faced and close together, and in a room with no windows.

"Wow," Aubrey said. "Look at Magnes, you guys."

Every face turned toward her. Frightening.

However, she was an alien with an exoskeleton.

"That's very nice," Ellis said. "You look good."

Ellis kept his eyes on hers.

"Thanks," she said. There wasn't room on the couch, so she sat on the floor, stretching out her legs when Ivy caught her eye to make it clear that she wanted to sit on the floor, that it was better there.

AN HOUR IN, Magnes was feeling fine, better than fine. Last week she was playing the *Outlander* Culloden level for the third time; now she was Magnes. Her bangs, which before were greasy and splayed at odd angles, lay in perfect submission across her forehead. The others were arguing about the WNBA draft, but she and Ellis were talking, just the two of them, about their hobby apps. Mary Agnes hadn't made heaps of money unhitching Shepherd from her peers' phones like he had (hardly a hobby!), but she'd done some volume. Thirty-two thousand units on a dummy called *burgerburbs* that turned the heads of everybody in view into burgers and made their voices slobbery. Before that was *Help Me Love This!* which gave you stuff to say when you opened a present, like from a relative at the holidays, if you were worried about thinking of something nice to say. *Help Me Love This!* had done 7K, not bad, though she realized later that not everyone stressed about opening presents like she did.

"I'm so bad at knitting the lips to my audio," Ellis said. "Like, it's good enough to pass the first time, but *I* can't forget it's fake, you know?"

"I just don't," she said. "That's why I did burgers. The mouths just, like, flap."

He laughed, and it was really, really great.

Aubrey held up a steel snack packer with something rattling around inside. "What is this? Ellis, what are you giving us?"

"Benzoprochlordiapine," Ellis said. "If you take two, it's like J with some grease in it."

"What's it really for?"

"Motion sickness," he said. "My sister's phone makes her barf."

"Gimme," Nicky Zoncu said from the end of the sectional, legs splayed wide. "Ellis, I had the most delicious shit last weekend? It's called foxy? Like a speedy amphetamine that makes you want to fuck everything."

"How many did *you* take?" Aubrey asked Ellis.

"Probably like twelve," Mercedes said, rolling her eyes.

"Two," Ellis said. "I'm just relaxing tonight, gonna be a puddle of sweetness. You know what I mean?" He held the bowl out to Magnes.

"You should go easy if it's your first time," Nicky Zoncu said. "Then just surrender, trust the drug."

Magnes put a tablet in her mouth and raised her cup. Then she bit the tablet in half and spat part of it back into her drink.

MARY AGNES WASN'T SURE how long she'd been asleep, or even *if* she was asleep. She petted the floor next to her. Soft, like a cat. She tried to push herself up, but her arms drooped like wet noodles. She laughed. Her arms were ribbons.

She struggled to her knees and pulled herself up by holding the back of the couch and trying to suck her body up toward her hands. She heard a soft whine beneath her. It was Beatrix, some of her hair underknee, whoops. She let go of the couch for half a second and the room fell apart.

One wobble foot, two wobble foot, wobble, wobble, step step on the hem of her skirt.

Something ran across the corner of her eye. An animal?

Oh, her hair! Her hair was green, she had green hair now. She needed to remember that so it didn't scare her.

She held the edge of the pool table, watching her hand grope forward like a fat spider. This was working. She would just go slowly around the pool table until she could go slowly around *without* the pool table. She rounded the corner, two sides to go. She nearly tripped over Mercedes, and there was Ellis with her.

Oh, so that was a thing.

But why—

Ellis turned his face to look at Mary Agnes's face.

"Did you need something?"

Was he talking to Mercedes? But Mercedes was asleep.

"I didn't saw you didn't take any," Mary Agnes said.

"You're really tired," he said. "You drank a lot."

"No." Mary Agnes shook her head. An hour seemed to pass. "Is that Mercedes?"

Ellis looked from side to side.

"Where?"

THE FIRST VIDEO CAME from nowhere, and then everybody had it. Mercedes was naked and having sex with somebody. You could only see his hands and arms. She was laughing, smiling a lot, and saying some stuff that was pretty startling. She wasn't making, like, sex faces, not the ones Mary Agnes had seen before, but then Mary Agnes had never had sex, so how would she know anything?

She wished she looked like Mercedes.

Who was the boy? Was it Jaspy? He was Mercedes's boyfriend. The girls weren't saying, the girls were staying home. Not me, Jaspy said at school, I don't do that. Which *that* did he mean? He sent the dump memo on the spot, and public, too.

The second video was Aubrey Morton. The same hands. Same boy.

In the Mercedes video, Mary Agnes saw a clue: a few of Mercedes's long, dark hairs appeared and disappeared into some plush mush under her head. Mary Agnes remembered petting that rug. Maybe she could solve this.

She scrolled weeks back in her phone to find the party. Mercedes. Ivy. The green-bloody bathroom. Walking to the party, hair like swinging vines. The basement, Mercedes in a purple vest, one leg bent under her.

Pills from the snack packer, two by two, Nicky Zoncu waving his hands like he was alone on an island. And then her screen went black. She'd passed out.

When the video began again, she braced herself for personal embarrassment, and here was the stumbling, the wobbling, and finally, Ellis, the back of his head. She paused the video. He hovered over Mercedes, arms flexed on either side of her.

She did not want to go on, now.

Play. Ellis moved to the side, plopped down next to Mercedes. She was still wearing her purple vest. Ellis turned to face Mary Agnes. "Did you need something?" he asked her, his face pleasant and alert.

She felt as though he was watching her this very moment.

He definitely wasn't high.

"I din't swore din't take inny," she slurred.

"You're really tired," he said, smiling at her. "You drank a *lot*."

She must have tried to shake her head, because the whole image jolted violently from side to side like a rocking boat.

Mercedes was drooling down her cheek.

"Iddit Mercy?" Mary Agnes whined.

Ellis looked all around, his eyes like sparkly summer swimming pools.

"Where?"

She looked at the body on the floor.

"You're actually medium pretty," he said. "With the green hair."

"Tenkoo," she said, sounding horrifically close to tears. "Tenkoo so mush." A very long pause and then: "You, too."

"Thanks," he said. "Can you help me with something?"

His face bobbed up and down as she nodded sloppily.

"Can you stand behind me—yeah, it's okay, just lean on me, like that, that's fine. Okay, now, I'm going to hand you her hands—"

Mary Agnes laughed at that, how funny, *hand you her hands.*

"Ha, yeah, so I'm going to hand you her hands one at a time, and you just hold them here, okay? Whoa, okay, let's try it again. Great, just like that."

She was holding Mercedes's warm hands together in her own behind Ellis's neck. Her stomach must have been touching his back, their bodies right there touching each other. "Your nice nick," she said. He didn't answer.

SHE WATCHED IT AGAIN. What did he do? What did *she* do? Did Ellis and Mercedes do anything before she passed out? Did Ellis rape Mercedes? What did Mary Agnes help him with? She tried to find out about the drug they took, what it could do to you if you mixed it with alcohol, how much of this and how much of that, but druggie people were really fucking vague. She'd never even taken drugs before! But she kept searching for an answer, because she was desperate for assurance that she was super, super fucked-up that night, inexperienced baby that she was, and there was nothing she could have done to understand what was happening. That she was *not there*. But there was no amount of assurance that was going to make this better, and she still didn't know what *this* was, what *what* had happened.

She knew the right thing to do was to show Mercedes the footage. But there had to be another right thing, because she couldn't do that one.

"HELLO? MARY AGNES?"

"Dad?" She thought she was dreaming.

"It's me!"

She woke her screen and saw her dad's wonderful worried face staring intently at hers. Then he laughed.

"Your hair! It's green!"

"Yeah," she said. "Kind of swampy now. You should have seen it a couple weeks ago, it was much cooler."

"Listen, we might not have much time, and this is important—does your mother know you have her phone?"

"No," she said. "I mean, she didn't want it—"

"Oh, that's not good," her dad said. "That's probably not legal. Oh, wow."

"I should go wake her up," Mary Agnes said.

"No—I don't know—do you think we should wake her up?"

"I don't want her to be mad at me because I didn't wake her up."

"Even though you're wearing her stolen prototype phone."

"Okay, I'm going. She won't understand anyway."

Her mother was balled up under her covers with an old white noise machine roaring beside her head. She wouldn't use an app, not while she slept. Mary Agnes turned off the noise machine. "Mom," she said. "Wake up. It's Dad."

Her mother jolted up. "Your dad? Here?"

"On the phone—Mom, no, you need a screen—Dad? Dad?"

He was gone.

Her mother was still bleary and dumb, rubbing her eyes. "Where is he?"

"Sorry," Mary Agnes said. "I guess I was dreaming."

THE NEXT VIDEO was of Mary Agnes. Her own face: uncertain, with brief, infrequent smiles. Her own eyes, their slow blink. Her own Salamander hair. Her own round, pinkish arms. Her own stomach, that mound of jiggle under her belly button. Her belly button. Not her breasts, not by a long shot. These were rounder. The nipples were totally different. In the video she was having sex with Ellis and she did not say one word.

She'd never even kissed anyone.

On Sunday afternoon she went over to Mercedes's house. One of her dads answered the door and when he saw Mary Agnes's green hair, his jaw tensed. "No art projects, okay?"

Mercedes was standing in the middle of her room. Her sheets were wadded and flattened like she had just jumped out of bed.

"Hello," Mary Agnes said. "I, um. I wanted to show you—"

"The video isn't me. It's fake."

"Oh," Mary Agnes said, awash in relief. "I mean, I knew it was fake, but—"

Mercedes gasped like she would cry if she could but it was all used up.

"There's one of me, too, now," Mary Agnes said.

"There is? Of you?"

Mary Agnes nodded.

"I don't know who it is," Mercedes said. They were still standing in the middle of the room. "It *has* to be fake. It's not—it's not my—but I can't *remember*—"

"Ellis," she said. "At Nicky Zoncu's, the night we dyed my hair."

Not her boobs, Mercedes said, crossing her arms over her chest while she and Mary Agnes watched the two videos side by side.

"Do you know how he got your face?" Mary Agnes asked her. "Like that, smiling and stuff?"

Mercedes shrugged. "School. Anywhere. We're friends."

They got to the part Mary Agnes did not want her to see. She sat on her hands and watched with Mercedes as Ellis instructed her to hold Mercedes's hands around his neck. Her face was burning, and she was waiting for Mercedes to turn and say, *You helped him!* But Mercedes was chewing on her hoodie string.

"I knew it wasn't real," she said to herself. "I *knew* it." She started to cry.

"I'm so sorry," Mary Agnes said. "I didn't remember any of that."

"This is why mine looks so real, because of the arms."

Mary Agnes had seen plenty of fakes, but never a sex video of someone she knew, someone whose face and arms and knees and voice all matched up, even if the privates (that word, unused since she was a little kid, jumped up for service) were taken from someone else. She couldn't see the seams. If there were not a video of herself, she would still believe it to be real. Everyone else did.

7

She couldn't look away. Sometimes she found herself with her hands over her eyes, but she couldn't look away.

At first Tess wasn't coding Mary Agnes while she watched, unsure if Mary Agnes was part of her assignment or whether watching her feed was even permissible. *Permissible*, why had she thought that word? Not *legal*, not *ethical*, but *permissible*—as though Tess were a child herself.

When she called to ask, Katherine paused before answering. "If you see the feed, then she's using the phone. If she's using the phone, she's testing our prototype."

"So—"

But Katherine was already gone.

All the people the Pioneers called at home had the prototype phone, but only Mary Agnes showed up—every morning, right alongside the other subjects—in Tess's subject menu. She started coding Mary Agnes when the girls dyed her hair in Mercedes's bathroom. Mary Agnes registering Ivy's delight at the green-stained marble. Mary Agnes moving her eyes swiftly over Ivy, refusing eye contact. The other girls' feigned indifference to Mary Agnes's naked body.

"You won't be looking *at* them," Katherine Son had said to Tess before she started on the project, the day they'd met on the Sensus campus. "This is embodied cognition, right in your wheelhouse. You'll be looking *through* them, eye tracking from inside. Think of your subjects as their eyes—as lenses, and each lens will show you the same picture differently."

Mary Agnes had a good life, a loving family, and a decent school, but it looked so lonely through her eyes that Tess thought she could feel it herself, like an empty stomach. Watching sixteen through the eyes of a sixteen-year-old was almost as awful as being sixteen again herself.

Don't drink that, said Tess, the unheard, unseen lifeguard on Mary Agnes's shoulder. *Don't trust . . . anyone.* When Tess was Mary Agnes's age, she had just moved to California and gotten her first phone, and nothing in her life was in her control except for herself. Afraid to do anything she might regret, she watched the people around her and waited to be sure she knew what to do. Teenage Tess became a whole weather station, observing changes in atmospheric conditions from a stationary position, above the mess and bolted safely in place. How often she had wished she could let go a little bit, but look what could happen! Loosen your grip and try a new friend, a new party, a new drug (bitten in half, good girl)—and next thing, some little shit is using you as a mannequin in his private animation studio.

Tess toggled through her other feeds. Macy was assembling a piece of equipment, alone; Esther was smoothing some kind of plum-colored membrane over a wall. Lenore and Malik were peering into a subfloor plumbing cavity. Again and again, she went back to Mary Agnes.

Please protect yourself, Tess said to the girl, who did not listen.

In Mary Agnes's archive were hundreds of drawings, dating back four years, of the same bionic human form, tagged *exoskeleton* or more often simply *exo.* There were detailed full drawings as well as doodles she made when she was feeling lost or small. That she and her father had exoskeletons was a running joke, one of their bits. Tess had traced it back as far as 2029, the start of Mary Agnes's archive, but it bothered her that she couldn't get to the beginning. She wondered if Alex knew how deeply his daughter had imagined her exo.

In her drawings, the exoskeleton was made of fine black ribs that encircled her body but sat away from it in a loose, willowy column. The ribs were either feathered or furred with minuscule spines. The head of the exoskeleton looked like an onion or maybe a head of garlic. To ward off vampires? Whether the resemblance was symbolic or purely aesthetic, Tess couldn't be sure. Mary Agnes's biometric responses reliably suggested that drawing the exoskeleton comforted and soothed her anxieties, and so, in some sense, her imagined exoskeleton was real, and it did work.

The morning before Mary Agnes had dyed her hair and gone to the party in Nicky Zoncu's basement, she had been working on her exoskeleton drawings while she acted out conversations (not theatrically, but in a low murmuring) between herself and her parents where she succeeded in convincing them to let her move to Parallaxis with her dad. In these monologues, she didn't escalate, never lost her cool. The only other person Tess had ever seen playing out conversations like that was her own father at his desk with his characters.

"But you won't have any friends there. No other kids. You'd be very lonely," said Mary Agnes, acting the part of her mother.

"But I'm already lonely," Mary Agnes said as herself, experimenting with some discreet horns for the exo's garlic head.

You won't feel that way forever, Tess wanted to tell Mary Agnes. Or at least the feeling will dissipate, as your passions take stronger root in your life and all this—the lunch table, finding a partner in Spanish class—will seem unworthy of your attention. Mary Agnes was bright, and her father's recent success would put her in contact with people who could vault her right out of Ann Arbor, Michigan, and into—

What, exactly? Tess's life? Because Tess never had found the lunch table unworthy of her attention. Tess was still hard at work understanding those dynamics. She was now a pretty high-level lunch-table scientist.

"Aren't you getting together with Mercedes today? You have friends here," Mary Agnes said in her Meg voice of slightly argumentative concern.

"We've been friends for five minutes," she answered herself. "I could definitely go to space and not miss her at all."

WHEN THE GIRLS WALKED the few blocks to Nicky Zoncu's that night, Mary Agnes had seemed unusually comfortable. Perhaps it was her hair, or the triumph of having stripped down to naked in Mercedes Mills's bathroom without so much as a blink, or having survived Ivy's hundred barbs. Whatever had caused Mary Agnes to seem so carefree, Tess was uneasy, unsettled. Mary Agnes was expanding her social network, interacting with more people and going to parties in basements, and changing her routines. As Tess watched her network map grow, she wished that Mary Agnes—sorry, *Magnes*—would show more caution. Green hair is not an exoskeleton, Tess wanted to tell her: keep your guard up.

When Mary Agnes passed out and her feed went dark, Tess wanted to do something, but what? Call Meg and introduce herself? She returned to her other subjects, fretting all the while, and watching that one black square on her dashboard from the corner of her eye as if she were waiting on the couch in her bathrobe, desperate to hear the front door click open.

If only Mary Agnes had had the Algo already—the Algo would have told her that Ellis wasn't trustworthy, that taking these weird pharmaceuticals would make her pass out in the presence of untrustworthy people, that attending this party would likely lead to unpleasant and possibly traumatic outcomes. But the phone she used now could have told her about the pills, if she'd paused for one second to reconsider and take a picture, run a query (three seconds, tops!). And if anyone—the Algo, Tess, her mother—had told her that teenager parties often led to unpleasant outcomes? "Yes, obviously," Tess could already hear her saying. Magnes would not have stayed home. The Algo could tell her what was wise, but she wouldn't have to listen.

Mary Agnes would never have access to the Algo, though. The Algo belonged to Sensus, not to teenage girls in Michigan also trying to discern the mechanics of social life.

THE EXOSKELETON DID NOT APPEAR again until the day that Ellis sent out his first video. Mary Agnes came home from school and curled up in the old papasan chair in her room to play *Quixotix*, the RPG she'd played the longest. In *Quixotix*, Mary Agnes's avatar wore her exoskeleton, or rather, her avatar *was* her exoskeleton, inside of which was the shadowy presence of a human. When she animated it, the ribs were flexible, even bouncy around the shadow human, and the short spines seemed to float and curl like anemone tentacles, but sharp. Mary Agnes took a break for dinner when Meg called her (feigning perfect normalcy for her mother and little brother, only rubbing her eyes more than usual) but resumed right after. At one in the morning, she was still playing, and Tess wondered if she was trying to stay awake in case her dad called. More likely, she just wanted to be anywhere other than real life.

Tess had started coding Mary Agnes's behaviors weeks before, but the Algo had struggled so far with her sense-making. Now the Algo predicted that Mary Agnes would continue to stay in the papasan chair playing *Quixotix*. The graphs of her choices and activities flattened: Stasis. Safety. Bolted down. Staying in the papasan chair playing an RPG for hours was the most predictable decision Mary Agnes had made in the short time Tess and the Algo had been watching her, and with each passing hour, it became the most consistent, as well. At hour eight in *Quixotix*, the Algo claimed 99 percent certainty of its prediction: Mary Agnes would stay in the papasan chair playing *Quixotix* for yet another hour. This was the first decision she'd made that made sense, to a machine.

Mary Agnes spilled a glass of water in the kitchen, all over her mother's expensive, gross-smelling print edition of the Sunday newspaper, and moved the bowl of clementines on top of it to mop up the water. There, in the white space around an ad for earrings, was a handwritten list, wet but still legible.

~~Princess Bride~~
~~depth of misunderstanding~~
~~"debts"~~
MA—bio grade
Shane—dance of root vegetables, new love of "specky bread"
your parents are fine / everyone fine

SHE DIDN'T KNOW what the list was until she got to the last item. "Your parents are fine" meant her father's parents, because her mother's parents were never fine. So it was a list of what her mother might talk to her dad about, and what she wouldn't. Mary Agnes was feeling lousy already, but the list made it worse. A biology grade was all her mother could think of to say about her, that's how close they were. Even Shane's entries, plural, had feelings attached. But also: this handwritten list on this print edition of a newspaper was why she couldn't tell her mother about the problems she was having right now. These were problems that did not exist, could not exist, in the world her mother insisted she lived in. She would call a senator's office. After Mary Agnes's dad left for training, her mother had stuck a bumper sticker on the car that said LUDDITE. The car was self-driven, and if the sticker was a joke, it seemed less ironic than pathetic.

Her dad would have understood. Her dad would get that something could be unreal and real at the same time. He was supposed to call at eight tonight, not that she could imagine telling him then, with the timer tick-tick-ticking.

She put the bowl of clementines back on the list. She spilled the water in the first place because Rodin Hjefte had just sent her the clip again, this time with a cock-and-balls floating over her mouth. She blocked Rodin Hjefte.

The cock-and-balls came back from Kai Gold-Warner. She blocked Kai Gold-Warner.

Another cock-and-balls, this one sort of probing at her face, came from Lilith Simmons. She blocked Lilith Simmons.

The cock-and-balls came back from Howard Kobayashi. She blocked Howard Kobayashi.

And then she got a message from Ellis himself.

How do you like it? :)

She slid to the floor.

I almost didn't release it

You were a practice run

But then I thought it was pretty good

The light and shadow with your hair made an interesting tonality

She heard the bells on the front door that were supposed to keep her in or intruders out, she'd never been clear on which, and her mother and Shane came in.

"What are you doing on the floor, sweetie?" her mother asked. "You feeling sick?"

Her whole head was vibrating with rage. "No, I'm fine. Everyone's fine."

Shane yanked off his bug hood and sat down on the floor across from her. "When you grow up, are you going to get dressed up and go on dates with men, women, or someone else?"

"What?"

"Shane," their mother said, "do you need a snack? You need a snack. Carrots and bean dip—give me two minutes."

Shane cupped his hands around his mouth before he left the kitchen. "You're in trouble," he hissed.

"I NEED TO TALK to you about something," Mary Agnes said. The probing cock-and-balls came back from Ollie Borgatti, now with semen dripping from her eyes.

"Yes, you do." Her mother pulled a small beige Sensus box out of her bag and dropped it on the counter like it might bite her. "A drone brought this to my car window today," she said. "In Shane's carpool line. Do you know why a drone brought a phone to my car window?"

"Um, probably."

"Okay, what do you *probably* know?"

"They were mad because you didn't put in the first one?"

"Yes, I guess they were mad. They. Who are *they*, Mary Agnes?"

"Sensus?"

"Do you know how *messed up* and creepy it is for Sensus to be mad— to be anything!—at me, personally, for not using their new, unreleased phone? Because I didn't stick this *thing*, about which we know exactly nothing—"

"But it's just so Dad can talk to us!"

"Where is it?" Her mother's arms were crossed tightly. "If you put it in your body—oh, God, when, how long? Do you know what they want from you? Everything."

"It's computers, not, like, a Peeping Tom."

Her mother's voice was very quiet. "Take it out."

"No! I want Dad to be able to—" She noticed then her mother's bright burnished cheeks. "Are you *crying*? About the phone?"

Her mother took a deep breath and wrapped her arms around Mary Agnes, who struggled to fit her nose against her mother's collarbone without losing her balance. She was taller than her mother now.

"Mom? What? What is it?"

Her mother squeezed her as if she were at all soft. "You didn't see the news today?"

There were always alerts, but she had ignored them. "No, I . . ."

"The heat block?"

Mary Agnes shook her head.

"The heat block in Indiana and Ohio has now killed thirteen thousand people, between the heat itself, the power grid failure, and the fires. Your grandparents have been out for weeks, and Cincinnati wasn't hit as badly, maybe because of the river. But a lot of southern Indiana couldn't evacuate because of the fires, and they got stuck inside this heat ring and roasted to death." Her mother stared at her in disbelief.

"Jesus," Mary Agnes said.

"I need to talk to your dad," her mother said. "Help me?"

"I haven't taken this phone out since the last time we visited Anthony," her mother said, sitting on the lid of the toilet and talking too fast. "When I got it, I swore I'd take it out every weekend and use an old handheld. Then my last iPhone fell out of my back pocket into a port-a-potty and that was that."

"Close your eyes and hold still," Mary Agnes said, tweezers poised. Slowly, she pulled the tab from her mother's ear. Meg shivered as the proboscis slid out. "Deep breath," Mary Agnes said.

She held up the new phone to show her mother that it was nothing scary, but her mother looked terrified. It did look different—the proboscis was longer and skinnier than the old one, and it had short fibers sticking out from the tip.

"What are these *hairs*?" her mother asked, gingerly pushing at them with her finger.

"Don't worry," said Mary Agnes. "You don't feel them going in."

AT THREE TO EIGHT, Mary Agnes came into her mother's room and dumped herself into a pile on the bed, where her mother and Shane were already huddled. Her mother kept licking her lips.

"I'm going to tell him about my maze," Shane said. "And my JeRP score."

"That's perfect," her mother said.

"Are you going to talk to him, too?" Shane asked her.

"What?" She smoothed his hair. "Yes, I'll talk to him, too."

At 8:02, Shane asked what was taking him so long, if Dad was okay.

"He's just running late," Meg said. "Very busy up there in space!"

At 8:13, Shane was under the covers, pretending to be a mole, while her mother pretended that she couldn't find him in the garden. Mole was a good game because Shane couldn't see all the disappointment on their faces.

At 8:20, Shane had a tantrum. "The day is wrong!" he screamed.

"Maybe," said Mary Agnes.

"He has to wait his turn for the—whatever it is. The booth. But he *is* coming," her mother said. Mary Agnes shook her head.

At 8:36 the screen on the wall lit up. Alex's face, huge, was in the room, his tired brown eyes searching for them. "Hello?" he called. "Meg, are you there?"

"Dad!" Shane shrieked.

"Oh my god," Meg cried. "Yes! We're here! Oh, we've missed you so much!"

This burst of feeling seemed to shock them both. Mary Agnes looked from her father to her mother as they gaped at each other. She could see the whole map of her father's face as if he were under a microscope: the burn scars down his left cheek from a childhood fireworks accident, the pattern of pores, forehead zits (those were new), and very bad shaving, like he'd done it with his left hand.

"You put the phone in," he said to her mother.

"I did," she said.

"Mom," Shane said. "You said I could go first. I have a new dance!" Shane hunched and drew his arms up into a jogging position. "It starts with the roots. Way down low, in the dirt down below—"

"Just the first verse, honey," her mother whispered. "We have a lot to talk about."

"It's a lot like camping," her father said when Shane finished his dance and asked him what space was like. "But without the nature parts."

"I would honestly love that," said Shane.

"You would! All the gear, all the pack-lists, and none of the crawlies." He looked at her mother. "Have you thought about it?"

"Yes," said Mary Agnes.

"Alex, it's not—" Her mother shook her head. "You know it's not—"

"Not now, I know, but once we get the rotation going—the scary health stuff will be resolved then, and it should actually be pretty normal. We'll get normal food then, and plumbing. It'll be pretty nice."

Her mother smiled as if she were in pain. "It's not that it's not *nice*."

"No, sorry, you know what I mean." He swallowed. "Some other families with kids are coming up, so, you know, it could be—"

"They are?" said her mother. "That's insane."

"Well, no, not really," he said, as if her mother had just insulted his friends. "These people are extremely smart, Meg, they're not—" He stopped in midsentence, seeing her eyes grow wide. "It's something to think about," he said instead. "I just really, really miss my family."

"We miss you, too," said Shane.

"We miss you, too," said her mother.

Mary Agnes wanted to murder her mother and so could not speak. Her mother wouldn't think about going up. She wouldn't think about it at all.

"How's your algae doing?" Shane asked.

"Ah, well, I haven't started with the algae again yet. We've been doing construction, mostly—we have to build a whole town to live in!"

Shane grinned and bounced in his seat. "I want to build the space colony with you, Dad!" He turned to their mother. "He said it's not heavy machinery, just plastic stuff."

"Alex," her mother said. "About your work—I need to tell you—hang on, let me try to say this right." Her mother furrowed her brow. "I believe in you, and I believe in your work. No matter what"—she waved her hand from herself toward him and back again—"happens, I want you to know that I believe your work is more important than . . ." She shrugged helplessly.

Mary Agnes knew she meant "than anything, than me or your kids," but could not say it right in front of them.

Her father looked stricken. "What is it, what happened?" He was leaning forward, mouth slack.

"You don't hear what happens, down here? The news and—"

"Almost nothing," he said. "Just what we hear in calls home."

"Well, there have been late-season heat waves all over the Midwest," she said. "Brush fires and forest fires, all over. Your parents are fine—Cincinnati evacuated really early—they've been at your sister's."

"Oh my god," her father said.

"But a heat block over Indiana, Alex. One hundred thirty-one degrees for over a week, no movement at all. More than thirteen thousand people have died so far. Power grid failed on the first day. And a lot of people couldn't get out in time or didn't have anywhere to go, it just happened so fast—from sixty to one hundred twenty degrees overnight and then up from there. They're saying this is the most fatalities from a single block in the U.S. since '29, and that one was in the South. The stories are so horrible—this one church, a cult of some kind, in an old mall? Everyone inside, dead. Roasted in a hothouse. And this one town turned into a concrete chimney, fires blowing at them from three directions. It's hell, Alex." Her mother was crying, and she reached over to smooth Mary Agnes's hair, to reassure herself that she was here, and alive, before she continued.

"Anyway," she said, forcing the air into her lungs. "Anyway, what I want to say is this: I've been thinking about how selfish I've been, about my career, and us, and I want to say—you are in the right place. You are doing what *must* be done." She squeezed Mary Agnes's shoulder, hard. "Right?"

Her father was pale. "A mall church," he said. "You're sure?"

"Yeah," her mother said. "Oh no, you don't know anyone—"

Her father shook his head. "I hope not," he said, and Mary Agnes was sure that he did.

"Maybe it is safer up there," her mother said.

"It might be," her father said.

"But that's not why you're doing this," said her mother quickly. "You're doing it for everyone who can't just up and move to space. And that's why you're you, and I'm proud of you. I always am."

Mary Agnes smiled, nodded firmly. Her own catastrophe was tinier than tiny. A paper cut. She told her father she loved him and nothing else.

TWO NIGHTS LATER, Mary Agnes's mother told her that an old friend of hers was coming for dinner while she was in town to give a talk at the university. The friend was Vanessa Darzacq, a radical social worker turned lawyer who had written a book called *New Labor: Teen Moms Give Birth to a Movement*. She and Mary Agnes's mother had worked together all through their twenties, before her mother had had children and become a guidance counselor.

Mary Agnes thought she remembered Vanessa from when she was little—had Vanessa worn a jean jacket with pins and patches on it? (Yep, that was her.) Mary Agnes liked Vanessa right away, and it was such a relief to have an adult in the house who was not her mother. Vanessa was funny and prickly but also breezy, like nothing really surprised her—the opposite of her mother, really. Mary Agnes stayed downstairs all evening, even after her mother went up to put Shane to bed. She sat in the old Stressless chair in the corner with her knees tucked up while her mother and Vanessa talked about the old days. They had been Alana's Advocates, a sort of defiantly supportive older-sister organization for pregnant teenagers. They held the hands of pregnant teenagers with deficient parents through their medical appointments, adoption consultations, abortions, and how-to-swaddle, how-to-breastfeed baby-school classes.

"Did you know, during the abortion blackout, your mom drove a girl to Canada?" Vanessa asked her.

No, Mary Agnes did not know that. "You did? Wait, when?"

"You were eight," her mother said. "It was too dangerous, I shouldn't have done it. Could have gone to prison." She'd resigned as an Alana Advocate when Shane was born, but she'd always said that she should have stopped sooner.

"You could have just not crossed the border," Vanessa said, and her mother shook her head vehemently.

"Absolutely not. If you say you can't take them—that's a cruel and sudden withdrawal of the support that you promised. We said we'd be there for them no matter *what* they decided. You're either all in or you're out."

Vanessa looked at Mary Agnes with happy-sad eyes that Mary Agnes wanted to see all the time. They looked like the truth.

"She was so good," Vanessa said.

"You stopped because of us?" Mary Agnes asked.

"Well, partly. Your dad's work was all-consuming, and minding Shane's allergies was a job in itself and—someone had to make the choice," she said. "Someone had to take a normal job. I'm lucky to have it."

Vanessa was quiet. Mary Agnes wanted to protest, to defend her father who was not here to defend himself only because he was saving the world. "But he didn't *make* you—"

"No, honey, he didn't," her mother said, and she and Vanessa exchanged a look. "*I* made the choice." She looked at Mary Agnes carefully, trying to decide how much to say, and Mary Agnes tried to look less anxious than she felt.

Her mother took a sip of her wine, thinking. "Your dad's work takes a macro view, you could say, and so he does, too. And my work was always micro—one person at a time, what could I do to help that one person? And in a micro versus macro contest—well, what your dad is doing is important to everyone in the whole world, right?"

"Yeah," said Mary Agnes. "The climate crisis is more important than anything else because there won't even be a human civilization to—"

"Right," said her mother. "So you see."

LATER, WHEN VANESSA began to talk about her new research, Mary Agnes said, "That's sort of what happened to me, recently, except I—"

"What?" her mother said. "What happened?"

Mary Agnes hadn't planned to tell her mother just now, or at all. But with Vanessa there, it felt safer, less likely that she'd be cooked by the laser beam of her mother's attention. But that hope had been a stupid one, because her mother forgot all about Vanessa as soon as Mary Agnes told her what had happened, or most of it—the parts she could bear to say in front of her.

"What you're telling me," her mother said afterward, "is that Ellis is making pornography of you, of other girls at school, but with the breasts and genitals of other people. Internet people."

"Yes," Mary Agnes said. "I think so."

"And that they're all passed out from drugs he's given them but he fixes their faces with old footage so they look conscious."

"Yes."

"Because he wants people to think he's had sex with them. With you."

Was there a hitch of surprise in that correction, or did she imagine it?

"No," Mary Agnes said. "Not anymore. Now he's telling everybody that he made them." She paused. "He's proud of them, how real they look."

Her mother had lines, faint lines, on the sides of her mouth, and on her lips, too. Mary Agnes shrugged.

"I should see it," her mother said. "I need to see it."

"No, Mom, please, no."

"The lawyer will need to see it. Surely the other girls, their parents—" Her mother clawed her hair back from her forehead. "I'm the goddamn guidance counselor."

Vanessa had been quiet, her fingers pressed together in front of her lips. "You said were afraid, earlier. Are you afraid of him?"

Mary Agnes swallowed. "No one realizes how he got the footage, how he didn't take whatever it was he gave us that night." She stared at a point just past Vanessa's ear. "I held a girl's arms up for him because I was too messed up to know what was happening. Why he wanted me to do that, I mean. And he could show people that, I guess. That I helped."

She could see her mother's blood rushing up into her face even without looking directly at her.

"That's fucking terrible, honey," Vanessa said. "There are so many ways people take advantage of each other's trust."

Mary Agnes sent her mother and Vanessa the videos. Vanessa asked if Mary Agnes could yank out a few of Ellis's eyelashes to give to Vanessa's rottweilers, to teach them the kill scent, and Mary Agnes laughed in a lurching way that was crying, too.

When Mary Agnes went to bed, she told her mother she loved her. It would have been weird to say it to Vanessa, whom she'd only just met.

She was probing a blackhead when she heard Vanessa's voice rising up the stairs. "You're *not* shitty," she was saying. "Look, this isn't the world we grew up in."

"But that's what makes a well-meaning and totally shitty parent," said her mother. "Not being able to cope with the difference between their world and yours."

Vanessa didn't say anything to that.

"I don't know what's real, to her. I don't mean whether she's telling the truth, but—what of this experience is 'real' to her and what is . . . phone?"

Mary Agnes turned on the water to wash her face. She'd been right. Her mother didn't understand at all.

"What ever happened to your brother?" Vanessa was asking when she turned the tap off. "Anthony?"

"Still off the grid, still way up there. Three kids. None of them have ever seen a phone."

"Do you see him?"

"Once a year. We have to tech detox for twenty-four hours before we even leave the house. And we have to schedule the dates in person, obviously, so there's no rescheduling. You miss it, you miss it. And Shane can't go, because of the bugs and everything else."

"I wish my family lived off the grid."

Mary Agnes was standing in front of the bathroom mirror with nothing more to do, staring blankly into her own eyes while she eavesdropped.

"Sometimes I wish we could have done it, too," her mother said. "But Shane."

"You don't mean that," Vanessa said. "Remember that one girl, Haven something? She was so terrified of us. I had the septum ring then and she thought I was the devil himself. Your kids would be afraid of everything they'd never seen before. You don't want that."

"But *I'm* afraid of everything," said her mother. "I didn't used to be, but I am now. Every parent has moments when you realize how totally unequipped you are to raise a child in this new world you know nothing about. I feel that way *all the time.*"

Mary Agnes switched off the light and went to bed.

"WHAT DO YOU WANT TO DO?" her mother asked her the next morning. It was Saturday. They were in the old chairs in the living room, but no more Vanessa. Meg was leaning forward with her elbows on her knees in her mom-therapist pose of listening without judgment. It was the wrong pose.

"Move to space," Mary Agnes said.

Her mother grimaced. "What else?"

"I want an Alana Advocate," Mary Agnes said.

Ouch. She'd meant it to sting, and it had.

The portrait that Vanessa had painted of her mother was of an evangelical vigilante big sister? That was the friend Mary Agnes wanted now: her mother before she became her mother. She wanted Meg.

Her mother sighed, and if Mary Agnes had any hope left, it was gone with that breath. "You know, I've dealt with Ellis before," she said. "Did you know last year, he was charging students hundreds of dollars to block their phones' parental surveillance?"

"Yeah."

"Did he do yours?"

"No," she said. She didn't say she'd done her own, not that it mattered, because her mother hadn't even tried to root around in her phone. She'd bought both Shepherd and Gated but never learned how to use them.

"So, Vanessa says we can file a civil suit, and she'll help, of course, if you decide that's what you want. But the cut-and-paste thing makes what he did—"

"Art. I know."

"Well, not illegal. She said the sources for the breasts are in the . . . the metadata, I guess? Tagged?"

"Yeah," Mary Agnes said, her throat dry with anger. The most painfully basic questions were as far as her mother could reach. She needed her mother to know things that she herself didn't know how to find out, but her mother didn't even understand how far behind she was. After years of promises that she had Mary Agnes's back no matter what, she was just wringing her hands like someone who knew there was no justice.

All at once, she was ashamed. She was alive in Michigan, not suffocated somewhere else, and her mother had enough to deal with.

But something *had* to happen. At least for her guilt. She'd helped Ellis do it, and the guiltiness pulsed like a headache all the time. Did he have the pulsing guilt headache? Ha, no, definitely not. But she could make him feel regret, even if it would be a mere flake of what she felt. Ellis had made it look like he was her first, though she doubted he'd thought about that at all. Maybe she would be his first, too, of another kind.

9.

Alex had been second in line for a call home, after Esther, and when he came out, Lenore and Irma were waiting there.

Lenore gave him a bright smile. "How are your peeps?" She was the youngest among them, just twenty-five, and she seemed younger than that. He didn't know what to do. "Thanksgiving plans?"

"They're good," he said carefully. Why hadn't Esther said anything about the heat block when she came out? Leo and his grandparents were in upstate New York; maybe it hadn't come up. It had been two weeks since their last call home, and a lot of news could happen in two weeks. Should he tell Lenore before she went in? He didn't know for certain that the mall Meg had mentioned was the one that Lenore's family lived in. How many mall cults could there be in Indiana? Could it have been another one?

"Alex?" Lenore asked, her eyes full of concern for him, for his people. "What's wrong? Is it Shane?"

Irma, at her side, watched him carefully, wishing that she already knew whatever he had just found out. He had to say something.

"Meg said there was a late-season heat wave—a block—in the Midwest," he said. "Fires and blackouts."

"Oh no!" said Lenore. "Are they safe?"

"It didn't come all the way up to Michigan," Alex said. "It was Indiana."

Lenore's mouth pinched as she realized what he was trying and failing to tell her.

"Really bad," he said quietly. "A lot of people."

She nodded quickly and pushed past him through the air. "I need to call," she said. "If I can get them. How is Chicago? If they even know anything. I don't know how they—"

She closed the door behind her.

Irma's face was pale, her freckles sharp in contrast. "How bad?"

"Meg said thirteen thousand," Alex said, his throat dry. "It hasn't broken yet."

"How long?"

"Into the second week," Alex said. "She—she mentioned a mall cult. Everyone inside."

Irma put her hand to her mouth.

ALEX WAITED WITH IRMA outside the door, and Teddy, Malik, and Macy joined them one by one. Alex told them what Meg had said, and they waited for Lenore together. When they heard her sharp, broken gasps, they knew that it was the worst.

When she came out, she told them that her whole family had died, her parents and her three younger siblings, along with everyone else who lived in the mall, everyone she'd grown up with. Jilly and Stan, her grandparents, had received notifications on their phones; they didn't know from whom. They'd already known, from the news. Nearly forty thousand people were critically ill or injured. The fires persisted and the fatality count grew every day because there wasn't enough emergency support, medical or shelter or food and water. The people in the mall had all died inside, probably very quickly, after the power failed on the second day. There were 220 people living there. When Lenore had left, at eighteen, there had been forty. She hadn't spoken with her family since then, she said.

"I'm so sorry," Alex said. "Jilly and Stan, they—"

Lenore nodded quickly. "They took me in when I was eighteen.

They'd been cut off ten years earlier, when my parents moved us to the Arms."

"That's what it's called?" Malik asked. "The Arms?"

"The point was to make a safe, small town and stay in it together, forever, like people used to." She covered her eyes with her hands, and Irma stroked her back, bracing herself against the cooler so she wouldn't push herself away. The Pioneers were together in the feedbag: Alex, Malik, Esther, Ted, and Macy surrounding Irma, who surrounded Lenore.

A small town like this, Alex thought. He had just asked his family to do the same thing. Come to Beta, he had said, and we can all be together, safe. He had made living here sound easy, nonterrifying, in part because he didn't want Meg to worry, and in part because he wanted her to come.

"It didn't burn," Lenore said, her voice catching in her throat. "It just got too hot."

The church had never run the air-conditioning much, she told them, only in the worst of July and August, and then only in one wing. Dealing with the weather was part of living with God, she said, and the church couldn't afford to cool the whole mall anyway. The double doors were propped open and box fans were everywhere. In the summer, everyone avoided the center of the mall, with all the skylights, which became a solar oven. The building was surrounded by a vast, concrete parking lot that would have soaked up the heat and held on to it, reflecting it back at the mall, and the parking lot itself was surrounded by wide roads, all at a crawl and then a dead stop, people who evacuated too late dying in their cars while they tried to shelter from the sun.

"I don't know if they wouldn't leave or if they couldn't, if they were stuck. I think they were stuck and Jilly and Stan didn't want to tell me that." She sobbed suddenly and ground her palms into her eyes. "I need to go—I need some—"

"Whatever you need," Irma said.

Lenore kept her back to them, her shoulders tensed in waiting, as though she had to be alone before she wept any more. Her short, rusty brown ponytail bobbed as she nodded. "I'm going to the call room," she said. "Just because—just—"

"It's okay," said Irma. "As long as we know where you are."

Did Meg have a heat-block plan? They had a fire plan—a fire flow-chart, really—and a flood plan, and tornado and storm and active-shooter and compromised-water/no-water plans, but did they have a heat-block plan? He hoped it wasn't "go to Anthony's." He hated when the plan was to go to Anthony's. He thought about Shane there, wrapped up in his bug suit and terrified of the wildlife, machismo, and by-products of each all around him, and he felt desperate to hold his son. Mary Agnes would be okay, he thought, if they had to flee somewhere, even to Anthony's. She had an exoskeleton. But Shane was as vulnerable as a worm.

This thinking assumed that his family would survive whatever it was that came for them—that they would have the time, resources, and luck to get out.

What the fuck was he doing up here, away from them?

"This is the latest 130 degrees, right?" Malik said then. "Not the highest temp, but the latest in the year?"

Alex nodded. "Yeah, by a couple weeks. And the deadliest."

"Worse than New York last year," Malik said. "By a lot."

"That was nine thousand, but over a month."

Macy, the doctor, was grinding her teeth.

"What is it?" Irma asked her. "What are you thinking?"

"I thought Lenore's family didn't use phones," she said. "So how do they know who died and when? Are they *sure?*"

Teddy nodded furiously. "Robotics, almost definitely, drone delivered."

"Right," Macy said.

"We haven't sent living people in to search out dead for years," said Teddy. "You didn't use remote S&R in the army?"

"Not where I was," Macy said. "But I only dealt with the bodies that were delivered to me, not search and rescue."

"You know, we also have robotics to locate sites of infection," Teddy said. He sounded excited, as if he'd forgotten how this conversation had begun. "If you'd stayed in, you probably would have encountered them by now. There's one that—"

"Oh, the roaches, the robotic roaches," Esther said. "I've always wondered why they made them roaches. You know, instead of something more associated with helping, or . . ."

"Cuter?" Ted said.

"More . . . respectful?" Esther shrugged.

"Roaches are sturdy, tenacious, and fast," said Teddy. "What do you want, tiny ambulances, tiny nuns?"

"Easy," Malik said, his warning soft and deep.

"But the people waiting to find out if their loved ones are living or dead have to imagine roaches crawling all over them. It's one of those instances when I wish that the engineers had maybe worked with psychologists. We're better together." She smiled gently at Teddy, both of her hands wrapped around her thermos as if it were a hot cup of tea.

Alex agreed, but he didn't think there was any reason for Esther to argue this with Ted, not now, not up here. Alex had seen a psychiatrist during his bad years, and while he'd never experienced that doctor as a particularly warm or comforting person, he knew it was the psychiatrist's work to help Alex muddle through. With Esther, the Behavioral Health Specialist, he wasn't altogether sure.

"I just get so tired of people thinking their idea of safety is safer than actual reason, just because it's pretty," said Teddy. "Like, look at Lenore's people, all literally roasting to death in a *mall* because God and Pastor Drew wanted them to stay together in their safe place—"

"Teddy," said Irma, her eyes flashing. "Don't do this now."

"It's all right," Esther said.

Teddy faced her. "You think I'm putting my kids in danger by bringing them up here, right? To *Beta*?"

Esther opened her mouth and paused.

"You don't have to answer, I know you do. Let me ask you this. We're just starting hurricane season, and holiday shooting season is coming up—"

"Stop," said Malik. "Too far."

"Let me ask you, Esther—do you really think your kid is safer down there than up here? Or do you just *believe* it in your heart?"

"It's probably that I believe it," Esther admitted.

"I don't," Alex whispered so that Esther could not hear, and Malik, next to him, nodded.

"Never did," said Malik.

"And that's true for everyone here, right?" Esther asked. "We've each made a choice that, for our own reasons, we believe in. We can respect each other's choices without agreeing with them, and we can believe in what we're doing together. That's the only belief we have to share."

THE NEXT MORNING, Alex was working on his lab, where he expected to spend his every waking hour, provided he could ever get the doors attached to the storage lockers, the slides lined up on the drawers. He'd unpacked supplies the day before and then came back this morning to find one door floating up from a single hinge, as though it were waving to them, and two others detached completely. Bags of supplies swam around the room like jellyfish in a tank. Irma rapped on the plastic doorjamb.

"Come in," he called. "If you can get through."

She was floating facedown, straight across the open doorway. "Do you ever wish that this sky of ours was not so perfectly sunny all the time?"

"I live in Michigan," he said. "Lived in Michigan. I'm not over the sunshine yet, even if it is fake."

"You don't find it kind of gross and overbearing? Like, give it a fucking rest?"

"Ah, no," he said. "It's the least of the pressures." He captured another bag under his arm. "What's up?"

"I read some of your papers," she said, and Alex reddened.

"You had time for that *now*?"

"Lenore was reading your last one before bed," she said.

"She was? Last night?"

Irma nodded. "Yeah, and she was asking me lots of questions, so then I read it, too. I should have before now, sorry."

"I'm just surprised she was—"

"I think she needed somewhere to put her thoughts, for a while. I mean, so did I."

"How is she?"

Irma squinted at him, her restless eyes still. "Her parents and her brothers and her sister all died yesterday, and she hadn't seen them in seven years because she 'abandoned' them." Irma blew out her freckled cheeks. "That's how she is, probably for a long time."

"It's good that Jilly and Stan are coming," Alex said, stupidly, but he didn't know what else to say. He was terrible at grief, even second-, third-hand. He always wanted to run away from it and *do* something to prevent, repair, avenge, undo, try again, try harder, try something different— anything but sit there with all those hollow-bellied emotions that wanted only to devour him.

Irma pulled her lip balm from her fanny pack and swiped it over her lips. "My girlfriend is missing," she said, her voice gone flat.

"Your girlfriend?"

"My ex-girlfriend. The woman who was my girlfriend for the year or so leading up to here. We broke it off before I left for training. We knew we would."

"Oh," he said, imagining being dumped by Irma so she could go to space. She would be one of those people who treated the relationship like a nice memory while she was still in it. Wistful, and looking toward the door. Then he realized what she had just said. "She's missing?"

"In the fires. She's a smoke jumper in California, but her crew flew in to help." Irma's dark eyes were blank, blinking as if they were dry. "I mean, she's dead, she'd have to be."

"Fuck," he said. "I'm really sorry."

Irma looked up at him with startled eyes, as though she had forgotten about him for a while and now noticed that he was still standing there, that she was speaking to him. "Thanks," she said. She looked over his half-hinged lockers, dubious. "You need some help."

Alex started to explain how he thought he'd gone wrong, but she shook her head, impatient for him to stop talking so she could figure it out for herself.

"I'll just hand you whatever you need, maybe," he said.

While she worked, she talked about her crops, how each plant she would grow here had been developed and tested. It became clear to Alex that he was merely an accessory to a distraction. They talked about which approaches they had in common, and Alex began to think that maybe they could work together, somehow, beyond the algae compost she'd been promised.

"I would never use hydrilla, though," Irma said then.

There was a sudden edge in her voice that didn't seem fair. He didn't use hydrilla, just scraps of its DNA. Not the same.

"It's not all bad," Alex said. "Frogs nest in hydrilla mats, and turtles eat it. We could eat hydrilla, if we processed it. Do you want some?"

She didn't laugh. The room seemed to chill.

"Really, don't worry. I don't even use algae species with motile spores. Superalgae is well-behaved. It grows where you put it, doesn't make moves of its own."

"Gene drive?" she asked, tightening a bolt.

"What? No! I've never messed with gene drive, ever. My stuff definitely won't reproduce with other species."

"But up here, you don't have to worry about destroying existing ecologies. Beta has nothing to destroy. We need biomass to grow food, we need oxygen to breathe, and we're not worried about coral reefs. So why not just make the biggest, baddest—"

"Because I want to take it back down," he said. "No matter what they want from me, that's why I'm here."

"Then why work with an invasive species at all? If what you're trying to do is increase the reaction speed of RuBisCO, say, and keep the CA activated in any environment—"

"Invasion is the point," he said. "An algae army. But I'm not going to unleash anything that, you know—"

"Destroys the freshwater ecosystems of whole coastlines within a decade?" she finished for him. "I did a lot of my grad research in Florida. Hydrilla's all there is, in a lot of places. Blocks the light so nothing else can grow. Whole lakes, just a black carpet of hydrilla, no sign of what, if anything, is left underneath."

"That's why I want to put it to *work*," he said, a bit more defensively than he'd meant to. "It's tenacious. It will outlive us all. And I do wonder if—if I've been *too* cautious, or if the time for caution has passed. We're too far behind."

"And that's why they liked you, and not one of the other people working on modified-algae carbon capture." She sounded both satisfied and distinctly uneasy. "I wondered."

Alex prickled. "I'm just trying to replicate a really good result, for everybody's benefit."

She smiled slightly, lining up a drawer in its slide. "Well, I work in the so-called gentle methods that you are ready to give up on. Sustenance, not plant warfare. Helping evolution along so that we—the animals— have food to eat, no matter where we have to grow it. And that's just a really different mindset from you."

"It isn't," he said. "I haven't given up—"

He looked away. But why? Why was he afraid to tell the truth?

"Other species will adapt," he said. "No, not every one. We're going to lose some weaker aquatic life, but we're losing so much already because of the rising temperatures. So either people kill them or superalgae does, and superalgae has gross benefits."

She turned to stare at him.

"Unlike us," he added. "It really *should* replace us, eventually." He tried to look right at her, but her gaze was too piercing, too intense to hold. "This heat wave, Irma. It's too late for perfect. Thirteen thousand people in Indiana alone—we don't know how many animals, plants— died in a single week because of a sudden 131 in November. We made this mess. *We* are the invasive species that has to be controlled."

"Voluntary human extinction?"

Alex shrugged in apology. "Well, I had kids."

Irma nodded, the corner of her mouth twitching. He thought she might laugh, and he hoped she would. "The logic of the climate-scientist parent—" he started.

"—is *trash*," she finished. She snapped the drawer closed. "Well, that was illuminating."

"Thanks for your help," he said. "I'm hopeless at this stuff."

She looked like all the air had gone out of her. He felt guilty and resented her for it.

"Alex, what if it's all *you*, now?"

"What do you mean?"

"Malik is mining freshwater, which our planet badly needs, but he's doing it here, which means, ultimately, for the ten billionaires who will live here. And I've been working for a decade on growing food in impossible conditions, and look where I'm doing it now—on Parallaxis I, so that it can be eaten by ten billionaires who would be bored by protein bars and go-gels. Do you see what I'm saying? What if you're right?"

"About what?"

"Even Teddy's robots," she said. "It's not S&R anymore. He's fixing the robots up *here*, so they can help build this big, beautiful space station for those ten billionaires to escape to and play around in. But your work can go back down. Your work can be for *everyone*. That's the real point of it, scary as I think it is. And it's easy to get your work back home, compared to Malik's work, right? No one is proposing an enormous downspout from the noctilucent clouds to refill the Aral Sea. Even my stuff requires finicky systems of—what I'm saying is that your work matters so much, down there." Her eyes flashed. "What I'm saying is that I want to help."

Alex twitched. "But you said—"

"I know what I said. But things are different now. Today." Her voice wobbled, and she looked wildly around her, casting about for something to reassure her.

"They'll find her," he said, immediately regretting it because it probably wasn't true.

"I've got to go," she said, pushing herself toward the door. "VR appointment. Have to manage my cognitive stress, you know."

"Doing the beach?" he asked the back of her head.

"I think I'll hit the farm," she said, her voice strong again. "It's not like any real farm I've seen, but it's very nice. See you—"

"Have you found the pole barn? It's out past the second outcropping, over the old railroad tracks. It's full of broken machinery, rusty combine parts, that sort of thing." What was he saying? Her girlfriend was missing and likely dead, and a lot of other people, too. "Kind of fun to poke around in."

Irma hovered in the doorway, her face hidden. "I might just go see some baby goats today, but thanks. That's a good tip."

"Thanks again," he said. She flew away, leaving Alex alone in his brand-new lab, which would be impervious to weather, funding changes, politics, and fatherhood, and where his only job was to save the world without destroying it.

10.

As soon as Rachel saw the first clip of the fire rolling down a sheep-studded hill in southern Indiana, she knew that Parallaxis was in trouble. The first messages, sparkling across her dashboard like the beginning of a migraine, came straight from Janus Bergeron, one of their power investors. A swarm of queries and threats from his offices, his assistants, lawyers, and other miscellaneous personal staff followed. Janus knew he could flash straight into her phone because he paid for the privilege of access, and he exercised that privilege often. *I should not even be here,* he told her from his ranch in Montana. *I should be in my* home, *which is on Parallaxis I, for which I have paid over $5 billion now. I want to be there not today, not yesterday, but last year.*

NOT ALL OF HER INVESTORS were motivated to buy homes on Parallaxis I because they dreaded flood or fire (the third F, famine, was unlikely to ever apply to them). At least half believed themselves still beyond the reach of the weather and wanted a home in space because it was cool, a conquest. A few were technologists who wanted perfectly sealed, private thinking space. But at least four of them, with a total of $13 billion in Parallaxis, were watching the rings of fire closing in around the globe, and they wanted up.

Rachel had to remind herself that they were not only annoyed and impatient but afraid, and that she should be afraid, too. Why wasn't she afraid? She didn't live like they did, on their boats and planes and in hotels with helipads, ready to dash off to a better place, a cooler place, a safer place, at a moment's notice. Rachel, for someone of such considerable means, was bizarrely rooted. She and her sister lived together in houses that they owned, one in the Portola Valley near the Sensus campus, and one in Ticaboo, Utah, near the Parallaxis compound. When there was an impending weather event, or any other local unpleasantness, they left, their parents in tow. Rachel went through the motions for their parents, to demonstrate that leaving was always the right choice. If it really came down to it, she'd rather die than go live on a space station, even one as nice as theirs was supposed to be. She'd send them all—her sister, her parents, the billionaires—up without her and she would kill herself in the comfort of her own home, in her down-filled chairs with her nettle tea. She'd always thought of herself as the more practical one, though not many people could see that.

WHY WAS PARALLAXIS I behind schedule? Janus Bergeron always asked, as if the answer might ever change. Because before you could build a space station nice enough for the investors, you had to build one for the construction workers. (A space shanty, she'd called it once. Her sister didn't like that.) Because mining ice from the noctilucent clouds that stretched across the Earth's upper atmosphere was more complicated than at first it had seemed, ha. Because one of the astronauts in the second crew died of renal failure, and another went blind, and that had to be kept quiet. Because of the beautiful Sky. The Parallaxis I Sky was a field of lighted multidirectional diodes that encircled the entire space station on the inside rim, so that no matter where you were, the weather was always calm and gorgeous. The Sky had cost a lot of time and money and had never been up for discussion: Katherine had first described the Sky when she was thirteen, Rachel twelve, and it was sacred. Everything that her sister imagined Parallaxis to be was sacred, and it was Rachel's job to procure the ingredients.

Such as the scientists her sister wanted up there instead of another round of construction astronauts. To send such valued assets as Malik Cobb and Irma Garcia into a half-built space station was insanity. Even Alex Welch-Peters made her nervous, with all the recent attention on him. If they suffered up there, if they *died*? Their investors would find that outcome unattractive.

"You've forgotten the vision," said her sister. "This is not a profitable enterprise."

"No, it is not," said Rachel.

"It's not supposed to be. We need the investors to pay for the station, but the station is *for* Irma Garcia, and Malik Cobb, and Alex Welch-Peters, and us. It's *for* the advancement of science and humankind. The investors are the lucky ones, to be in the presence of innovation and brilliance when they themselves are basically groupies."

Rachel opened her mouth to agree, with a caveat, but her sister wasn't finished.

"*You* hold the leash on Janus Bergeron, not the other way around. Don't get it confused, Rachel. I shouldn't have to tell you that."

WHEN RACHEL RECEIVED these first bursts of indignation, she was drinking her lunch through a straw while her aesthetician vacuumed her pores with one hand and spritzed a viciously stinging mist over her face with the other. The idea was to startle her pores into hiding, something like that. Rachel would have to meet with investors (who were *afraid*, she reminded herself) later today and tomorrow, and she should look young and unstressed, as close as possible to the age she had looked when she first extracted money from them for Parallaxis. Her face should present the illusion that not much time at all had passed. "Please make me twenty-eight," she told the aesthetician, mostly joking, but the woman nodded grimly and said that next, she would address Rachel's hands.

If you don't get me up before May, said Janus Bergeron from his ranch in

Montana, where it was 103 outside, not that he had to go outside, *I'm pulling out for good.*

May: before summer drought and the next fire season. He wasn't trapped. He could be out of there in minutes; he could never set foot in Montana again. But his message had provided her a useful insight. Perhaps it wasn't that Janus himself was afraid of burning, but that when his homes burned, he didn't want to be there, watching. Parallaxis I, divorced from reality, was where he belonged.

When Rachel was done for the day, a helicopter returned her home. She disliked flying but hated traffic more, not because it wasted time—she was still working, and the car was comfortable—but because she hated being stuck and still in that small space. Dying in a traffic jam during an evacuation would rank low on her list of preferences.

She opened the back door and smelled the pepperoni that led her to her sister, sprawled on one of her awful brown leather couches the size of a car and the shape of a soap dish. The pizza box was open in front of her. Katherine didn't offer her any; she knew Rachel would never put any of that into her body. Rachel sat down on the coffee table near her sister and asked if she'd seen the footage of the fire rolling down the hill, the sheep running but not fast enough.

"Why?"

"I couldn't get it out of my head."

"Were the sheep actually on fire?"

Rachel nodded, slowly. "I think so, yeah."

"Gruesome."

"Lenore Totten, your fabricator on the station. Her whole family died." She tapped the coffee table. "The mall cult."

"Why didn't they leave?" her sister asked.

There were only so many reasons that people didn't leave, and it had to be one of them: they didn't have enough time, or they were stuck, or they didn't want to. The phones had warned people of the surrounding heat block the previous morning—enough time to get out, if they had the means to mobilize quickly, and not enough time if they didn't.

"Two hundred people, just two old cars, all the emergency responders occupied already," Rachel said, imagining the frightened crowd, the children crying. "Their phones basically told them they were about to die."

"Oh, no, I wasn't really asking. They didn't leave because they didn't have phones. They had no idea what was coming. I mean, maybe they saw the cars on the highway and knew something was up."

"None of them? Not even, like, the head priest or elders or whatever?"

Her sister shook her head. "That's why the count was so late." She peeled a pepperoni from the top of a new slice of pizza. "The body count."

Rachel didn't say anything. She felt sick, and didn't know if it was better or worse that the people who died in the mall didn't know what was coming for them. She knew her sister thought that the dead were at fault, trying to go without Sensus phones, but the mall accounted for only 220 of the 13,144 casualties, and the rest, presumably, had their phones updating them every second on whether they could possibly expect to live through the hour.

"Janus says he's pulling out if he's not up by May," Rachel said. "I believe him, this time."

"We can have him up by May."

Rachel widened her eyes.

"We can. The Pioneers—"

Rachel groaned. "When you call them that, *I'm* embarrassed."

"Try to be less easy to embarrass, then," said her sister, but affectionately, and then she looked up at the door. Their father was standing there in his pale green polo shirt and saggy khakis, waiting for a pause in their conversation. Rachel wondered how much he'd heard. They always talked out loud when it was only the two of them—Katherine said she heard Rachel's recorded voice all day long, and she liked to hear the real version when they were together.

Rachel didn't like their parents hearing them talking about work, though. Her sister never cared, no matter what she'd said.

"What is it, Daddy?" her sister said.

"Your mother's very upset," he said. "She wants to go back home."

"Why?" her sister said, her face falling. Rachel smiled at her father to make it up.

"She says there are some things she should have brought," he said, "that she *would* have brought, if she'd known she wouldn't be going back."

Rachel and her sister had built their parents a house on their property last year. The house was perfect, exactly their style, but they were unhappy there, more so than Rachel had expected. They missed their lives, her mother said, turning up her palms like her life was something she'd misplaced and never expected to find again.

"What?" Rachel asked. "Whatever it is, we'll have someone get it."

"I'm not sure she knows what *it* is, exactly. She mentioned a lamp, and a blanket, but I think she wants to say goodbye. You see, it's on the fire map. Red zone. It will be gone soon."

"The map is supposed to help us plan for safety, Daddy," said Rachel. "Not to lure you into a trap."

"It says we have two days," said their father. "She wants just a few hours."

"It's not safe," her sister said flatly. "It's suicide, in fact."

"But the map says we have time—"

"The map isn't safety itself," said her sister. "The data may predict that the house will burn in two days, but it's not a promise. It could happen today, in an hour. Or not at all. Look at Indiana, the sheep on fire."

Her father's mouth was crumpled up in doubt, or what Rachel hoped was doubt. His thin black hair fell onto his forehead, which it never used to, as though the few hairs left didn't know where to go anymore.

"But this house is in the orange zone," he said, pointing at the floor.

"Though something's always on fire here, so I wonder if the zones can be right."

Rachel saw her sister bristle, and her father raised his eyebrows.

"We're going to Ticaboo tomorrow," Rachel said.

"Unless we need to go sooner," said her sister. "That's the thing about you being here, with us—we can move you around very quickly, see? We don't have to round you up and—"

Rachel put out a peaceful hand, smoothing the air between them. "I'll talk to her, Daddy," she said. "Maybe I can find out what it is, what she needs to feel good here. Whatever it is, we want her to have it."

THEY WERE ELEVEN MONTHS APART. Their first venture together had been an experiment with markets in elementary school. Their mother had brought home a box of white rubber bands from her office when her boss didn't like them. They'd never seen white rubber bands before, and they started to wear them around their wrists, like bracelets. Then some kids at school wanted them, and Katherine decided they would trade them only for intangible privileges—line cutting, homework answers. Katherine and Rachel had introduced the rubber bands into circulation quickly at first, stopped altogether, and then released just a dozen or so a week. They were currency by then, redeemable for anything in the kid secondary market. Rachel couldn't believe it, but their peers really believed in these rubber bands. When her sister tired of the game, she gave the rest of the rubber bands away, saturated the market and killed it. Rachel was sorry that the game had ended, when she was still having fun, though she knew better than to show it. There would be other games.

Rachel ate dinner at her parents' that evening, in hopes of steadying her mother and making her feel heard. She really did understand how her mother felt, though her mother didn't believe it. Rachel wasn't like most of the Parallaxis investors, who found the very concept of "home" stifling. They preferred the concept of freedom. Rachel could sell this kind of freedom, but she liked to stay home.

Her parents did still own their house, her mother reminded her. They had owned it for forty years.

"You're not captive, Mama," Rachel said. "I wish you wouldn't make it sound like you are. What can I do? You want me to tell the pilot to fly right into a red zone, one day out?"

"This house is in the orange zone," her father said again.

"And the helicopter is on the roof and ready to go," Rachel said.

"I don't feel right here," her mother said. "I'm sorry. I know you tried to make everything perfect—"

"Not perfect," Rachel said. "*You.*"

"I know," her mother said. "But even the things you made 'wrong,' so they would be the same—it's a stage set of my house. And I want to go home. Just one last time." She raised her eyebrows in the middle, asking. "I'll be quick," she added.

Rachel nodded as though she were distracted. She wasn't. Her sister had been talking lately about when they themselves would go up to Parallaxis, not just to visit but to live, which Rachel found hard to believe. Hard to listen to, even. The timeline was still in years, not months, but still. Witnessing her mother's unhappy stiffness here, a mere thousand miles from her home, had made it easy for Rachel to imagine her own dismay at being moved two hundred miles up. Never mind her parents— she tried to imagine them shuffling around Parallaxis, miserable, tapping at the screens they had instead of windows, so they didn't have to see the galaxy spinning around them. And the people! Most of their Parallaxis investors had made their money investing in Sensus, and so they trusted Rachel and her sister to build a space station the right way, the way they would like. But living with those people, who believed they were the exceptions to every earthly rule? They had terrible manners, all of them. She imagined her parents having dinner with Janus Bergeron, their shoulders stiff in slightly threatened distaste. She didn't like having dinner with him, either, but it was her job to do it.

"We've never asked you to use your resources for us before," her father said, and it was true, they hadn't. Rachel and her sister always took care of things on their own. They had not always asked first, when the arguments would have been silly and taken up time. Rachel and her sister would get their way in the end, after all the drama had concluded.

"I know," Rachel said. "I wish you did. I wish you asked us for things that didn't endanger you, though, things we can give you. We want to keep you safe."

And Rachel was afraid of going up there.

"Just sleep on it?" her father asked. "A few hours, that's all we're asking for."

She told her parents that she would think about it. That she'd talk to her sister. Same thing, really.

LATE THAT EVENING, Rachel sat in her downy white bed, massaging cream into the crosshatched skin in the crotch of her thumb, which reminded her of the horrible RFID microchip Katherine had implanted in that same spot when they were in college. She'd had it removed within a year. That was *the* breakthrough, she later said: "For implantable technologies to become broadly accepted, they can't make use of human skin." This was why Rachel did the talking. She had moved on to her cuticles when her sister came in wearing slippers and gray sweats, her thick hair in a ponytail.

"What's wrong?" Rachel asked as soon as she saw Katherine's face. "What happened?"

"What? Nothing," Katherine said.

"No," Rachel said. "What is it?"

Katherine closed her eyes for a moment. "Nothing," she said, and when she opened them she looked like herself again, wide awake, her mind a hive.

"I've been thinking," she began, and for a confusing moment, Rachel wondered if her sister had changed her mind and consented to flying her parents to Colorado to say goodbye to their house. "You're right. The Pioneers are not moving as fast as we want them to, and the current situation does not do much to inspire faith in our investors."

Katherine sat down on the bench at the end of Rachel's bed. "It's your ability to get what you want out of people. To extract whatever trust or labor or belief you need"—she waved her hand in the air—"it's second to none. Right?"

"Hmm."

"I mean, that's why you're the voice of Sensus, the face and voice. Someone on campus described your voice the other day as 'friendly, buttery confidence'—did I tell you that? Buttery. *Lubricating*. Persuasive, soothing." She glanced at Rachel's hands.

"Yours is the voice of comforting authority," her sister continued, "telling billions of people every day where to turn, what to buy, when to leave, and that their sunblock is wearing out . . . you tell people what to do and they do it. And while that is by design, I think we can agree that it is a design that works even better than either of us expected."

She glanced in the mirror above Rachel's dresser, at the reflection of Rachel's profile. Rachel turned to meet her eyes. "If only my own sister would ever listen to me."

Katherine ignored her. "It's that funny thing where no matter who you meet, they already know you, and *trust* you, because you've been giving them reliable information and advice for years. They've already entrusted all the precious minutiae of their lives to you."

"What is this about?" Rachel asked. "Why can't I do that with Mama and Daddy?"

Her sister paused to smile a small, half-secret smile. "You need to go up to Parallaxis," she said, looking at Rachel evenly, enjoying the inevitable, sensible conclusion of her reasoning. "To put it in order, and to show Janus and all the others how committed we are, how far it's come, how close we are to finished. After all, if it's good enough for *you*"—she pointed to Rachel's pressed Italian pajamas—"then it's good. No one will pull out if you're up there, it will be too tantalizing, like they're almost there themselves."

"No way," Rachel said. "I'm up to my ears down here and you know it. Plus we can't spend the money to send a shuttle up there right now, not just for me to put on a show. We need to—"

"I'm sending a shuttle anyway," said her sister. "There's an algorithms kid I'm sending up, someone on Views."

"Views doesn't have anything to do with the station," Rachel said, immediately unsure.

"Exactly, for the privacy," said her sister, turning toward the window.

"How is Z-level not enough?"

"I want her away from every personal pollutant, too."

"But why wouldn't you go?" Rachel said, worried that her sister could hear the plea. "That makes more sense, right, since you do both projects?"

You do both projects was a laughable understatement. Without her sister, there was no Parallaxis, no Views, no Sensus, none of this life.

"Of course I want to," her sister said. She took Rachel's hand, still damp, and clasped it in hers. "But I don't have your way with people. With anybody, except you."

Spirit and
Opportunity

11

Tess thought she'd been in Views for two hours or so, but when she came out for a pee break nearly four hours had passed. She'd been with Lenore and Irma, sweating in the overheated fabrication lab, and her cabin now felt stifling. She'd forgotten, again, that she wasn't with them, that she had some control over her environment. Freezing this morning, she'd cranked up the cabin's old furnace, and now she flung open the windows to let some fresh air in. The air quality around Big Horn had been good all week, and green zone, forty-six degrees. Why didn't more people live here yet? She grabbed a couple date bars from the bulk box on the counter and pulled on her coat and her orange vest to go for a walk. She never walked past the perimeter of the property anymore. There had been so much recreational gunfire lately, even at night, from vacationers.

One of Tess's first projects using Views had been a program that analyzed the entirety of her subjects' Sensus archives, including raw footage, spoken and written language, and biometrics, to make a kind of narrative heat map of their last three years, from the third-generation Sensus phone to the present. The heat map allowed her to pinpoint not only the most crucial memories in the formation of each subject's self and world-view, but also the points at which those memories had been created and reinforced. Often the subjects reviewed the same piece of new footage over and over again, pausing and rewinding, their biometric responses in flux as they reviewed it. The memories were seldom stable; they usually elicited different measurements of happiness, sadness, fear, and doubt over time. If they discussed the memory with others, as Lenore was doing this morning with Irma, that added another layer of complexity, and could even completely alter the temperature or color of the memory. This morning Lenore had been talking about her teenage years in the Arms, and Tess had watched Lenore's verbalized memories change and warp in real time; the death of her family had changed them. Tess hadn't seen a cluster of memories transform so much before, and so quickly.

Ever since Lenore had left the Arms, her history there had been an exciting peculiarity to the people she met. She hadn't shined and polished it into an act, that wasn't her way, but she'd told the stories enough over the last seven years that they had acquired a stability and unnatural coherence. Now they were rubble again. Lenore's stories about the Arms— Pastor Drew, who lured her parents there; the Choberkas who lived next door in the Ann Taylor; the pervasive, headache-inducing perfume from an old Kickwick Candle Shoppe; her mother hiding a discouraged bottle of ibuprofen in Lenore's clothes; the echoing shrieks of babies that bounced off the terrazzo floors and concrete walls—the stories were drifting apart like a broken ice floe. Her family was dead and so was everyone else, and it all looked different now.

The Algo had already processed 3.7 million choices, from microdecisions to decision clusters, that Lenore had made in her daily life in the last three years: acknowledge or avoid, assert or submit, choose among items, recount an event, etc. Before the heat block, the Algo had been predicting Lenore's decisions with 88 percent accuracy—the highest of any of the subjects, at that point. Because she was easiest for the Algo to get a handle on, Tess had not spent as much time with her, until recent events. The heat block had thrown Lenore's perceptions, reactions, and memories into disarray and made her interesting, algorithmically speaking. This did not detract from Tess's empathy for Lenore, someone she cared about a great deal. They were separate interests.

TESS WAS CHEWING A DATE BAR and staring at a pair of twin fawns grazing behind some barbed wire when the message dropped: a meeting at 11:10 a.m. MST to discuss the progress of the Algo. Thirteen minutes.

She scrambled back to the cabin. She threw off her coat, cap, and vest and washed her face with the sense of dread that she was about to get in trouble, but why? She knew that her work on the Algo was good, she absolutely *knew* it. But was it not good enough?

"You were born waiting for the other shoe to drop," her mother had once said to her.

"Did I have a fetal twin? Is that why I'm always thinking there's something I don't know?"

"Not that I know of," her mother said. "If you did, you must have eaten her pretty early on."

After she checked her teeth for date skin and pulled back her hair (unwashed, extra greasy from the cap), Tess looked for somewhere to sit that was suitably plain and blank. She would be embarrassed for Katherine to see the cabin, the wreath made of turkey feathers, the iron-and-rope light fixture. She didn't know why. It wasn't her house.

She clipped her camera to the front curtains, so at least the light would be good. She had just taken down the print over the sofa, a Labrador with a fish in its mouth, when the black square appeared.

"Tess," croaked the voice of Katherine Son, who sounded as though she were lying down. "Happy birthday. Belated."

"Oh," Tess said, startled. Last week, she had been watching Macy's physical therapy when she'd realized it was her birthday, and if it hadn't been so boring she might not have remembered at all. "Thanks." She tried to focus on the black square, knowing that Katherine could see her.

"This stuff with the malleable memories—you're doing great. Your reach is fantastic." She was very pleased with Tess, she said, and she wanted her to go up.

"Up," repeated Tess. "To Parallaxis?"

"We want to test what you've done on the algorithm against the lived reality," she said. "Move among your subjects, see what they see, to compare with how you've trained the algorithm to process Views."

Tess's heart had been racing for ten minutes, so she wasn't sure what to call whatever it was doing now. *Go pour yourself a glass of water*, purred the soft voice of Rachel inside her phone, her head.

"I can't go up there," Tess said. "It's not ethical, it would muddy—"

"How else can we be sure the algorithm is seeing the right things, making the right sense? Just for a couple weeks. You can squat in an empty owner pod."

Tess's brain was full of bees. "What could I possibly be doing there?"

"You mean what will you tell them? That you're in algorithms at Ground, and you're up there to work on a possible responsive microclimate. Rachel is going, too, and she'll cover you. She knows I'm sending someone on Views."

Tess opened her mouth to clarify and then, remembering that she had no way of knowing what transpired between Katherine and her sister, she closed it again.

"All right," said Tess. "When?"

IT WAS NEARLY CHRISTMAS. Tess had been watching Views for nine months now. Soon she would be in the same place with the subjects; they would see her, talk to her. That night in the honey oak bathroom, fluorescent light overhead and toothpaste blobbed at the corners of her mouth, she tried to see herself as though for the first time. Her skin was pale and clogged, and the light tan that she'd long kept up to hide her acne scars had faded away. She looked like a saltine. Or like Katherine Son, as though she didn't care how she looked. She pulled out the toothbrush and gave a tentative, jarring smile. *Yikes.* She heard the criticism as if Mary Agnes's former friend Ivy were assessing her. *Seriously disturbed.*

She did care how she looked. She was going to meet Rachel, and then the Pioneers, who would have reactions to her, and they wouldn't be able to hide them, not from her. Tess wasn't very good at meeting people—the opposite of Rachel, really. She got along well enough but was always a little off. She never became who was wanted, who was craved.

This time would be different, though, because of what she had learned from Views and the Algo. She knew never to pretend with Irma that she knew about something she didn't, that Irma was better disarmed by frank admissions of ignorance. With Alex, she would affect a bit of self-doubt, a slight wariness of authority. With Malik, it was important to take advice that you asked for. He didn't like to feel that his time had been wasted. Macy was that way, too. Tess knew just how to be.

Her stomach fluttered. Most of her hookups had started online, after exchanging the most polished, artificial reductions of themselves. In a way, meeting the Pioneers would be the opposite. Her relationship with them was the most intense she'd ever had. Not sexually, exactly—she wasn't sexually attracted to any one of them consistently, anyway. The attraction between Lenore and Irma, despite the warnings against fraternizing they'd all received in training, was a development she paid close attention to, though. That she thought about, sometimes. The heat between them, the sweetness of it. And at the end of calls home, Malik and his wife, Colette, would say benign things to each other that transmitted such overwhelming desire, such unwavering devotion, that Tess wanted to wrap herself up in it—not one of them, individually, but what stretched between them that she could not see or measure.

Why did she care so much about Alex? She was only attracted to him when he was talking about his wife, and then just a little. He needs me the most, she had caught herself thinking. But none of them needed her at all.

She thought of Olivia, the woman she had seen for a few months before she'd left for Wyoming and the Pioneers. The sex was boring, in her memory and when she went back and watched it. Now this, now this: rote.

All of it was boring now. The attention that Tess gave to the Pioneers, though, their feelings and perceptions, had tightly attached her to them, and she didn't want it any other way. She was going up.

RACHEL, UP CLOSE and impossibly dewy, her skin like mother-of-pearl, her lips a soft cool pink and balmy. Her black hair was rounded perfectly over her skull, her iconic center part a white line dividing her. She cocked her head toward Tess and her hair fell forward like a curtain she had drawn for their conversation, blocking out the hive of Ground activity around them.

"Tess," she said. "I'm so pleased to finally meet you."

Her voice, low and soft, so much fuller in real life than it was in Tess's head.

"It's such an honor," Tess said, as she had planned.

"Oh!" Rachel laughed. "God, you're so young!"

Even though this was just the reaction that Tess had wanted from Rachel and that Rachel wanted from Tess, Tess felt herself flushing as if the exchange had been entirely spontaneous.

"You're so gorgeous," Tess blurted out as if she could not help it. She bit her lip. "Sorry."

Rachel raised her eyebrows. "I know your kind," she said, teasing. "But generally I do the buttering around here."

"In real life, I mean," said Tess. "You think you know what someone looks like, sounds like, but in real life it's just—"

"I know," Rachel said. "And I hear 'that' voice all day, too, and I forget that it's me. Isn't that crazy?" She smiled and very slightly crinkled her nose.

"Yeah," Tess said. A sudden tremor of doubt, quiet and alarming: was she certain that Rachel knew who she was? "That's funny."

"You'll have to teach me a little about responsive microclimate this week," Rachel said, and Tess's unease spread from head to toe. "I don't know anything about it."

"Of course. I'll—I'll—" Tess faltered.

Rachel looked at her sharply. "You'll need to present much better than that," she said. "Have you been trained in your cover? You can't wing it, not with the engineers."

Tess's relief must have shown on her face.

"Oh," Rachel said. "Oh, I see. Did you think I didn't know you were on Views? Writing algorithms?"

"No, no," Tess said, though for an awful moment, that was exactly what she'd thought.

"You did," Rachel said, nodding. "We're partners, my sister and me. You'll want to remember that."

"Of course."

Rachel gave a half-bright smile, her eyes glancing past Tess. "I'm so excited to finally see the station," she said. "We meant to go together, but I couldn't wait any longer."

A chasm opened. Tess looked at the floor so that Rachel couldn't see her face. If Rachel thought she could lie to Tess, she could not know that Tess was watching her.

But Katherine had said—

"Lunch is served in the lounge simulation," said a Ground guide. "If you'll follow me, please?"

Tess glanced at Rachel, whose eyes had decidedly relaxed, whose jaw was soft as she nodded as if to say that whatever Tess thought, the situation was entirely within her control.

During the Pioneers' training, they had been warned about muscle loss, that their untaxed calves and quadriceps would melt into their flesh as soon as they neglected to use them, and bone loss, because without the constant stress of gravity, the body would stop producing new bone cells and the old bone would waste away. Unused calcium would leach into the bloodstream, causing constipation, kidney stones, and occasionally a kind of psychotic depression too dull and deep to see the edges of, let alone the door. For Rachel and Tess, there were no such warnings.

"What do we need to do to prevent muscle loss?" Tess asked their Ground instructor, glancing at Rachel. "And bone loss, and our eyeballs changing shape into eggs. And—"

"You won't be there long enough for that kind of damage," he said, and Rachel exhaled.

"But I've read the rat study, they lost a third of their muscle mass in ten days—"

"Recent research suggests a longer time frame," he said with a curt smile. "But we'll practice some exercises, absolutely. Always a good idea."

At the end of each day, Tess sat on the bed in her single room—unlike the Pioneers, she and Rachel did not share the bunkroom—and went over Rachel's reactions to the day's training, pinning her heart rate, her blood pressure, her breathing, and her blink rate to the corresponding occurrence. Tess now had many of Rachel's facial expressions, too, because she was so often watching her, stealing glances whenever she could. This new angle was incredibly rich in information. Katherine had been right to send Tess up to observe, she thought, as risky as it had seemed. Anyway, Rachel paid Tess little attention. It took everything she had not to show that she was frightened, that she dreaded her journey to Parallaxis.

Tess had known that before their training. What she still didn't understand was why Rachel was going anyway. The answer had to be in the holes, the hours of Rachel's life that Tess couldn't access because Katherine was there. When she dwelled on this, she found herself circling another doubt: she had no evidence that Rachel understood how tightly the Views project was linked to Parallaxis I, that the station and Sensus were joined not only at the top, but all the way down to the Pioneers, and to Tess, and to Rachel herself.

The Pioneers didn't know they were subjects in the Views project, and Tess hadn't bothered much about that, had she? Not since the day she had taken Katherine's offer. To worry about Rachel Son, of all people—

But if Rachel's own sister had done it? Not the corporation, whom anybody could expect to be essentially evil.

The one Tess worked for.

No, stop it. She was exhausted, from training in the day and catching up with the Pioneers and the Algo every night, from being in the same room with other people for the first time in a year, pretty much, and having to talk to them, move her face in response to them, resume life as a social being. It was absurd for Tess to worry about the cofounder of Sensus, of all people. Rachel was focused and discreet, and she had decided that Tess was awkward and uninteresting, not someone to trouble herself for.

Tess saw the faint blue glow at the corner of the window first and pressed her cheek against it for a better look, forgetting, for a moment, the helmet that bumped her away. The noctilucent clouds at the edges of the Earth's atmosphere looked carved from ice. As they drew nearer to them, Rachel looked panicked, her eyes opening and closing too tightly.

"We go straight through that?" Tess asked, as if Rachel's fear were her own.

"They're just clouds," Rachel said.

The clouds seemed to glow and pulse along the bottom edge. They became more forbidding every second until they were a wall, a frozen ocean wave.

"You're sure," Tess said.

"Yes," Rachel answered her, but she shut her eyes, and so did Tess. When she opened them, the clouds were gone.

Tess was first to see the station. "Look," she said, trying to let go of her straps, but her hands had nearly cramped shut around them. The silver ring was perched among the stars at a jaunty angle, like a hat. It looked so small, as though the people inside must have to wiggle through it on their bellies. The people inside! She couldn't believe it, couldn't scale it in her mind.

"Mozgov has been in that thing for eight years," Rachel said.

"I can't believe it hasn't killed him," Tess said.

Rachel didn't answer.

They drew close enough to see the Helper, docked to the inside of the ring and as unlike Parallaxis as could be: a cylinder, dirty and scratched, a tin can.

"Just about there," said the voice from Ground. Tess glanced to the side out of habit, forgetting as she had all day that in their suits and helmets, she could barely see Rachel at all. Tess felt a far, low tremble, like an earthquake too small to notice without warning. Rachel moaned.

"And we're in," said Ground. "Great flight, textbook. Are you all right, Rachel? We're docking you now, should take four, five minutes, about twenty more before we open the airlock to the Helper."

"Oh, thank God," Rachel half whimpered, half laughed, sounding on the verge of tears. "Thank you, thank you."

Tess was staring at the airlock door. "We made it!" she said in weak celebration, mimicking Rachel's tone. She was about to meet the Pioneers.

IRMA CAME FOR THEM. She took Tess's helmet off, smiling almost maternally, and Tess gasped at her closeness, the warmth from her body, the sensation of a dissolving wall. "Hi," she barked, but her voice was small and tinny in the sudden crowd of people around her. She saw Malik, and the gray fuzz he'd grown since his last shave on Earth, and Ted, his smudgy eyeglasses strapped tightly around his head, helping Rachel out of her helmet. There was Macy hanging back, watching. The airlock door opened and Carl Bouchet floated there, smiling through clenched jaws, eyes screwed up to inspect them. Tess could see that Rachel didn't recognize everyone there. While Rachel stared at the choir of round, babyish faces as though she couldn't tell them apart, Tess felt her nerves climb into her throat.

"Hi, hello," Tess said. She gave a little wave. She hadn't meant to lower herself from the start, but she was too nervous to manage any-thing between badly feigned arrogance, like a drunk, or apology for ex-isting. She glanced at Rachel and saw her reaching up to feel her floating strands of hair. She was smiling, showing off her dimples. Even now, she was so pretty.

"Are you all right?" Irma asked Tess. She reached backward toward Macy, who handed her a water bottle. "Here, drink up."

When Tess, hands shaking, finished with the bottle, Macy took it from her and handed her a new tube of lip balm.

"Oh, thank you," Tess said. "I guess you know everything I need al-ready, huh?" She sounded, blessedly, like her normal self.

"Yep," said Macy. "I remember this well."

Tess felt her limbs floating up, but she knew from having watched the Pioneers' first minutes without gravity that she probably appeared stiff and frightened, that she might feel like a jellyfish but look like a thrown doll. Rachel did. The Pioneers laughed at both of them in a friendly, wel-coming way, and the sound of that laughter, in real life, was as wondrous to Tess as floating. She knew her whole face was blooming in uncontrol-lable joy and that the others would think it was because of the floating. She glanced at Rachel and saw that though she was still smiling at the Pioneers crowded around her, she'd gone quite pale and pulled her chin into her neck. She was on the verge of vomiting. Only then did Tess no-tice the peculiar stink of the bodies around them.

Rachel caught her eye and Tess frowned.

"Do you need a—" Tess turned to Alex. "She's going to barf."

Macy swung the bag up to Rachel's mouth with not a moment to spare.

"Weightlessness will take some getting used to," she said. "Your guts are floating, too. I was nauseated for days."

Rachel nodded, keeping her mouth covered.

Tess tried to look at the Helper, to express the expected wonder, but she wanted only to stare at the people around her. On Earth, Macy had been so lean and muscled, almost sinewy, but up here she was yeast risen. Teddy's and Malik's faces looked softer in person, too, almost mushy, as though if Tess pressed her finger into a cheek, it would sink right through. All the flesh and the blood and fat beneath had floated up. They looked alike now, like a family.

"Where's everyone else?" Rachel asked her.

"Working, we're working all the time," Macy said. Tess saw the fatigue hiding in the pink rims of her eyes, the way they were tucked far under her puffy eyelids.

"Welcome aboard," said a low, hoarse voice. Josef Mozgov, long and thin, shoulders hunched high: a dark heron. He folded his arms in front of his chest. His clothes were ragged, worn fleece sweats with a big hole in one thigh. Tess could see his bluish skin, the dark hair on his legs. He was tethered to his control center at both hips. Rachel stared at him.

"Your clothes," she said.

"I have more, I just like these best." He pulled one hand from his folded arms just enough to brush the air. "Go on, Carl will take you around, try to get comfortable. We'll meet up later."

"Yes, let's do that," Rachel said, buoyant. "Carl, show us the way."

The way, Tess knew, was through the Helper toilet. Tess thought she was prepared for it, but she was not, and she knew that she would stay in her diaper as long as she could stand it.

"It's unacceptable to have to pass through that space," Rachel said on the other side. She breathed into her elbow.

"Don't worry, you'll probably never see him again," Teddy said. A low chuckle, taut smile, and then he and Malik left them, said they had to get back to work.

THE PODS THAT TESS had watched the Pioneers work eleven, sometimes fourteen hours a day to build looked shoddier in person. The walls of the feedbag had jagged seams where light shined through and were smudged with fingerprints, toe prints. Rachel pecked at them with a fingernail.

"It must be so much harder to do everything in zero-g," Tess said.

"The schedule doesn't leave much room for a learning curve," Carl said.

Tess nodded. "It's incredible how much you've accomplished in such a short time."

Rachel twitched. Her sleek helmet of hair had been transformed into dandelion fluff.

"It's worse than I was briefed," she said. "Worse than it looks on video." Worse than she had promised her billionaires. She pushed away from the wall and bumped into a clump of loose wiring. Tess winced.

Rachel gave a tiny gasp. "Are these live?"

"Those shouldn't be loose. I'll take care of it," Carl said. "So sorry, Ms. Son."

"Rachel," she corrected him. "Rachel's fine." She brushed at her thigh where the wires had touched her. They had not shocked her, but she was acting as though they had. "Let's push on."

Carl hustled past the barracks, where he and the Pioneers still slept each night, and then Macy's clinic, Esther's office, and the labs: Teddy's robotics lab, Lenore's fabrication lab, Irma's greenhouse lab, Malik's air and water lab, Alex's algae lab. The staff homepods were only partially built, and Tess peered into the open wall cavities to see all the snaking tubes stuffed inside, the machinery that would keep them all alive, clean, breathing. Some of the Pioneers' homepods had been put together perfectly, beautifully even. She looked up at Carl and smiled. He was attractive in that big-faced way that actors were, chiseled and toothy.

He was watching Rachel and biting the inside of his cheek. Tess followed his eyes to Rachel and to the sudden end of the floor. The subfloor should have been completely installed by now, but here was a gap of the length of a few schoolbuses where the dense maze of systems that ran under the floor of the whole station was exposed, unprotected from dust, hair, and human clumsiness.

Rachel, ankles dangling, put her hands in her hair and tried to smooth it down.

She ought to have understood that any shortcomings were the fault of Ground and their ignorant expectations. The amber light from the Sky, set to sunset, bathed her face. She pointed silently up to a dark panel up ahead, on the right edge. Tess hadn't noticed it, but once she did, the Sky seemed to crack apart into its grid of light panels, and the walls around them closed in.

A blue puff of gas shot out from a hole in the wall. "What is that?" Rachel asked.

"Bluebreeze, for the odors," Carl said.

"Sort of blue-raspberry?" Tess said. That was how Macy had always described it. "Plus dryer sheets."

Rachel would have said "cheap." The station was builder-grade, dirty, raggedy edges everywhere. Pod walls that were supposed to have the pearly glow of nautilus shells looked like packing material. Tess swallowed.

"This is lovely," she murmured as she ran her fingers along the pebbled ground of the central promenade. She meant it. The texture felt nice under her fingers.

"It'll keep us from slipping," Carl said. "We'll be walking in a bowl, perpetually uphill, once we're walking again."

"It'll get filthy," Rachel said. She hadn't done a single flip.

TESS HAD PLANNED to get to dinner before anyone else so she could let the Pioneers choose to come to her, if they wanted to. There were three tables in the feedbag, each with a ringed pedestal for clipping a leg leash. Tess chose the farthest from the doorway and tried to manage what her face was doing, but not too much. Rachel clipped right next to her, which was a surprise and a strange relief.

Alex and Lenore came swooping through the door first, and then Malik and Teddy. They were all so elegant and economical in their movements, like dancers. Tess smiled, waved her weird, shy "hi," hoping Alex and Lenore would come over. Malik and Teddy joined them instead. Tess had hoped to work up to this interaction, practice with safer people first. Of all the Pioneers, they were most likely to ask her detailed questions about responsive climate systems.

"Overwhelming," she said quickly when they asked her how her first day had been. "It's just incredibly impressive, what you've built here." Malik smiled at her—appreciative, she thought. She knew he saw every flaw and more besides. She relaxed. She knew them, and she would do fine.

Dinner was called Smoked Tofu Steaks with Shoestring Squash and Green Matter. "It's one of the better ones," said Teddy.

Tess watched Rachel note its familiarities: the black grill marks, a smearing of russet-colored sauce. Still, she squeezed her tofu steak out of its bag with tight-throated trepidation, and Tess did the same. The squash was spongy; the greens were dark and chewy, reconstituted but familiar.

"You want to work the sauce around a little bit," Malik said, massaging his tofu bag.

"So, Tess, what exactly do you do?" Teddy asked her.

"Algorithms," she said, careful not to be so blasé that she sounded as though she were concealing something. She felt Rachel's attention. "Optimizing some of the station's automatic processes."

"Which ones?" Teddy asked. "I handle our robotics."

"Microclimate, mostly for human comfort. It's an experiment still." Tess expected Rachel to corroborate, but Rachel didn't say anything. In another month or two, the Algo could help Tess through this conversation, but not quite yet.

"Your tofu is flying away," Teddy said. Tess pushed off the table and tried to grab it, but her leash yanked her back down. Malik was already unclipping himself, and he flew after the lost tofu. Tess felt everyone's eyes on them.

"Thanks," she said when he returned it to her. Rachel had turned around to face Irma, who had just addressed her from another table. Tess was on her own.

"No problem," Malik said. "How micro? At the pod level? I do air and water engineering, oversee the ice mining. I'm surprised we haven't been talking."

Tess beamed. "Oh, I know all about *you*—I mean, we're all huge fans, at Ground. We've been working on a responsive climate, pod-level, working from your biostats. Conditions look pretty trying up here, and we want to make it more comfortable for you all." She glanced at Rachel again.

"Great," Malik said. "Air circulation is an issue already, and it's only going to get worse. The hair. Not mine."

"Yeah, we've seen that. I think we should start vacuuming everybody's heads every morning." She smiled. "They're working on a different fan for the barracks. That's where it's worst, right?" Tess could handle this. She knew all about the issues they faced, albeit from a different angle.

Around them, the other Pioneers kept up a labored chatter between their eating choreography; Tess had never seen a group of people try so hard to conceal their collective fatigue. Rachel might have reminded the subjects that they needn't pretend for her—they would have liked that—but she looked very tired and didn't seem to have it in her to comfort anyone. Or she saw no need. They all lived here now and there wasn't anything they could do about it.

As dinner was ending, and the people around them were beginning to unclip and repackage their refuse, Lenore floated by them.

"Lenore, hi, I'm Tess," she said. "We didn't meet earlier. I'm an engineer at Ground. How are you?"

Lenore, her eyes hollow, smiled sadly. "Well, you didn't bring me any different news, did you?"

"No," said Tess, and she let her real sadness for Lenore right into her voice, didn't try to hide it or mask. "Lenore, I'm so sorry. We are all so, so sorry."

"Thanks," Lenore said. "I appreciate that, I do."

Rachel was watching her.

"Please let us know if there's anything at all we can do," Rachel said, but it sounded late, and canned. Lenore flew toward the door.

When she was out of sight, Teddy turned back to Rachel.

"The family option," he began. He looked almost feverish, perspiration clinging to his upper lip. "It's still on, correct? As soon as we're spinning, correct?"

"Correct." Rachel blinked at him. "As long as they are physically and mentally sound—we don't want anyone to get hurt—we plan to bring them up as soon as we have gravity."

"Plan to?"

"We *will* bring them up." Rachel was off her game, Tess could see, distracted by the way her shoulders kept creeping up toward her ears without her knowledge, by the way her filmy new clothes fluttered against her skin. "That's why I'm up here, to make sure everything is operating as efficiently as possible, to help you get to that point. Once we have gravity and finish the build-out—"

"Yes, right," Teddy said. "It's just that—we're working so hard, and what if we get there and then you all decide—"

"Teddy," Rachel said, trying for warmth. "You're not being tricked." She sounded impatient, like he was asking stupid questions at the end of class and keeping everyone there.

"It's not generosity," Tess said, and Rachel tensed.

"Ground wants to study their experience on Parallaxis, too," Tess said, glancing warily at Rachel as though she expected to be reprimanded. Her head was light with the thrill of her transgression. "They want diverse data."

"Right," said Teddy.

"Symbiosis—more reliable than kindness," Tess said, drawing up one side of her mouth. Teddy would see now that Tess was on their side.

Rachel smiled, tried to squeeze into the developing camaraderie. "Don't worry, Teddy."

Teddy frowned but seemed to settle back into himself. "We'll keep at it, then," he said, and then he turned and glided away.

Tess had learned so much from Rachel over the last year, much more than she'd realized, about how to be however it was best to be. She'd learned it in her head, but now she was doing it herself, with her face and voice and body, in real life. Better than Rachel, even. Rachel would bounce back—she was muddled from the journey, Tess knew. Tess had spent a lot more time getting used to life here than she had.

Invasives

12.

Alex and Irma built out their labs together, moving back and forth between them as if they would be shared. They were often together for hours at a time without seeing anyone else—like being part of a couple, especially when he noticed something else about Irma that reminded him of Meg. Her freckles, her tenacity. Thick thighs and wild hair, no polite laughter. He still wanted Meg, and familiar, comforting, boring, end-of-the-day married sex, with more jokes than fire, in their own bed with their old cotton blankets, and then to go to sleep with his nose buried in her neck for five minutes or so until she pushed him away because he was slobbering on her and she needed some space. He did not think she would appreciate this fantasy, but it was the truth.

He'd never *not* wanted Meg. He'd been loyal, always, in that way. But he'd neglected to hold up his end of their marriage, possibly (probably) because he was sure she wouldn't drop hers. He'd been wrong about that, too.

"Did you talk about her this much when you were married?" Irma asked him. They were installing strip lighting in her six cylindrical greenhouses, each tower stretching from the pod's floor to its ceiling.

"No," he said. "Who knew that everything on a space station would remind me of my wife, the technophobe." He paused. "Semi-ex wife."

"You can just say Meg," said Irma.

"Do you want to talk about—" Alex grappled for the name of Irma's semi-ex girlfriend who had died fighting fires, but Irma hadn't told him.

"Erin. And no, I don't think so. Not today."

She blew out her cheeks and sighed, and for a moment Alex thought she'd changed her mind.

"All right, that was the last strip. Ready?"

She turned on the lights, and they stared. The greenhouses were miniature skyscrapers, grids of lit windows and empty rooms. Soon they would be filled with climbing plants, and then they might look like abandoned buildings reclaimed by the natural world, every potted pothos trailing longer and longer, over desk chairs and along cubicle walls, after the people had gone.

"I could start planting tomorrow," she said, hushed and giddy at the same time. She turned to him, and the fatigue that had clouded in her huge brown eyes for weeks had vanished. "Tonight, maybe."

"We'll do the trellises tomorrow." He laughed. "It's really happening."

"Wait, strike that," she said, sobering up. "Tomorrow we'll do your light install. We have to catch you up, so you can start growing as soon as we're spinning, as soon as our feet hit the ground."

"No, no," said Alex. "If you can start now, you should. I'll be fine."

"You sure?"

"Yeah, yeah," he said. "I've gotten much better at doing this stuff in zero-g, thanks to you. Grow us some goddamn salad, please." He pulled his canteen from his belt.

Irma did the same, and raised her canteen in a toast. "To the family farm."

As they drew closer to the spins, Alex began to avoid Irma, and everyone else, too. The pressure in his head became a snare drum, hard to think through.

Yesterday, Irma insisted at breakfast that he let her help, that she refused to bail on him, and waved her off again. He needed to deal with lab supplies that came up in cargo with Rachel Son and Tess, he said; there was no helping to do. This morning he skipped breakfast altogether and went straight to his lab. He believed that he could replicate Tray 182, given the chance and the right conditions, but what condition was *he* in? Look at what he'd ordered: full-spectrum and 75 percent lights; rolls of polygon mesh in 23, 73, 160, and 225 microns; two brands of soluble phosphorus that were identical in composition and should not have made any difference. The key to Tray 182? Probably not the mesh! He skipped lunch, too, and ate two go-gels.

Irma knocked on his door in the afternoon. She had brought him a bag of pudding.

"Great, thanks, yum." He tried to sound calm. Calm and normal. "How's it going over there?"

"No germination yet. I'm helping Malik now, unless there's anything I can do to help you—"

"Nah, I've got it."

"I was thinking it might be faster if you—"

He held up a hand. "I'm fine! I've got my own timeline, okay? Everything's fine."

Irma jerked back.

"Sorry." Alex closed his eyes. "I'm—I'm bad. It's bad." He took a fast breath. "Oh, boy."

"Hey," she said, and the concern in her voice undid him. He should have replicated 182 before he came up, obviously he should have. The algae was not going to grow fast enough and then Irma wouldn't have enough biomass to feed the crops and their families would never escape to Beta, his fault entirely. The planet would burn while he was up here tangled in rolls of mesh—

"Are you freaking out?"

He tried to answer but couldn't get it out.

"Hey! It's okay. We're in this together. Look, let me see your—"

There was a knock at the door, and Alex looked in the direction of the sound as if doom itself were calling.

"Alex," Irma said. "Deep breath. What would Meg say?"

"Oh, God." He buried his eyes behind his hands.

"I meant she would know what to—"

"I know," he said miserably.

"Hello," Rachel said, peeking in from behind the door. "Just making the rounds, checking in on our gardens."

Irma looked at Alex and then turned back to Rachel. "Alex is freaking out," she said, like Rachel was their friend. "After twenty years of trying to stabilize global warming all by himself, the pressure is getting to him."

"Ah," said Rachel. "But you're not trying to do anything new up here, you've already done it."

Alex's throat was dry. "Replication isn't—replication is its own—"

"Is there anything you need?" she asked. "We can get you anything at all, just say the word."

Alex shook his head. "I'm fine. It's going to work just fine. I'm probably drinking too much coffee."

Rachel smiled at him tenderly, her dimples winking at him. "Can you give us a minute?" she asked Irma.

Alex didn't want to be alone with Rachel. He was still weirded out by the sound of her voice coming from a real human body, as though he were conversing with a robot that had become sentient. "Irma—"

But Irma was drifting out the door already. "Yep," she said. "I'll come by later."

"Alex," Rachel purred when she was gone. "Listen to me. You're not here to save the world. We didn't bring you up here thinking that *you* would be able to *save* the *world*. I mean, my goodness."

"But you said Parallaxis wanted to support—"

"We do, we do!" she said. "We want to support this particular science, and the people doing it. That *is* the whole point of Parallaxis. But you can't put the weight of the whole planet on your shoulders, that's absurd. You're just one man." Her eyes were gentle, a kind teacher's eyes. "All we need from you is enough carbon fixation—I'm probably not saying that right, forgive me"—she fluttered her hand—"so that the people who live here can breathe. You seven—nine, with the astronauts—and the people who will come to live here with you."

"Their families," he said.

"Yes, and then the other Parallaxis owners. So, a few dozen at the most. Not nine billion." She laughed. "Does that help?"

"Yeah," he said, laughing back, not knowing why. "Got it."

"I'm told you've managed other methods for carbon capture with your algae, is that right? Not the brand-new-species thing but something else that would work for Parallaxis? Hang on, they sent me the title— 'Pre-irradiation of aquatic growth medium . . .'"

"Allows algal species to make use of one hundred percent of the visible light spectrum," he finished. "That's not a solution. I just wrote that because—"

"I'm told that you say here that it *does* work."

"As a method for enhanced carbon capture, yes, but it's brutally expensive, it doesn't scale, and it's ecologically more costly than the amount of problem it solves."

"Well, it seems like it would help the people on this space station," Rachel said, raising her eyebrows. "We don't need it to scale."

"But—but it doesn't address climate stabilization—"

"Down there, on Earth, I understand," said Rachel. "But we need clean air here. So maybe this is Plan B, if you don't have your algae doing what we need it to by our gravity deadline? Yes."

His panic was shrinking, and then so was he.

"Good," she said. "No need to get torn up. Having Parallaxis work as it should *is* saving the world, as far as I'm concerned."

She paused in the doorway, one hand wrapped around the frame. "Oh, and don't skip your VR sessions, or your time with Esther."

"I don't have time for VR," he said.

"You don't have time for a nervous breakdown, either," she said. A hand over her heart. "Please, take care."

THE PIONEERS HAD A CALL home that night, and when Meg asked Alex about the algae, her questions made him squirm with a new dread, a kind of embarrassment. His wife had given up her own career, one where she made a difference in people's lives every single day, where girls called her in the middle of the night because they thought only Meg could help them (and they were right!) so that he could chase this dream. His ego had conned them both. But not the Sons or Ground—they had seen him from a distance and known exactly what he was good for: making some nice air for billionaires, so they wouldn't need to solve the climate crisis anymore. They could just leave.

He couldn't tell Meg any of this. She would say that he needed to talk to the counselor on board—Esther, right? That this new pressure, after so many years working on the margins, was bound to unsettle him. And that she loved him, though not like that, and that Rachel was wrong, and fuck the Sons, fuck Sensus for—

He didn't tell Meg any of that, on his call home. He told her, and Shane, and Mary Agnes, that from the large circular window in the observation lounge, he could see the Earth, and that it was huge, and that he and the others could see hurricanes as they formed. He told them about the Sky, how eerily real it was sometimes, and how the designers had solved the problem of the sun's brightness and location by having sunlight pour down from just out of view, so you'd never be able to look right at it and see that it wasn't bright enough to be real. He told Mary Agnes about the fab lab, where Lenore made everything they needed out of foams and plastics. Like Santa's workshop, he said to Shane, who giggled conspiratorially because last year, he'd gotten in on the joke.

"I want to come, too," Mary Agnes said. She said it differently this time, without urgency, as though she knew it were impossible.

Alex looked at Meg, who had reached up to stroke their daughter's green head. "I wish you would," he said. "All of you."

THE NEXT MORNING, Tess, the young Ground engineer who had come up with Rachel, came to see Alex's lab. He had talked with her a little at dinner a few times, and she struck him as either reserved or uncertain, someone who preferred small talk. She waved a small "hi" before every conversation and paused on the third or fourth word of each sentence as if she had to wait for the rest of it to land. After months stewing in the intimacy of the Pioneers—the casually probing questions, the knowing looks, the yawning, the arguments that paused and started again over weeks or months, the butt scratching, the closeness—Alex found his superficial conversations with her to be a relief.

She had asked him at breakfast if she could visit his lab and hear more about his research—she knew all about it, she said. She called it "super, super cool." Alex said fine. It wasn't as though he had anything to hide, really, except his doubts in himself, in the Sons' intentions, in the whole Parallaxis enterprise. Come by whenever, he said.

"Hey, hi," she said, waving from the door. She bumped into the door frame. "Whoopsy," she said under her breath.

"It takes a while," he said, laughing to put her at ease. "Well, for me it did. Some people got it right away, but they must have been fish in a past life."

Her eyes darted up at him in surprise, but she didn't say anything.

"So," he said, "what can I show you?"

"Your lab looks ready to go," she said. "These are the racks for the algae trays?"

"Oh, it's not ready," he said. "I mean, this is the easy part, right? This is just insert tab A into slot B."

"But even that looks super hard up here." She swung an empty rack back and forth in the air. "Nothing does what you expect it to."

"I didn't mean *easy*," he said. "It's taken us almost five months to get this far, when at home this would be the work of a few weeks, tops."

"I'm starting to understand how three years turned into nine," she said, keeping her head tilted down and her light eyes up. "Or whatever. A long time."

He watched as she trailed her fingers along the cursed rolls of mesh, lashed together and floating like an island in the middle of his lab. "What are these for?" she asked, peering at the labels. "What are the different sizes?" She asked him question after question about the materials in his lab and how they would work together, but when he started to ask about her work on Parallaxis, she winced.

"I'm not allowed to talk about it," she said. "I'm sorry."

"Oh," he said.

She groaned. "That's not true. I mean, I'm not allowed to talk about it with people outside Parallaxis, obviously, but I'm sure I could talk about it with *you*. I'm just in a weird place, you know? Like, who am I up here?" She laughed nervously. "Yikes, sorry."

"No, it's okay," Alex said. "I understand, seriously."

"Is that a paper book?" she asked, pointing to the notepad that did not quite fit in his fanny pack.

Back to the questions. He nodded and shrugged. "My wife still uses them and I'm used to it," he said. "I guess I find it comforting."

"I thought you and your wife split up last year?" she said, looking at him with such benign curiosity that Alex felt like an idiot for using the word *wife* at all.

"Yeah," he said. "Common knowledge, I guess." He nodded down at his belly, toward the notepad. "Well, they're good to have for backup in case of a power outage."

"But if there was a power outage, we'd all die!" Tess said, and when he looked at her in exasperation, he was surprised to see her smiling. She was joking with him.

"Ha, yes," he said. "So many ways to die up here."

"So . . . how's it going for you?" She sounded uneasy, as though she meant to tell him that her work wasn't going great, either.

"Well, I'm trying to do this thing that should be easy for me because I've done it before." He shrugged again, more of a twitch at this point. "But it hasn't happened yet, and people are waiting on me, and—I don't like to disappoint people."

"Yeah," she said. "Me neither, and I always am." She sighed.

"Oh, I doubt that. It's tough up here, in this environment. The expectations are the same, much higher actually, but the environment—it's like trying to do tasks in a dream, you know? The car is on fire, the extinguisher is floating away."

She laughed. "What's the . . . what's the bugbear?"

"Oh, I just have a few things to work out, still, things I thought I'd have gotten by now. Hiccups. Bugbear. Haven't heard that before." He was trying to brush her questions away, but she was homing in, and he didn't like it.

"That really sucks," she said, too earnestly, and though she was two meters away, he felt as though she were leaning into him. "What happened?"

"Nothing. Nothing *happened*," he said. She swung the trays back and forth in their racks with her fingertips. "It's not like I'm being tasked with saving the world, either, it's no big deal."

"No big deal? Your work? Do you really think that?"

"Well, it's just for rich people, it turns out. Not the whole planet." His mouth filled with sourness. "Anyway, everybody has anxiety about replicating results."

"What do you mean?"

"Who doesn't have nightmares where they don't deliver, right? What if there's an error?"

Her eyes flashed. "You think there's an error?"

"No!" he shouted. He hadn't meant to shout. "But what if there is, you know? I don't think so, but what if there is!" He had not meant to say any of this to her. He didn't even *know* her, and how was he having this conversation? "The air's a little thin, isn't it? Oh, ha ha, that's my problem!"

He had said so much more than he meant to, and he didn't know why. The room got smaller with her every question, and he had nowhere to go.

"The pressure . . . that sounds really hard." She swallowed. "I mean, it is hard. For me, too."

That sounds really hard was what Meg said to help someone, typically a teen on the brink, open up about their troubles. It meant she could be trusted not to dismiss them, that she believed their struggles were real. But Alex didn't want to open up. He wanted her to leave. He wanted people to stop coming into his lab and pulling his feelings out of his throat, stretching them across the light to examine them, crisscrossing them until he didn't know how he felt anymore.

"Well, I really need to get back to work," he said. "Enjoy your time here—it'll be over before you know it."

"Yeah," she said, wistful. "I don't want to leave, though. Everyone here is super interesting, such a rich and varied group of people."

"Rich and varied," he repeated. "Yes, we are."

13

Tess left Alex's lab and hurried back to her own pod. She wanted to watch their interaction from his perspective and cross-reference the biometrics. She went to his feed, but before she could enter the time marker where she wanted to start, she saw him in real time, flying down the promenade toward Irma's lab. He rapped on her door and didn't wait for her to answer before he flung it open.

Irma was snacking while she inspected her root modules. "Whoa, what?" she said when she saw Alex.

"I can't believe I'm the one worrying about replicating. You're contaminating everything right now," he said.

"Jesus, are you okay?"

"Why does everyone keep asking me if I'm okay?"

"Uh," she said. "Close the door."

"I'm fine," he said. "I just had kind of a weird conversation."

Tess felt her face getting hot. She pressed pause. She shouldn't watch this, she knew. But this was important data, wasn't it? She opened Irma's feed, too, so she could see Alex's face as he talked about her.

"You ever talk with Tess?"

"Not much," she said. "Just the basics."

"She's small-talky, right? Like, markedly so?"

"Yeah, I'd say that."

"Well, she came to my lab to check things out and—it felt like she was rooting around in me," he said.

"What do you mean?"

His eyes were still while his mouth twitched. "Like we were having a pretty normal conversation, but then she kept asking me questions, non-stop. Facty-facts at first, and then a very fast acceleration to questions . . . like we're close friends, I guess?"

Irma snorted. "Maybe she likes you?"

"No, no," he said. "Not like that. Like she was . . . I felt like I was being scraped by a person, if that makes sense. Like bits of information were flying out of my mouth and she was just collecting them in a bag—"

"Alex," Irma said flatly. "Listen to me."

"Like she was riffling around in my brain for anything *interesting*, I don't know. But you should have seen her, when she found it. She looked like she'd had a fucking blood transfusion." He drew his shoulders up—Tess knew he was doing an impression of her, she knew it instantly—flung his eyes wide, and pinched his mouth in perverted excitement.

Tess tried to pull her shoulders down. It was from the typing, that her shoulders got hunched up like that. From coding.

"What did you tell her?" Irma asked.

Alex let his arms flop. "That I'm worried that my algae isn't going to work, that maybe there's an error."

"Because there could be an error, or did you tell her there was an error?"

"The first one. I think. I mean, it is the first one. But she might not know the difference, you know? You know what she called us? 'Rich and varied.' The same language people use to describe data sets."

"Alex, she's working on algorithms on a space station. And she's, what, twenty-five? This is probably the first place she's been that isn't school. You've got to calm the fuck down—"

"Just be careful," he said. "When you talk to her, be careful. You'll feel it. It's like she's pulling stuff out of you and you don't know, and then you feel it—this empty *thunk*."

THIS IS PROBABLY *the first place she's been that isn't school,* Irma had said about her. Translation: Tess doesn't know how to act with people, how to behave. It stung even more than Alex's impression.

She replayed Alex's Views of their conversation in his lab twice to look at herself, and then she watched his conversation with Irma again. Horrible, to come upon a friend doing a nasty impression of you, and still worse to watch it again knowing that it was coming, which gestures and grimaces he would use to create "you" for someone else—for someone he actually liked. Alex was not her friend, even though she believed that, to some extent, she was his, because she cared about him.

When she'd asked him if there had been an error, her eyes had glinted slightly—at least, that's how it must have looked to him. A human response, excitement at a secret of any kind. In her future conversations, she would have to hide her feelings better.

14

Whenever Rachel had guided potential investors through the virtual tour of Parallaxis, she had quoted an edited list of Simon Vaswani's inspirations: honeycombs, seashells, the inside of a perfect croissant. She liked this mix of mathematical brilliance in the natural world and the civilized one. The Hourglass Nebula had been her addition, for the grandeur of space in the human imagination.

Simon had also been inspired by the massive superyachts designed for Russian oligarchs, by a drawing of an underground ice castle from a storybook he'd loved as a child, and by the Guggenheims New York and Bilbao. He'd told Rachel a story about himself as a teenager, looking through his worn and cruddy art history textbook, and seeing a picture of a white building wearing a weird brown hat. The building was a chapel, Le Corbusier's Notre Dame du Haut, and looking at it, he felt like believing in something, he said, even if that something was the building itself. Vaswani himself was agnostic, but he'd designed nine churches, from a small private chapel in Utah to the stadium-sized Light + Way in Florida. Designing belief, he told Rachel, was one part fantasy, one part nostalgia, and two parts lighting. When Katherine had told him about her dreams for Parallaxis, he'd heard a familiar desire for both childlike awe and childhood security. She wanted a church, a place designed to teach its visitors to believe in her vision.

Rachel flipped through the snack selections in the dispenser. Go-gels and proteoats, go-gels and proteoats. In ten minutes, she would have to tell her sister that this was not that place.

Her second evening on Parallaxis, Rachel had gone alone to find Mozgov. Teddy hadn't been kidding, she understood now: he would not seek her out.

She didn't remember very much about Josef Mozgov from when she'd known him on Earth. He was one of the last people that Katherine had dated before she lost interest in the labor of traditional romantic relationships. They were together a few months and then Katherine had ended it and hired him for Parallaxis instead. It was unlike Rachel to have absorbed so little about someone in her sister's life, but Katherine had met Mozgov when Rachel was entangled herself, for once distracted.

All she remembered about Mozgov then was the intensity between him and Katherine about Parallaxis, and how relieved Rachel had been to escape that particular obsession. Grateful, even, to be excluded from those conversations.

Rachel fretted at the top of the ladder, where a device she did not know how to use kept her from entering the Helper airlock.

"Code 154 for the toilet," Mozgov said from the speaker.

"I don't need the toilet," she said. He didn't respond. She punched the toilet code and entered the Helper airlock, a box as empty and banged up as a freight elevator. The door on the other end had a TOILET label slapped across it.

"Mozgov," she said.

The door slid open. Carl, dutiful and grim, slipped out and shot past her. Rachel pulled herself through the toilet and into the Helper. She didn't breathe until the toilet door clicked shut.

"It's best to have the toilet between them and Control," he said, gesturing with one hand, arms crossed. "Keeps everyone where they're supposed to be."

"Is something wrong with your other hand?" she asked him.

"No," he said. "All things considered, I'm holding up well."

She stared at him, looking for a person she recognized instead of a collection of features: a dark mat of hair, one badly crooked front tooth, dark eyes that didn't keep still.

He had remade the Helper to suit him. In the bunk area, he'd cobbled together a private cubicle for himself. Screens and cameras meant for the workroom covered two of his homemade walls—made from what? What was missing elsewhere so he could have these walls?—lashed together with zip ties. On one wall he'd rigged some straps into a make-shift gurney that she supposed, from the greasy gray spot where his head must go every night, was his bed.

"So you've come up to make us look good," he said. "You want a bag of coffee?"

The pouch he offered was the size and color of a mouse. "I hear you never come out, ever," she said.

"I don't like mingling," he said. "You'd think I'd want to meet the new people, wouldn't you? And then they all showed up."

He sounded loose, too candid. She had not spoken with him often—twice in the last year, another handful in years before that—and always alongside her sister. He'd always sounded judicious, if wary. But then, she herself had always been soft, encouraging, and it seemed unlikely that she could be that way now.

"And Carl?" she asked. "Is he ready to take over for you?"

Mozgov shrugged. "He'll do as he's told."

With one finger hooked through a zip tie, she brought the coffee bag to her lips. "Oh, God," she said. "This isn't coffee."

"It is inspired by the thought of coffee."

"We'll have better coffee soon," she said, nodding to herself.

"Yes, soon," he said. "Just as soon as we get spinning. Everything will work perfectly, just like it does on Earth."

The smile he gave her then surprised her with its hostility. On Earth, seeing him on video, she had mistaken what the years without gravity had done to his face as evidence of his relative health and good spirits. His forehead bore no creases, no telltale signs of wear, but his eyes were the dull gray of gravel. Everything seemed to shift then—the room around her, the man before her, and the woman he thought he was speaking to. Mozgov didn't look forty-five, he looked like another species.

"It's much worse than I was briefed," she said.

He didn't answer.

"Much worse than she knows."

"Katherine, the tycoon," he said, as if her rise had ever been uncertain. "She's not a scientist." He turned back to his console.

"If Ground is the problem, tell me when and how, and I'll fix them. You have a witness now who cannot be disputed. We'll put it right, and then can get you home, finally." She paused. He was wearing a navy blue sweatshirt, threadbare, something from Earth. "You do need to talk to me, though, tell me what's going on."

"What's going on?"

Rachel closed her eyes. "Let's start with the missing stretches of floor. The dark skylights. The wide-open client homes, systems exposed."

He sucked from his pouch and shrugged. "The client stuff is their job."

"Mmm. All of this is your job," she said. "And now it's my job, too, to make sure it's good."

"Why only now, though?" he asked. "Why did this just become your job? You hate this, you always did."

"I made this place happen," she snapped. "I've been working on it for even longer than you have." She shouldn't have said this, but she didn't regret it.

"Did you get married? You were going to, she said that's why you weren't working on Parallaxis, back then. I don't think I ever met him."

Rachel shook her head. "I didn't, no."

Ishaan: he'd taken a job in London, still lived there. They'd run into each other once, at a private concert. He was married and divorced. She'd said she was married to Sensus. "And to Katherine," he'd said, and she'd laughed, hollow. "I'll remind you that you moved across the ocean be-cause *she* told you to," she'd said, and they'd laughed about everything. It wasn't as though they would have decided differently, now.

Was Mozgov smirking? He, who had lived in this tuna can for eight years, seasoned with his own filth? "If you're smiling because I care more about my company than anything else, you're right. I do. But I've ne-glected this part of it, and now we need a plan."

"To make it look good to her," he said.

"To us, and to our investors," Rachel said, as though she hadn't no-ticed what he was trying to do. People—men, always men—thought they could stick a few pointy remarks into the sisters' relationship and, with a few quick swings of the hammer, drive a wedge into forty years of partnership. Maybe she hadn't been around as much back then, but that had been one year of forty. "Why are you still in the Helper? Control was supposed to be moved out of here months ago. It smells like rotting death."

"Is that your Katherine?" he asked, and then Rachel hated him.

"We have two issues here," she said. "We'll treat them separately. The first is that we need the station to look better. That, I can help you with. The second is that you've been, let's say, glossing over some of the issues up here with Ground and, more seriously, my sister. I don't know how or why you thought that would work. What I can do is help with the first issue in hopes that it mitigates the impact of the second. How long will it take to at least finish the floor and fix the dark light panels?"

He didn't answer. If there was a better way to approach him, she did not have time for it. Two weeks: some cosmetic renovations and a few good angles for the investors. Her sister, though, would have to hear the truth. She dreaded it.

THE WEEKLY CHECK-IN with Ground was scheduled for Rachel's fifth day aboard Parallaxis. Her sister would be on the check-in call, too, and so, for the very first time, would Rachel. The night before, Rachel had received Ground's agenda in her phone.

HELPER CHECK-IN 560

Latest reading on carbon ppm is above upper bound for date

Latest reading on microplastics ppm is 4.5% high in fabrication lab, 8% high in promenade area. Need L. Totten's plans to reduce emissions and stay on schedule.

Can air filtration from Helper be repurposed?

Can manufactured items be transported into airlock for off-gassing period without compromising schedule?

Concerning pulmonary reading in L. Totten

Client residences suffering odors? Client residences must not be subject to staff odor.

She stopped reading. She was still queasy all the time, her guts see-sawing daily between diarrhea and constipation (preferable). She couldn't sleep strapped to a wall in a closet—her pod, Malik said, wasn't hooked up to the ventilation systems yet, and Rachel hadn't even gone to see it. Her skin itched, everywhere. When she looked out the great, magnificent window in the Lounge at the Earth below, all she could think about was the real life happening down there without her there to supervise it. Katherine could be messy in how she talked to people. She'd be rude ("honest"), tactless ("candid"), or a huge bitch ("why pussyfoot around?") without a thought, and then Rachel would have to clean up the mess: with their parents, with the Parallaxis investors, with the politicians who got all worked up about Sensus every two years, like clockwork, and cost Rachel a lot of time and Sensus a lot of money. Two weeks gave Katherine a lot of time to say the wrong things to the wrong people.

"It would make infinitely more sense to send someone else," Rachel had argued to her sister. "Someone who knows what the fuck is going on with the superalgae and fab lab kit-outs and noctilacent—"

"Noctilucent," her sister hissed. "They're clouds, Rachel, just say *clouds* if you refuse to remember even the most basic facts about half of our business."

Rachel had turned away to fume alone. They had been in the long gallery between their suites, where last year Rachel had placed a series of enormous agate sculptures. She stared into a green stone tower until she noticed her sister's reflection, and then she closed her eyes.

Half their business?

"I need your help," Katherine said, pleading. "You know I can't do this on my own."

A FEW MINUTES before the appointed check-in time, Rachel opened the door of her cot-closet and jerked back. Esther was floating right in front of her.

"Fuck," Rachel said, hand to her chest. "You scared me."

"I need to talk to you," Esther said.

When Rachel had first recruited Esther years ago, she had been baby-faced, downy even, with a pink softness to her cheeks and lips that was gone now. While life in zero-g had made many of the other Pioneers look younger, Esther was thinner, whiter, and drier.

"Absolutely," Rachel said. "I'll come by your office this afternoon."

"No, now," Esther said, her brown eyes unnervingly steady. She crossed her arms tightly over her chest, and Rachel noticed the dry pink rash creeping along her neck from her ears down into her shirt. Was that what her itch would turn into? "You told me an hour to call home, and what we get is a *scant* ten minutes. I have a kid, and that is not enough."

"I'm on my way to talk with Ground right now," Rachel said. "Right this minute. We will fix this for you. That's why I'm here—to see what's wrong and make it change." She smiled at Esther in a promise of her own power, but usually she could feel that power herself, and right now she did not. The promise felt like a lie.

Mozgov did not answer to her shouting at the door of the Helper toilet. Rachel waited until Macy slid the airlock door open behind her, needing the toilet, and then she went to the call room alone. At one minute to, he still hadn't showed. Rachel peered at the panel on the side of the call screen. "How do I use this?" she asked her phone in desperate habit.

At 10:04, the screen lit up on its own.

"Hello, Rachel!" a Ground tech said. Not someone she knew, just another youngish man with the sagging, unfrightened face of someone who did not live in space.

Another window popped open, this one blank. Her sister. Rachel heard her slurp from her mug of tea and was filled with relief and dread in equal measure. "Nice to hear you," she said.

"Hey! Oh my god, look at you! You're really there!" her sister said. "Where's Mozgov?"

"You know, I really don't know," Rachel said. "He didn't answer the door—the door of the toilet, that's how you have to get to him. Which, actually—"

Never say *actually*, Katherine had warned her time and time again.

"Tell me everything," her sister said. "God, you being there just—it makes it real to me."

"I have concerns," Rachel said, and she stopped.

The Ground techs—there were three of them now, all lined up—watched and waited. The black square indicating her sister's presence seemed to vibrate with expectation. Why was she nervous? None of this was her fault. Ground got constant, detailed readings on everything from the photovoltaics program to the inhabitants' bodies. If that information did not include things like "feels cheap" and "no floor over there" and "lighting looks like a prom," it was not Rachel's fault.

She swallowed, looking for a smoother path into the truth. "Lenore

Totten, in the fabrication lab, and some of the others have requested to finish the staff projects before addressing the client homes. Because of the size of the station, moving between the regions causes—"

"We can't compromise the schedule," Ground said. "Not at this stage—"

"The schedule is already compromised. Severely. I want to minimize—"

"We're not talking about the research scientists, right? Just the staff—the doctors and Lenore?"

"Right," Rachel said. "The scientists haven't been assigned owner work yet."

"Yeah, no," Katherine said slowly. "If the staff finish their own pods first, they will be less motivated to complete the owner homes on time."

"I don't think so. The buildings they constructed first are pretty bad. We should let them train on their own pods first, to build their skills for the owner homes."

"Bad," Katherine repeated. "What do you mean, bad?"

She and her sister should have had this conversation alone, but it was too late for that.

"Ragged edges, loose corners, cracked plastic, zip ties, smudges, shoe marks—"

"They don't have shoes," said Katherine.

"It doesn't look good," she said. She shrugged, helpless, to show Katherine that she wished she weren't saying this in front of Ground, that it might have been better to discuss this privately.

"Are you sure you understand what you're seeing?" her sister asked. "I mean, you're not the target audience."

Her sister always talked this way, but she did not talk this way to Rachel in front of other people. Certainly not some Ground techs, who stared at their laps.

"It's not possible to misunderstand," Rachel said with a cool smile. "Not even for me."

She looked into the black square. "The first structures—their canteen, this call room—are ugly, and look like Simon's design as built by a child." She pointed to the wall behind her. "It doesn't look rare or impossible, it looks . . . builder-grade. There's an entire stretch of the ring, maybe fifteen percent, that's currently sealed off with a plastic sheet. A huge stretch of floor is missing, meaning that the systems are all exposed to dust et cetera. Loose wires floating around. The Pioneers—that's what they call themselves now—have rashes, dry coughs, and digestive problems. The lighting looks cheap, as do a lot of the surface finishes. They are far behind, as you know. A live tour for investors will not be compelling, not at this stage." She raised her eyebrows. Yes, she understood what she was seeing.

Katherine was silent.

The heat in Rachel's chest began to drop. "It's because everything takes longer up here than it should," she added. "Until they have gravity—"

"It's not gravity," one of the Ground techs said. "It's a fictitious force within a noninertial reference frame."

"Whatever it is that puts our feet on the ground," Rachel said. "The worse problem is that Mozgov never leaves the Helper. He feels above the job, with civilians, so they have no manager."

"They're managed from here," one of the Ground techs said. "Management of the new team isn't Mozgov's role."

Silence from the black square. Not like Katherine, not like her at all.

"We have to get spinning in March," her sister finally said, as if nothing had happened. "We need to show the investors something—you, up there, *happy*—next week at the latest."

Rachel nearly snorted. "I can't renovate your space station in one week, no." She couldn't see her sister's reaction, but she could feel it. They never fought in front of other people, not even close.

"It sounds like there might be a misunderstanding between—" one of the techs began.

"Stop," her sister said, and Rachel heard from the black square the snap of elastic. Katherine had pulled her hair back. "If she says it's a mess, it's a mess. My sister deals with people better than anybody. We're lucky she agreed to go up there."

Rachel saw what was coming before she believed it.

"Do your thing," her sister said. "Let us know what you need, however we can help move them forward. I'll check in next week, okay?"

"I'm coming home in nine days," Rachel said.

"Take the time you need," said her sister.

"Katherine, no, what the *fuck*—"

The black square shrank into a dot and disappeared.

WHEN SHE CAME OUT of the call room, Esther was there again.

"What," Rachel said in a voice that wanted to murder someone.

"No, I wasn't—I was just going to remind you about the VR," she said, suddenly nervous. "A lot of us have found it really helpful."

Rachel stared at her.

"You haven't done one yet, but these are the tools we have for processing this experience, emotionally, mentally, and . . . for performance." Esther looked about to smile but decided against it.

"Thank you, Esther," Rachel said. "I'll be sure to avail myself."

IN THE MIDDLE of the night, Rachel unstrapped herself from her cot. She wanted to see her own pod now.

Lenore had given her a pair of black fingerless gloves with LED lights encircling each wrist and sticky patches on the palms. "So you can creep along the floor or the ceiling," Lenore had explained. "The lights are a new thing. I just have bracelets."

Rachel snapped on her fanny pack and pulled out the gloves.

On the promenade, the walls were inky and shimmering, like an ocean at night. The stars in the Sky would have been enough light to guide her if she felt familiar yet, but she needed the station map on her phone. She pulled her body along, hand over hand on the string line that ran along the side of the promenade's floor, for now. She found the doorway and opened it.

At first all she could see was a giant window and the bright wedge of glowing Earth that loomed outside it.

She blinked and looked around, curled down to inspect some faint markings on the floor. A double line, like a track, in a rectangle around the oval room, made of tiny spikes. She brushed her fingers over them and it didn't hurt, but when she pulled her hand away one had stuck into her skin like a sliver. She couldn't see it, but she could feel the sore spot. Her floor was the soft golden color of melting butter, and translucent, milky, when she shined her lights on it.

She remembered the night that Katherine had showed her the design for her own bedroom, spare and dark, somehow cloaked in icy clouds. A trick of the light.

"I'd like the opposite of this," Rachel had said, laughing, drawing a circle around it with her finger. "Tell Simon's people the exact opposite of whatever you said to get this."

"Simon, hi, my sister wants your basic bitch sunset," her sister had said to her phone. "White sands."

"Less ice effect, more turtleneck," Rachel had said. "Think 'hot tea and Savonneries.'"

"Also, can we send up some dogs for her? Soft ones," her sister went on. "Like maybe three dogs that all look the same, and a walking stick?"

The track of spines would hold a carpet, the Savonnerie she'd joked about, but made of hypoallergenic and nearly weightless polymer fibers, and printed in the fab lab by Lenore Totten. Katherine had tried to show her the design the week before she came up, but Rachel had too much to do: "a lot of balls that I'm trying to superglue into the air," was how she'd said it.

Her pod was shaped like an egg, her bedroom a small oval inside a larger one. The ceilings were coved, with an off-center skylight in each area from which to view the Sky.

She used her gloves to creep along the floors. Peel, crawl, stick. She found two more rug tracks, one for her bedroom and another for her office. The bathroom was crescent shaped, along the outside curve of her bedroom, and clad in that same hard-candy material, this time a deep, smoky lilac. She could imagine Katherine admiring this design, approving the colors. It was just what Rachel would have wanted, if she had wanted to live here.

Except for the window, which was big enough to ride a horse through, and arched, to better welcome her into the abyss. But a tiny window would have acknowledged Rachel's enduring resistance to this place, and that wouldn't do at all.

She thought of the snap of her sister's hairband during the check-in, a sound of frustration. Had Rachel embarrassed her, was that it? Any embarrassment at the station's flaws should have belonged to Ground. And Katherine could have, should have, come here herself—or, at the very least, ensured that she and Rachel had a private conversation before the meeting. She'd asked Rachel to be her eyes and ears: she would have to hear what came from Rachel's mouth.

Why hadn't she come up? Now that Rachel was here, seeing every detail of the design that her sister had pored over for years, she did not know. She didn't understand at all.

Was she that afraid of disappointment? Yes, if she'd sent Rachel up in her place. Katherine refused to be disappointed, and then Rachel had forced it on her, and in front of Ground. A betrayal, that's how it must have felt to Katherine, who had been dreaming and drawing and scheming toward Parallaxis since they were children, when Rachel had taken a quick look around and said it's ugly, cracks everywhere, and smells bad, too. Parallaxis mattered to Katherine more than Sensus did now, and even if Rachel resented it, she should have found a way to treat her sister's dream as her own until it was.

I'm sorry, she said in her mind, and then to her phone that did not reach her sister, or anyone. "I'm sorry, I'll fix it," she whispered aloud, unnerved that it sounded like a prayer.

15

Mary Agnes first made a comparable video of Ellis: his face, his voice, and his body except for the whole dick region, which she got from TV, apparently having sex and enjoying himself immensely. It wasn't difficult; he'd provided the blueprint, and her crush on him had provided plenty of usable footage from the party alone. She'd looked at him so much. But her video was not comparable in the most crucial sense, which was that it would not hurt him, and the making of it made her feel even sicker.

But she wanted him to feel like he'd made her feel. She tried just his face, no shopping, no tweaking. She enhanced the yellow tinge she remembered from the basement. She had good enough voiceprints to put some different words in his mouth, and she made it very clear that someone off-screen was unconscious. The resulting video was of the very real face of Ellis Evans chatting comfortably about the girls he had raped. *That* was comparable.

She reviewed her work at first with satisfaction, but then a panicky heat shot up her limbs. No, no, no. Horrible. She couldn't do it.

But on Monday, she watched the back of his head in the cafeteria. Mercedes was there, sitting just three seats down from him.

Was Mary Agnes the only one who hadn't let it go? She thought about it all the time, Ellis looming over their sleeping bodies in the basement, taking them in with his eyes, point by point, making sure to capture every curve and hollow and hill, every joint. Raw material, something fun to work with. And then he had invited her to help.

Mercedes didn't talk to him or laugh at him, but she was there, in her same seat, as though she couldn't move. She caught Mary Agnes watching her and twitched slightly, as though the sight of her was unexpected, and then nodded. Mary Agnes nodded back at her. That was all. Ivy sat right next to Ellis—she was supposed to be Mercedes's friend!—and when Ivy leaned her laughing face into his shoulder, Mary Agnes's metal water bottle fell out of her hand, clanged off the table, and clattered to the floor. Ellis turned at the sound and when he caught her eye, he smiled, lightly, like they were old friends. Then he turned back around and resumed his lunch.

Mary Agnes felt more capable of revenge after that.

THE IDEA CAME TO HER on a Tuesday night while she was looking at old magician posters online, looking for stuff to draw. She saw a silvery incubus, his outlines blurry and undefined, hunching over a sleeping woman, and shuddered.

By Friday afternoon, she had created her first virus. Sometimes while she was making it, she felt sick, like a thick, ugly, bile-y feeling all the way through her, but it was just because of so much Ellis in her mind. She was saturated with hatred. The question of how to use the virus, how to deploy it so he would feel as invaded as possible, remained.

Shane stood in her doorway scratching at the inside of his elbow. "Hello," he said. He leaned forward until he was teetering over the threshold. "Hello!"

"You may come in," she said. "Thank you for waiting."

He went right to the window and slipped behind the sheer curtains to watch her through the gauze. "What are you doing?" he said.

"Nothing," she said. "Just thinking."

"I did something really bad." He opened his mouth wide and tried to bite the curtain. "I poured juice in my booster seat."

"What do you mean you put juice in your seat?"

"On the ride home! It hurts my butt! The straps are too tight."

"On your butt?"

He laughed. "On my front butt." He sat down and stuck his spindly legs out under the hem. "Why don't you have green hair anymore?"

"It just faded. Kind of a pickle-brine color now."

"It looks really disgusting. You should do it green again."

She still had some green dye. "Maybe you're right. You wanna help me?"

In the bathroom, she sat on the lid of the toilet and let Shane brush out her hair, trying not to wince when he hit a snarl. "Don't worry about those," she said. "We'll just dye the tangles, too."

She got out the tub of Vaseline. "Okay, now we rub this all over the sink."

"Why?"

"To keep it from turning green. I hope. It makes, like, an invisible fence for dye."

"Why is it called dye? Will it make you die?" He laughed.

She sat on the floor and spread the dye along the top of her head while Shane, standing next to her, pulled it down to the ends, patting it gently into each ribbon of hair. When they were finished, he took his green-baggied hands and placed them on his own head.

"Me ne-ext," he sang.

Mary Agnes groaned. "There's not enough left," she said, though now his hair would be spotted regardless.

"There is! I have, like, barely any hair!"

"You'll get in so much trouble. Well, I will."

"I need green hair for space," he said.

Hers had washed out in just weeks. Shane's hair was two inches long, tops.

"Okay," she said. "Sit on the toilet"—he chortled here—"on the *lid*—and I'll put it on you." She squeezed the end of the tube directly onto the blond crown of his head.

"It's cold," he said, shivering. "And smooth. I only like smooth things."

"Smooth like how?"

"Not itchy," he said. "Or prickly."

She spread the sticky paste over his head, plastering all his hair flat. "Like things that hurt your allergies?"

"No," he said, defiant. "Like itchy and rough. Like grass."

"But grass hurts your allergies, too."

"That's *not* why I hate it," he said. "I hate it because it's poke-y. And, like, those sticks that poke through pillows sometimes."

"Feathers? We don't have feather pillows."

"Those are *feathers*? From *birds*?"

"Aunt Merisa and Uncle Anthony have feather pillows," Mary Agnes said. "I don't like them, either."

"Aha!" he shrieked. "A detail, you said a Miami detail!"

"You got me," she said guiltily. She wasn't supposed to talk about Miami, which was the name she'd given, when she was little, to the nameless off-the-grid settlement where Uncle Anthony's family lived. If they talked about Miami then their phones would know about Miami, which was Miami's number-one nightmare for reasons she had never really understood. Shane had never been there, never met his uncle or aunt or cousins. Aunt Merisa had pots of herbs growing in the kitchen, flies buzzing in and out, and her cousins kept little tanks of their favorite bugs right in their bedrooms.

"The space station is smooth," he said. "Everything there is nice and smooth."

"Now we wait," she said. "It has to dry."

He patted his head gingerly. "How long?"

"Until it's hard, like plastic. Go get a book. I have to do homework."

She hunched forward and stared at the white wall. She needed a big blank screen for video editing. "Just don't let your head touch anything," she said. "Be super careful."

He nodded slowly, trying not to let his head disturb the air around it.

"Here, let's wrap it up so it doesn't get on anything."

Their bath towels were black, because Mary Agnes had chosen them when she was twelve. She wrapped both their heads in turbans. "Okay," she said. "I'll tell you when it's time."

WHEN HE'D LEFT she looked out her bedroom window and saw her mother in the back yard, tending the sunflowers that were supposed to keep the stinkbugs distracted from their family. The sunflowers were traps, sacrificial plants, netted and surrounded by buckets of soapy water for her mother to drown the bugs in. The rest of the yard, front and back, had been ripped up and replaced with pea gravel. The Welch-Peters' property was ugly to insects and neighbors alike. It wasn't enough, though, and her mother said that every year the stinkbugs were worse. Mary Agnes wasn't convinced that was true. Sometimes she thought her mother *talked* about them more every year, but that was it. She said the only place in the country that wasn't yet crawling with stinkbugs was Wyoming, but Wyoming was crawling with everything else, and the stinkbugs would get there, too.

Her mother sat back on her heels and looked up at Mary Agnes's window. Mary Agnes jerked back, startled, but her mother waved.

"Shane's pizza sticks," she shouted, cupping her hand around her mouth. "I forgot about them."

Why couldn't she just use her phone like a normal person? Did everyone in the whole neighborhood need to hear about the pizza sticks? Mary Agnes nodded and hurried away from the window.

She had stitched the Ellis virus to a weirded-up ad for his father's concierge medical practice that she saw all the time. She'd flipped Dr. Evans's smile upside down and made little black flies buzz out of his eyes as his name glittered behind him. Ellis, his parents, they'd see the fuckled ad and click through, *what the fuck is this*, and then the virus was in. She targeted the ad to the Evanses' GPS coordinates. A tiny ad buy, only cost her $629 of her *burgerburbs* money, which she'd been saving for ages for something worth doing.

What she wanted was for Ellis to see himself like she did, and for the people Ellis took most for granted to see him that way, too, and, accordingly, revile him. She wished she could see their faces when the video took over their screens, their confusion as they tried and failed to make it stop. They would not be able to make it stop. The video would stop and begin again randomly, all day long, at work, at school, eating breakfast, walking to the bathroom, ordering takeout, at a work meeting, eating some ice cream, on the toilet, lying in bed. Sometimes they'd get twenty, thirty minutes without it popping up again, sometimes only four. The only way they could stop it was to go to sleep.

Good luck with that.

SHE HEARD THE SMOKE ALARM before she noticed the smell, and then she heard the back door slam as her mother raced into the house. Shit, the pizza sticks. Mary Agnes jumped down the stairs three at a time. Her mother was yanking off her gloves, shedding her bug suit in the mudroom.

"Well? Can you get the alarm, please? And the pizza sticks?"

"Sorry, sorry, sorry," Mary Agnes said, already dragging a kitchen chair under the smoke alarm. Why did they still have an alarm like this anyway? She jabbed the buttons with the broom handle and when it finally stopped, she heard her mother bounding up the stairs, running down the hall to Shane's room. "Where's Shane?" she heard her mother sing.

Mary Agnes climbed down from the chair. Something was wrong. She didn't know what, but time was slowing down in that syrupy bad way. She looked at the stairs.

"Shane?" her mother shouted upstairs. "Where are you, buddy?"

She heard a thud as her mother fell to her knees in the bathroom.

When Mary Agnes got to the bathroom door, her mother was on her knees with the EpiPen in Shane's thigh. "Emergency," she was whispering. "Emergency, emergency, emergency." She scooped him into her arms and the turban fell off. His hair was encrusted in what looked like green plastic.

"Oh no," Mary Agnes whispered.

Her mother looked up and took in the black turban, the green smears creeping out from underneath.

"*You* dyed his hair?" she said. "Were you trying to kill him?"

"I—I didn't think—it's all-natural—"

"Get his bag. And find the container. Bag it up and bring it to me."

"I'm sorry," Mary Agnes said, frozen. "I'm so sorry."

"Please hurry. The ambulance should be here any second."

They went to the hospital without her.

EVEN AFTER SHE had a message from her mother that Shane was okay, or would be okay, Mary Agnes paced around the downstairs loop, kitchen to dining room to living room to mudroom, for hours, every piece of her family's clutter newly bright with importance and the suggestion that she did not deserve to live among them. Shane worked so hard at getting along, the little bright-sider, not like her at all, and she had poisoned him because she forgot not to. She forgot not to poison her brother. She forgot not to poison her brother because she was distracted trying to hurt Ellis Evans the way he'd hurt her. She knew Shane's allergies, not as well as her parents did, but plenty well enough not to let him squeeze hair dye that she'd bought online after considering it for all of nine seconds because it was the one that promised the fastest-acting, brightest color without a separate bleach step. She remembered laughing with Mercedes and Ivy at the all-caps warning on the label that said CAUTION: DO NOT LET MIXTURE COME IN CONTACT WITH SKIN because it was such an ass-cover move, for hair dye: ha ha, they had said, squirting it all over her scalp.

Her parents had argued before Shane started kindergarten because the administrators at his allergy-free private school wanted all the kids, even the kindergartners, to have phones inserted, for safety. Her father had been ready to capitulate (the school knew best, right?) and her mother had said no, the whole point of the allergy-free school was that they knew how to keep all these highly allergic children safe from harm, and if they couldn't do that without phones then what was the point? Shane was one of just three kids in the school who didn't have a phone installed. If he'd had one, it would have alerted Meg as soon as the dye touched his skin. But if Mary Agnes had been paying attention, that wouldn't have been necessary.

Her mother and Shane were at the hospital all night. She wished that her father would call, even though if he did, he would get her mother in the hospital, and she would tell him what had happened. But he'd missed his last scheduled call, and there hadn't been a new one set up. He wasn't going to call. He didn't want to anymore.

Two nights later, Mary Agnes had fallen asleep in her papasan chair again—she didn't sleep in her bed lately, like she didn't deserve that kind of rest or something (stupid)—when she heard her mother's soft night-voice in the room.

"Honey," her mother said. "I need to talk to you about something, and it's very serious."

Mary Agnes blinked. Her mother's face was looming before her. It was still mostly dark in her room, but there was some blue light coming through the curtains now.

"I'm so sorry, Mom," she said, her mouth thick with sleep. "I feel *horrible*. He asked me to do his hair and I was thinking about other stuff, I guess."

Her mother's face drew back. "What other stuff," she said. "I need you to tell me what other stuff."

Then Mary Agnes saw the bubbles, dozens of bubbles, on her dashboard. They were all from Mercedes.

Ivy says ambulance at Ellis house

Effie unconscious

No sign of Ellis

Effie Evans was Ellis's younger sister, in ninth grade. The pills that Ellis had passed out were hers, he had said, prescribed for phone vertigo or something like that. She was quiet but smiley, pale with wispy brown hair and splotchy pink-blue arms.

probably just her phone making her sick again

I thought it might be related to the other thing

That sounds super sick I know but like

That thing where I think everything is about what I'm obsessing about

wake up and talk to me!

god can you imagine if your phone made you sick all the time

just never let you live

what would u even do

"Honey, listen, I got a strange message from Principal Singh," her mother said.

"What did he say?"

Her mother shook her head. "You know I can't. But I really need you to tell me what's going on."

Mary Agnes looked up at her mother's face and fell apart. She hadn't cried in front of her mother in years but now could not stop. Her eyes stung with tears.

"I should have stopped him," she said. "Ellis, I mean. I watched the footage again and again and every time I see myself helping him, just like, sure, I'll do whatever you say. Like, you know how whenever there's a rape video, you know that somebody was watching, not doing anything? And it's me, Mom. It's me. I'm that monster."

"You're not a monster, you were just scared—"

Mary Agnes covered her face. "Don't tell me what I was!"

"—and he didn't rape anyone, did he? You didn't watch anyone being—"

"But what *is* it, then? If someone makes a fake video of having sex with you and shows it to everyone you know and they all think it's real until *he* tells them it isn't, what is that?"

"I don't know," her mother said. "I don't know what to call it."

"And Mercedes—you know, she didn't know for sure that it was fake." Mary Agnes wiped the strings of snot from her lip. "Nothing was going to happen to him. And so I—I—"

"Oh, honey, what did you do?"

"I wanted people to see what he was," she said.

Her mother got a strange look on her face and Mary Agnes knew that she was having another conversation at the same time, or someone was sending her messages.

"What?" Mary Agnes asked. "What is it?"

"Take it out," her mother said. "Take it out right now."

"What?"

"I'll get the tweezers," her mother said, and when she came back, she turned on Mary Agnes's bright desk lamp. A cloud of dust puffed around them when she flipped the switch. "Now."

Mary Agnes scuttled up in her bed like a crab, pulling her legs tight around her. "Mom, you're scaring me," she whispered.

"I'm very scared myself," she said. "No? Fine." Her mother grabbed the desk lamp by the neck and dragged it over to the bedside. The cord wouldn't stretch, so she cocked the metal shade up like a spotlight.

"I'm doing this to protect you," she said. She pulled Mary Agnes's hair back from her ear and pinched the tab between the tweezers. She gave the stem a yank, and Mary Agnes gasped as the end sprang out, wet and red.

"It's bleeding, you're bleeding." Her mother stared at the phone for a half second and then dropped it on the floor. She grabbed one of Mary Agnes's boots and began to beat the phone with it, but the rug was too soft. She kicked the phone across the room toward the door, where the wood was bare, and smashed it with the boot until the casing cracked apart.

"Mom!" Mary Agnes was shouting, cradling her ear in one hand. "That is NOT how it works!"

"What else," Meg asked, "do you suggest we do?"

Mary Agnes began to sob again.

"Dear Jennifer," her mother dictated to her phone. "It is with great regret that I must leave my position at Allied Schools immediately. My son is having a medical crisis, and with Alex gone, there is no way for me to ably perform my duties and obligations. Please accept my resignation and my sincerest apologies. Very best, Meg Welch-Peters. Dear Dr. Kleinberg: Due to a family emergency, Shane will be out of school for the remainder of the month."

"What are you doing?" Mary Agnes cried.

"Please send me the home education materials when you can, and we will ensure that he doesn't fall behind. Very best, Meg Welch-Peters. Oh my god. Alex, where are you?" Her mother rubbed her eyes hard enough to hurt. "Go pack a bag," she said to Mary Agnes. "You need clothes, toiletries. Some paper books, maybe."

"*Books?* Where am I going?"

"Where do you think? Where can I keep you safe? From *yourself?*"

"For how long?"

"I really don't know. But I have to go pack for me and your brother, so let's get on with it, okay?"

Let's get on with it was what her grandmother said. It meant she did not have time for your endless feelings. It meant shut up.

"But, Mom—"

"Listen to me. Effie Evans is in the hospital because she tried to kill herself because she had a virus in her phone that wouldn't leave her alone. A video, something about her brother, that she couldn't shut off, and it was terrifying, and the virus came from *this house.*"

"Oh my god," Mary Agnes said. "Effie."

"I have spent years of my life worrying about something happening to my children," her mother said as she ransacked Mary Agnes's dresser, throwing clothes on the floor. "Viruses, cancers, guns, angry men. Child predators. The lead in the water, the droughts, the stinkbugs. And the bullies." She slammed the bottom dresser drawer shut and glared at Mary Agnes with eyes that seemed like they could kill her on the spot. "I worry about you both, all the time, never stop. That people will hurt you, or just be *mean* to you. I worried about bullies every which way I could think of, except this one."

Shane was in the doorway wrapped in his blanket. "What's going on? Why is she crying?"

"We're going to take a little trip to visit Uncle Anthony."

"All of us?" Shane asked.

"But he doesn't know we're coming!" Mary Agnes said.

"Someone will find us," her mother said. She grabbed the stem of her own phone between her fingernails and ripped it out.

16.

You look like twins, people had said to Rachel and Katherine all through their childhood. Their mother hadn't meant to dress them identically, except for a few frilly ensembles at Christmas, but Rachel had managed it on her own with hand-me-downs. The same haircut, too, bobbed with thick bangs, and Katherine didn't mind. She liked the doubling, often found it useful. Who was to say whether it was Katherine or Rachel who had been heard saying that rude word or doing that bad thing? "Are you sure it was me?" Katherine would ask, turning the adult unsure. "That sounds more like Rachel," and Rachel would laugh silently, in on the joke.

Rachel was prettier, their mother told her, and when Rachel said it wasn't true—angrily, tearfully—her mother was embarrassed. She'd been trying to help, Rachel realized later. By then Katherine had started high school, and she was attracting even more attention than her parents had expected: she was a genius, which Rachel had always known, and a pill, disrespectful of her teachers and a nightmare when she was bored.

Rachel didn't want to be the pretty sister, but Katherine had said that it was good. "I'm not jealous," she'd said. "One of us needs to be pretty, for our team. The team that's us. You'll see."

RACHEL COMPILED A LIST of the station's hazards and shortcomings and assigned blame for each. She talked to the Pioneers one by one, ferreting out problems and their causes. In most instances, she blamed Mozgov. Even if the hazard wasn't his doing, the failure to deal with it was.

This list was long. She revised it, first eliminating all of the problems reported by the Pioneers that could be neither seen nor proven remotely, including her own complaints that fit these criteria, even if she'd noticed them, recoiled from them, immediately upon her arrival. Visible failures and only the most urgent hazards: the missing floor, the loose and exposed wiring that floated its tentacles all over, the dark grime that collected on the hard surfaces, the zip ties everywhere. In the owner pods, the wall plastic meant to glow when lit from behind like marble skin sometimes looked like a foam to-go box, but she needed to see it on camera; maybe it was fine. Ditto the lighting. The scary hot spots in the walls would have to wait, as would the situation in the cafeteria, how the walls were sometimes "dewy" with condensed saliva in the morning. Would the dust pollution show on video? Why was there so much dust?

"It's the hair," Malik said. "We have a very sophisticated air cleaning and circulation system, but it is clogged by hair. Not mine."

"Show me," Rachel said. "Show me this hair, and then we'll know who needs a haircut."

Safety issues had been ignored, mangled, and masked, but if Rachel could just make the station beautiful, her sister would be happy. Rachel could handle the rest from home. She would become much more involved.

Now, to motivate the team. What support structures would be most helpful? she asked. What was holding them back?

"Holding us back?" repeated Teddy. "You mean, from going faster? The schedule is stupid. The people who make this schedule have never built houses in zero-g. We're working as fast as we can."

The schedule might have been unrealistic, but they were not working as fast as they could. Why would they? Katherine's solution would be to make their calls home conditional on their performance. Rachel saw how they anticipated these calls, planned their conversations with their teammates. No, Rachel wouldn't do that. For the station to look good to investors, she would argue to her sister, the people who lived here must already be believers, too.

THE NEXT CALL HOME was scheduled for Rachel's eleventh day aboard, and at breakfast the Pioneers were tense. She could see how much was hidden in the soft, placid faces around her now. What had been the happiest event of the week had become, because of the heat block, a source of dread. Teddy fretted about the alleged end of the hurricane season, which had been lighter than in recent years, and how all those Category 5 false alarms, dwindling to 3s and 2s every time, had likely made people insensible to threat. Those were exactly the conditions that had allowed Esme to obliterate the Gulf Coast in '31. Every town between Fort Myers and Galveston had been under an evacuation order that went largely unobserved. Rachel worried about her parents, that they could have absconded without Katherine noticing.

"We'd see a storm like that," said Alex. "We'd be able to see it from up here."

"Does that make you feel better?" Teddy asked.

"We couldn't see the heat block," said Irma.

"Just get them up here, okay?" Teddy said, turning to Rachel. "I'll do anything you ask, just get them up here."

"As soon as we have gravity," she said, nodding. "You're a bit behind, though, and your families wouldn't be feeling good about that, I think."

Irma and Alex turned to look at her, and Rachel smiled warmly but tiredly, like the understanding mother of another child, someone who couldn't help you but certainly wished she could. Irma and Alex smiled back, tentative and dutiful, but Teddy didn't. Rachel waited. You are my employee, she thought, pulling the corners of her mouth back a little tighter, until he was forced to do the same.

Rachel was anxious, too. Her check-in would be the first call tonight. She would show Katherine that she understood now, that she saw it her way. And then she would go home.

SHE DIDN'T BOTHER with Mozgov. Let him hide, she thought. Rachel floated into the call room alone. She had put on a new combo for the occasion, deep red. She was ready to see her sister's black square and greet it with a triumphant smile. When her connection went through, she saw only two sweaty male faces, flustered and unsure.

"Where is she?" Rachel said, staring at the spot where the black square should have been.

"She's not here," said one of them.

"What? Is she all right?"

"We have been ordered to suspend all calls home," said the other.

"I thought she might want to do that," Rachel said. "It's not the right strategy. I'm here now, and I—"

"Sorry," he interrupted. "We just now got the order or we would have canceled. No more calls home until after the investors are virtually toured, which is probably end of Phase I."

"This will not make our team more efficient," Rachel argued. "It might even—let me talk to her."

The techs glanced at each other. The other one cleared his throat. "I think it's also that, uh, now that we know that things aren't, um, up to snuff? They could talk, in calls home. Negative information would leak."

"They know they can't talk about the station," Rachel said. "And you're watching them anyway to make sure."

"Well, but, with these more intimate relationships, they don't have to say anything, strictly speaking—they can just insinuate? You know?"

These more intimate relationships. Yes, Rachel knew about those.

"You want me to tell them they have lost all contact with their families because they are behind schedule," she said. Her fingertips were growing hot.

"She gave the order," he said. "We're just doing what she said."

He flinched, and Rachel could have sworn that the second Ground tech had elbowed or swatted him, out of frame. The way he was speaking to her, as if she were no one.

"Let me talk to my sister," Rachel said. The heat had spread through her hands and raced up her arms, her neck, her face. She was a bundle of live wires. "There are no 'orders' until I talk with Katherine."

"I'm sorry," said the Ground tech. "She said—"

He looked to the other one, pleading.

"Not just them," he said. "She said no home calls for you."

"The hell she did." Their little boy faces, mouths shut tight like they were covering their braces. "Fucking hell she did!" she roared. She leaned into the screen, let her face fill it up. "That is not for her to say!" she screamed. She reached up and grabbed at the loose tile edge from the ceiling and yanked it down, and the whole grid of curved tiles came apart and began to float up and out, like a slowly exploding igloo.

Teddy's face appeared above her first, arms out against the floating tiles. "What's going on?"

Rachel could hardly see. Katherine had stranded her in space. *Her.*

The swarm of Pioneers and Tess floated up over the roofless call room, looking down at her. She couldn't see their faces.

"I didn't get a call home," Rachel said.

"Well, you didn't need to destroy our call room," Irma said, grabbing a tile.

"Shh, we'll put it back together," said Esther. "What happened?"

"When the connection went through, it was Ground," Rachel said. "They are suspending all calls until we complete Phase I." She didn't want to face any of the Pioneers, so she looked at Tess, whose face quickly arranged itself into dismay.

Rachel knew what acting looked like, and too-late acting was obvious. She could see, in the corner of her eye, signs of real shock and fury: Lenore putting her hand to her mouth, and Teddy arching his back, but she kept her eyes on Tess, whose cheeks were flushing pink. Her neck, too, blooming from the neckline of her plum-colored shirt.

"What?" Teddy shouted. "What is wrong with you people?"

Rachel blinked and broke her gaze from Tess. "I promise you, this is not me," she said. "My sister—" But she stopped there as though she'd been yanked back.

"Is this meant to make us work harder?" Esther asked. "If so, this is not a good choice."

Macy's mouth twisted. "It's real, real messed up."

Rachel looked back at Tess. She didn't know what she was looking for, but something was there for her to find, she was sure of it. One by one, the Pioneers followed her eyes to Tess. She was from Ground, after all.

"I don't know anything about any of this," Tess said hoarsely, all eyes upon her. "This job isn't what I was promised, either."

"That's not good enough," Malik said.

"None of this is good enough for you, for any of you," Tess said, looking at each of them in turn, every one except for Rachel.

The Spins

17

Alex had lived and worked on Beta for 224 days. Built a whole village, or at least an asylum. Today, they would start to spin.

"Go on about your day," Carl told them in the feedbag before breakfast. "Keep to the schedule. It's not like you're strapping in for a Tilt-A-Whirl—it'll take all day to get safely up to speed."

"You think we'll be able to work right through," Teddy said, a corner of his mouth lifting.

Alex, squeezing a grapefruit go-gel into his mouth, tried to imagine what tomorrow would be like—lifting his toothbrush, scratching his head. Picking up his legs and setting them down. He saw his feet flopping against the floor like wet spaghetti. Nope.

"Oh, no," Carl said. "It'll pull you down like a rug."

"*What* will, Carl?" asked Irma, one eyebrow up.

"A fictitious force within a noninertial reference frame," he said, and a single huff of laughter escaped.

Alex grinned, and without his direct permission, his head lolled backward. He was delirious with fatigue. His muscles were dangling threads. His spent brains folded in on themselves like stacked lunchmeat. They had finished building this flat-packed labyrinth in just over seven months, working well into the night since Rachel had arrived. None of them had spoken to anyone outside the station for over two months. These last fifty-six days were the longest of his life.

Teddy, who had often driven them all crazy with his demands to work harder and longer to get to this day faster, had collapsed the night before, just before dinner. Exhaustion, a sudden shaking in his faith that all his hard work would be rewarded, as promised, by the heaven-like appearance of his husband and children.

It was Esther who went to comfort him. She brought him back to the barracks and tucked him into his cot. They all needed a good night's sleep to prepare for the new gravity.

"But maybe don't stray too far from the pods," Macy said now.

"True," said Carl. "I'd rather you stay close in, in case I have to scrape you up and drag you home."

Alex, whose eyeballs felt like cracking eggs, saw worms wriggling around on a wet sidewalk.

Lenore rubbed her eyes. "Somebody gonna tell Rachel?"

"That we're about to spin?" Alex said. "She knows. Let's just take care of us."

ALEX HELD A ROLL of greenhouse plastic much larger than himself tight in his embrace. His arms just made it around. "I wonder if we should try to face the right direction," he said. "In case it kicks in and I get squashed under this thing."

"That's not how it'll happen," Irma said. "You'll get squashed very, very slowly."

"I think I just felt something in my hands." He shook out his left arm.

"You probably have a cramp," she said, but then she stopped, and they stared at each other.

The roll of plastic was sinking toward the floor, Alex astride but upside down.

"Oh, wow," Irma said, giggling.

"Help!" Alex said, and Irma reached out to turn him over, but already their bodies were becoming different, less easy to control in the ways they'd become used to.

"Just let go!" Irma said.

Alex bumped the floor with his left shoulder, and the rest of his body followed, soft as a drop of vinegar in a jar of oil. He let go of the roll of plastic and it landed next to him, soundless.

Irma pushed off the floor with her hands and bobbed up slightly before coming down again. She couldn't stop giggling. She arranged herself on all fours and then tried to stand, but her feet wouldn't stay put. As soon as she landed a toe, she bounced off again.

They went to find the others, bounding along the promenade. "I feel like a cartoon," Irma said. But Alex was too startled by the shift in his surroundings: A floor, underfoot. The Sky, overhead. All the switches, levers, and windows they had installed in the last months were suddenly in the right places. Real life. Then his feet went out from under him and he hit the floor.

He'd turned his ankle, and he wasn't sure he could get up again. He wasn't bouncing.

"Are you—?" Irma asked, looming over him, but before she could get the question out, she was on the floor, too, on her knees and then on her side. They were spinning faster.

"I thought it was supposed to be gradual," Alex said, massaging his ankle.

"I don't think it's done yet," Irma said. "Carl said all day, and it's only two."

They crawled to the feedbag, growing heavier with every minute. He should have worked out more. Lenore, Teddy, and Tess, also on all fours, were approaching the feedbag from the other direction. They laughed at the sight of each other and then huffed and wheezed for breath.

"Tess," Irma said. "Not you, too!"

"I should have done the PT," Tess said, blushing. "I guess the bluebreeze has run out. Can you smell us? We smell so bad."

He prickled, always, when Tess said *we* like that. It shouldn't have bothered him—Ground or not, she'd been up for two months.

"You can't smell as bad as the rest of us," he said, and then he looked up at a forgotten sound: the soft rhythmic thump of bare feet hitting the floor. Rachel, walking.

She glanced down at Tess, and Tess stared at the floor, her mouth tight in embarrassment.

"I guess somebody did the PT," Lenore said, and Tess's face relaxed.

No one spoke to Rachel.

"WE CAN LIE DOWN in our own beds tonight," Malik said, legs flung out in front of him, back slung against the wall. "We're going to *lie down*."

They were sitting around the perimeter of the feedbag floor. Tonight would be their first night apart after 224 nights sleeping together in the barracks, their small, dark room that stank of wipe-washed bodies and the dead-dust smell of space. Alex had learned to sleep with his arms crossed over his chest, like a vampire, and strapped in just loosely. This was how Macy had slept from the start. Ted strapped extra blankets in around his body to swaddle himself, and Malik left his arms floating free, like a zombie. Esther hated the feeling of the straps against her skin and had wrapped hers in spent T-shirts. Irma and Lenore both slept on their stomachs, facing the cot, which Alex had tried just once, unsettled by his floating feet.

They would all be starting over again, tonight. Same station, same people, new physics. None of Malik's snoring or Teddy's muttering in his sleep, Irma's occasional groans, their collective gas. Very quiet, it would be. Very still, in his one-man pod. He should have been more excited about it.

"If we can get there," Esther said. "To our own pods. I'm not sure I can get up."

"We should have gone straight to our pods as soon as we felt it happening," said Macy.

No one answered. Macy was right that they were only going to get more stuck with each passing hour, but who wanted to endure the sinking alone?

"What's it like, Tess?" Irma asked. "To sleep in your own pod."

Tess shrugged. "I never did it any other way."

That night, Alex, Macy, and Malik stayed in the barracks. Their cots were the lowest to the floor. Those with cots mounted high on the wall went to the new pods: Irma and Lenore stayed together in Irma's pod, and Esther and Teddy went to their own pods, alone. Alex woke up shortly after eleven, gasping, sure he was having a heart attack.

"It's the weight, it's just the weight," Malik said from across the dark room. "We're okay."

IN THE MORNING, Carl came for them. He was walking unsteadily, holding the wall.

"Macy," he said.

"What?" She said it as though she were bolting upright, but only her arms moved, fumbling for the buckles on her straps.

"Mozgov had an accident," he said. "Some unsecured glass. He's at the base of the ladder, cut up pretty bad."

Macy fell out of her cot and collapsed onto the floor like a dropped towel. Alex was next. Malik hesitated. "I can do it," he said.

"Stay, rest," Macy ordered. "We've got it."

Carl held the barracks door open, and Macy and Alex crawled out behind him like a pair of old dogs.

By the time Carl, Macy, and Alex got to Mozgov, he had been bleeding for more than an hour. He was on his back on the floor with broken glass all around him, both long black shards and fine grit. A piece of the Sky screen had fallen on him while he climbed down the ladder. The blood was coming from under him. Macy's infirmary was twenty-eight meters away. Alex didn't have any idea how they would get him there.

"Get my kit," Macy told Carl, and he turned back down the promenade.

Alex expected Mozgov to groan or whimper, but Mozgov was silent, eyes shut, his chest rising and falling heavily. Alex hadn't seen him since their first day. Whether their hermetic captain had been isolated too long to stand other people or despised the Pioneers more specifically, no one knew. But last night, he had tried to come down the ladder.

"Okay," Macy said. She was panting. "Okay."

"Okay," Mozgov whispered back.

Macy quickly inspected his chest and stomach for more injury, more glass, but it was all under him. "I have to flip him over," she said. They were weaker than they'd ever been in their lives, it felt like, and Mozgov couldn't move at all. Macy sat next to Mozgov with one foot braced against his ribs and the other against his hip. "Does this hurt? I mean, can you stand it?" she asked him. "We're going to try to flip you over now, and it's going to be unpleasant. Alex, can you—"

"Sompersha," Mozgov whispered.

"What?" she asked.

"Oh!" said Alex. He nearly laughed. "Yeah, you will feel some pressure."

"All right, here we go," Macy said. Feet braced, she reached forward to take Mozgov's far arm and pulled it toward her, or rather tried to let her own weight do the pulling, but she was not heavy enough. She moved both her feet to his ribs and directed Alex to push his feet against Mozgov's hips, and they tried again. Alex was a dead weight against Mozgov, a concrete footing and nothing more. This wasn't even Earth-level gravity. It was light, Carl had said—more than a swimming pool, but someone straight off the planet would be prancing.

Macy's thighs were the strongest muscles they had among the three of them, and by pushing Mozgov away with her legs while she held his arm tight, Alex rooted against him, they flipped him. Alex heard the tinkling clatter of glass hitting the floor when she finally got him up and over, and then she fell backward herself.

Mozgov's back was all bloody shirt, glass shards still sticking through it and into him, and doubtless many tiny pieces that they couldn't see and maybe never would. Carl returned with the kit, and Macy tended him right there on the floor.

"He's saying something," Alex said. "Hang on, listen."

He and Carl leaned down close to Mozgov's face. His brown eyes looked a hundred years old, and his breathing was ragged with the pain and the weight.

"Get me . . . back up," he wheezed. "The Helper."

Carl nodded, but he looked worried. The Helper was on the inside of their spinning ring, so it turned very slowly. It would have the least gravity of anywhere on Parallaxis now. The Helper was now up through the ceiling. To get there, Mozgov would have to climb a ladder that went up into the Sky. There was no way.

Why had Mozgov come down the ladder in the first place? The real question was why he hadn't before, when it was safer. "What did he need to do out here?" Alex asked Carl, and then he looked down at Mozgov and redirected the question to him. "Do you need us to do something?"

"We'll move you to an empty pod," Carl said, glancing at the ladder. "Until you're well enough. I can handle—"

Mozgov grunted, and then Macy extracted a shard of glass that made him hiss in pain.

"We have to stop," she said. "The rest of these will need to work themselves out over time." She ground her teeth. "We need to get you back up there," she said to Mozgov. "The force is too much for your body, too much, too fast."

Carl gave her a wild, hopeless look, and then he nodded. "All right," he said.

It took them nearly twenty minutes to get to the ladder. They took turns dragging Mozgov by his feet, very slowly, so that he could stay on his stomach.

"I can get him up," Carl said, leaning on the wall and panting. "The bottom is the hardest part."

They strapped Mozgov's wrists together around Carl's neck, and Carl hauled him up the ladder on his back. For the first two rungs, Alex watched in silent terror of the two men falling, Mozgov landing on his back.

"Every rung, they get lighter," Macy said quietly.

Two more glass shards fell from Mozgov's back as Carl climbed, but the rest were clotted in tight. They disappeared through the airlock. Macy let out her breath.

THREE DAYS WOULD PASS before Alex could walk unsupported. Rachel recovered the fastest, having spent, along with Tess, the least time in microgravity. Like a ballerina, she swept past the Pioneers lumbering along the promenade. Tess blamed her sedentary lifestyle for her slower recovery, claiming that unlike the Pioneers, who had been pretty fit at launch, she had no real muscle base to work back to. She mentioned this several times, as if she were embarrassed to be in such poor shape. But as Alex watched Tess's knees tremble and quake at the snack dispenser, he suspected that she was exaggerating—that *us* business again. She was trying so hard to align herself with them, but Alex hadn't forgotten that she came up with Rachel. Tess was Ground, had her own pod from the start and work she couldn't talk about. She knew more than she let on about the machinations down there, the people who decided exactly how the Pioneers could live, and when and if they would ever call home again.

For ten weeks, their only information about life at home, on Earth, had come from watching their planet from above. They saw the fire that burned for three weeks from Quito all the way down to Santiago, the fire that curled around the entire east coast of Australia, and twin lines of fire in northern and southern California that crept closer together each day but did not meet. They saw a mass of white forming over Washington, DC, for two days before it grew to cover the mid-Atlantic and then whipped northeast through Quebec and Newfoundland, finally dissipating a week later in the Labrador Sea. They watched in horror as an extratropical cyclone appeared to ravage the northeastern United States and eastern Canada, and they despaired of what they could not see beneath the clouds.

It was hard to remember weather, what it really felt like.

They gathered at the window in the lounge before breakfast to check on the storm, but it was harder now that they were spinning. The planet whipped past them. Alex felt like a dog watching a thrown ball.

"It's not going south," he said to Malik, whose family was in Durham.

"And nothing too bad in Miami, not this year," said Malik to Teddy.

"Don't say that yet," said Teddy, dry throated, and then, seeing on Esther's face that she didn't know if her son and his grandparents who lived in upstate New York had survived the storm they watched, he said, "I'm sorry."

"I should have been at home."

"Here you are," Rachel said. Alex turned around to find her standing gracefully next to an empty chair, one hand resting lightly on its back. "I've just come from a check-in with Ground. I know it's been difficult to go so long without calls home, especially with this storm, and they promise me that it will be reinstated very soon. In the meantime, I'm extremely relieved to report that all your selected contacts are alive."

Alex stared. "Well, that's something."

"All of our families, or all of our contacts?" Irma asked.

"Your contacts, which, it would stand to reason—"

"No, it wouldn't," said Lenore with uncharacteristic sharpness.

An alarm, a low, soft *pumm*, sounded in Alex's phone. *It's time to begin your workday.* The words of Ground, their remote control, in the voice of Rachel Son. He'd known this voice and relied upon it for years, but now it had an owner, and its owner was Rachel. Her grip on their fate never let up. Every time his phone reminded him to do something, go somewhere, change his combo, hydrate, make this deadline, or manage that ration, he heard in Rachel's low, supple voice the control she had over him. Her voice wound through his head all day long, reminding him of what he owed, and what he'd lost to come here.

"Tess," said Rachel, ignoring Lenore, "your father is in a hospital in Modesto. He was critical but is now in step-down."

"Modesto," repeated Tess. She was standing with her back to the window, passing her canteen back and forth between her hands.

"I gather the Bay hospitals are compacted," Rachel said. "They're taking people farther inland."

"But the fires usually go—"

"That's all I know," Rachel said. "But step-down is good news, isn't it."

She didn't ask it like a question. "Questions make back-talk," Alex's great-grandfather had reportedly said about bringing up children—a sentiment Rachel must agree with, about keeping the Pioneers to heel.

"Alex," she began. "I'm told our carbon levels are too high to sustain eight more lives."

She did not look worried or angry so much as expectant. She kept talking, and Alex could feel the others' eyes on him, but he did not hear what she said. *We're already five minutes behind schedule,* said the other Rachel. Or five months, five years, who could say? It did not matter to Rachel that their home was besieged by hurricanes, fire, heat waves, and heat rings that killed thousands of people every day, sending massive crowds of weather refugees into regions that could not or would not support them, and causing endless fear and misery. She cared about the climate that her clients had paid for.

"You can fix that, yes?" she asked.

Alex nodded. Yes, he could give her what she wanted. But then what? He imagined the confusion on his daughter's face when she learned that he had left the planet to work without distraction on scalable carbon capture, and had instead created the perfect closed system for billionaires, which he would operate for three years, until she was finished with high school. He imagined the look on Meg's face. He couldn't sell out, not here, not now.

WHEN THEY HAD BEEN spinning for eight days, Irma reported shoots in all six of her greenhouses. At ten days, the two robots that Teddy had programmed to help Lenore distribute furnishings followed her down the promenade to her family's pod and positioned her grandpa Stan's freshly printed rowing machine. Lenore stood by only to point and confirm. At fifteen days, all the staff pods had plumbing, and Malik took the first (short, misty) shower. On the sixteenth day spinning, Alex knew that it was morning only when Tess showed up at his lab bearing coffee and a packet of jerky. He'd worked all night, again, thinking he finally, finally had it.

"Can you believe Irma's greenhouse?" she asked breezily. "I thought vegetables took, like, months to grow, but this morning she showed me the speed beans. Have you seen the speed beans? Everything's planted in these little beads, I don't know what it is, but it looks like couscous."

She paused for Alex to respond, but he didn't. He was busy.

Tess passed her eyes over his algae racks, all filled with water and the thinnest layer of delicate green lace. "She says there's other stuff she can't do until she has more biomass from you, though."

Irma had stopped coming by to chat, was maybe even avoiding him.

"And of course with more people coming up next week, the carbon situation—"

"Yeah," he said. "I know."

What Alex knew was that he was out of time.

"Sorry," she said. "I always say the wrong thing."

Alex turned to hide his irritation. Tess loved to remind everyone that she was "so awkward," or "bad at people," or "always saying the wrong thing." Then stop, Alex was often on the verge of telling her. But he was hardly one to talk.

"I mean, I'm more worried about the air," Tess said. "We can go-gel as long as we need to, it's not like we'll starve to death."

"Yep," said Alex, jaw clenched. "But aren't you going home soon?"

"I don't know." She shrugged. "I'm sort of stuck up here as long as Rachel stays."

"I thought she was going home in the return shuttle, once the families arrive."

"Yeah, that's the plan," she said, looking around, looking anywhere but at him. "But, like, the plans are always in flux, you know?"

He nodded, but he did *not* know that the plans were always in flux. It seemed to him that the plans never changed, no matter the circumstances or obstacles—Ground and Rachel just pushed ahead as if they saw nothing in their way.

"What do you mean?"

Tess was leaning against the wall, obscured by racks of algae up to her shoulders, but Alex could see her shift her weight from foot to foot. "Just how, like, they aren't going to send the families up here until the carbon situation is resolved."

"Yeah," he said. "So I've heard."

"It's a really shitty situation," she said.

"Yep," Alex said, forcing his feelings down. Tess seemed to feed on them—the slightest whiff of emotion and he felt all her attention on him like suckers. "They want their Plan B." He was trying to sound light, blithely disgusted instead of cornered, and it was not working.

"I know," she said softly. "Listen, I'll wipe this conversation before my team sees it. But I think you need to know—the families are already together at Ground. They're quarantined, they're training. Ground is kind of . . . waiting for you."

"What *is* this?" Alex shouted. His vision was going splotchy at the edges, and he reached out to steady himself on an algae rack. "This is not science, not research—it's—it's—"

"You need to sit." She looked at him with round, worried eyes. "What's so wrong with the Plan B?"

"What's wrong with it? What's wrong with it is that it's *wrong*!" He was shouting now. How could she not understand? "If, after all this time trying to help everybody who needs help, I instead gave my help to a handful of billionaires on a space station?" His voice was shaking, but he looked Tess hard in the eye. "Indefensible. To my kids. To myself. To anybody who cares about this stuff, at all." Had her eyes grown so huge because she understood now, or because he sounded, to a young Parallaxis engineer, psychotic? "And why is this so urgent? We have a very sophisticated microclimate up here—in fact, isn't that your job, isn't that why you're here?"

"Well, yeah," she said. "But it's predicated on carbon fixation from your lab. I mean, we're good for a while, but the system *will* require it." She lowered her voice to a whisper. "Just because you can't do it your way now doesn't mean you won't ever. There will be time, later."

"It's not about it being *my* way," he said. "No, I'm almost there. I know it."

She looked wild, exasperated. "You're not going to—"

Alex shook his head, his jaw clenched so tightly that his teeth threatened to crack.

"No Plan B, no exclusive climate for billionaires." Either he would replicate in time, or he'd call their bluff. He wasn't going to break.

THAT NIGHT RACHEL confirmed it: the families were already at Ground, training for launch in two weeks, if all went according to plan. She did not look at Alex when she said this, but she didn't have to for him to feel pinned to his seat. Home calls were restored, as promised: Esther spoke to Leo, who was safe with his grandparents in a cabin in the Finger Lakes, but their house in Ithaca had been destroyed by Maya, the storm they had watched unfurl from above. Irma's sister and her family were alive in New Jersey but renting a stranger's basement a hundred miles from their flooded home, and her ex-girlfriend, the smoke jumper, was confirmed dead. Her body had been located in northern California. Macy's mother had been named Tampa Bay's #1 Realtor: Retail/Hospitality Sector 2033. Alex could not reach Meg or Mary Agnes. They were missing, off the grid, which could only mean they had gone to Anthony's. Right? He worried for Shane, who shouldn't be there, but he might have been with Alex's sister while Meg and Mary Agnes paid their yearly visit. That he couldn't reach them was, in a way, reassuring. If anyone were seriously hurt, hospitalized, or dead, their phones would know. Rachel would know.

Teddy and Malik talked to their families for nearly an hour each, because they were at Ground, well secured. Alex could hear their laughter, the shocking ease of it, through the flimsy walls, and a knot of jealousy tightened in his stomach. Then Lenore went in to call Jilly and Stan, and he felt bad. Meg didn't want to be married to him and didn't want to come to Beta with their kids, but at least they were alive.

Lenore did not talk about her lost family. She seemed to funnel all her feelings into excitement for the launch. The Pioneers had finished seven tidy apartments—studios for Alex, Esther, Irma, and Macy; and two-bedroom family apartments for Malik, Teddy, and Lenore. Lenore printed a garland of purple pom-poms out of a mixture she called "trash smoothie" to decorate Teddy's twins' room, but she couldn't stop there. She printed their names, Lola and Julian, to go above their beds, and a shag rug that was slightly sticky underfoot, and a set of not-quite-human figures with articulating limbs, and a dollhouse, and a spaceship that docked on the dollhouse roof.

The spaceship-dollhouse made Alex's heart heavy. Shane would have loved it, too.

For Malik's children, who were older, she made the name banners (Inaya and Sebastian) but didn't know what else. Inaya was seventeen and Sebastian was thirteen. At that age, all she had wanted was freedom and "the truth," and she did not know Inaya's and Sebastian's relationship to those concepts.

"They have access to both," Malik said. "Sebastian's sax is too heavy to bring up, and that hurts. But you can't print a saxophone."

"I'll find a way," Lenore said.

There was a second track running alongside the excitement, though. Malik's wife, Colette, and Teddy's husband, Homero, were fit and healthy adults. But the Parallaxis shuttle would also carry two small children, two teenagers, and two senior citizens into space. The Pioneers did not have the same faith in Ground's expertise that they'd had before their own launch.

"We know how the sausage is made," Alex said to Macy.

"We live in the sausage factory," Macy said.

Macy would acquire eight new patients, and she made no secret of her belief that none but Homero and possibly Inaya were at all suited to a life in space, even with pseudo-gravity. The children's bones were still growing, and Jilly's and Stan's bones were deteriorating. Jilly already had osteoarthritis and Stan had bone spurs, and that was just their skeletons. Maybe, as they both anticipated, life in lighter gravity would ease their aches and pains, but Macy didn't like the new variables.

Alex remembered when Mary Agnes was three or so, and Meg had wanted to take her to the Michigan State Fair. The entire day he'd fought to smile through his thrum of worry that there would be a mass shooting. He hadn't let the fear keep them from going, and he didn't want it to ruin his little family's joy at the pens of piglets or Mary Agnes's first fifty-cent honey stick, so he'd kept it to himself. His worries for his friends' families, soon to be reunited after a few short hours of space travel, were like that—to share them would be a burden. He kept them to himself. Besides, there was still no guarantee that they would get here at all. He— no, *Ground* still stood in their way.

BY THE NEXT WEEK, Alex's cyanobacteria mutants filled all thirty rotating racks of six trays of twelve wells each: 2,160 wells. The next day, he added twenty more trays on the floor, lining the perimeter of the room, and fifteen or so sterilized food containers that he was supposed to return to the feedbag for reuse. Warning messages from Ground and the Helper about his high water usage blinked across the top of his dashboard in an endless red ribbon that Alex ignored.

Malik showed up first thing the next morning, unannounced, probably to hassle him about the water. Alex was at his computer. Malik looked around at the mess and rubbed his hand over his scalp.

"Time for another shave already," he said. "I'd forgotten how fast it grows."

He had shaved his head again the week before, wanting to clean up for his wife and kids. No more of this sloppiness, he'd said.

Alex tried to smile. "Will you get to talk to them before they come?"

Malik shook his head. "Not unless something goes wrong," he said. "Delays, you know."

Alex did know.

Malik gave him a lopsided, apologetic smile. He was a good friend, and Alex hadn't been, not good enough. "I'm sorry about this," Malik said gently. "I know you're under a lot of pressure."

He paused, and Alex knew something bad was coming. Was it the water? Maybe he should have started on Plan B. Just started it. He could keep working on replication, and he wouldn't be keeping his friends' families away from here because he refused to sell out to the Sons. *Sellout*. The word itself was juvenile, implied an understanding of the world that had been stunted at eighteen years old.

No. One of these trays would work, and then their families would come (not his).

Had he refused Plan B because he was jealous? The thought was so startling and so ugly that Alex turned away from Malik, not wanting to be seen.

Malik knocked on the doorframe as he left without a word. Alex didn't turn around. He was staring at his computer screen, the photosynthetic analysis for section 2, tray 1, wells 1–6. The numbers had changed.

ALEX EMERGED FROM his lab nearly four hours later, just in time to catch the end of lunch. He ran. He saw Esther and Macy first and blew past them, his lungs bursting, and nearly fell down in the doorway of the feedbag. Lenore and Irma were still sitting at a table together, and when they saw Alex, crumpled and panting, they froze.

"What is it?" Irma said. "What happened?"

Esther and Macy were behind him now, asking him if he was okay.

No Teddy, no Rachel, no Tess, and no Malik. Where was Malik?

"It's working," Alex said, one hand on the floor. "It's finally working."

"Water," said Macy.

Alex yanked his canteen from his waist and took a drink, splashing himself. "Not just one well, not just one tray. Every well of every tray I've looked at so far in section two. Every single one."

Malik stepped out from behind the snack machine. He'd been hiding there, hiding from Alex.

"When you say 'working,'" said Irma. Her eyes were screwed on to his as though she were looking for the trick. "You mean—"

"Photosynthesizing at close to 140 percent efficiency of the control. I've measured 130 wells so far, and each one has about 5×10^8 cells per milliliter. It's real."

"It's real," Malik repeated. "It's real?"

Alex burst out in shocked and sloppy laughter, years of tension flying out all at once.

Lenore and Irma were on their feet. "Well, I want to see!" Irma said. "Let's go!"

But Malik was still, his head thrown back and his eyes cast upward.

"Malik," Alex said.

"Thank you, Lord," said Malik. "And thank you, Alex." Alex could see the relief coursing through his veins, his muscles slackening. "I knew you were about to get it," he said. "I knew you were right there." Alex didn't believe him, and it was okay. He had it now, and that was all that mattered.

Macy was messaging Rachel, and then Teddy, too, and Irma said that she shouldn't go in right away, not until Alex had secure samples. She shouldn't risk cross contamination from her own lab. But maybe she could use just one fresh lab suit and save it for visiting Alex—no, even that was—how quickly could he secure samples, she wondered—

"Somebody tell Ground," Malik said. "Tell them we're ready."

How strange it was to slide open the door of his lab that afternoon with excitement instead of the mix of dread and determination that he'd grown so used to. The warm humidity wrapped around him, welcoming him back. He had 130 wells of success, an isolated variable, and the joy and support of his friends and colleagues. He wanted to call Meg—and Mary Agnes, who would be almost as proud of him but with less complication. They wouldn't get a home call until after the families arrived. He'd have his whole lab growing superalgae by then.

He had grown a single variant under three different light regimes, and the superalgae was in the second of the three groups. He knew exactly how he had grown it and could do it again: same culture, conditions, methods, timeline. What if they all died, like 182 had? No. He could set that worry aside for now. He would close the air intake vents, wouldn't let anyone in the lab. This time, he had it under his control.

ALEX WOKE UP in bright white light, stiff and aching. He heard the racks whirring as the trays rotated their positions and the gentle hum of the water pump. He was on the floor of his lab. His shoulder ached from sleeping in a strange position. He didn't remember lying down.

It was almost four in the morning. He had stayed in the lab through dinner, but when had he fallen asleep? He sat up. His cheek was damp and hot, imprinted with the crisscross texture of the floor. He scratched it, and it burned. His hands were streaked with raised red hives. Then the stench hit him: like rotting vegetables and cat litter, septic and chemical all at once. A toxic algal bloom. He stood up. His stomach rolled and his head pounded, the room spinning around, the racks of algae flying by. He sank back to his knees, too dizzy to think.

He made it toward the door of the lab and slid it open, gulping the fresher air. He slammed the lab door closed behind him and sat back against it.

Maybe it was one of the other sections, and not the superalgae.

Malik's face yesterday, the relief he could not hide. Tell Ground, he'd said. Tell them we're ready.

Alex raked his hands down his face and gasped at the burn. He needed a shower. A sealed suit. And a respirator, to go back inside.

Lenore had one in the fab lab. He had about two hours before anyone woke up. He'd missed dinner, so he couldn't miss breakfast, not without worrying anyone. He had worried everyone enough. This was his mess, and he would clean it up.

18

Tess woke up worrying about her parents. She didn't know where they were, only somewhere in Modesto, where she had never been. She didn't trust Rachel to have told her everything important. What condition was her mother in? Was she well enough to take care of her father, or did she need Tess, too? They shouldn't be in a hospital without Tess to look out for them.

She was still bleary from sleep when she went into Alex's Views and saw him killing his algae. It looked like he had done all the trays in one section and most of another. He was probably in a hurry to get the super-algae in every tray. It was only once she grew awake that she noticed the round edges of the goggles, the respirator mask over his nose. He had been wearing safety glasses in the lab, but not this. And he was disposing of the algae water as sewage, not gray water, which was odd. She needed to see the footage from the night before. Something was wrong.

WHEN ALEX STEPPED INTO the feedbag for breakfast, Tess nearly knocked her chair over trying to get to him before anyone else did. He stepped back with his hands flexed before him as though she were an unpredictable dog.

"Whoa, are you okay?" he said to cover his flinching, and Tess gave a small smile that she hoped looked gentle, reassuring. She'd planned to ask him how the rest of the day went yesterday, since they hadn't seen him at dinner, but Alex had already turned his back toward her. He grabbed a pouch of dry smoothie from the rack and stood at the tap, filling it with water.

Tess heard clapping behind her. It was Malik, with his big, unstoppable smile, Lenore and Irma right behind him.

"Super Alex," Malik said to greet him. "Super Alex of the super algae!"

Alex's pouch of smoothie was overflowing down his hand. His top lip was frozen in a smile while his chin trembled.

"You just needed someone to believe in you," Lenore said. She spread her arms wide as though to encompass not just the Pioneers there in the feedbag but all of Parallaxis, Ground, the entire institution that had believed in Alex and brought him here.

Together they cheered for him, clapping and shouting, Irma whistling. Teddy came running in, cupped his hands around his mouth and barked. When everyone else had joined the applause, Tess did, too. Alex smiled down at his feet.

Come on, tell them what happened. She found herself pleading with him to tell the truth, even as, at the same time, she wanted the Algo to have the lie.

THAT AFTERNOON, Tess tried to see Alex in his lab, but he yelled through the door that he was too busy with the new algae to chat, and he couldn't have visitors. Contamination, a fragile environment. Tess, standing on the other side of the sliding door, heard his voice doubled: she watched and listened from her phone as he killed the rest of his algae. The super-algae, the control, all of it. Dead.

When he stripped off his gloves, she raced back to her pod, worried that he would come out and find her still there. But he went to his workstation.

The interface wasn't familiar to Tess, but she understood enough. He was in the climate systems logs, changing some of the reported numbers from his lab.

She had never thought him capable of deception like this.

The Algo updated its predictions for Alex: a pattern of deceit, withdrawal from social life, a general inclination toward secrecy—

Tess wanted to correct the Algo's model. That was not Alex; the model had to be wrong. But the model was right, and Alex was broken.

—and friendship-ending, career-ending humiliation once he was found out.

What could be done? What, Tess asked the Algo, could fix Alex? The Algo offered two possibilities. One, Alex could correct the numbers and tell his colleagues what had happened, what he had done afterward.

He would, wouldn't he? Tess thought so—within a day or two he would think better of it and come clean.

Unlikely, said the Algo.

Okay, what else?

The second possibility: should Alex be re-embedded in his primary network—his nuclear family—he would behave more like Alex again.

Impossible. And not only because the Algo marked Meg as "lost." Tess was pretty sure she was off the grid, at Anthony's.

A summons bobbed onto her dashboard: at three a.m., she was to report to the call room for a meeting. No one was to see her go in.

SHE WAS IN THE CALL ROOM early, jittery. At two minutes after three, the black square appeared.

"You've made some interesting progress," said the voice she knew well by now. "You're really integrating into the community."

"I have to," Tess said easily, casually. "To some extent, anyway," she added. "It would be odd to them if I didn't." She waited for Katherine to say something about Alex. She would know, somehow.

"Still having trouble processing conflicting information, though," said Katherine.

For a moment, Tess thought she was talking about Tess herself, but of course Katherine meant the Algo. "Oh," Tess said. "Yes." The Algo was missing too much social information that was clear to Tess when she compared their readings, she said, and the gaps were worst in conversations among three to four people. The Algo still couldn't read denial, or unstated ambivalence, or standard impostor syndrome, when the actor in question was reacting to two or more actors simultaneously.

Tess was talking too fast.

"You're making great progress, just keep at it," said the black square.

She wasn't going to bring up Alex. Tess was surprised at how relieved she felt. Her shoulders went slack, and she took a long, shallow breath.

"Can I ask you one thing?" she began. "Would you know if—sorry— do you know anything about my dad? I haven't been able to reach them since the fires."

The black square didn't answer right away. Bad news.

"He's out of the hospital," she finally answered. "They're in temporary housing nearby but planning to leave California."

"My mom's retiring?"

"Stanford's done with physical classes after this, I'm sure. They have to be."

Throughout Tess's years there and after, parts of the physical campus had shut down—for pandemics, to conserve water during the hottest months, when high winds threatened to blow down electrical wires that would then ignite more fires. Still, life continued online until it could resume in person, and it always did, eventually.

"Too many people are displaced . . . injured . . . A lot of the campus is reparable, all that stone, but the new undergrad complex, the old grad housing, and the surrounding neighborhoods are totally charred. They've got nowhere to put anyone."

She sent Tess a tour: her parents' condo building, their whole faculty village, blackened and skeletal. The streetlights and path lights still stood, black spines rising from the sidewalks, surrounded by rubble. Why had they been home? Why hadn't they stayed in Minnesota?

"Your dad's thing was lungs, not burns," Katherine said.

"Smoke inhalation," said Tess.

"And particulate. This smoke is full of stuff."

"But he's okay now. He's out of the hospital." And her mother was fine. They would say goodbye to Palo Alto, to Stanford, and go back to Minnesota, where they had lived until Tess was seventeen. She would bet on it. They still had lots of friends in the Twin Cities.

"Yes," said Katherine Son. "So to prepare for your departure—"

"I wish I had just a little more time," Tess said.

A pause. "How much more time?"

"Oh," said Tess, not looking at the black square. "Not much. Another month or . . ."

Katherine laughed.

Tess stared into the tour of her parents' cul-de-sac. It looked like any California fire ruin. No people, no little dogs. Some odd colorful scraps on the ground, maybe pieces of flowerpot or bike helmet. Then she was thinking not of her own family, but another one: Meg and Mary Agnes swatting mosquitoes in Anthony's off-the-grid settlement, Shane in a now-filthy bug suit, which he'd have to wear all the time, probably sleeping across Meg's lap half the day after being stuffed with antihistamines. In her imagination it looked like the set of an Old West theme park.

"Anything else?" said Katherine Son.

"There's one more thing," Tess said. She paused. "I understand that Meg Welch-Peters was approached about joining the project some time ago but declined, and—I think Ground should try again. Meg, Mary Agnes, and Shane. It would be best for the Algo to have Alex's family here, too. But then, they're off the grid right now, so it's probably not possible."

"Not Meg and Shane," said the black square. "They're in . . . Rochester Hills, Michigan."

"Oh," said Tess. "With Caroline, Alex's sister. And his parents."

"Meg and Shane aren't phoned, but everyone around them is."

"And Mary Agnes is alone?" Tess's vision began to swim, and the black square seemed to shimmer. Had Meg taken her to Anthony's settlement?

"You want them all up there," Katherine said.

Tess nodded, flecks of light colliding in front of her. She hadn't had a migraine in years. "I could get more out of Alex if Meg were here, too. And if the daughter were here, relating to the other teenagers, that would be a rich vein, as well." *The daughter.* She had said it to convey distance, a scientist's objectivity where she no longer had any.

"We can look into it," Katherine said.

In the moment, Tess thought the voice sounded amused, though because she could not replay her conversations with Katherine, she knew her recollection was slippery, at best. That helped, later, when she began to feel regretful about the conversation. She couldn't know exactly what she had asked, what she had said or implied, no matter how badly she wanted to. It was just a memory now.

THE NEXT DAY AT LUNCH, Rachel announced that the families' launch had been delayed. Just a few days, likely the first week of May. There was no reason to panic. Some additional training, probably, or maybe someone had a cold that he or she needed to get over before they brought it up to the station and snotted it all around.

Tess watched Rachel deliver this news with little to no affect: no persuasive warmth or apology, no nothing.

"This is it," said Teddy, who had been waiting for just such an announcement. "This is the final fuck-over."

Rachel rolled her eyes. "Give it a rest," she said. "Surely you can appreciate the complexities of getting your *six-year-old children* to a space station."

Tess glanced at Alex, who was more than usually pale.

"It's okay, guys, these things happen," said Lenore. "Really, we should have expected it." She nodded as she spoke, revising her own expectations.

"We of all people know how little things can add up to delay, right?" She looked at Malik, whose eyes had gone still with doubt. "They're coming," she reassured him. "I know it."

He gave Lenore a tight-lipped nod. "Let's not go to pieces now."

"Whatever it is will be resolved in short order, I'm sure," Rachel said.

Tess looked at her lap. *We can look into it,* Katherine had said when Tess asked about Alex's family. To think she could have such power in this organization had been ridiculous, but as soon as the delay was announced, she wondered if she did.

FOR THE NEXT SEVERAL DAYS, Tess worked long hours in her pod coding the Pioneers' reactions to the delay and testing the Algo's readings of their small group conversations. The Pioneers stayed close to one another that week. It wasn't just those with families quarantined at Ground who were anxious; the families' launch and Ground's exploitation of it had become their common cause.

Tess focused on concealed emotions, from the simple, such as the way Alex's heart rate surged when he had to talk about the algae with his colleagues, to the complex, like the way Lenore toggled between her tendency to accept bad news with a powerless shrug and the behavior she was trying to adopt from Irma, which was acceptance with a blithe shrug. The former was easier for the Algo to read, due to the biometric evidence. What Lenore was trying to change about herself was more nuanced, trickier to teach the Algo.

The Algo didn't have any trouble with Alex now. Its predictions of his failure and humiliation were painful in their certainty.

He was not her child, her parent, her brother. He was not even her friend.

Tess had an Algo to tune. The delay, a fresh stressor, had been a boon for the Algo. She ran the feeds in real time on all of her screens, the Algo's models changing and shifting by the moment as it scraped and processed information. It was doing most of the work now. She made small adjustments, stunned and gratified by the Algo's increasing speed and facility. She could run six screens of Views at one time now, sitting back in her chair like a security guard as Views from all over the station played in front of her.

On her top left screen, Malik climbed the ladder to the Helper with the idea of demanding answers, and Tess watched as he took in Mozgov's shrunken body for the first time. She heard Malik swallow, and his eyes darted away before he forced himself to look into Mozgov's eyes. Malik had no history of embarrassment around people with illness or disability, and it was only on Tess's third go-round that she got it: Malik, having worked with astounding focus to achieve gravity, had not until now considered how that achievement would disable Mozgov, who had been here a lot longer. He and Mozgov had both worked toward the spins knowing that each day floating damaged them a little more, but Mozgov would have known what their eventual success would cost him.

Carl, sitting at Mozgov's right, looked at Malik steadily as if to caution him.

"This delay," Malik began. His voice, usually as round and earthy as a mushroom, quavered.

"I know nothing," Mozgov said, and he refused Malik's eye contact. "This is my concern," he said, sweeping his arm toward Control. "Nothing down there. Nothing about you."

"Nothing about us?" Malik repeated. "We're doing everything we're asked. I'm building apartments, I'm getting us water, I went *outside* six days in, and you still tell me—"

"Carl shouldn't have done that," Mozgov said. "It wasn't safe, and it wasn't necessary."

Carl gave his head a small, firm shake. Just once, side to center, and Malik stared at him. He and Carl had not been friends, no, but Carl had been their teacher. What was he now?

In the corner of Tess's eye, she saw Lenore's face bob into Irma's

Views, her lips open and almost smiling, her big nose ducking in laughter. Tess looked back at Malik's screen, trying to focus on whatever Carl was trying to conceal, or keep concealed, about the station. She put her hands up on either side of her eyes like blinders.

"He's right," Carl said. "We're each responsible for one piece of this—"

She stole a glance at Lenore again and saw the edge of her jaw, her long neck stretching. Irma staring, and very close to her, almost touching. Tess muted Malik. A second later she killed his feed and pulled up Lenore's there instead. She saw Irma there, just from above, her wild hair and the tops of her thick eyelashes, her cheekbones.

"Taste one," she said. She held up a pea shoot, a single green curl.

"We should share them with the others," Lenore said.

Irma tucked it into Lenore's lips, her thumb grazing her bottom lip. Lenore bit her finger and Irma laughed, still staring at Lenore's lips. Tess stared, too, hungry, jittery, jealous. Then, Lenore's great swallowing brown eyes, looking right at her.

Tess held her breath. Irma cupped Lenore's face in her hands and kissed her. Lenore held very still at first, and then she pulled away.

"No?" Irma whispered.

Lenore leaned in fast and kissed Irma, who stumbled backward. The Algo raked through their archives for newly significant detail, and the information between their ties exploded. They stood there kissing each other, their screens going black when they closed their eyes, and shadowed and blurred when they opened them so close to each other. Lenore had her hands in Irma's hair, and they whispered words that Tess would have to go back to get later; she couldn't make them out now. Irma kissed Lenore's neck up under jaw, where she had stared before, and pulled the neckline of her shirt out and kissed her shoulder. Tess licked her lips. Lenore tugged on the hem of Irma's shirt and then her hands disappeared under it, wrapping around Irma's waist. Tess could see her hands moving through the silky fabric—

"Tess," said a voice. Loud, like Tess hadn't heard her the first time.

Tess disappeared the feeds. Her screens were all code now. She un-locked her door from her workstation. "Yes, come in?"

Rachel stepped into the pod and quietly closed the door behind her.

"What's up?" Tess asked her, trying to sound casual, which was stupid because this had never happened before, Rachel showing up at her pod, and Tess could have, should have, sounded as startled as she was.

Rachel crossed her arms and tilted her head to the side, looking at her feet. When she looked up, her face was almost unfamiliar to Tess, one that Rachel had never shown her before. Her dark eyes were worried and her mouth a bit sick, pinched.

"Are you all right?" Tess asked.

"No," Rachel said. "I'm still up here. Are *you* all right?"

"Oh, you know. I'm . . . a little shaky."

"Mmm," Rachel said, her mouth twisting in one corner. "Are you?"

Tess had started consulting the Algo before she encountered Rachel—made a solid, reliable plan before she tried anything other than small talk. She'd noticed Rachel looking at her critically, as if she thought now that Tess was someone who might matter. Talking to Rachel had always felt more dangerous than talking to the other subjects, and now that Katherine had stranded her here, it was worse. Tess hadn't even glanced at Rachel's Views or even the Algo's Rachel model, since the day before. She didn't have any of the tools she needed.

"I know it's not as bad for me as it is for you," Tess said. "I don't mind being up here. I like the people."

"But you keep away from the people," Rachel said, squinting. "Your pod is way, way out here, and you haven't been coming in at mealtimes."

"My work—"

"Yes, what is your work?" Rachel's eyes crawled over the six screens of code behind Tess's head. All of it would be gibberish to her, but Tess was still anxious. A few crumpled food wrappers and a wad of dirty socks that she hadn't composted yet were on her desk. She didn't want Rachel seeing any of it.

"Algorithms. For Views," Tess said. "You know I can't say more than that."

"Not to me?"

"I'm not supposed to talk to anyone," she said, trying to sound young and confused. "But, you, I guess that's different?"

"Is that why—" She paused, pursed her lips. "Are you why I'm still here? Because you have to be here, and you're late?"

"Oh, no," Tess said. "I hope not. I don't have, like, a single set of deliverables, so—"

"So there's no end point," Rachel said. "Your project up here could go on indefinitely."

"No, no, they need me to come back down, to implement—"

"Is the shuttle delayed because you don't *want* to go home yet?"

"No!" Tess said. What she needed to do was pause, stop Rachel right there, and run the Algo so that she could find out exactly what Rachel knew and what she suspected and proceed from there, but Rachel did not pause, did not wait for Tess to catch up.

"Is your direct line to Ground? Or to my sister?"

"What are you talking about?"

What are you talking about? was the guiltiest response to any accusation, and when Tess heard one of the subjects resort to it, she groaned. But now she had fallen back on it, too, because when someone guilty is accused of something and she is not yet sure exactly what, *What are you talking about?* is all there is. There was no move she could see that would not worsen her situation.

"It's to my sister," Rachel confirmed.

Tess wanted to disappear into the wall, close herself up in one of her star-freckled plastic storage closets. "No," she lied, shaking her head. "No direct line to anybody. I just code and they retrieve the code—I don't even know who actually does that."

Rachel was nodding as though it didn't matter if she believed Tess or not. She stopped and made her face completely still, as if every muscle were at work to not move. "No," she said. "I have a different idea." Her voice, low and even, sounded murderous despite, or perhaps because of, its control. Even as Tess struggled to find her footing, she knew the Algo could use this perfect example of concealed loathing.

Tess swallowed. "An idea for what?"

Rachel's eyes wandered past Tess and behind her, over her screens. "I would like to get home, Tess. To my life, my company, my parents. I would like to see my sister. This *was* supposed to be a two-week trip, of that I'm sure, because of the supplies they sent up with us."

Her eyes stopped. Tess knew she'd disappeared the Views on her screens, there was nothing to see. To turn around would only confirm that she had something to hide. She stared straight at Rachel, feeling as though she'd finally gathered herself.

"Do you code?" she asked Rachel. "Maybe you could help me with something? I'm not allowed to ask Teddy or I would have."

Rachel didn't answer. Tess spun around. On her top center screen was Lenore's stomach, the deep gold ripple of her combo's shirt, pushed up on her ribs, the brown mole just north of her navel. The picture blurred and darkened. Irma's feed—these were Irma's Views—as she kissed Lenore on her stomach.

Tess had set up the override a few nights before. It was supposed to pop up a subject's feed if the Algo determined that she was missing important action in real time. Tess had set it up because a few times since she'd been up here, she'd been so bogged down in code that she missed real-time action that changed things, even what she was doing that very moment, and she'd had to go back and rewrite, revise. She'd thought it wasn't working because there hadn't been any pop-ups yet. This one was the first.

Tess closed the window. Lenore's feed popped up on the screen next to it, Irma's eyelashes again, her closed eyes. Tess turned it off.

She blinked at the black screens. She didn't want to turn around.

"This is what you mean by 'algorithms for Views,'" Rachel said to the back of Tess's head. The air was suddenly icy, and Tess's skin prickled all over. "The Pioneers are your Views, and you . . . watch them."

"I'm training the algorithm," Tess said, and her voice came out cracked. "You can't build an AI like this without human oversight, obviously."

"Obviously," Rachel repeated. "We're lucky you pay such *close* attention to the details."

Tess's ears burned. "You are lucky," she said. "You're lucky it's me, and not someone else. I care so much about this project. I've given up so much for it."

"Oh? Have you? What have you given up?" She asked it lightly, and Tess could see her silhouette in the reflection of the screens in front of her. She had cocked her head gently to the side. "It must be a lot," she said, almost cooing. "It must be a whole, whole lot if you can't even begin to say what it is that you gave up."

Tess didn't answer.

"I understand that you're worried I'll tell your friends," Rachel said. "The Pioneers, I mean."

What Tess understood was that even now, Rachel didn't think she could be one of the subjects.

"Please don't tell them," Tess whispered. "Please."

A shocked noise from Rachel's throat like swallowed laughter.

"I'm almost done," Tess said. "Then it will be all yours, to do whatever you want with."

"Mine," said Rachel.

"You'll have a machine with infinite capability to understand people, to predict them. You'll be richer than—" She didn't know who was richer than the Sons. "You'll have power that compounds," she said, her voice catching. "Just please don't tell them about me."

"No," Rachel said. "I would never. That wouldn't help me. The algorithm is, as you say, mine."

Tess nodded.

"Turn around."

Rachel's face was pale as chalk. She raised her eyebrows and gave a small ironic smile. "Just tell me what you need to finish. Let's get you caught up. I'd like to go home now."

Tess felt as though she had just stepped out of the path of a speeding bus. She let out her breath and blinked, nodded into her lap.

"Yes," she said. "Okay."

What she needed were more comparisons, more times when people said things that weren't what they meant, or were different from what they'd said before, or changed their mind. It was hard for her to get them without coaxing the Pioneers toward their most sensitive topics, which, as she'd learned that awful day in Alex's lab when he felt like she'd scraped him, she could not do. But there was someone who could, whose job as their psychiatrist gave her the cover to try.

"Esther wants to help them," she said. "She's tried to do sessions— like, therapy sessions?—but they don't want to do it because it's weird, to do therapy with someone you—" She paused. "With one of your own colleagues. But if that therapy became compulsory . . . if they had to do it . . ."

"I see," Rachel said. She let out a short, choked laugh. "I'll manage it."

"You can't tell Esther—"

"I wouldn't dare," she said. "And then you can do your job better, too."

Reunited and
It Feels So

19

Rachel.

Rachel, get out of the shuttle, said Ground to her phone.

Rachel did not let go of the straps around her chest. The shuttle was the same shuttle she had come up in, but there had been only two seats that time, one for her and one for Tess. Now there were nine: nine new people on the station, and nine empty seats returning to Earth. She was going home in one of these seats.

It's not leaving with you or anyone else.

She had done all that Katherine asked, all that she wanted. Always. She had treated her dreams—every dream, now—as her own. It hadn't mattered, because the person who mattered now was Tess. Katherine had given Tess the direct line to her that she'd told Rachel was not possible. Rachel, who had given her whole life.

There was nothing she could say to Ground or to her sister now that she couldn't say better with silence, inside her space suit and strapped in tight. She would not eat or speak; she would pee in the diaper. If they wanted their shuttle back, they would have to bring her with it.

SHE STAYED IN THE SHUTTLE for thirty hours before she gave in. She struggled with the latches, her hands shaky and weak. Her space suit was heavy and an unbearable joke, besides. She pulled off the helmet and dropped it on the floor.

When she emerged from the airlock, Tess was waiting for her with dinner, boxed up, and water. She wanted to help Rachel back to her pod, to make sure she could move all right, and Rachel allowed it.

Rachel understood her role now. All her life she'd thought of herself as her sister's partner, her sister's sounding board, her sister's relied-upon, her sister's surrogate. Up here, she was a decoy. Katherine knew Rachel would play any role she was given. She always had.

At the door to Rachel's pod, Tess looked at her with her troubled young eyes and said, "I'm sorry they won't bring you home."

Rachel gave her a pitying smile, which made her feel better, momentarily, even if the pity itself was put on. "You're so small," she said. "You don't realize. But everything you do for her will haunt you. You watch."

Tess blanched and Rachel realized what she'd said. *You watch!* She shrieked with laughter, and Tess looked frightened. Rachel leaned back against her doorframe so she wouldn't fall down.

The Pioneers hated her, really, and why shouldn't they? They heaped all their suspicions and grievances against Ground upon her, and as long as she was here for them to do that, maybe they wouldn't look too closely at the other one. For years, she had shielded her sister from view. Up here, she did the same for Tess.

20

At first, her father felt like home, even with the huge beard and hollows around his eyes. Mary Agnes had burst into tears at the sight of him, waiting in the airlock. They had fallen toward him, shaky and limp, and he'd gathered her and Shane together in his arms and smoothed her hair, *shhhh*, kissed them all over their heads. Her mother stretched her arms around this messy bundle, and it was like stumbling out of the snow into your warm house. But within an hour that feeling was gone: her dad was in a different room in that house, one where she was not allowed to go. Something was wrong with her dad, and what was wrong was that they had come to join him.

THE THREE FAMILIES had trained together in Ticaboo, but the Welch-Peterses had been late arrivals, unprepared outsiders from the start. There had been an older couple who had left the compound, deciding at the last minute not to make the trip. That's what their trainers had said. But Inaya said she hadn't seen any signs that they didn't want to go. "Jilly and Stan were psyched out of their minds," she said. "One of them must have really fucked up to get kicked out."

Mary Agnes didn't know what to do with that. She had really fucked up, too. That's why her mother had brought them here. Sensus would handle the case, her mother had said, not looking at her. What it must have done to her, to turn the care of Mary Agnes over to *them*.

THE WELCH-PETERSES WERE GIVEN—assigned—what her father said was a rather large pod, made up of a common living area, one bathroom, and two bedrooms. "A really nice family pod," her father said. He smiled uneasily. Every gesture and all the different pieces of his face were *off*, like he was her father's twin she'd never known about, and who didn't know her at all.

None of the rooms were straight-sided. They fit together more like scales or feathers. Mary Agnes stood in the room that she and Shane would share and tried to understand how big it was, in normal terms, but the way the walls bowed and curved made it hard to decide how much of the floor or the space was "room." She felt squeezed by the walls. Their beds were triangular and nestled tightly in opposite corners, one high and one low.

"Did you build this?" she asked her father.

He shook his head. "Just put the beds in. I mostly worked on another one."

He did not say "another one where I lived, alone," but she understood. "You didn't live here," she said. "Who was supposed to live here?"

"Another family," Alex said. "But, you know, plans change."

"Where are they?" Shane asked. "Did they pick a different pod?"

"Remember, the people who decided not to make the trip?" her mother said gently. She squeezed Mary Agnes's shoulder and Shane's at the same time, like they were twins.

"Did they say anything about why?" her father began. "Lenore had no idea—"

"We didn't meet them," said her mother, and the sadness Mary Agnes saw in her mother's face was unbearable. Her dad had said he wanted them to come; he'd said it over and over. But he hadn't thought they would, and it showed.

"Let's continue our tour," her mother said with uncharacteristic softness. "We have a lot to learn, Alex—we got to Ground about eight days ago, and everybody else had a month. So we might be, you know, a little wobbly on the particulars."

Her father nodded. "Everybody's a little wobbly," he said. "But we'll take care of each other, won't we?" He looked down at Shane and she could practically see his heart cracking through his shirt. Mary Agnes felt a small change in the atmosphere, an unstiffening, and for just a moment it seemed possible that they had just had a bad start, that her family might be all right.

There was no kitchen, just a tiny fridge and an electric kettle, a basket of snacks she did not recognize. No labels on anything, like at Uncle Anthony and Aunt Merisa's, but all in thin pouches. The pouch material was so thin that it was disgusting, you could feel what was inside too clearly.

"What do we eat?" she asked her father.

"Ah!" her father crowed, and his voice bounced off the walls. "We eat in the feedbag. I think officially it's the 'dining lounge.' Meals are communal—well, I assume they're still communal, going forward—at seven, twelve, and six. You can take snacks around with you, though." He pulled at his pockets and a smattering of packets fell and smacked lightly on the floor. He squatted and looked at them like they were special rocks he found, not snacks that had fallen from his own pocket. "Gogels and cottonseed bars," he said. "Proteoats. But several familiar meals from home, too, pouch versions, we'll have more variety now, for you guys. The gravity has changed things around here so quickly, I'm not used to it yet. The neighborhood has really changed."

Her mother laughed. Ha ha ha.

Shane picked up a pouch and started to open it.

"Honey, wait, I need to check that first," her mother said, grabbing his hand. "Let me see it for just a minute."

"He can have it," her father said. "I checked it."

Mary Agnes looked away, embarrassed to see her parents confused about, of all things, each other. She noticed the little holes sprinkled along the wall like freckles. Or stars. Right, everything like stars, probably.

She hooked one with her finger and it opened. Storage. Empty. Inside was a bit of ripped and scraggly plastic stuck where the shelf met the wall. They didn't have anything to store.

"What are we supposed to put in here?" she asked.

"You'll accumulate different items," her father said like she was nine and he was teaching her how to play *System Shock 2.* "I know it feels like you left everything behind, but you'll be surprised at how quickly you forget about all of it."

A silence like an empty attic.

"The trappings, the stuff," her father muttered hopelessly. "It's much simpler up here. Like living OTG, in that way. Of course, in most other ways, Beta is far more complex."

"Beta?" asked her mother.

"I'm going to go see Inaya," Mary Agnes said. Her mother started to protest, and Mary Agnes waited for her to realize that this was normal and good: look, Mary Agnes had a *friend* she wanted to see, just like a nontroubled human teenager ought to. Her mother smiled a small brave smile.

"Be careful," she said. "Just be careful."

"I will," Mary Agnes answered, and then she was out the door.

She raced past the other pods on her toes and then, when she didn't know where she was anymore, slowed down, turned down a narrow passage. A tunnel.

She crept through the tunnel like it was the white belly of a snake that she was trying not to wake up. Not that she could help how light her footsteps were; her socks against the floor made all the noise of falling slices of bread. The tunnel walls gave off a soft purple glow, a dawn-light color, near the floor, but when she looked straight at them they had a rippled texture that seemed to vibrate and breathe. They looked kind of alive. She couldn't tell how dense or delicate they were, whether they would support her leaning against them or kicking at them with her toes, or whether they would ripple or tear if she so much as touched her pinky finger to their surface.

She looked both directions down the passage and then tried to plant her feet to feel sturdier, but it didn't really work. She always felt about to tip over, up here. She leaned in close to the wall. It was nubbly, pebbly, with fine creases everywhere, like expensive leather. She extended her index finger very slowly and brushed it against the white skin.

Plastic. The pebbles were hard, the creases stamped. All her breath ran out in relief and disappointment. She tapped her nail against it and heard the plastic *tic-tic-tic*. It only looked alive.

This was where she lived now. This was her home.

THE COBBS' POD was almost exactly like their own—two bedrooms, one for the parents and one for Inaya and her younger brother, Sebastian, though Inaya's dad had put an orange plastic partition up between the two ends of the room to give them each some privacy, and purple banners with their names arced along the walls above their beds.

"I like the orange, actually," Inaya said, "but it's aesthetically a little ad hoc. We need a scheme." She looked up. "Maybe a ceiling feature."

"Mint," said Sebastian. "A little splash of mint."

Inaya wrinkled her nose. "Maybe," she said. She turned toward Mary Agnes. "A splash of mint is honestly his solution to everything."

"It gives some freshness," Sebastian said.

"Cute of our dad to do this, though," she said. "He does try."

At training, Mary Agnes had been dazzled by Inaya and sad about it, because it meant that they wouldn't or couldn't be friends. Inaya was seventeen and beautiful, willowy and unimpressed. She spoke her clipped declaratives in a slightly stretched drawl that made her seem utterly sure of herself. She was going to become a lawyer for the environment—not an environmental lawyer, which was what Mary Agnes's mother had thought she meant, but one whose client was the planet. The only thing that scared her about coming to Parallaxis, she said, was boredom.

But Inaya and Sebastian had brought her into their fold without hesitation. "We *love* a buffer," Inaya had said the first time she asked Mary Agnes to sit with them, and Mary Agnes had been grateful to oblige.

"Our room is just plain," said Mary Agnes now. "Only the beds, and they look like they got shoved in yesterday."

"They probably did," said Inaya. "Because Jilly and Stan probably would have had one big bed."

"Yeah," said Mary Agnes. "I wish I knew why they left—I feel like people keep looking at us like, 'Why are you here?'"

"It's not like *you* kicked them out," Inaya said. "People are just confused about what happened. They were there and then they weren't, and you guys showed up."

"I hate that," Mary Agnes said. "I actually feel really bad about it."

"Well, stop."

Mary Agnes nodded.

"Everyone'll get to know you, and it'll be so fine."

Inaya and Sebastian's mother, Colette, came in then with their father, holding hands. Mary Agnes glanced at Inaya to see if this was normal or if she was embarrassed, but her face showed nothing amiss.

Colette beamed at Mary Agnes. "How are you doing, sweetie?" She squeezed Inaya's father's hand. "It's just about dinnertime, I understand, and your mom and dad are going to wonder what happened to you—"

Mary Agnes felt her cheeks redden. "Yep, I better get back," she said. "Thanks so much for having me, Mrs. Cobb, Dr. Cobb." Even if everyone hated her family for stealing Jilly's and Stan's spots, at least they would see she had been raised with good manners.

"Malik, up here. Just Malik," said Inaya's dad. He was a little shorter than her dad, but bigger, softer, and when he smiled at her, he had the same deep dimples that Sebastian and Inaya did. "I've heard an awful lot about you this last year."

Mary Agnes nearly dove out the door, and the glow of the Cobbs' happiness, their warm fleeciness, followed her halfway home. There was no one inside her family's pod. They had already left for dinner and thought she'd meet them there. It was such a small thing, no big deal at all at home—on Earth—but here it was not right. They needed to walk to dinner together, like the Cobbs were going to. Now everyone would see right away how weird and choppy they were together.

But they knew already, because the other people, the people who had been here with her dad, they knew her parents were separated. There were just so many ways that her family wasn't supposed to be here.

Her last day at Uncle Anthony's (she hadn't known it was her last day; she didn't even know what day it was), she had been helping her cousins wash aluminum foil sheets and dry them for stacking when Aunt Merisa came down into their cave and waved Mary Agnes over, dripping with slush and mud just inside the door. Their house wasn't really a cave, but it was mostly underground and made of mud, an "earth shelter" that was dark inside, and brown. She didn't mean cave like it was a *bad* thing.

"Benny saw a car," Aunt Merisa said. "We think it's your mom. It's the same one she had last time." She pulled off the wool hat that she wore over her old blue baseball cap and scratched her hairline.

"The silver one?"

"Probably about an hour ago, now. We should get you packed up, kiddo."

"Oh," said Mary Agnes. "Yeah, okay."

"I'll make you a snack sack," said Aunt Merisa, pulling off her boots. "In case she's in a hurry."

Even if her mother wasn't in a hurry, Aunt Merisa would be. This "visit" of Mary Agnes's had gone on forever, halfway into April. Even though Mary Agnes knew her uncle and aunt loved her, her being there so long really freaked them out. Their kids were homeschooled, and they thought it was fun to ask Mary Agnes to check the facts in their books, if they were still true, as if Mary Agnes were a visitor from the future.

Which she was, kind of. At first it had been okay, just little things, but then they had started turning to her during their mother's lessons on biology—"Is *that* true?" they would ask her, giving their mother teasing looks. Usually, Mary Agnes would nod vigorously, because really she didn't know—all the *facts* her little cousins were charged with memorizing were foreign to her because she hadn't had to learn them herself, not in the same way—she didn't have to store all those little shreds of information in her actual brain. So then what did she learn in public school? they wanted to know. Well, she said, more like how to do stuff. Like the processes and stuff.

"But, like, it's silly for me to know the life cycle of a frog or whatever when it's all in my phone," she explained, "and, you know, frogs are mostly dead anyway. In the US." She wasn't sure actually. "And, like, bee behavior is weird to learn about now because it's super in flux, because of climate change. Like, our neighbors down the street were beekeepers for a while, but the colonies kept collapsing, and it turned out their neighbors' 3D printer was venting out the window right at the hives, just spewing plasticky steam at night? They thought they still had some live bees, but they were actually fake bees, like drone bees sent out by the university to study colony collapse?"

The children were delighted, and they had many questions to which Mary Agnes had no acceptable answers. After that, Mary Agnes was sent out on outdoor chores during their morning lessons, or read a book, anything less disruptive to schooling.

Benny had been correct: it had been her mother in the silver car, twenty years old, a manual driver that didn't even have nav. She rented it from one of the settlement's few trusted outsiders, a woman who'd left because her diabetes wasn't compatible with the OTG way of life. Mary Agnes's mother, when she showed up, didn't even stay for dinner. They had a long drive ahead, she said, almost eight hours.

"We're not going home?"

Her mother shook her head. She looked exhausted. Awful, really. Lines fanned out around her eyes as she squinted, even behind her sunglasses. First, she said, they had to return this car to its owner and pick up their real car, then they would pick up Shane at Caroline's, in Rochester Hills—that was where they'd been staying for the last month, while her mother got everything sorted out—then the three of them would fly to Salt Lake City, where they would be picked up by Parallaxis reps and helicoptered to Ticaboo for training. In only nine days, they were going to the space station.

Exactly what Mary Agnes had wanted.

"Why can't we go home?" she said, her voice dry.

"Well," her mother said. "It's complicated for us there, right now."

"Because of me."

Her mother paused.

"There's a libel suit, which—it's just money, and we don't have much to take." She giggled nervously. "But I've been advised that for the hacking, the virus, they will charge you criminally, possibly as an adult." She paused. "I think that's bonkers, but because of what happened with Effie, they have the leverage—"

"I'm sorry," Mary Agnes whispered. "I'm so sorry. Can't I say I'm sorry?"

"I know," said her mother. "I know you are." She bit her lip. "But they are not interested in mediation or restorative work. The good news is there *is* somewhere we can go, and that is this space station where your father happens to have gotten a job. What are the chances, am I right?" Her mother gave her a delirious grin. "You will get to be the very first criminal to flee to Parallaxis! Just like the brochure!"

"Lucky for me," Mary Agnes said quietly.

"I love you," said her mother. "I see how this all went wrong, and I want you to know that I see it. Okay? If you were smaller I'd grab your chin to say it. You hear me?"

Mary Agnes nodded, lumpy throated. "Whatever I can do to help," she began, trailing off because she knew there was nothing, absolutely nothing.

MARY AGNES DIDN'T REALIZE she had gotten lost in the station until she heard someone call out to her. "Mary Agnes? Are you looking for the feedbag?"

"Yes," Mary Agnes said, annoyed to be lost and relieved to have been found.

She recognized the shorter of the two women who approached her. Tess had been with the waiting crowd when the families disembarked from the shuttle earlier that day. Now her dark hair was held behind her ears with clips, which made her big eyes look even larger, and she had put on a second pair of socks. But it was the other woman—tall and gangly, with a long nose and a short chin—who had spoken to her. Mary Agnes had not met her yet.

"Come with us," she said. "We're headed that way."

"Thanks," Mary Agnes said, and her throat swelled with gratitude. For fuck's sake, she told herself, don't cry.

"I'm Lenore," said the woman. "I run the printer."

Mary Agnes was suddenly cold and unsure. This was the granddaughter of Jilly and Stan, the people who had left training.

"That's a bit of an understatement," said Tess. "She makes everything we need: hair combs to teacups to gurneys."

"Just one gurney," Lenore said, wincing and smiling at the same time. "Don't scare her, she just got here." To Mary Agnes, she smiled tenderly. "I'm sorry I wasn't there today when you arrived, I had to do a few things to get your rooms ready. And I'm so sorry you didn't have name banners to welcome you! I'll have them for you tomorrow, promise."

"Oh no!" Mary Agnes said. "I mean, you didn't need to—I know we were last minute—I know your—"

Lenore shook her head. "Listen," she said. "We are all *very happy* to welcome you here." She smiled with her lips closed and pressed, as if her smile were to make a point. "Now come on, let's go to your first dinner on Parallaxis I."

Mary Agnes had been walking in the wrong direction. This was Billionaires' Row, Lenore said. She would have gotten to the feedbag eventually, since the station was circular, but it would have taken a long time and might have been a little stressful, on her first day. When they arrived at the feedbag, her mother and Shane were facing her father, his shoulders slightly hunched. Her mother's mouth was hanging open, her eyes wide in giddy disbelief.

"Oh my gosh, look," Lenore murmured to Tess, grabbing her arm. "Quick, look at Alex's wife."

Tess put her hands to her mouth. "Right," she said. "She didn't know."

"Didn't know what?" Mary Agnes said.

"You better go sit with your folks," Lenore said, giving Mary Agnes a gentle push on the shoulder.

"Honey," her mother said. "Here, sit down—no, sit with your dad." Her words tumbled over each other. Mary Agnes wanted to feel excited, too, but she only felt anxious. This day had chewed through too many surprises already.

She sat down next to her dad, plucking at the fabric on her knees. Her first uniform was the color of overcooked broccoli. Her dad's—his combo, he called it—was dark purple, sort of a plum, and not a color he'd ever worn at home. His legs were skinnier now, she was pretty sure, but that felt weird to notice. Still, he was here, next to her and familiar. Then his right knee jerked and started bobbing, and Mary Agnes jumped in her seat. She looked up at his face, extra scruffy and pale.

"What is it?" she asked. "What's going on?"

Her dad looked down at his plate and tilted his head, considering.

"Alex!" her mother said. "Tell her!"

Mary Agnes looked at her dad and waited. She saw something in his eyes that she didn't recognize.

"He solved it!" Shane burst. "He solved the algae!"

"Really?" Mary Agnes said. "Really, really?"

Whatever she had seen in his eyes just a moment before seemed to have disappeared. He laughed one of his deep huffing laughs, eyes half-closed.

"Yeah," he said. "Really."

21

Meg, all five and a half feet of her, stretched out in the big bed facing him: radiantly freckled, negligently sunburned across her nose; limbs leanly muscled from running around on Earth in all-out panic; the streaks of gray at her temples thicker, witchier than when he left. She was here, and she was talking.

Shane, rushed to the hospital, unconscious. Mary Agnes essentially on the lam. Anthony furious with Meg for showing up at the settlement without warning and leaving Mary Agnes, whom he dearly loved (Meg imitated him pressing his hands over his heart) but who was diseased with the toxins of mainstream society (Meg couldn't argue with that, not anymore). Within the first week, Anthony's children had put acorns in their ears and were talking sassily to each other, pretending to order toys for same-day delivery. Listen, Anthony had said before Meg left Mary Agnes there, this girl needs her parents right now, not the sense that she's being placed in off-site storage while you make a plan. I'm sorry, Meg had told him, but I need your help.

She had taken Shane to Alex's sister's house in Rochester Hills, which was (so far) a reliably sealed and filtered fortress against the wrath and indifference of the natural world, where for a happy month he was doted upon by his grandparents and Aunt Caroline, who welcomed every available convenience and entertainment without suspicion or discomfort and thought Meg really ought to relax, go play with wooden blocks herself if she liked them so much. The Evanses filed suit: Meg was served by a drone in the pharmacy drive-thru. Meg did not know what to do. Every idea she had was a reaction and a stall at best.

The invitation had reached her through Caroline. Parallaxis had spots for her family and would love to have them aboard.

"That's not a solution," Meg had said.

Caroline had grasped her forearm. "They will fight the lawsuit for you, Meg. And any criminal charges, too."

They can't do that, Meg was about to say, but Caroline's comfortable mouth had twisted in impatience. They could do anything.

"You can get your daughter out of this," her sister-in-law had hissed at her. "So do it."

Meg jerked her arm back.

Another sleepless night, and then she agreed.

SOMETHING HEAVY CROUCHED on Alex's chest. "I'm so sorry," he said. "I'm sorry you had to do all that alone," he said. He hadn't thought the Sons could have any more power over his life than they already did, denying him, these last few months, even the sound of his children's voices. Now they had his family in hand, too. He wished he had never told Meg about the family option. Life here had looked a little more promising, back then.

He wondered if Sensus in fact wanted Mary Agnes's case, if it mattered to them particularly. He suspected, with a shudder that he hoped Meg could not see, that it did.

He reached out to trace the bridge of Meg's nose. She'd closed her eyes. Her eyelashes were blond on the topsides. He'd forgotten that.

"What? What are you thinking?" he asked her.

She opened her eyes and fixed her blue eyes on him with such determination that it seemed like it must hurt her to look at him. "That's the thing," she said. "I might have had to do all that alone even if you had been home."

"Not *as* alone?" he said. "I'm sorry, Meg. I get it now, I do."

She cocked up one side of her mouth. "It was worth it, though."

"What?"

She laughed, one short, soft bark. "You'll slow global warming. You really, really will."

He shook his head. "No, no. I'll capture enough carbon for the station, for the people who will live here, but—I mean, methane is the worse—it's not—"

"What do you mean?"

"I mean don't give me too much credit," he said. He was trying to tell her the truth, and he was almost there. "It's not perfect yet."

She propped her head up on her elbow and stared at him. "You created a new species of algae for radically enhanced carbon capture, right? What you've been trying to do for twenty years? No, it doesn't solve every problem at once, but it does go a long way on one of them. What am I missing?"

Last week, having killed off every specimen and cleaned his lab entirely, Alex had sat down to examine his original culture. He did this with dread, unsoothed by his drumming insistence to himself that he would find nothing wrong with it. His cyanobacteria was not easy to isolate, but he was always careful, and his cultures were always clean.

He never would have seen the hitchhiker had he not been searching for it. Among the cells in his culture, minuscule and wedged between cell walls, was a single cell of a different species. He didn't recognize it. Something he had done—the light regime maybe, or the temperature changes—had triggered this second species, causing the rapid algal bloom that had filled his lab with phycotoxins.

What Meg didn't say, and didn't have to: that she had given up so much for him to chase this dream because they had agreed that it was bigger than them both. Now, with his wife by his side, looking like she might give him another chance, and his children sleeping safely in the next room, nothing could make him confess that he had lied to them. He would get his clean culture, and then this part wouldn't matter.

ALEX HAD BEEN ORIENTED, more or less, by Mozgov and the two remaining astronauts of Crew 3. He hadn't thought of them in ages, and he wondered now how they had readapted to life at home: the speed of information, the noise, the relentless chaos of weather. Meg, Mary Agnes, and Shane would be oriented instead by Alex.

He first took his family to the fabrication lab, where Meg, along with Colette and Homero—"the other faculty spouses," Meg said tartly—would work with Lenore to furnish the client homes. They met Malik and Colette, who were on a similar tour, just outside. Colette Cobb was forty-two, a restaurant consultant back home. She and Meg were about the same height, but both Colette's carriage and her hair made her appear quite a bit taller. It was braided up her scalp to the crown, where it exploded into a coppery bloom. While Meg was starting her first day with a kind of reedy, frazzled determination, her gray streaks nearly taking flight from her temples, Colette had all the calm authority of someone who had always meant to be here. Someone prepared. Alex took Meg's hand and squeezed.

The fab lab was bright and hot as usual, stacked high with mattresses that looked like slabs of tofu. Lenore peeled off her mask and winced as the suction pulled at her skin, leaving a purple ring. "Hi, welcome," she said. "Sorry it's so hot."

"Is it always like this?" Colette asked her. "How do you stand it?"

"Just when we do big things really fast," she said. "It's the materials, not the machinery. Freshly baked couch, basically."

"Malik said we were working construction," said Colette, turning to Alex and lifting her eyebrows. "But I've never swung a hammer."

"This is more like LEGO," Alex said. "It's . . . it's kind of fun."

Colette frowned. "Don't overdo it," she said, and Malik laughed.

Alex looked at Meg, startled to find her looking back at him. She turned to Lenore.

"Up here it's all snap-and-lock, pop-pop-pop," said Lenore. "The stuff that came from home is flat-packed in the door and window cavities of the pods, and then what-all's too bulky to ship, we make here. Like today, I'm doing couches and beds."

"You're *printing* couches?" Mary Agnes asked. "Out of what?"

"High-resilience polyurethane foam. Herf. Pillows and other soft portables in a latex pincore unless we got allergics." Lenore ran out of breath and closed her eyes for a long second. "The answer to your question is 'foam.' Lots and lots of foam."

"And this just for the . . . client homes," Meg said, and Alex gave her a nervous glance. He knew she would hate this, but he'd hoped that the children's excitement at the 3D printer cranking away, so much more sophisticated in its capabilities than anything they had at home—would smooth over or drown out her political objections. "As opposed to—"

"The staff pods," said Lenore.

"We finished the staff pods first," Alex said. "So we could live in them."

"Ground didn't like us doing that," Malik said, rolling his eyes. "Privileging our own comfort over—"

"The people who don't live here yet?" finished Meg.

"Sounds about right," said Colette. She and Meg exchanged a look that gave Alex hope and anxiety in equal measure.

"You should see the things they have us making for the client homes," Lenore said. She coughed and thumped herself on the chest. "Well, you will!" She pointed to a tadpole-shaped chaise at the edge of the room, which Shane immediately ran to and flopped down upon.

"Oh, don't sit on that," Lenore said, wincing as she rushed to the chaise. "We can't get them dirty."

"I'm not dirty," Shane said. "There's no dirt up here anyway."

"Oh, there is, sweetie, you'll see." Lenore brushed off the seat when Shane stood up again. "These will all get covers, but those will come up with the clients, so it all has to stay pristine until then. Until they see it." She coughed again.

Alex looked nervously at Meg. Be like Colette, he found himself pleading. You can recognize the problem without making a huge deal out of it.
Her lips were tightly pursed, but she didn't say anything.

"This doesn't look pristine." Colette pointed to a ridge of bubbles running across the back of the sofa. "This looks burnt. Blistered."

Lenore sank to her knees to inspect it. "Oh no," she said. "No, no, no."

"I don't think it'll show," Meg said. "Not when it's covered."

The hollows under Lenore's eyes were dark as bruises. She tapped one
of the bubbles with her fingernail and it caved in. She gasped.

"Like a macaron," Colette said.

Alex caught Meg and Colette looking at each other again—Meg's
eyebrows scrunched together, Colette's lip curled—in a wordless
conversation that anyone could overhear. They didn't understand: a
puckered couch meant delay, which meant an angry and possibly vengeful Ground.

"Can we see a client home?" Mary Agnes asked. "Are they really different?"

"Yeah," said Lenore, brushing off the flecks of foam that clung to her
shirt. "I mean, yes, we can see one, and yes, they're really different. Here,
let's take a cart of mattresses down. Many hands make light work!"

Mary Agnes looked at Alex, and he shrugged. "Yeah, sure."

It took four people to heave each warm, floppy mattress onto the cart.
Meg, Colette, and Mary Agnes were doing most of the work, it quickly
became clear.

"Wow," Lenore said. "You guys are so strong." Meg and Colette
pushed the cart from the back while Lenore guided them down the
promenade, stepping between the wheels and the walls whenever they
veered out of line. Not yet recovered from her weightlessness, Lenore
used her body to passively correct their course instead of pushing and
pulling the way Colette and Meg did.

Alex and Shane hung with Malik. "Not going?" Alex asked.

"Just trying to give them a little room. She doesn't want me telling her how it's all supposed to go."

"Yeah," Alex said. He didn't know what anybody wanted.

"You too, Shane," Malik said. "You have your family here, but you're also on your own adventure. You'll see everything in just your own way."

"I've really been planning for this," Shane said. "But I'm still very surprised. You could even say shocked."

Alex's laughter came in falling breath, a shock of his own. "Yeah," he said. "I feel that way, too."

THEIR OWN PODS were compact and practical; the mansions, as Colette immediately christened them, were cavernous in comparison. Each one was different, Lenore said: this one was a cluster of alcoves off a large central atrium; another was S-shaped; another, like a submarine, with the doors to the bathroom and closets hidden flush in the wall.

"What's going on with the windows?" Meg asked. "I mean, those are windows, right?"

There were three ganged together in the living room, each frame as tall as she was. They were recognizable as windows only because of their placement; the recesses were still packed tight with materials. Meg leaned toward one of them but did not step closer, as though she might get sucked out into the infinite darkness.

"Oh, yeah," Alex said. "We just haven't installed the screens yet."

"Screens?" Meg asked.

"For the video feed," Malik said. "Like you have."

"You're not really looking out into space," Colette said as though she were teasing a little bit, as though Meg couldn't possibly have believed that from her humble staff pod, she could really look out into space.

"We're not," Meg said, making the question into a statement.

"We're spinning, Mom," Mary Agnes said.

"Right," said Malik. "The view would be whizzing by every three minutes. Falling down, or rising up, I forget which direction we're going."

Alex knew this wasn't true. Malik absolutely knew which direction they were spinning.

"Really barfy," Mary Agnes said.

The window in their family pod was on the far wall of the living room, behind their own foam love seat. Meg had gone right to it when they'd first walked inside together, stared down at the blue world with wonder and gratitude. "See there," Alex had said, pointing. "That's Mexico." It was a video feed, and he knew it so well that he hadn't thought to tell her.

"Right, of course," Meg said, turning away from them all. If she had thought about it, he knew, she would have known: of course they weren't real windows. The station was spinning. The floor she walked on was the outer wall.

Alex made his way to her side and bent his head toward her. "You just haven't had time to soak it all in," he murmured. "You've had a lot on your mind."

IN THE AFTERNOON, Meg had her intake session with Esther. When Alex came back to pick her up, she was stepping out onto the promenade, Esther behind her in the doorway. Meg turned to say something and Esther smiled quickly and then shut the door.

"Hey," Alex called. Meg looked rattled. "Everything okay?"

"Not here," she whispered. She nodded up ahead.

When they had walked silently for a minute without seeing anyone, Meg stopped. "You should have told me," she said. "You should have told me she has a son at home."

"Oh, God," he said. "Of course. I'm so sorry."

Meg looked up toward the ceiling, the perfect Sky, like she was trying to keep from crying.

"Here, the Lounge is right up there, come on."

He opened the door to the Lounge and saw the last sliver of Earth disappear from the window—the real window. Meg stared into the starry dark like it was any window, anywhere.

"It really took a turn," she said, "when I told her that I didn't want our kids using the phones up here, because our son is too young for one and, actually, our daughter is, too, and she said, well, they need them for safety, and I started to argue with that idea, and then she said—'If your son had been wearing a phone during the hair dye episode—'"

"What?" Alex said. "How did—"

"From his medical records," she said. "Weird power move, right?"

"Yeah," Alex said. Esther had never talked to him that way.

"And that kind of caught me off guard, and I said, sorry, what is your deal with phones? Because I know this whole project is on Sensus money, but you seem *very* invested in everyone using them, and she said that if you brought your children to live on a space station, it seemed odd to then worry about them using phones." She shrugged, trying to shake off Esther's judgment. "I don't belong here."

Alex put his arms out to bring her in. "I don't, either. It's a space station. Nobody belongs here."

"Oh, God," she said. "What have we done?"

"Brought our kids up for an incredibly unique adventure in a hypo-allergenic environment with impermeable cybersecurity," he said. "Rescued our marriage, maybe? Or just," he added quickly, "you know, decided to try again? All good things."

"I don't know what I'm doing," she said.

"Oh," he said. "It's okay. You're a Pioneer now."

The Earth rolled into the window frame, and Meg gasped.

It was different now, he told her, with the spins. Sometimes the view whipping by made him feel like—

"Like death is coming faster?" she said, watching their planet slide away. "Like in an old movie where the pages fly off the calendar?"

"Before, it was the opposite," he said. "We were frozen, and you all kept living."

"Let's go get Shane," she said.

The promenade was glowing softly, its golden hour setting, and Meg was right beside him. Shane was at Teddy and Homero's, playing with the twins. Mary Agnes was with Malik's kids, whom she seemed to really get along with, and Malik had offered to have Mary Agnes intern in his lab along with them. Alex was astonished that his family had been so welcomed by the others. As long as he got his own shit straightened out, they could be remade here, could thrive here.

"I haven't seen *your* lab yet," Meg said, startled.

"I know, I know," he said. "We'll do it tomorrow."

"But I want to see what—"

"If I go in, it'll be hard not to start checking things, fiddling around," he said. "And then . . . you know how that goes. I want to give you the whole day." He tried to smile. "It's so great that the kids are all getting along. Shane told me Lola was 'born for this.'"

She laughed, and he relaxed, a little, for the moment.

As they passed Esther's office again, Meg's arm stiffened, and then they heard the sound of the children's laughter, Shane's piercing squeal and Lola's husky giggle, coming from inside.

Meg pulled her arm from Alex and pushed open the door.

Homero was sitting on the floor with Julian standing behind him, his arms wrapped around his father's neck. Lola was standing with Shane in a bridge formation, their small hands clasped in the air as they leaned in to each other. Esther was in her chair, smiling and watching them.

"Shane," Meg said sharply, and his face fell in confusion. "Come here."

"I can't let go. Lola will fall down."

"I won't fall," Lola said. She released Shane's hands and he stumbled forward, catching himself on Homero's back.

"Come here," Meg said again, tenderly this time, and when he did, she picked him up and held him against her hip like a much younger child. "What are you doing?" she asked Esther.

"Playing," Esther said with a weariness that Alex knew, without a doubt, would make Meg want to twist her head off.

"Just puzzles and games," Homero said. "Esther has a few things, thank God."

On the wall was a blinking maze in bright turquoise and pink, its walls and tunnels shifting slightly every few seconds. The children's wobbly routes, where they dragged along their index fingers, wound through it in yellow.

"We weren't allowed to bring any games or toys," said Meg.

"Good thing Esther has some, then?" said Homero, his heavy-lidded eyes blinking at her in exquisite patience.

Meg didn't notice. She was staring at Esther, eyes flashing. "Why were you allowed to bring toys and games for my children, who you don't think should even be here, but I was not?"

Esther seemed to be searching for a reasonable answer to an unreasonable question and not finding it. She looked at Alex to see if Meg made sense to him, but he only cleared his throat.

"There's no way it's just games," Meg said, glancing at the maze. "What are you studying, here? Whose research project is it? Are you the principal or are you collecting data for a larger project?"

"This is the larger project," said Esther. "Life on this space station."

Alex cleared his throat again, like that action alone amounted to anything, and shifted his weight back and forth. He had to say something to back her up, even if she did sound a little—a little—

"Might be better to talk about stuff with the kids with us, beforehand," he managed to croak.

Meg, still clutching Shane, looked ready to bolt.

"It seems to me like you could have approached me differently," she said to Esther, using her most careful voice. "Given that this was your goal."

"This?"

"Making my children the subjects of experiments."

Shane wriggled down. "Mom? Why are you mad?"

"I'm not mad," Meg said. "Come on, let's go get your sister."

But before they were out the door she turned around to face Esther. "You should have asked."

Esther only studied the children's routes through the maze.

"IT'S CALLED COGS," Colette said. She handed Meg a cup of tea. "We all have to do them, and we talked about—well, you must have missed that day."

"Totally therapeutic, I'm sure, and definitely confidential," said Meg.

Colette gave her a hard look.

"You think I sound like a lunatic," said Meg.

"I just don't get why you're surprised," Colette said. "It's the price of admission." She was perched on the arm of her foam sofa, as comfortable as if she'd lived here for years. She wore her first Parallaxis combo, dark orange, as if it were high-end loungewear. Malik stood just behind her, not an inch farther than politeness required.

"I thought the somethings being exchanged were different," said Meg. "I didn't think we were here to be full-on lab rats."

"Hey," said Alex. "Hang on."

"What, you thought you were getting to come up here to move couches?" Colette said. "Because you already expressed your surprise that you have to do that. So which is it?"

"I thought it would be more like an experiment we were all doing together," Meg said. She picked at a dried spot of food on her shirt. "Not like being a lab rat. Who moves couches." She gave Alex a look that was angry and guilty at the same time. She knew she sounded naive, spoiled, worse.

"What did Esther ask you this afternoon?" she asked Colette. "In your intake session."

"A few minutes of chitchat and then we went straight to Cogs. Tests to see how I'm adapting. Spatial awareness, speed-logic, some short-term memory stuff."

Meg slugged her tea like it might be something stronger.

Colette sighed. "Why did you come?" she asked gently. "We came *for* our kids. They will lead more exceptional lives because of Parallaxis. They will not be gunned down at the store or swept away in a flood. They are *safe* here—"

"My kids and I are just poorly suited to life on Earth," Meg said, trying to make it sound like a joke even though it wasn't.

"We all are," Alex said, trying again for that solidarity he'd so badly failed at, down there. But Malik caught his eye and gave him a look he couldn't quite read, or maybe he didn't want to. He thought of Jilly and Stan, their alleged jolliness and can-do attitudes, and hoped Malik and Colette weren't thinking of them, too. It wouldn't hurt Meg to remember that they had displaced others, even if they hadn't done so intentionally, and maybe show a little gratitude for this chance they'd all been given.

THAT NIGHT, Meg and Alex lay under the flimsy blanket facing away from each other.

"I know you're awake," she said.

He didn't answer quickly enough.

"Will you turn over and look at me?"

He did, and he couldn't see her, not really, but after a year of sleeping alone, her presence a foot away from him was both overwhelming and not close enough.

"You asked us to come," she said. "You said you wanted us."

"Oh, Meg," he said. "I did. I *do*."

Meg moaned some subverbal sadness into her pillow.

"Are you mad I talked to Rachel?" she asked.

That evening, after dinner, Meg had banged on the door of Rachel's pod, as though it were her unquestionable right to do so, to lodge her various complaints. Alex had been bewildered at first, and then humiliated, though he couldn't say exactly why—not to her, and not even to himself.

"Not *mad*," he said. "It's just—" He licked his lips. "It's hard to hear you complain."

"What?"

"To complain now, when the station is so nice, and the food is so much better, and everything is clean. It did not look like this, or feel like this, when I started."

"I'm not complaining about *you*."

"Well, but, you are, kind of. Because we've all worked ourselves down to nothing, all day, sometimes all night, every day. We pushed ourselves to our limits over and over to build this thing."

"But for Sensus? For Parallaxis? Why?"

He remembered the night Rachel had come out of the call room and told them that there would be no more calls until they had finished Phase I, the look on her face when she told them, as though she couldn't believe it, either. She had worked on pod construction, too, in the owner homes, taking items from their to-do lists as the Pioneers fell behind. Never with them, always alone—preferable, because when she made her rounds to check their work, she seized any opportunity to remind them of the people at home, the children and parents and partners and friends, who were waiting to hear from them, or, in some cases, to see them again.

"To get you here," he said. "All of you."

Spiderhands

22

Mary Agnes had wondered once before if her father was maybe having an affair. The weirdness, the secrecy. But now *wondering* didn't seem strong enough. Tess had been skulking in the corner of her father's lab when Mary Agnes, Inaya, and Sebastian had come by. There wasn't any good explanation, either, though Tess had bouncily offered a few casual excuses. Mary Agnes watched her wind her away around the algae racks to the door, very familiar, very comfy, and was pierced by a hot needle of hatred. She was what, twenty-five? And those tiny, creepy hands, her fingers dry and spindly. Spider hands. "Later!" Tess called in her too-quiet, too-blurty voice. Mary Agnes looked back at her father, who watched Tess's back until the door closed behind her.

Inaya was looking at her father's screen, even scrolling, and Sebastian was poking around in the lights. Only Mary Agnes stood still, not touching anything, and trying not to barf on the floor.

Her father took a quick breath before he turned around. "Here's the thing—you should be careful around her," he said. He twitched at the sight of Inaya at his workstation but didn't tell her to move.

"What?" asked Mary Agnes. "Why?"

"Just avoid her, if you can. She has this really intense way of getting into your head. Definitely don't tell her anything personal—"

Inaya's eyes went wide.

"Then why are *you* hanging out with her?" Mary Agnes asked.

"I wasn't hanging out with her, I'm working. We're all working."

"What's she doing in your lab? Workwise, I mean."

"I don't really know," he said, sighing. "Why the third degree, Mary Agnes?"

That he looked angry startled her, even though she was angry, too. Mary Agnes had seen how Tess looked at her father at dinner, her stolen sideways glances from across the room. At her mother, too, and even, once or twice, at her. When she felt Tess's attention on her family she wanted to spin around and catch her, but she never did. Instead, she just sat there and felt gross.

"Come on," Inaya said, her voice softer than usual. "My dad's waiting for us, anyway."

Had she meant to emphasize *my*, or had Mary Agnes imagined it? Inaya wouldn't shy away from the comparison. Malik was expecting them, wanted them, had given them important or at least pseudo-important experiments to do on air and water quality. Mary Agnes loved working in his lab as long she didn't pause to ask herself why it was impossible to do this with her own father, or why he thought it was.

"Fine," Mary Agnes said. "We'll go."

Everyone knew you didn't choose your parents, but her eyes were stinging with embarrassment anyway. She tried to shake it away. She should be happier for him, she reminded herself, and the world he was saving.

THEY HEARD THE CLATTER of the little kids' feet before they saw them. Mary Agnes's mother was in the fab lab today, and it was Homero's turn with the herd of them.

As soon as Shane saw her, he stopped and threw up his hands.

"Can you believe this sky?" he shouted. He lowered his hands to his hips like a recent retiree at his new beach condo.

"No," Mary Agnes said once she was close enough to speak at an appropriate volume. She looked up into the chlorine blue and puffball clouds. Her family was from Michigan; a sky like this didn't feel like home. Why not planets, why not stars? The galaxy, the one right there on the other side. This wasn't how Parallaxis was sold to them. Well, she didn't know, actually—she wasn't pitched, her mother was. No one had ever needed to sell Mary Agnes on Parallaxis. She had wanted to leave the planet, and high school, to be with her dad again and to help him with his work. The promise of being lifted up.

Pretty different mindset, back then.

But she'd listened to her mother spin a gorgeous sci-fi adventure tale for Shane, and she had fallen for it, too, a little bit: their family, together again, but with new specialness and heroism. Heroism! Ha. Ha ha ha.

Her father was having an affair. That was it. That was why he'd been so weird since they got here. Distant. Not distant like preoccupied, like he was working through a problem in his brain—that distance, she was used to. Distant like he didn't *want* them getting too close to him. She had been sure he was lying about something, she just didn't know what it was. Did it even count as an affair, since her parents had been separated until her mom had shown up all of a sudden to remind him of the messed-up family he'd left behind?

Her baby brother was the hero here, if anyone was. He'd never gotten to go anywhere outside of his sterile school (the Sanitarium, she'd called it, talking to Inaya and Sebastian), and now he was gallivanting around a zazillion-dollar space station like a wild pony. Bare legs, bare arms! No face shields, no bug hood!

"Another beautiful day in space," Shane said. "Homero's going to teach us about comets versus meteors versus trash."

"That's great," Mary Agnes said. "You'll tell me later? Because actually, I have no idea."

Her voice sounded hollow and far away. She smiled at Shane—lopsided, but she managed it. She wished she could be alone right now, because the thought of watching Inaya, Sebastian, and their dad enjoy one another's company—the corny puns, the long-running jokes, the comfort that bounced right back up when they teased each other, never collapsing—it was a little more, at the moment, than she could take.

LYING ON HER pointed bed after dinner, Mary Agnes picked at one of the scalloped plastic tiles on the wall, worrying its edges with her thumbnail. In the month she'd slept in this bed, she'd fucked up this one plastic tile considerably. Inaya was stretched out on the floor and picking at her own favored wall scallop. Her parents were having a date night, which they definitely didn't need to tell her, she said, since she and Mary Agnes hung out here after dinner most nights. Gross, Mary Agnes had answered, but there was a grosser part of her that was jealous, a little.

How was your home call? Did you get to talk to Zoya? Mary Agnes messaged.

She wasn't there.

Sucks.

She probably has a new best friend. Probably Fleur.

Mary Agnes laughed. *Fucking Fleur.* She wanted to ask Inaya if she had seen it, earlier, what she had seen in her dad's lab. She wanted to ask her, but also she really didn't, because Inaya would definitely tell her the truth. "What's she like? Zoya, I mean."

"Hilarious," Inaya said. "Super confident, and, like, confident *about* her confidence, if that makes sense. She just does her thing, even if it gets weird. Like you."

"ME?"

"Yeah, you don't care if you look goofy. No offense."

"I care," Mary Agnes said. "I just can't do anything about it."

There were so many scalloped tiles, thousands of them across the ceiling and the one wavy wall. Was it supposed to look like a fish's skin? She picked off another shard of plastic, so satisfying. No one would ever notice this bad one, right?

"I think my dad is having an affair," Mary Agnes said.

Inaya didn't say anything at first, and Mary Agnes thought maybe she hadn't heard her. "I think maybe my dad—"

"Zoya's dad had an affair last year," Inaya said. "An emotional affair, which is worse. And, actually, it was—no, this is too—never mind."

"What?"

"So, her dad never talks—supernerd, soaked in tech—and I always thought that's just how he was. Stays inside his own head, right?"

"Like my dad."

"But what Zoya said was an emotional affair proves he *can*, like, connect with someone. Just not them."

A long silence. The lights dimmed, and the pinprick constellations in the wall storage units and the ceiling glowed on. The covers on her bed seemed to change color from blue to a murky violet. Eight o'clock.

"Like he was cheating on their whole family by actually caring about some lady's day and what she ate for lunch and stuff," Inaya said.

"I got it." Mary Agnes dragged her face with her hands. "I mean, it's no wonder. My mom up here is like . . . a fly that's stuck in a car. And I'm all—well, she basically left me on the side of the road when she found out about the virus."

"It's so messed up that you did that," Inaya said, and Mary Agnes froze, unsure if it was a *yikes-ha-ha* messed-up or something worse. Inaya was still talking, but her voice might as well be underwater, because the something-worse was already filling Mary Agnes's head.

"Back at home, was your dad, like—"

"Gross?" Mary Agnes finished. "Like, was he a gross dad, salivating at baristas—"

"—Asking them about their *plans* in life, and all the interesting courses they're taking, and giving himself an advice-boner—"

"No, he wasn't," Mary Agnes said. "You think it's emotional?" she asked. "The affair?"

"*I* don't know what kind of affair it is."

"Can we call it, uh, the alleged affair?"

"Sure, but you're the one who's alleging it." She paused. "Spider-hands?"

Mary Agnes heaved.

She did want to know the truth, but wanted the truth to be that her dad was not having an affair, because that made her feel angry, and she had proven to be a vengeful person who made terrible decisions under the influence of anger, and she did not want to negotiate with that feeling again.

"What he said about her listening all the time," Inaya said.

"I mean, she's Ground, so . . ."

Inaya smoothed the edges of her plastic tile like she was trying to soothe it. "You think Ground is listening to us all the time?"

"Or watching us, or tracking us or whatever."

"But, like, *listening?*"

"Mmm . . . yeah."

"Don't tell your mom that," Inaya said.

"Seriously."

A long pause.

"As long as it's not Carl," Inaya said. "That would be . . . my death."

"Handsome Carl," Mary Agnes said, teasing her.

"You're never going to let that go, are you? Hot is just not . . . terribly descriptive. It's, like, sweaty and squinty but what *else?*"

"And handsome is?" Mary Agnes, grateful for the distraction, wanted to keep Inaya on the subject of Carl, of flattering adjectives, of anything that wasn't her messed-up family. "Handsome sounds like a big face? An old, big face?"

"Hellooooo," Inaya sang in a high, soft voice. "Hello, Ground!" She dropped to a whisper. "Is her dad having an affair with Spiderhands? If yes, flicker the lights."

"Oh my god," Mary Agnes said. "I gotta pee." She swung her legs down to the floor.

In the bathroom, she shut the door and sat down on the lid of the toilet with hands over her eyes. Her parents had been separated, before. Maybe she was being stupid, childish, to be upset about this. Maybe her mom knew.

The door opened, and her dad covered his face with his hand. "Sorry!" he said. "Sorry." He slammed the door.

Mary Agnes stood up and flushed the toilet, willed herself to calm down. Calm *down*. She opened the door.

"I didn't know you were here!" he said.

"Where else would I be?"

"Where's your mom and Shane? I'm just getting a fresh combo, I've got to go in tonight," he said. "Won't be home. Burning the candle at both ends. That means—"

"I know what it means." She turned her back on him and went into her bedroom and shut the door.

"Whoa," Inaya said. "You okay?"

"I don't know," Mary Agnes said quietly. "My dad is a liar. Can we get out of here?"

"Wanna go poke around the mansions?"

Mary Agnes shook her head. "I got caught this morning. Rachel."

"What!" Inaya sat up. "I can't believe you didn't tell me!"

Mary Agnes had said she had to pee and fled Malik's lab, but instead she had kept walking. When she reached the corridor that led to Rachel's pod, she hesitated. She'd wandered into it her first day, and then Lenore and Tess had told her she was lost and brought her to the feedbag. This morning she had turned into the corridor again, this time to the mansion across from Rachel's. She pushed open the door, silent as ever, and stepped into a house elsewhere in the universe. The room was inky blue, with walls that curved up and met each other, like a chapel. Just above her head there was some kind of silvery fog, thicker in some places than others. She'd reached up to touch it, wondering if it would feel damp and cold, and saw the light hit the palm of her hand. It was light. She couldn't see where it was coming from.

"This is my sister's," Rachel had said behind her. Mary Agnes spun around. She thought Rachel would tell her to get out, but she didn't.

"It's beautiful," Mary Agnes said. "Like an abandoned church in a lost city."

Rachel, looking at the floor, gave a single slow nod. "She'd like that."

"Sorry," Mary Agnes said. "I'll just—sorry." Rachel still stood in the doorway, and Mary Agnes passed by her close enough so that their clothes brushed against each other. She smelled the same vanilla-mint cleansing wipes that they all used. She heard the click of the closing door behind her and hurried back to Malik's lab.

"What did she say?" Inaya said, sticking her thumbnail between her teeth.

Mary Agnes heard her mom and Shane coming through the front door. *Should we go to the feedbag?*

It probably still stinks from dinner. The window?

"Mary Agnes?" her mother called. "Are you here? Have you seen your dad?"

You walked for an hour here to end up exactly where you started. "Anywhere but here," said Mary Agnes, knowing there was nowhere else to go.

23

Tess knew her hands were small, a bit bony, her skin always dry, but she hadn't thought they were *spidery*. She was surprised by how much the girls were willing to say when they believed they might be "overheard." Even their suspicion that she was having an affair with Alex was not sensitive material to them—just gossip, even if it was gossip that one of them found stressful. Given a similar suspicion, their parents never would have talked about the same things they did, but the girls' generation was used to it—"it" being either the sensation of being monitored by machines *or* a more timeless childhood-feeling of being watched by one's parents, Santa, God. Regardless, their suspicion or belief (unclear how strong it was) did not seem to change their behavior.

She wasn't surprised that Mary Agnes had gone to "affair" as an explanation for Alex's distance, given the circumstances, and Mary Agnes had noticed Tess looking at Alex and Meg a couple times. That she herself figured in this explanation, though, was fascinating. She felt Mary Agnes's attention on her like an electrical charge, as though the next thing she touched would bring a shock.

For Mary Agnes, her father having an affair would be less of a betrayal than the one Alex had committed. The same was true for Meg. That Alex would lie to *them* about his superalgae was beyond the possible—literally outside their perceived range of possibilities, according to the Algo—and, Tess worried, unforgiveable. The Algo had marked Meg as Alex's primary stressor, above the algae, above his lie about it. What that meant was that Meg was the reason Alex hadn't told the truth yet.

THE FIRST TIME Meg and Alex had sex on the station, on Meg's fourth night aboard, had been less than successful. Expectations were too high and too fraught, the walls too thin. Alex was embarrassed by the changes to his body, which he hadn't fully realized until he saw Meg's body again. Meg wished she could have a glass of wine first and felt guilty about that. The faint but constant hum reminded her they were spinning around, that she didn't know what she and Alex were now or what she wanted them to be. Alex was preoccupied by fear, by what he didn't want her to know. They hadn't done it, Tess was pretty sure, since before the separation—at least a year, probably eighteen months.

When they kissed each other, Meg twitched and hesitated, and when Alex asked what was wrong, she said it was different, his mouth tasted different, and then they both apologized. He smelled different, too—Tess could tell by the uncertain way Meg pressed and repositioned her face against him. The strange diet up here, probably. The newcomers smelled too earthy, gamey even, to the Pioneers; Tess herself had noticed it.

Meg climbed on top of Alex and he tried to lift her up from the hips, but he couldn't do it anymore, he wasn't strong enough. Instead of laughing about it and trying something else, they just gave up.

When the Algo connected this new information to old information, it read a distinctly human problem that until this point had been inexplicable in machine learning: Here were two people who wanted to want to have sex with each other. They did not fully want to have sex with each other, but they *wanted* to want to. The Algo was learning about so much: human ambivalence, human desire, human sadness, monogamy, mythology, ritual and practice. Theirs wasn't a dynamic that Tess could have understood before the Views project, but together with the Algo, she read it just fine.

Their second time, three days later, was good. Meg couldn't fall asleep afterward because of the sex fluids on her thighs and creeping into her butt crack, sticky, wet, and itchy. She tossed and turned as though she hadn't expected it to bother her—it probably hadn't, back when she was used to it, when she could roll over and snuggle into him and never mind it. Tess could see it perfectly, how Alex would surround her afterward and pull her hips into his.

But now that sticky itch was too unfamiliar to ignore. She squirmed. Finally she got up and crept to the bathroom to pee and wipe off with a towel. Instead of putting the towel into laundry disposal, she brought it back to the bedroom with her, wadded up, as if it were somehow incriminating. The Algo noticed this detail before Tess did: Meg did not regard the towel as her own. Her towels were not hers, which meant: this was not her home, not yet. She had been invited to Parallaxis, and she still thought of herself not as a "citizen" but as a "guest." But since Alex treated all station supplies as if they were his own, and Meg had traditionally drawn from the same shared supply as her husband ("household," "common property," "marriage"), then Meg must have seen herself not just as a trespasser on Parallaxis but as a trespasser in her own household, common property, and marriage. And it was the used towel that taught the Algo this math, which meant the Algo was learning unconscious human mixed symbolism: sex, towel, hiding, ownership. Tess was pleased and proud. Good job, Algo.

She looked at Alex differently at breakfast the next day, noticing things about his face and body that she hadn't before. His shoulders were broader than she'd realized. She found herself looking at his forearms and hands, his lips and long fingers. Meg helped Shane get seconds in the breakfast line, bending over to mix his oatmeal, and Tess stared at the wide flare of her ass, wanting to hold each side of it in her hands as Alex had. She glanced at Alex and saw him watching her, too.

It made sense to focus her training of the Algo on sex right now. There had been so little of it for so long, and now there was so much. Teddy and Homero, often in reunion after an argument that Teddy had started because he was horny. Macy and Carl: at a mutually agreed upon time, usually in the middle of the night. They seemed to be merely scratching an itch; neither wanted anyone to know about it. Malik and Colette often did it in the early morning, before anyone else was awake, about every other day after the first week. One of them would reach for the other in bed and find them half-asleep, waiting to be awoken by the other. He often buried his nose at the base of her neck after he came, in the well above her collarbone. She ran a finger along his neck, behind his ears, while she caught her breath. The completeness of the intimacy between them was unfathomable, no matter how many times she witnessed it.

And Lenore and Irma, which Tess watched with lonely hunger. The first time, Tess had stopped breathing as soon as Irma pulled Lenore's shirt up over her head and nosed into her bra, seeking the undersides of her breasts with her lips and tongue. Tess made sure her door was locked and pulled Lenore's Views up, too, so she could watch them side by side. Lenore knelt and filled her hands with Irma's thighs, pushed them apart, but then she closed her eyes. But Irma kept her own eyes open, and Tess stayed with them until she heard Lenore's feet padding down the promenade, passing Tess's pod on her way back to work.

Tess was no longer so afraid of being found out. The new subjects regarded her as someone who'd "been here," neither mysterious nor suspicious, and the first Pioneers now thought of her as someone stuck, like Rachel, but more helpless and less deserving of her fate. She had a certain privilege of anonymity that was seldom questioned anymore, except by Alex. She still hadn't been able to recover his trust.

In June, Alex got his clean culture. The uninvited guest was gone, to his incredible relief and to Tess's, and for the next few days, the Algo read his relief everywhere, from the jokes that he made to Meg and his children to his blood pressure. But at the beginning of his second week working with the clean culture, he began to tense up again. The algae was not working. At the end of the month, he had not replicated. Maybe the genes had mutated over their months in space; that could happen. Maybe he had introduced a new variable, or an instability specific to a space lab. Or maybe the trespasser species was responsible for both his successful replications and the toxic algal bloom in his lab, and he could not have one without the other. This last explanation was the one that kept him up at night, wrapped around Meg for comfort.

The Algo allowed a slim chance now that Alex could solve the problem and his lie would pass undiscovered, but Tess did not. The Algo didn't see that the lie itself would hold Alex down, like wet cement he'd poured over his own feet, thinking he had enough time to step out before he got stuck. When Alex was found out, the reactions of the other subjects would be good for the Algo's training. She repeated this to herself as often as she needed to. She couldn't protect him from himself.

In the month since the families had arrived, Tess and the Algo had made stunning progress. Partly this was due to Esther's weekly sessions with the Pioneers: both her Views of those appointments and the notes she took on them had proved invaluable. The more contrasting perspectives of the same experience she could feed the Algo, the better it got at processing the thousands of nuanced perspectives the subjects created each day. All the time now, the Algo picked up evidence that Tess hadn't yet. If a scrap of Views had the slightest whiff of importance— nervousness in the eye movements, say, or it corresponded with a slightly elevated heart rate—the Algo knew exactly where to dig for the rest.

And partly, the Algo's rapid improvement was due to the conditions in which her subjects lived. Tess had watched strangers become intimates in a very short period of time, with little alternative. It wasn't just the absence of "noise" in larger society that made the subjects' quarantine a clean arena for study, but that the shared experience of their quarantine was a fertile ground for their relationships. Lenore and Irma were falling in love with each other, but they, too, wondered if their feelings would have arisen the same way, had they met on Earth, had they not both lost people at home as soon as they left, and had they not been selected to live this strange life, together, in space.

When Tess was a little girl in Minnesota, her father had brought home two pet rabbits, strangers, who would have to share a cage. He put a soft towel on top of the clothes dryer and sat the two rabbits on it. Then he put a few items in the dryer and turned it on. As the dryer rumbled beneath them, the frightened rabbits crowded together. "This is how you bond them," he'd explained. They were inseparable after that.

The Height of
Her Powers

24

Tess watched Esther's counseling sessions carefully, more carefully than Esther did. She checked Esther's notes and sometimes changed them slightly to better prepare her for the next session. She'd started to add her own games to the Cogs sessions, too, to trigger the kinds of reactions she needed the Algo to process. All that aside, she could see that Esther was right—the counseling was good for the Pioneers, and they often left Esther's office a little lighter than they came in.

One Sunday afternoon, when Esther was usually preparing the weekly group coordination game, she was instead watching a memory in her archive. Leo was playing with a wooden railway, lining tracks up on either side of a bridge that collapsed when he pushed the red plastic button at its center. He pushed an engine up to the bridge and pressed the button. The train fell through the bridge, and Leo giggled madly, turning to make sure she had seen. Then Carl Bouchet, the astronaut, had tapped at Esther's office door and stuck his head inside. She minimized the footage but didn't close it, left it suspended on her dashboard, just above his ear, as she welcomed him.

"I've never done therapy," said Carl Bouchet, sitting down and scrunching up his handsome face. "Of this kind."

Esther was surprised, and so was Tess. Neither of the astronauts had ever come to Esther for anything. Carl wasn't one of Tess's subjects; she had no idea what was coming. She crisscrossed her legs and adjusted her lumbar pillow.

"This is a complex environment," Esther said, her hands clasped loosely in her lap. "We have good coping tools, the games and the VR—I'm not sure if you use it?—but they're not a substitute for, well, *venting*. Especially in a closed group like this."

Carl nodded. "How long have you been with Parallaxis?"

"About four years now," she said. "I'd always hoped to come to the station, but there are five of us in the Behavioral Health Module. I didn't know who would be chosen."

"Do you know why they picked you?"

"They said I was selected for harmony."

"You don't make trouble," he said.

"Never." She laughed. "Well, I do my best for our group. Sometimes I have to push."

"Their therapy sessions."

"Yes," she said. "I pushed for those."

Tess smiled. She couldn't see Esther's face, but she could hear the soft pride in her voice.

"Were you part of the selection team? Did you hire *me*?" Carl asked, and Esther shook her head. "They used to say at NASA that the main obstacle to long-endurance missions wasn't technical limitation, but personalities," he said. "How to select the right people."

Tess held her breath. This was why Carl had come today. He was testing Esther, evaluating how much he could trust her.

"What do you think?" Esther asked.

He gave her a sideways grin and jogged his knee. "Are you asking me if I'm the right people? Yeah, I think so."

"You were trained at NASA, right?"

"Oh, yeah, most of us still come out of NASA. They train us, then the money picks us up at the door. That's starting to change, there are a few private training programs now. But I did everything by the book. I hadn't planned on leaving, but I was almost forty, and it wasn't going to happen there."

"Space flight," she said.

He nodded. "They get it, the funding just isn't there." He paused and drummed his foot, two soft beats. "How did *you* get up here?"

"Like you, by the book," she said. "I did a four-month isolation sim with NASA when I was in grad school, at the HI-SEAS lab in Hawaii. Then I went back as a postdoc on the other side—my PI was developing VR tools like ours. I applied to Parallaxis, worked at other projects, but, you know—I always hoped I'd get that call. I was pregnant when I got it. And my husband and I moved to Ticaboo."

"He's still there, with your son?"

She shook her head. "Leo is in upstate New York with his grandparents," she said. "My husband died last year. Over a year, now."

"Oh," Carl said, drawing back. "I'm sorry to hear that."

Out of habit Tess tried to run the Algo on Carl, forgetting that she had no Carl-model.

"Thank you," Esther said. "He—he really encouraged me in my work. Whenever I had doubts, he said we'd figure it out. He was like that." She said this last part too fast, as if she were helping it to escape. She cleared her throat. "Is it what you expected, up here? The food is better than I expected."

Esther had never, ever said so much about her husband to any of the Pioneers.

Carl nodded, considering, perhaps relieved that she had redirected the conversation. "The food is pretty tolerable," he agreed. "I'd prefer a real window in my pod. Our living quarters are so protected from the authentic experience of life in space."

"I thought you lived in the Helper?"

"No," he said. "I'm just in there all day."

"What did you mean by authentic?"

"Oh, how we're babied, like we can't handle the sight of the real thing. We're here because of a desire to live in space, and yet"—he swept his hand around her office, at her plush chairs and her fake fern—"it's designed to feel as *grounded* as possible. To feel safe. I mean, look at the toilets."

"What about them?"

"The Helper toilet is an astronaut's toilet. Your-all's toilets are just bad bathrooms."

"I'll take our bad bathrooms any day." Esther had opened the memory of Leo with his train tracks again and let it play, floating over Carl's face.

Carl pushed himself farther into the seat of his chair, a pose that looked half-relaxed, half-frustrated. "Life in the Helper station is very different from what you all experience out here." He looked off to the side and let his eyes wander her office's empty walls. "You don't even know how anything works," he said. "How Mozgov runs the station."

There it was. He wanted to tell her about the Helper—about Mozgov.

Esther minimized the footage. "Do you think we should know more about it?"

She understood.

"Mozgov's having a hard enough time handing the reins over to me," he said. "I don't know who selected that personality, or maybe he was different before, who knows."

An answer, of a kind.

He leaned forward and clasped his hands over his knee, which started jogging again.

"Are you in an unsafe situation?" Esther asked him.

His knee stilled.

"Carl," Esther said. "I'm listening."

Too much. She had scared him.

"Not more than anybody else," he said.

"Are *we* in an unsafe situation?"

He scratched his chin. "You didn't want to bring your kid up, like the others?"

She shook her head. "I didn't think it could be safe."

"Even in the best conditions," Carl said.

Esther nodded, looking at her knees.

"My grandma raised me," he said. "He'll be okay. Lucky to have them, right?"

"Yeah," Esther said.

Carl said he had to get back to the station. As soon as he was gone, Esther returned to her chair. She typically reviewed parts of a session and made notes afterward, but this time, she drew her knees up to her chest and wrapped her arms around them. Then she pulled up the Leo footage again, picked up right where she left off. Leo turned to her, laughing in amazement at the collapsed bridge, again and again.

Tess drummed her fingers on her desk. Esther claimed that people needed to talk, to vent, so that the weather in their brains did not consume them. But what to do when Esther herself was consumed?

Tess wasn't a therapist, schooled in getting people to open up about their worst fears and desires, but she didn't need to be, not now. She knew everything about Esther, including all that she didn't say. She could help Esther talk.

Tess turned off the feeds. She stood up, brushed the crumbs off her combo, and locked the door of her pod after her. She could be in the right place at the right time. It would be good for Esther, and good for the Algo, too.

THE PURPOSE OF Esther's isolation sim at HI-SEAS, she told Tess, was to troubleshoot and optimize group dynamics for long-duration space flight, meaning that for the time they were together, the six crew members pretended they were on Mars. They lived in a yurt under a volcano and emerged only for "missions" in the lava rock around it, wearing their space suits. In the tent they had roles specific to a long-duration space flight scenario. They had been chosen for their interests in this kind of work but also for key elements in the ideal personality: self-discipline, self-sacrifice, self-care, and the ability to consistently prioritize coordination over individual choice. She laughed.

She was ambitious, always had been, and it had been challenging for her to relax her own will in relation to others'. She'd had a crush on one of the other crew members, and since even mild flirtation among the crew was strongly discouraged, she'd had to learn to sublimate that, too, for the sake of the group and the experiment.

Two years after the simulation, she went back to HI-SEAS as a post-doc, observing a mission much like hers. Two months in, one of the crew tore his retina and had to go to the hospital. The sim was broken, the mission aborted, all the data thrown out.

Her own mission group had kept in loose touch, and she knew Ben Berlinski was still in Hawaii. That was his name, the crew member she'd had a crush on. She decided to text him while she was there with, for the first time in many years, nothing to do.

He was still there? Tess asked. What was he doing?

Dissertating remotely, dragging his feet. He was studying actuarial science—the odds of disasters, basically—and there was never a worse match between a person and the path they'd taken. She laughed. Staying in Hawaii didn't make it easier to sort through reams of data for fourteen hours a day.

They made plans, and she almost canceled, she was so nervous. But when they met, he pulled her into a hug so sure that she stopped worrying. "You smell better than you used to," she said into his shoulder. He said that she did, too.

Did he look the same? Tess asked. Was he like you remembered?

Esther nodded slowly. The way he moved, his gait. He was lean and rangy, almost ropy in his limbs, as if his actions started in his extremities, instead of from his head. She laughed. This is the kind of thing you think about, in isolation together.

She told him that she hoped to get hired at Parallaxis. He told her that he wanted to drop out of his program. This was the next morning, in the kitchen of his shared apartment. He was standing at the counter wearing worn-out running tights and eating pickled herring out of a jar. A month later, she canceled her flight home and canceled it again.

They went back to Ithaca, to his parents' basement, when she got pregnant. That she was going to have a baby with him was astounding. There were hair ties she'd known longer. But what could possibly better prepare two people for partnership than HI-SEAS had, right?

In Ithaca, Ben took a job in a big insurance office where he wore sweater vests every day so he wouldn't have to iron his shirts. Esther volunteered at the VA hospital and applied to work with special forces groups in the military, newly terrified that she'd let herself fall behind. But Ben believed in her, and when she got the call from Parallaxis Ground that they wanted her in Ticaboo, he didn't hesitate at all. We're going, he said. She was seven months pregnant.

"Out there, it was like we were back in an isolation sim, Ben, me, and Leo. It's Mars in Utah, you know how it is around Ground. Our apartment looked right out over the canyons."

At first, Ben loved the canyons, but when Leo learned to walk, they looked different to him, suddenly. Leo always wanted to look over the edges, and yanking his hand away, and running too fast. He didn't like having his hand held. It only got worse.

One night, Ben woke her up and said they had to leave, that the canyons were too dangerous a place to raise a child. When she mentioned all the other children, he said that the canyons were making him nuts. The windows from their apartment tortured his imagination. "Someone's going to kidnap him and disappear down there. We'll find him in the spring if we find him at all."

Esther didn't think the canyons themselves were the issue, but she thought she had time to understand what was and to find him the right help. They switched apartments to one without a view, and he got better, for a while. Then, when Leo was two, he got worse, and she misjudged the size and redness of the flags. Ben killed himself that spring.

Esther put her hands over her eyes.

"I was so *angry*," she said.

It clawed up through her grief, through her guilt that she had brought them there, her shame that she had misunderstood his suffering. Her training was no match for it. Ben had left her a single mother, with a two-year-old and $150,000 in debt to her name. How was she supposed to teach Leo to survive, to bounce, to bend, to try and try again, when his father had given up? She knew she was wrong, but she could not stop thinking it.

At night, in her bed in her tiny pod, she talked to Leo as if she were praying, but then Ben would appear in her mind and catch her up short. She had made a terrible mistake.

Tess went to her. She pulled Esther to her feet and wrapped her in a hug, rubbed the center of her back, rocked her back and forth, until Esther pulled away and wiped her nose with the back of her hand. She was embarrassed at all she had said, apologizing. But she was also lighter, softer, slack, her eyes bright. Tess had her own embarrassment to hide. There was so much of importance that she hadn't seen, let alone understood.

IN HER POD, she went over the session again. She had already known about Ben's suicide, how they had met, the frantic moves back and forth across the country during Esther's pregnancy, the debt. Still, Tess had got it wrong. She and the Algo thought that Esther joined Parallaxis to escape grief and debt—to run from her life. That Esther herself believed she came up to prove she was stronger than her dead husband? That, they had not seen, and what Esther believed about herself was at least as important, if not more so, than what was true. That was perspective, the point of all these Views.

Sensus still had Ben Berlinski's archive, and once Tess had the file, she ran the Algo on it. Even without his Views, the Algo predicted even three months before his death that Ben Berlinksi would attempt suicide. The Algo marked depressive behavior, often angling toward self-harm, 430 times in the year leading up to his death. His death, when it happened, was not a surprise.

Ben had hidden many of those signs from Esther and the other people around him, and so the Algo had much cleaner information than Esther, than Ben's parents, and maybe even than Ben himself. The Algo knew Ben better than any of them. The Algo could have saved him.

TESS SENT A MESSAGE to Katherine Son that she wanted to stay for a couple more months. She owed it not to Sensus but to its users to train the Algo as perfectly as possible. The Algo was not yet sensitive to denial, to the untruths people watered and fed to protect themselves from pain.

It wasn't just Esther. Malik had not expressed any doubt in Alex, what was happening or not happening in his lab. He was in charge of their air and water quality, and yet he never tried to get into Alex's lab, not even out of normal scientific curiosity. He accepted the numbers as he encountered them. The Algo didn't see the problem yet, but Tess did. His family was here with him. As far as he knew, they were safe here, and he would not go looking for any threat to that safety.

Tess received a quick answer from down below: yes, for now.

Tess imagined her parents' faces, her mother's wry and knowing eyes, her father's furrowed brow, when she finally came down from the station. "I've been observing rabbits huddling on top of a clothes dryer," she would tell them. No, she couldn't tell them that. It was too close to the truth.

Many years after the rabbits, when their family had moved to Palo Alto, Tess had gone to her father's study one afternoon—it might have been a Sunday, she remembered a sense of melancholy—to ask him about something homework related.

She knew the memory she was after, and she knew how to find the

292 · REBECCA SCHERM

scene in her archive. Tess and her father, alone, in his study. There were thousands of those, and many where Tess stood in the door but did not step inside. She added the word *entertainment* to the search, and there it was.

She had opened the door to his study and been startled by how upset he looked, pale and haggard, like he'd just gotten some awful news.

"Are you okay?" she asked him, her teenage voice fighting to hide her anxiety.

"Fine," he said, blinking rapidly. "Just working."

"I thought your work was fun, just making stuff up."

Her father crossed his arms, pulled up his shoulders in what Tess now saw as protective self-importance. She missed him so badly.

"Yeah, I make stuff up. What I do is I make up some people, and then I start to care about them, all their hopes and dreams and fears. Then, for the next few years, I torture them for the entertainment of others. So, what's up?"

Tess stopped the footage there, her throat hot. She was only watching the subjects, she wasn't hurting them. And it wasn't for entertainment, either. The Algo could do so much good, once it was out in the wild.

25

At the last check-in that Rachel attended, two months ago now, the Ground techs didn't even offer an excuse. "Did she say she'd be here?" she had asked.

"We didn't get confirmation either way," said the older one. "I don't know if it's her assistant, or . . . I don't think she's been in Ticaboo this month."

Katherine was in contact with the head of Ground, and with Mozgov, they said.

"With Mozgov," she'd repeated. And, of course, with Tess.

But not with her. Rachel walked out of the meeting, planning to go straight to Tess, to demand to speak to Katherine through whatever means Tess had. She stalked down the promenade as if she still had the power to fire Tess herself, or to wrap her up in a sheet and shoot her out the airlock. Then she saw Lenore and Irma disappearing into one of their pods, like any couple returning to their apartment after dinner out. They had managed to find some happiness here in spite of her, Ground, this place, and her sister. She thought of Tess, sitting in her pod with her screens all around her, salivating.

Doing work so very *special* that Katherine had kept it a secret from her.

She turned back and instead climbed the ladder to the Helper. I'm going to stay in here all day, every day, until she next contacts you, she told Mozgov and Carl. And then she'll have to talk to me. She got used to the smell soon enough. She slept there, too.

THERE WAS A STORY Rachel and her sister liked to tell about one of the few times their father had taken them back to Seoul. They were thirteen and fourteen then, and he brought them to the hagwon where he had practiced baduk after school as a child. Their father had started playing baduk—the game of go, in the States—with Katherine when she was four, and Rachel had joined as soon as she was able. Outside, the old men in plastic chairs playing on the sidewalk might as well have been the same old men who played there when he was a kid, he told them. The hagwon was on the second floor of the building, and a childhood friend of their father met them upstairs with his two children for a friendly game. Katherine and Rachel had quickly vanquished the other children. They then played as one, whispering together, against the other father, in a game that stretched on for hours and made them late for dinner at their aunt's house.

The first time Rachel heard Katherine tell this story, Rachel hadn't remembered any of that. When she admitted so to Katherine, later, her sister said that Rachel hadn't played baduk with her at the hagwon, actually—she had only come up in the last hour, and then she had played maybe one game with one of the kids and then sat, bored and waiting, as Katherine played against their father's friend, and lost. Before that, Rachel had been at the Body Shop on the ground floor, which had replaced the pharmacy her father remembered from his youth.

At the mention of the Body Shop, that afternoon had come back to Rachel. As soon as she had seen the sign, so familiar but teasing with difference, she itched to go inside and touch everything, smell it, see what was the same and what was different from the Body Shops in American airports. She had rubbed body butters and shimmery eye shadows on her skin until she had noticed that it was getting dark outside, and then she had gone upstairs to the hagwon.

She didn't have to ask Katherine why she told the story differently. She herself told Katherine's version from then on. White people especially loved the baduk story, and Rachel ended up telling it often, over the years—the two sisters, united against the patriarchy, kind of, and sharing one mind and strategy, past dinnertime.

It wasn't that she had disappointed Katherine, but that her sister's expectations of her, in fact her sister's need of her, was simply much lower than she had realized. Possibly this had been the case since they were children and she was finding out only now just how lesser, how merely decorative, she was in their lives and projects. Right now, she was meant to decorate Parallaxis. Katherine wanted no boundary between their identities only as long as she was in charge of both.

Nobody knows what we can do, Katherine had once whispered to her when they were girls, they think it's just one-person-you and one-person-me. They don't understand.

It looked different, now—now that Katherine had pushed her look at it, had left her no other choice.

MOZGOV HADN'T BEEN SLEEPING because of the blisters on his back where the minuscule shards of glass were slowly working their way out through his skin like tiny teeth.

He leaned forward, and Rachel gingerly pulled his shirt out from his back. She'd learned not to take in the whole battlefield at once, but to focus on one blister at a time. She needed the magnifier anyway. She tapped her tweezers on a shard that looked as though it had poked through to see if she could tug it out.

"Hold still," she said.

Mozgov hissed through his teeth, and she dabbed the blister with antiseptic. The low bell sounded that indicated a message from Ground.

"All right, that's the only one today." She let go of his shirt, resisting the impulse to smooth it with her hand.

"New agenda's here," said Carl from Control.

HELPER CHECK-IN 569:

Biomass significantly deficient for crops. Carbon ppm still
unmitigated by algae lab. A. Welch-Peters using excessive water.

Garcia using excessive water. Reduce water-intensive crops.

Mined water to be mineralized for consumption; status update re:
gray water

Low hydration reading in E. Fetterman, H. Gomez, R. Son

Microplastics ppm is 26% high in fabrication lab, 9.8% high in
promenade area. Need L. Totten's plans to reduce emissions and
stay on schedule.

Problematic pulmonary readings for L. Totten

Analysis of first biowaste package complete

High average daily calorie intake by T. Rokeshar and minor S. Cobb.
To be reduced 4% by next data package.

Very high average daily calorie intake by minor S. Welch-Peters. To
be reduced 12% by next data package.

Days until Residence Orion completion?

Days until Residence Cygnus completion?

Days until Residence Canis Major completion?

Requisition list for Day 493 cargo order: perishable foods,
dehydrated foods, medical supplies, pharmaceuticals, ventilation
filters. Owner-residence design materials equal approximately
1730 kilograms; ~305 kilograms for supplies remain.

J. Mozgov to prepare for return ~Day 494

"Will she be there?" Rachel asked Mozgov.

"I don't know," he said.

"Have you ever gone this long without her contacting you?"

"Never," he said.

"Mozgov to prepare for return," Carl read from the screen.

"I'm not going anywhere," Mozgov said.

Rachel didn't respond. Now she, too, was staring at the screen, at the line that said he was going home, but she was not. That still, she and Tess were not.

HER SISTER DIDN'T SHOW up at the Helper check-in.

"Get her," Rachel said. She was shaking. "I don't care what you have to say to get her. If she does not get me out of here, I am going to start behaving like a little sister. I am going to start breaking things that are hers."

"Yes, yes, ma'am," said the Ground tech.

Rachel turned away. For these men to see her like this was a humiliation that she could not bear. She heard them talking behind her about matters that she didn't care about and would no longer pretend to. Mozgov would return home a legend, admired and adored: the longest time in space, the most expensive mission, the first captain of Parallaxis I. Mozgov, who had lied to them all for years. She hadn't told Katherine or anyone else the extent of it when she'd had the chance, and why? To protect Katherine from disappointment? Now, she never would. Let it spin, like a top, and topple.

When it was over, Mozgov asked Carl to leave the Helper. Carl glanced uneasily at Rachel and then left without a word.

Rachel sat in front of the monitors, staring at the map of the station, the moving red dots that tracked every single body on board. In Teddy Rokeshar's living room, two dots crawled and two dots jumped and dashed. Ted and Homero and Julian and Lola, playing together on the floor. The red dot that was Carl slid through the Helper airlock and out into Parallaxis. The red dot that was Tess was still, alone in her pod, watching.

Mozgov pushed himself up to standing and looked down at his legs. "There's something I want to show you."

He leaned over the workstation, his weight on one palm, and pulled up his own vitals.

"This column here is my body, as I stand right here. I weigh six kilos. I can stand. I can walk from here to here. I can push myself up to sitting, standing. Occasional mishaps, yes, but look at this. Here is my body down the ladder, outside the Helper, given the pull on the station floor. I weigh forty-one kilos. I require a wheelchair at the very least. If I tried to go down the ladder by myself, I would fall by the fourth rung. You understand why I stay in the Helper."

"Why did they keep you here so long?" she asked.

He added a third column. "And this is a hypothetical me if I were to return to Earth now. I can't sit without support. If I try to push myself up, I will break my arms. Probably my heart is dying, and I may not be able to breathe without assistance for years, if I last that long." He paused. "There's no 'go home.' This *is* my home. I've been here too long to leave."

"You'll die here," she said.

"I'll live here first," he corrected her. "Then I'll die here."

Parallaxis was not Rachel's home, would never be Rachel's home.

She glanced at his body, nodded toward the third column. "Don't they know?"

"They think they do, and they think they can just put me in rehab. Not Katherine—she knows, she gets it." He bit his lip. "Or she doesn't want to see me, see what happened up here."

"Why didn't you leave when you could?"

"This is mine. My home." His eyes were wild and urgent and told her that she didn't understand. "They can't replace me in my *home.*"

Rachel drew her knees up to her chin and wrapped her arms tightly around them. She couldn't remember ever feeling so alone.

"I'm ready to hear it," she said. "Tell me when this all went wrong."

"After we had the Helper built," Mozgov said. "The mining operation up and running. Then we started with Beta."

He turned to face her.

"I had three crew up with me, and a two-month work order for the shell frame. All we did, fifteen hours a day, was lock the frame together. Outside. We wore diapers. One break for lunch, but when we fell behind, Ground wanted to get rid of that. I said no. They didn't want to hear about any delays. They wanted us 'on track,' 'caught up,' 'moving forward.' You know."

He was using her language.

"My crew was suffering," he said. "We lost Kriege, and it was horrible. Horrible. And you've heard about Heaney, too, his eyes. So imagine the endlessness of this single task—like doing a park-sized jigsaw puzzle, and you've got no fancy food, none of this stuff you have now, and I've lost one of our people already. They meant to use us up." He stopped to look at her.

She wondered who else knew that she, too, would be or was already used up. He did.

"We did the best we could, and I gave them what they wanted to see. It was the only way to take care of my crew."

"How?" she said. "You can't hide anything from Sensus—"

"This was years ago. You weren't all-knowing then." He screwed up his eyes at her. "If you start building an alternative . . . version of things early enough, it sticks, over time. Nobody can see it. They still don't."

Rachel's head was roaring inside.

"Put yourself in my shoes, Rachel," he said.

She put her head between her knees.

"You were supposed to use the robots to lock the shell in place," she said. "Not people."

"Heaney was the robotics engineer," he said. "When he went down, instead of hiring someone else, Ground programmed the robots themselves, to keep pace with *their* schedule, which we could not keep, had not kept. I couldn't tell them how I'd managed that, could I? My crew would have lost their jobs, their healthcare, breach of contract, careers destroyed, their families left with nothing but impossible debt. Parallaxis contracts are vindictive."

She reddened.

"Is that embarrassing to you?"

She didn't answer that. "They sent you Ted Rokeshar this time."

"I don't know why, I mean why *now*. Maybe it's different, since they're all doing double, triple duty."

"What do you mean?"

He stared. "What they're here for in addition to their work."

Oh. He knew about Views. He had known all along, because he knew everything about this place and always had. More than Rachel did, and, it turned out, more than Katherine did, too. Her sister's control over her empire was imperfect.

Rachel looked past Mozgov to the screen behind him, where, on the station map, a red dot was approaching the ladder to the Helper.

The red dot climbed the ladder. When it reached the top, Rachel saw Tess's face, her ever-surprised eyes, her pinched little mouth, from the camera outside the door to the Helper toilet. Mozgov frowned at the screen and glanced back at Rachel, as though she had beckoned Tess to them.

"Rachel," Tess said through the Helper door, nearly shouting. "It's important."

Rachel and Mozgov were as silent as if they were hiding.

"I didn't ask them to keep you here," Tess said. "I didn't want them to keep you here."

"It's Katherine," Tess said. "You can talk to her . . . through me."

Rachel, silent as dust, looked at her lap and shook her head no.

"You have to, it's the only way," Tess said, so quickly that it could only be a response.

Rachel blinked, twitched. She turned toward the door, where Tess stood on the other side, somehow knowing that Rachel had shaken her head.

Rachel's lips opened.

She was a Pioneer, too.

Tess was here, with her, all the time.

"Oh, God," she whispered. She covered her ear with her palm. She wheeled around and saw what Tess saw: Mozgov, the gray filth, the crusted food trays.

On the station map, Tess's red dot stepped back, fled through the door of the Helper toilet, and descended the stairs, then hurried down the promenade back to the pod where she watched all of her subjects, of which Rachel was merely another.

"I'm one of them," she said.

"How would you have escaped?" Mozgov asked.

Rachel stood up, holding the back of the seat to steady herself.

"When you see her—" he started. "Rachel, look at me."

He looked into her eyes then with such frightening intensity that it felt as though he were trying to burn right through them.

"Whatever you tell her, I made the right decision," he said. He was speaking through her, speaking to someone else through the conduit of Rachel. "Beta is whole, and Beta is spinning. I haven't lost anyone else. I made the right decision."

Rachel, tasting bile, reached into her ear and yanked her phone out.

26

Last week, Inaya and Mary Agnes had been changing a microbial check valve in Malik's lab, when Mary Agnes started spinning the fuck out. The sickening thought of her father and Tess, Ellis Evans saying that he liked her green hair in Nicky Zoncu's basement, and all that had followed: she was stuck in a spiral and she couldn't stop. Then Inaya straightened up suddenly, and Mary Agnes turned to see Colette gliding into the lab.

"Good morning, children," she said. "I wondered if we might borrow Mary Agnes today."

Mary Agnes straightened up, too. Colette's attention, directed right at her, made her feel like a bug. Even in her combo, this one a deep red, Colette looked like nothing could rattle her or frump her up.

"We've just installed sixty floor-to-ceiling plastic stalagnates—do you know what those are? Sebastian? Inaya? No? *Stalagnate* is a term for when a stalactite, the cave formation that looks like an icicle coming from the ceiling, connects to a stalagmite, which is the kind that comes up from the ground. Have you ever toured a cave, Mary Agnes? No? Yes? Which is it?

"I don't like them. But someone who will be moving here *really* does, because they wanted sixty stalagnates in their bedroom. And now the bedroom walls are to be finished in Vantablack. Do you know what that is? No? Sebastian does. Sebastian, tell Mary Agnes about Vantablack."

"It's the color that's so dark that you can't see it," Sebastian said. "It just looks like a hole."

"Applying Vantablack in a space station bedroom is, you'll understand, terrifying," said Colette, "because you feel like you are always about to fall out of it. Mary Agnes, your mom says you are not scared of heights at all, is that true? How about when the heights look like the end of the universe?"

"Well, but these aren't real heights," Mary Agnes said. "Just illusion heights."

"Perfect," Colette said, sighing. "You come with me."

The mansion's name was Cygnus, but they called it the Black Hole. The aspects of the Black Hole that so creeped out the grown-ups didn't bother Mary Agnes as much. It was like a virtual reality setting, basically, the way the stalagnates were arranged so that you were coming around a corner too often. But then these grown-ups hadn't spent much time with VR outside the station—certainly not her mother, not Lenore, and probably not Colette, either. Homero maybe had, but he was icked out by it, too. He said, his soft eyes narrowing, "It's not the design itself, no. It's knowing that this person is coming here soon, to live with all of us." He stared at the strings of dark stalagnates. "To be our neighbor."

"Is the other one freaky, too?" she asked him. "The other mansion you're working on?"

"No," he said. "That one we call Big Daddy's. It's pretty standard rich-guy stuff."

But Mary Agnes liked installing the Vantablack membranes on the walls, smoothing them out with the scraper, imagining that any moment the surface would break and her arm would burst through, because she knew it wouldn't. Her mother and Colette wouldn't touch it. They leaned away. But Mary Agnes found it strangely reassuring, how every time she was just a little nervous for a moment, and then every time it was all right. Again and again, she did not fall through.

THEY FINISHED WITH the Vantablack in four days. Mary Agnes went back to Malik's lab and felt right away that the dynamic had changed while she was gone. They had so many inside jokes; every three minutes she ran into another one. Inaya shrugged her shoulders and rolled her eyes to tell Mary Agnes it wasn't worth explaining, but Sebastian would always try. "See, we had this old dishwasher . . ." Mary Agnes was so much more clearly an intruder now. When she and Inaya and Sebastian had started out together, she had been an outsider, naturally, not because they made her feel that way but because she was. They were a family. But while she was away they had sealed up.

Malik had spent so much time with his kids, even on Earth, more than she'd thought possible for a scientist at his level. Inaya said he just brought them into the lab a lot and always had. So many of the jokes were lab jokes.

It was hard not to miss her dad, when she was with the Cobbs.

No one ever suggested that they check out her dad's lab, even though he was just up the way. It would be nothing, to stop by and say hi, check on the slime. But when she wanted to, it always got mixed up with the other feeling: she would also risk catching him at something, and the prospect of finding Tess in there with her father was enough to keep her away.

"OH, HI," LENORE SAID when she came back. "I missed you!"

Mary Agnes looked away, embarrassed, before she realized Lenore had been smiling lopsidedly, not making fun of her.

"Oh," Mary Agnes said. "Thanks." Then, feeling as though she owed some further explanation, she blew out her cheeks and said, "I think, to not feel like an outsider when you are one, you need to be in on at least thirty percent of the inside jokes."

Lenore grunted. She was examining the drawings on her screen, zooming in on an object Mary Agnes couldn't identify. Not furniture.

"Can you bring me some PEBA samples, since you're right there? P52 and P54?"

Mary Agnes brought her the samples, tubes of white polymer seeds. "What are you making?"

"Hide, like a hairy hide, from an animal. It's for Big Daddy's." She shook the tube and listened to the tiny rattle. "Let's do a test. Can you get me thirty grams of P52?"

Mary Agnes asked Malik the next morning if it was okay if she kept helping at the fab lab, and maybe she imagined the relief she saw in his eyes when he said sure, of course; maybe not. She still got to hang out with Inaya after work, but she felt better in the fab lab. Less jealous.

Mary Agnes didn't know what it was about Lenore, but she didn't feel like a weirdo around her, or like she had to work so hard to not seem like one. One afternoon, while her mother and Colette were out, she had even said this to Lenore, who told her that it was because she had no radar for what was weird and what wasn't, because of how she was raised.

"You mean, in a doomsday cult?" Mary Agnes asked.

"More the old mall part," Lenore said. "But is being raised by your dad totally *unlike* being raised in a doomsday cult?"

Mary Agnes's laugh was almost a bark. "True," she said, her voice cracking. "Completely obsessed with the end of the world, and it's, like, a known fact that I shouldn't exist."

"What do you mean?"

"People should've quit having kids way before me," she said. "This woman at my dad's work? Once, at the holiday party, she was drunk, and she told me and my brother that it was an act of violence to bring us into the world."

"Violence to the planet? Or you?"

"Both? I don't know, I was just, like, come on, Shane, let's hit the cheese cubes."

"I didn't hear about climate change, or the climate *period*, until college," Lenore said. "Whatever happened outside the Arms was God's will, and God was angry about the collapse of the family, the collapse of the parish."

"What's a parish?"

"All the members of a single church." Lenore smiled to herself. "All of this was preached to us in a converted Talbots."

"My aunt Caroline works for Talbots," Mary Agnes said. "She does their refugee-closet program." She remembered something she hadn't thought about in a long time. "My mom was going to go to work for this refugee org, a sub-Saharan refugee resettlement? But, like, climate refugees."

"But? What happened?"

Mary Agnes tried to remember. This had been two years ago or so. Her mom had badly wanted the job, had talked about it for months, and when they'd offered it to her, she hadn't taken it. She didn't know why. Her mother hated writing college recommendations.

"My dad, probably," she said, a sour feeling in her stomach.

"He didn't want her to do it?" Lenore asked. "Why not?"

"It's weird," said Mary Agnes. "I remember him being excited for her when she got it. But it was going to be a really intense job and I guess he would have had to . . ." The sour feeling in Mary Agnes's stomach had gone away. "Not enough time, I guess. With me and Shane and . . ." Mary Agnes knew she wouldn't say any of this in front of Irma, or Esther, or Macy, or even Inaya. Why had she only thought of women, just now?

Lenore didn't say anything, but Mary Agnes caught her sideways, wondering glance.

"Anyway my family is basically climate refugees, too," Mary Agnes said quickly. "That's why we live in Michigan."

Lenore only nodded.

Mary Agnes didn't want to be talking about her family anymore. It seemed that her mother and Colette had been gone a long time. "How did you leave?" she asked.

"The Arms?" Lenore sighed. "I waited until my eighteenth birthday, and then I crossed the highway to a Chipotle, and my grandparents were waiting there for me."

"You planned it?"

"Yeah," she said, and Mary Agnes could have sworn she looked guilty.

"I wonder if that's what my OTG cousins will do," Mary Agnes said. "But they won't know how to survive outside."

"They would need someone to take care of them," Lenore said. "I did."

"Once, we went to this wildlife sanctuary," Mary Agnes said. "And they said that wild sloths eat this exact combination of fifty toxic plants that all cancel each other out? But the sanctuary sloths just ate cantaloupe and dog food. They'd been there since they were babies, so they would die in the wild." She paused. "That's what would happen to my cousins."

"Living in the normal world is like learning to eat fifty toxic things in the exact combination that won't kill you?"

"Yeah," said Mary Agnes, and there was Effie again, on a ventilator or something, a mask over her face, because of Mary Agnes.

"You know, whenever you start talking about OTG, you compare it to something else. You never talk about the place itself."

"Well, I'm not supposed to," she said.

"With who? With me?"

"With anyone," she said. "You can't stay off the grid if people on the grid are talking about you."

"You're not giving me coordinates," Lenore said. "You were there for a month with no idea what had happened to your mom or your dad or your brother. You should be able to talk about it. It's just me."

"Well, and whoever else."

Lenore's wide eyes grew wider. "Who else?"

"Whoever listens to us. We're not, like, alone and privatized up here, there's no way. Like, I'm sure we're privatized against invaders, but—"

Lenore stopped scrolling and peered at her. "What do you think is listening to us?"

"I don't know." Mary Agnes shrugged. "Whatever. Ground, I guess, or some AI."

It was the first time she had felt crazy in front of Lenore and she hated it. "I'm not the only one who thinks—who assumes this is how it is," she said. "Inaya and Sebastian, probably other people, too."

Lenore nodded slowly. "Your parents?"

"I sure as hell wouldn't put that idea into my mom's head, no, thank you," Mary Agnes said. "But I don't know what my dad thinks. About anything."

"Oh, I thought you two were close?"

"We used to be."

Lenore looked at her, waiting, and then turned back to her screen.

Mary Agnes cleared her throat. "Actually, can I ask you something?"

"What?"

"Was my dad, like, involved with someone else up here? Before we came?"

"No, no," Lenore said. "And we all know everybody's business."

"Not Tess's, though," Mary Agnes said. Immediately she regretted saying it, wished she could stuff it back in her mouth.

"Tess? You think your dad and *Tess*? Why do you think that?"

"She's always looking at him. Like, I catch her looking at him a lot."

Just then they heard a rapping along the wall, right exactly on the other side of Mary Agnes's head. Inaya, telling her to come out.

"She loves doing that," Mary Agnes said as she jumped down to the floor, far too eagerly.

"Cogs?" Lenore asked.

"Yeah," she said. She regretted the entire conversation.

ESTHER TOUCHED EACH of them on the shoulder as they filed into her office. "Sebastian!" she said. "We're all so excited for your big dinner tomorrow."

For weeks Sebastian had been experimenting with mixed-packet cuisine, adding more liquid here and only partially hydrating there, trying to, in some way, cook. Colette helped whenever he asked her and chastised the girls for snickering. Tonight, he had secured adult permission to "cook" a meal for everyone, or at least enough for everyone to taste, provided he did not exceed rations. Sebastian aspired to cook regularly, perhaps hosting dinner parties, cooking birthday meals, etc. Mary Agnes couldn't tell from Colette's expressions what she thought about it, whether she was humoring him or not.

"Yeah!" Sebastian said, going up on his toes. "It's going to be *biblical*."

"What?" Esther said.

"He means, like, a big deal," Inaya said. "Dumb thing to say."

"Ah, got it," Esther said. "Okay, today we're playing a storytelling game, it's new. We'll see a series of images, and then you'll write a note of what you think it means, how they go together, whatever." She passed out notepads, their screens smeared with fingerprints. The little kids had been here already today. "Sorry, I should have wiped these down for you. As always, there's no wrong answer. Then we share, and we can talk about it—"

"We got it," Inaya said. "Let's go." She narrowed her eyes and gave a tight smile. She looked exactly like her mom.

Esther spun her chair around so she was facing the screen on the wall, too. "This is the first series."

A picture of some mashed grass, a litter pile with an empty bottle, and a deer standing on a hill, partly hidden by a tree.

When they shared, Sebastian had written, *The deer saw somebody litter and got up to chase them off.*

Mary Agnes had *Someone was lying in the grass drinking while the deer watched.*

Inaya had *The deer is drunk.*

"Wait, Magnes, what?" Inaya said. "That's a deer bed, not a human bed."

"You didn't even put a real answer," Sebastian said.

"Never mind," said Esther. "Here's the next one."

The second sequence was a photo of a swamp, a spaghetti-jumble of plumbing, and the sound of birds. The third was an image of a man hugging a woman from behind, both of them looking down, and a clip of a rapidly decreasing countdown clock.

"Okay, last one."

An unmade hospital bed, a black-and-yellow salamander, and a pink bicycle lying on its side in the middle of the road.

Mary Agnes's vision started blotching with panic.

"Ready?" Esther asked.

Sebastian: *A girl got bitten by a lizard and was allergic and had to go to the hospital.*

Inaya: *Girl is scared literally to death of salamanders.*

"Mary Agnes?"

Mary Agnes faltered and grabbed for all she had: *Scared of salamanders*

"Cheeeeater . . ." Inaya sang.

"That one was hard!" Mary Agnes said with fake lightness and great effort. She stared at the images. The creature was a salamander specifically, not a mudpuppy or a land lizard or anything else: Salamander like the label on her tube of hair dye. An abandoned bicycle, the universal symbol of a horrible kid tragedy, a crash or a kidnapping or something. And the hospital. There was no way this combination was an accident.

"Why would you do that," she asked Esther, and her voice was soft and babyish.

Esther and Inaya looked at her, their four eyebrows furrowed up in a gentle confusion.

"What?" Sebastian asked. "Do what?"

Her guts were churning. Someone had put these images together and shown them to her to see how she would react. But the dye hadn't been called Salamander when she ordered it. It had been something else, something stupid. She searched her archive for *salamander*.

Purchases: none. Tasks: none. Contacts: none. Media: A musician she must have listened to but didn't remember. Memories: A blue-spotted salamander crossing a leaf-littered road, about two years ago. A discussion about newts and salamanders with her dad, later that same day. A tool her mother had called her to fetch while unclogging a drain last year. The tube of hair dye, silver and taut, and its black cap with the white sticker that read SALAMANDER.

To know that salamander was any kind of black-magic word to Mary Agnes, you would need access to her archive, which meant access to the eyes that built it.

"What's happening?" Esther asked. "Tell me, you can tell me." Her eyes were wide and worried. She leaned in like she needed to catch each word before it hit the ground.

"It's you," Mary Agnes whispered from a dry throat. "You've been watching us this whole time." She turned to Inaya. "It's her."

Inaya was shaking her head and then shaking Mary Agnes's arm. "Come on, let's go."

The psychiatrist. Of course. "Even down there, before we came," Mary Agnes said. "She watched everything, that's what all this is."

"What do you mean, watching you?" Esther asked her. She sounded afraid, but Mary Agnes didn't believe it. "Tell me what that means."

"NO!" Mary Agnes shouted.

Inaya dug her nails into Mary Agnes's arm. "Listen to me," she said. "You are having a psychotic break, and we're going now."

Sebastian shook his hands in the air. "What *happened*?"

Inaya looked at Mary Agnes, checking to see if it was safe to let go of her.

"She's in our archives. Salamander's the color my hair was," Mary Agnes said, and it sounded stupid, coming out of her mouth. "The dye, it was the name on the dye tube. It's not in my purchase history. And the hospital bed. And an overturned bike, like someone got hurt. I know it sounds stupid but—"

Inaya loosened her grip. She didn't think it was stupid.

"I didn't make these," Esther said.

"Where did they come from?" Inaya asked.

"I got them in my phone," Esther said. "From Ground."

"What do you tell them about us?" Inaya asked.

Esther shook her head. "I don't tell anybody anything."

Mary Agnes heaved, and Inaya dropped her arm.

"Maybe you don't have to," Inaya said.

27

Tess stood up, blinking, trying to adjust to the dim light of real life. She had been sloppy with the Cogs, trying to do too many things at once. Because she was preparing for Alex's unraveling—fast approaching, according to the Algo—she had fallen behind on the other Views. Malik had had several conversations with Carl that she hadn't even looked at, and he had an Esther session coming up, too. She almost hadn't watched the teenagers' Cogs, forgetting until the last minute that she'd added one to the set. Now it was almost four, and Rachel was supposed to come to her pod to talk to Katherine for the first time in months. She didn't have time to deal with this.

She'd thought she could get just close enough to Mary Agnes's memory of the Shane-then-Effie near-death catastrophes to elicit an authentic response, but not so close that Mary Agnes would think it intentional. Since Mary Agnes's arrival on the station, she'd appeared to have back-grounded the events that precipitated her family's departure from their home and planet. She never seemed to think about her legal troubles. At the same time, the Algo repeatedly coded her as *anxious*, *lonely*, and *isolated* despite the close ties she'd developed with Inaya, Sebastian, and Lenore—closer and more comfortable than any of her friendships at home. Tess puzzled over the hierarchy of Mary Agnes's driving fears and anxieties: the Algo said that highest was her disintegrated relationship with her father; then the "affair," which was related; and then the bundled events of poisoning her brother, being the victim of a simulated sex crime, and unwittingly cyberbullying another girl into a suicide attempt, her family into a lawsuit, and herself into a cybercriminal. Tess had wondered if the Algo's ranking was correct and thrown together a Cog to check.

Mary Agnes had not responded as the Algo predicted. Inaya, Sebastian, and Esther kept talking and gesturing in front of her, but Mary Agnes didn't seem to process any of the conversation around her. She had fallen out of the present.

MARY AGNES WAS ALONE in her pod now, her adrenaline, heart rate, and blood pressure still elevated, swallowing and swallowing even though she wasn't drinking anything. Tess kept glancing back at the feed even though there was nothing to see; Mary Agnes was staring at the tiles on the wall while the voice of Rachel Son, unbidden, attempted to coach her through a box-breathing technique. Mary Agnes did not seem to hear it.

It was four o'clock. Tess ran to the door of her pod and stuck her head out into the hallway. No sign of Rachel. *She's not here,* she sent to Katherine.

Tess started Esther's Views feed from 3:54 p.m., as soon as the teenagers had left her office. Esther quietly chewed a fig bar. Then she looked at her office door for a long moment. She stood up and went to lock it.

Tess tried to still her bobbing knee. Esther didn't know anything about Tess's work.

Esther sat back down in her chair, a printed version of the Ekornes Stressless she had left at home, and drew her knees up under her chin. She began to look through her session notes in her phone. She didn't enter any search terms at first, just flipped through the sessions, reading bits here and there but never staying longer than a minute on any single session. Then she let down her knees and covered her eyes with her hands.

Tess huffed out the breath she had been holding. There was no reason Esther should believe anything that Inaya or Mary Agnes had said, and no reason that she should suspect Tess, of all people. Ground, people down there, that's who would see her notes. Not Tess. She was in responsive microclimate, a totally different area.

"Nothing is different, Esther," Tess said to the screen in front of her. "Nothing has changed since yesterday."

When Tess had occasionally made small edits to Esther's notes in advance of a session, she had done it in Esther's voice, Esther's style, and they had never given Esther pause. Tess watched to see if she would pick them out now, but she didn't. Now Esther was hunting back through her archive—searching for Ben, it looked like. But the conversation Esther pulled up was the one she and Tess had had about Ben.

Esther played the conversation from the beginning. When she got to the part where she moved in with Ben in Hawaii, Tess had said, "I never could have done that!" Esther paused there and rewound, played it again:

Tess gave a small gasp of delight. "I never could have done that!"

I never could have done that!

I never could have done that!

Esther watched this clip over and over. Tess didn't know why, and the Algo didn't, either.

She ran to check for Rachel. Nothing. She wasn't coming. As soon as she sat down again, she ran a search in all the subjects' archives. *I never could have done that* was a Lenore-ism, what Lenore said whenever she heard a story about something she herself had not done. It had an opening quality—the other person would almost always go on to explain exactly how and why they had come to do *that*, defend, contextualize, explain. It had been a good thing to say, at the time, to keep Esther talking about Ben.

She pushed her chair back. It wasn't weird for Tess to say *I never could have done that*; everyone had heard Lenore say it, anyone might have repeated it and probably did, and Tess would find the evidence of that if she looked for it. When people spent time in close proximity with each other, they began to adopt each other's language patterns and mannerisms. This was totally natural social behavior.

ESTHER LED HER next three Cogs sessions, none of which Tess had augmented. After she finished with Teddy, she locked her office and began to walk quickly toward Tess's pod.

Tess tried to plan what she would say, how she should act, but the Algo only said that Esther was angry with Tess and had been since she had first rewatched that clip, and that Esther would now verbally confront her. Tess chewed the inside of her cheek.

She made herself stay in her chair until she heard Esther's physical knock. She checked her workstation one more time to be sure that everything was really, truly *off*. When she opened the door, she made a face of pleased, albeit distracted surprise at the sight of her guest.

"Oh, hi!" she said.

Esther's hair was pulled into a knot. Her lips were dry and pale. "I need to know something," she said. "Why did Lenore's grandparents change their mind about coming here?"

Tess tried to hide her surprise before she remembered that surprise was correct and normal at such a question out of nowhere. "Oh," she said. "I have no idea. Why? What does Lenore say?"

"She doesn't know."

"Rachel?"

"I'm asking you."

Tess steadied herself. "Maybe it was too risky, at their age. Or the pay wasn't good enough." She grimaced. "There are only a few reasons to do this and about a million not to. But why? What happened?"

"Were they encouraged to rethink their decision, though?" Esther's arms were crossed tightly, both hands hidden. "Did it suddenly look riskier to them, halfway through training? Right when Meg decided she wanted to come with their kids?"

"Oh, maybe," said Tess, sounding sickened, as though they were gossiping about the exploits of someone they hated together. "Because Ground wanted more kids up here?"

"I never could have done that," Esther said.

"I know," said Tess. "Way, way too big of a risk for Leo."

Esther looked at Tess for a long moment, but Tess did not flinch.

"You must miss him so much," Tess said. "I can't imagine how hard this is for you."

WHEN ESTHER LEFT, she went to her homepod, not her office. She lay down on her bed and began to comb her contract for an out. There wasn't one: no possibility for early return from Parallaxis. If she breached her contract by failing at the work she had agreed to do, she would be fined $7.6 million so that Parallaxis could recoup its sunk investment. If she died, it said, her estate would be fined. A clause to discourage suicide.

But Esther did not read these words the same way Tess did. Esther's eyes hovered over the phrase *breach of contract* as though she were waiting for a gate to open. Maybe, to Esther, who was already deep in debt, another $7.6 million didn't matter much.

The shuttle to bring up the first clients was coming next month. It was already on their calendar. When that shuttle returned home, Esther vowed to leave with it.

At least that was how Tess interpreted the scene before her. The Algo, not inclined to dramatize, summarized it thus: Esther perceived the cost of leaving to be less than the cost of staying, and she had resolved to leave.

ONCE THE PIONEERS had all arrived at the feedbag for dinner, Tess went to the Helper. *Tell her it's about our parents,* Katherine had said. *And she should have a phone in. It's dangerous and stupid not to wear one, no matter how evil I am.*

Since Rachel had removed her phone, the Algo had stopped updating; its Rachel model was out of date. Even so, Tess knew that there was no chance of Rachel Son putting another phone in her ear. Not now.

Tess tapped on the Helper door. "Rachel? It's me."

The door slid open. Rachel had turned around in her chair to face Tess but looked at her with the thinnest patience, as though she'd let her in only so she'd go away again. Mozgov was seated next to her, watching the screens where he did all his own tracking, logging, fixing, predicting. The smell hit Tess like a wall.

"I know you hate me, but this isn't about me," Tess said.

Mozgov turned around. His mouth was just slightly open, as though he were concentrating on an idea, not on a person. One of his front teeth overlapped the other and whenever Tess had seen him, she'd wanted to reach out and set it straight.

"You're angry to be here," Tess said to Rachel, careful to keep her eyes steady. "You have to know that has nothing to do with me or anything I've asked anyone for—"

"I'm never going to *like* you, Tess," said Rachel.

"I just want you to know that I—"

"Does Katherine say what she wants us to feel and then you make us feel it? That's how she and I always did it. Or, with you, is it the other way around? Do you have a punch list of all the things you need to see a person do?"

"I would never hurt them," Tess said. "I care about them. I care about all of you."

Rachel's mouth made an ugly shape. "What else would you never do? When their launch was delayed, and we all lost contact with our families—you would never do that, would you?"

"I had nothing to do with that decision," Tess said, and it was true. It was true as far as she knew. "I wanted more time for them—"

"So you could watch. Do you need to watch us now to feel anything? To, as you say, *care?*"

"The work that I do," Tess started, but she couldn't continue. Rachel sounded so stupid, naive, and self-righteous. "The work that I do will belong to you and Katherine. To Sensus. That's the thing about it that disgusts me. You're not why I do it—you are last on my mind. This is science, and it's going to save lives. It's going to save people from suicide and murder and rape and maybe even from people like you, who look down over the world like it's one big mine. The Algo is going to teach us everything about people, how they act, what choices they have, how they think—"

"And how will it do that, Tess? Tell me, how will it get around the people running it? You don't know what she's thinking. You don't even know what *I'm* thinking. You have a story, I'm sure, that you've glued together from your scraps."

"Your story," Tess said, her voice shaking. "Here is your story. I am a research scientist at Caltech when I get the call to come into Sensus to talk about a potential project. The project is Views. I'll have blind subjects—they'll soon be under quarantine, so much easier to study. My first subject is my boss's sister, her partner, her right hand. Her face, even. At first, I think she's volunteered to be a sample subject for the good of her company—that *has* to be it, right?"

Rachel opened her lips. *Stop,* she mouthed, voiceless.

"It's ages before I begin to understand, because what I'm seeing is so not at all what I expected. The Algo gets it without my help, though, because the relationship is perfectly rational. The little sister is not the partner. She is the right hand, the face, and the voice. Not a whole person, really, but a tool for the older sister's will. And the relationship between these two actors has been running for so long, is so deeply and frequently reinforced, that the younger sister isn't aware of its nature. Her role in this dyad is so successful that she doesn't even understand it."

Rachel had turned away from her. Already Tess regretted everything, but she could not stop. "I couldn't believe it until we were in the shuttle together. You really didn't know."

"Are you the left hand?" Rachel asked. "Is that what you think?"

"Go home, Tess," Mozgov said. "Leave us alone."

Tess stepped back and stumbled. "Oh—she said to tell you it's about your parents."

THE FEEDBAG DOOR opened up ahead of Tess, and the Pioneers spilled lazily onto the promenade in their little groups and pairs, some of them alone. Dinner was over. Meg squatted in front of the children, telling them something, and Lola pointed at Tess and said, "Tess is crying!" Meg shushed her as she looked over her shoulder to see. "Oh no, are you okay?" she asked in a soft voice that Tess scurried past. Rachel was full of shit. Tess did care about them, far too much. Sometimes she had done her job imperfectly because she cared about them so much. Rachel was just angry because she hadn't been smart enough. Now she'd glommed onto Mozgov, also a big brain who needed her to be the body—that couldn't be lost on her, could it?

She had done nothing that Rachel or Ground or even the subjects wouldn't do if their own work were on the line. Just look at Alex. If Rachel knew how other people would have done her job, how lucky they all were that it was Tess up here instead of someone who easily forgot that they were human beings, that they mattered. It could have turned into the Stanford Prison Experiment, the subjects howling in corners while the coder watched from his pod and rubbed his chin. She had been careful, she *had*, not to do anything more than what was necessary, never to forget their humanity or her own. That was why she was still here, after all this time—because to tune the Algo right, to do justice by the project and its subjects and the billions of people who would be affected by her work, she had to go slowly, carefully, kindly. The work couldn't be kind to everyone, all the time. But Mary Agnes, for instance, she had been troubled already, for reasons that had nothing to do with Tess, who only studied the after-shocks. And Alex had been working on his Frankenalgae for most of his adult life, and she hadn't recruited him, Parallaxis had. She had studied how he reacted, how he handled the stress of his life up here. She hadn't made him lie. She had encouraged his family up here, but that had been a kindness to them, regardless of what it had been to her.

But Rachel's words hummed in her head, growing louder and louder like swarming flies. The right hand doesn't know what the left is doing, that was the saying. It was one of her father's favorites.

Tess wasn't the left hand. Katherine Son had hired her for this work, but Tess didn't think of herself as in service to her. It was the project, the Algo: she had always worked in service to the Algo. She barely thought about its owner.

TESS WENT TO MACY'S CLINIC the next morning, and when she returned, Rachel was leaning against the rippled wall outside her door. She had cleaned herself up. She must have gone back to her own pod, because she had showered, and her hair was still wet. Her sleek black helmet of hair had grown out into a bob like Tess's, or how Tess's used to be. She was wearing her own home clothes, a thin white sweater and a long cream-colored skirt, thick wool socks that gave Tess a pang of envy.

She stepped inside and lifted her chin. "How is this going to work?"

"I'm just going to message her that you're here." She gestured toward her office chair, and then went ahead of Rachel, got there first to brush off the dust and crumbs. Tess sat down on the corner of her bed. *She's here,* she sent down to Katherine.

They waited.

"I won't—I won't have to talk to her through *you*," Rachel said.

"I don't think so. I don't know," said Tess. "You could put your phone in?"

Rachel shook her head.

At last, a message dropped down into Tess's dash. *Lock your door and turn on your mic.*

Tess did as she was told. The lower left screen of her desktop workstation lit up, the bright black that meant Katherine.

"That's her," said Tess.

"I know," Rachel said. She swallowed.

Tess sat back down on the corner of the bed. Already her heart was racing.

"Rachel," said the black square.

Rachel raised her chin, defiant.

"Yes, I'm here." She turned to Tess. "You can go."

"No," said the black square. "She should stay."

Tess crossed her arms tight and looked down at her knees. She didn't want to stay.

"There is something I need to tell you," said the black square.

"Let me see you," said Rachel.

A silence, and then, captured on the screen, Katherine Son.

Tess had not seen her face since the day at Sensus that she had handed Tess a mug of tea and invited her into Views. She looked so different from how Tess remembered her. This woman wasn't soft in the face; she was sharp and drawn. Her hair hung over her shoulder in a thin ponytail.

Rachel's mouth had opened.

"You're not up there because of Tess," said Katherine. "You're up there because I'm sick, and I can't come myself."

"Sick," repeated Rachel. "What is it?" Her voice was flat, no breath in it.

"Cancer. It should have been completely fucking obliterated by now, but it isn't."

Rachel closed her eyes. "How long have you known?"

"It first showed up about four years ago," said Katherine. "I dealt with it. And then it came back. It came back."

Rachel clasped her hands together and squeezed the knot between her knees, as though it were the lock on her body that kept her from springing. "How," she began. "How could you keep this from me?" Slowly, she shook her head. "You need me there with you."

Tess drew a sharp breath.

"I needed you *not* here with me," Katherine said. "You're the only person I wouldn't be able to—to hide it from." Katherine looked up toward the ceiling. "No one knows except our doctors."

"What do they say?"

Katherine didn't answer, didn't look back at Rachel. Blue light from a window fell across her cheek. Her brow was furrowed. "I hate those bushes," she said. "The ones with the fried-egg flowers."

"What happens next?" Rachel asked her.

"You take care of Parallaxis, because I won't be able to come up this year. The progress on Views is good. I'll be finished with this thing and you'll be back home when it's time to select clients for the Beta."

Tess thought she might apologize to Rachel, but she didn't.

"What happens next *with your treatment?*" Rachel asked.

"I'm in CAR T therapy now, which is way more sophisticated than it was the first time. They've weaponized my immune system, essentially." She seemed out of breath. "Those bushes are so fucking ugly. The whole bottom half of them looks dead."

"Let me come be with you."

Katherine was silent. She pressed her lips together and glanced out the window again.

"All right," she finally said.

She was dying, wasn't she? Katherine Son was dying.

"Tess," she began. "In the event that you try to reach me in the coming weeks and you can't, you are to wait for my reply. I remain your only contact, even if you have to wait to hear back from me. Do you understand?"

Tess nodded. "Yes."

"If you so much as breathe the *vapor* of this conversation to anyone, anywhere, including your own notes and archive, I will destroy you in every conceivable way, do you understand?"

Rachel opened her mouth to soften—habit—and then closed it.

"No matter what anyone suggests to you," Katherine said to both of them, "I am in control. You are to do as I say."

If Katherine died, Rachel would have to take over. She would become the head of Sensus, alone. Views. And Parallaxis. She could not turn away at the mention of those vindictive Parallaxis contracts, embarrassed.

Tess looked over at Rachel, who was intent on her sister, leaning forward, eyes wide.

"Katherine," Rachel said. "I'm coming home."

"I'll be back in touch soon," said Katherine. "Don't disappoint me now, either of you. Please."

28

Mary Agnes's mother was lying on the floor again, eye mask on, her palms smashing it into her eye sockets.

"Oh no," Inaya said. "Another migraine?" She plopped down on the love seat and looked at Mary Agnes with bared teeth.

"Do you want some tea?" Mary Agnes asked her mother.

"Sure. Some plain sencha, do we have that?"

She raked through the packets. "No, not that one."

"Could you get some? From the feedbag?"

She was about to say yes, but it was almost time for dinner, and anyone who didn't want to see anyone else—Esther, for instance—would be ducking in right about now to pick up something to go. Or her father, Tess: there were too many people in this looping cave that she didn't want to run into by herself. Better to slide in once it was a noisy mass.

"We have other green ones," she said. "There's muskmelon green, roasted rice green—"

"Ugh, no, but thanks anyway."

"I just said, like, ten others—you can't stand any of them?"

Her mother's eye mask stared in disappointment.

"Let's get the tea," Inaya said, standing up. "I'll come with you."

She could read Mary Agnes's mind now.

ON THE PROMENADE, Mary Agnes apologized for being weird. "I didn't want to run into Esther."

"Good luck with that," Inaya said. She dropped her voice to a whisper. "Hello, Dr. Fetterman, I hope we're keeping you entertained!"

"Or Tess. Or my dad."

Inaya didn't answer that.

"I don't like flavored tea, either," she finally said. "It just tastes wrong."

"It tastes better, like *not* dirt," said Mary Agnes.

Inaya shook her head small and fast, like a little old lady. "It tastes . . . tacky."

"What!"

"If you like green tea, you want it green, not bluebreeze. How long are you going to hide from all these people?"

"Forever, or until I start screaming and can't stop?" Mary Agnes heard how actressy she sounded, like she and Inaya were doing a show together. She didn't mean to do it, but she couldn't stop. Inaya was doing it, too— the way she tilted her head, or held a pause, or drawled over certain words like they had a dozen meanings and she was trying to cover them all without going off script.

"Are you going to tell your dad you know?" Inaya asked her. "About him and Spiderhands?"

"I don't know," Mary Agnes said. Yesterday, she had gathered herself up to go to her dad's lab alone, her first visit in months. She wanted to talk to him about what had happened in Esther's office. He couldn't already know about her, right? He wouldn't keep that from her, that someone was watching them all the time. It had taken a sad amount of courage and fake-casual whatever-ness to get there, and then when she opened the door, there was Tess again, half sitting, half leaning on a table edge.

"He said it was the first time she'd come by in months, yesterday," she told Inaya. "*He* brought it up, at home after dinner. He said it to my mom, but he was really saying it to me."

"Gross."

Mary Agnes blew out her cheeks. "Yep."

"I've been thinking," Inaya said. "About . . ."

"What?" Mary Agnes asked.

"Never mind."

She didn't want to be overheard. Mary Agnes glanced down at Inaya's hands. They'd been writing on each other's palms sometimes, when they needed privacy. You couldn't look at your palm, only feel the line in motion. It started with one letter at a time, capitals only, but a shorthand was evolving fast. As of yesterday, the symbol for Esther was a sideways oval with a circle inside, one continuous stroke: an eye.

"Yeah," Inaya said. "Later."

THE ONLY PERSON in the feedbag was Sebastian.

"Oh no," Inaya said. "It's his dinner thing tonight, his mixing-shit-together night."

"No 'oh no,'" Sebastian said from behind the two tables zip-tied together that constituted his kitchen. "Don't bug me, I'm focusing."

Mary Agnes peered over the bowls. "Whoa. This smells not bad, actually."

Sebastian looked up from his snipping—something dark green and papery, little rings of it—and his slow smile spread across his face and pushed up his glasses.

"You have something on your glasses," Inaya said, reaching out to the red gob stuck on his mint-green frames.

"I know, don't touch it." His voice cracked and he cleared his throat. "It's concentrated chile paste. I need my gloves to get it off."

"Where are your gloves?"

"Somewhere? I don't know! Can you not bug me, please?"

"But dinner's in twenty minutes," Inaya said.

"I know!" His voice cracked again and he shook his head, jaw clenched.

"I'm going to stay here and help him out, okay?" Inaya had already found the gloves and was putting them on carefully. "You good, Magnes?"

"Yeah," Mary Agnes said. She found her mother's plain green tea and took two packets, rubbing them together in her right hand to hear the swishing sound they made. When she was at the door, Inaya called out after her.

"Sit with me, okay?"

"Of course," Mary Agnes said, and Inaya glared at her like she knew Mary Agnes wouldn't come back.

TODAY HAD BEEN A BAD DAY. There were good days, with a good solid feeling from time with Inaya or Lenore, and there were bad days. Sometimes the bad days had Lenore and Inaya, but Mary Agnes felt like she wasn't there herself. On the bad days she walked around with what felt like a sopping wet coat of hopelessness draped on her shoulders. It was about Effie and Shane and Mercedes Mills and Ellis, and her dad, and her mom, but mostly herself, and it was all mixed up together in one cold wet woolly clump. Sometimes she made patterns on her skin with her thumbnail, intersecting crescents, to try to snap out of it, but it didn't work or didn't work in time, and then she was going over everything again and again and again and—

She *knew* why she'd plagued the Evanses with the video, that was the thing. She had thought carefully, but she had thought wrong. This awfulness belonged to her "nose to toes," as her father would have said. She'd been like, Best_Revenge = max(x*pain_to_Ellis). Solve for x. Cool, now go do x! Collateral damage? What's that? And now she lived with the later calculations: Given that x = calculated and yet careless cruelty and Mary Agnes had done x, how different from, say, Ellis could she be? What she had done to Effie, even if she had not intended it, moved her from one group of people (people who did not do monstrous things) and into another (people who did, including Ellis (whom she'd had a crush on for *years* and that meant something about her, too, didn't it? (Yes))).

Before everything really bad had happened, she had imagined Parallaxis I as a fresh clean place, the sparkling answer to what was wrong at home. She'd even thought it could fix her family. The hole her dad had left behind: fixed. Shane's allergies to Earth: fixed. Her mother worrying about him every nanosecond: no more. And then, later it was Ellis: left below. Effie: not in the hospital because of her, her thoughtlessness. Shane: not in the hospital because of her, her thoughtlessness. *Whoa, thur, lil lady, you're talkin' 'bout a time machine.* And Mary Agnes herself: up, away, gone, poof. New and Improved, the Magnes of the Future. A Youth with Promise, like Inaya and Sebastian.

Shane's life was so good here. No suit, no bugs, no grass. Not a whole lot of choice in what to eat anyway, and he knew which packets to bypass. He *loved* go-gels, had gained four pounds and grown an inch, her mother said. He loved Julian and Lola, he loved Homero, he loved space school, he loved sharing a room with his big sister, he loved Cogs. That should have been enough. But Mary Agnes hadn't found any new and improved Magnes. Sometimes she felt like she was still floating, even though her weightless time was just the six hours or so it took to shoot up here. Now she was substanceless, or maybe a heavy gas, not a good one. Up here, she was still made of *wrong*.

"It's me, I'm back," she said when she opened the door to their pod. Her mother was still on the floor, curled up like a pill bug. "Wait, where's Shane?"

"Homero," her mother said. She groaned. "I'm coming to dinner, I don't want to miss Sebastian's special thing. I just need a couple more minutes."

Mary Agnes made her mother a cup of tea. Their fake space window was covered with a pillowcase, stuck up at the corners, to make the room darker.

"Do you need anything else?"

"Sledgehammer."

She didn't want to go to dinner tonight, but she couldn't be alone with her mother, not with the bats in her brain. "I'm going now," she said, but not until she was already closing the door.

HER FATHER AND SHANE were sitting together already, near Homero and Teddy and the twins. The two empty seats next to her father were meant for Mary Agnes and her mother, but Mary Agnes pointed toward the Cobbs. She sat down next to Inaya just as Sebastian stumbled toward the table with a platter that Mary Agnes had never seen before, or thought she hadn't until she realized it was a window-screen protector from one of the mansions. They'd popped them off just yesterday.

"Hokay," Sebastian said, out of breath. He held the tray high at his shoulder and looked down the bridge of his nose at them.

"Tonight, we have a Mushroom Bulgogi," he said, "inspired by a restaurant from my childhood in North Carolina, garnished with sesame seeds and chive rings, over millet and served in fresh Baby Bombe lettuce cups grown right here by Dr. Irma."

Colette gasped.

"Oh my word . . ." Malik said as he lowered the tray. Inaya grinned, enjoying her parents' shock and everyone else's, too, as people turned to see.

On Sebastian's platter were tiny mounds of mushrooms sitting in dainty green lettuce cups, their pale, creamy folds so unfamiliar to Mary Agnes by now that she did not at first recognize them as food.

Mary Agnes looked over at her father and Shane. "I want some," Shane was saying, craning to see. He'd always hated salad. He said it tasted like pool water. Her father was smiling limply, half-happy.

The lettuce, cool on her lips and crisp in her teeth, was dense and mild, as far from reconstituted collards and seaweeds as possible. Sebastian's careful mounds of millet and sweet, salty mushrooms were delicious, but it was the lettuce that persuaded people to try it.

"It feels wrong to eat it," Inaya said. "I want to, like, take care of it."

Mary Agnes looked back at Shane, who was petting the leaves on his own plate. Next to him was the empty seat where her mother usually sat, and next to her was Macy, who stared at the lettuce as though it could not possibly be real. Lenore was peering into her lettuce cup as if she were looking into the face of a puppy, and Irma watched her and laughed. She must have kept it a secret from everyone except Sebastian. And Esther, Ground, Rachel, whoever else they could not keep secrets from.

Sebastian himself, now sitting between his parents and being squeezed and loved and leaned into, spun his lettuce cup gently on its plate. Mary Agnes would ask to take one back to her mother, who would be deranged with joy.

A sudden silence made her look up at the door. She thought it would be her mother, but it was Handsome Carl. He rarely came to dinner. Next to her, Inaya rearranged her arms.

"Carl," said Mary Agnes's father into the silence, his voice tired and dry. "Have some lettuce."

Her father didn't look good, even for lately. He looked seasick.

Carl cleared his throat and smiled quickly, like it was an intrusion. He was still in the doorway, everyone staring and waiting, shifting his weight on his bare feet. He never wore his socks, Inaya had noticed, and all his combos were dark blue or black, as though he'd gotten to choose them himself.

"The kids could go read a story, somewhere," he said carefully. "Just for a few minutes."

A quiet panic filled the room like smoke. Homero stood up and took Julian and Lola, protesting, by their hands. Mary Agnes watched her father stand up uncertainly, and then Homero nodded and said, "Come on, Shane, come play in our pod." Her father nodded like yes, yes, of course, but Mary Agnes thought he looked like he was going to vomit. Shane looked at his friends, and her father said, "Go on, bud, have fun." And then Shane went, and Julian and Lola stopped protesting and ran ahead.

Sebastian and Inaya were frozen, trying to be invisible, she realized, in case someone mistook them for children and sent them out. Mary Agnes looked down at her plate, probably too late.

Once Homero and the children were gone, Mary Agnes let out the breath she'd been holding.

"What is it?" Macy asked, her voice flat like she was never surprised.

"The station is not safe," Carl said, the words rushing out.

Teddy snorted. "Well," he began.

"What I mean is that the station is less safe than it appears to be, both to us and—and to Ground."

"Ground—what do you mean, to Ground?" Macy asked.

Carl paused like he had a bunch of bad choices in front of him.

"Go on," Malik said. Whatever it was, he already knew it. Mary Agnes caught Inaya's eyes and saw, for the first time, fear in them. She looked from her father to Carl without moving her head and rubbed the edge of her thumbnail.

"Ground receives constant information about every function on Parallaxis," Carl said. "Every action is monitored and adjusted, if possible, from below, depending on the complex feedback they receive."

"Yes, we know this," Teddy said.

"Try again, Carl," Macy said in a low voice that made Mary Agnes's hair stand on end.

"The information that they receive has been, however, compromised. By Mozgov. For some time."

"Compromised how?" Macy asked. She looked at Carl like there was no one else in the room.

"The readings have been routinely overwritten to maintain the illusion that the systems are operating successfully." He swallowed. "Water readings, antimicrobial readings. And tasks that are not communicated by the data as well, build features that are off camera. And I've come to understand he has been doing this since well before we got here."

Macy pressed both her hands over her mouth. "You coward," she said.

Mary Agnes looked at her father. The blood had all gone out of his face now.

"How long have you known about this?" Colette asked. She turned to Malik. "And how long have you?"

"I didn't know the extent of it for sure until last week," Carl said. "It was hard to be certain, and I didn't want to—to scare anyone, if I was wrong. But I had doubts from the beginning, from when we first got here. Some of the data I had access to seemed . . . unlikely, and I worried about so many untrained people relying on—on us—but then I thought I had to be wrong. I *had* to be wrong. And then once I knew, I told Malik."

"Just a couple days ago," Malik added quickly. "We felt we should share this information when we were alone. Without anyone from Ground."

"Tess," Colette said.

"Right," Malik said.

"What's unsafe?" Lenore asked. "What, specifically?" She had not said anything until now. Her face was pinched and pained.

Irma, beside her, was looking at Mary Agnes's father, whose eyes were fixed to nothing, to nowhere. Mary Agnes stared, her coat of hopelessness growing tighter.

"Where to start," Malik said.

"I think we have to start with the carbon," Carl said.

Her throat made a noise then that she did not recognize, and Inaya's hand shot out and grasped hers. Her father's eyes swung toward her and he looked lost and wild, like an animal.

"Alex," Malik said, pained. "You should tell us now."

Mary Agnes watched her father's bloodless face, his slack-jawed fright, as he tried and failed to speak.

Carl was tired of waiting. "The carbon capture program has not—"

"It's not working," her father said.

"I knew it," Irma said, and Mary Agnes gulped for air.

"You lied to us?" Lenore said. "To *all* of us?"

"I didn't—it worked, at first, it did." Her father's eyes were fixed on the corner where the walls met the ceiling. "But then something went wrong, and—I thought I would be able to fix it."

"*What* went wrong?" Irma asked.

"I didn't have a clean culture," he said. "There was another species attached. A hitchhiker. A Trojan horse. I had an algal bloom—"

"A toxic algal bloom? In your lab?"

"Yeah," her father said.

"You could have killed us," said Macy. "How could you not—"

"I caught it right away," he said. "I've been trying to isolate—"

"Wait, so this whole time," Colette began, pressing her palms together, "the air revitalization numbers have been . . . fake?" She turned to Malik. "How? Did *he* change his readings?"

Malik looked at Alex, who did not answer. "Yes," Malik said. "I think so."

"We weren't in any danger yet," Alex said.

"You shut up," said Colette.

"We saw the overwrites in the Helper," Carl said. "And I saw Mozgov leave them."

"Why would he do that?" Lenore asked. "Why wouldn't he just tell Ground—"

"Because then they would know that the numbers can be changed from up here," said Inaya. "And then they would know that the numbers they see from us aren't actual facts."

Mary Agnes wasn't listening anymore. Even though she knew that her father was a liar and a cheat, she never, ever thought that he would have or could have lied about the algae. But she was looking at him now, surrounded by the people he had betrayed. He had done those things. And he had lied to her about them, too.

"What's going on?"

Coming through the doorway now, brushing past Carl and heading straight for the empty seat next to her father, was her mother, her eyes squinting in the light. She had come for Sebastian, and instead, there was this.

"Meg," her father said, and Mary Agnes suddenly felt even worse, much worse, because her father was about to humiliate her mother in front of everyone, and she, too, would have to watch.

29

Tess watched the dinner from her pod.

She had known what was coming, and she knew that she had to be out of the way for it. The unraveling would happen only without her. Last week, she had complained to Irma and Teddy over breakfast that she was suffering a spate of migraines. This was overheard by Meg, who then joined her in commiseration about their Earth triggers and speculation about their many possible causes on Parallaxis. She had stayed in her pod all day. The Algo had predicted with 64 percent certainty that Alex's exposure would occur at communal dinner that night, but that dinner had proceeded without incident. The Algo downgraded its confidence for the next night to 44 percent. On the third night, she had gone back to dinner, not wanting her absence to attract too much attention. This morning, she had gone to Macy to ask for stronger drugs, said what she had taken wasn't even touching the beast in her head, and gone back to her pod to watch that information travel through the station.

And then Rachel had been there, ready to talk to Katherine.

But there was no stopping it now. Macy and Carl had planned one of their efficient trysts for two thirty, if conditions allowed. After they'd had sex, Macy had mentioned to Carl that she had two migraine patients now, that there might be an unidentified trigger in their microclimate. Carl had gone to Malik's lab just after four, when Inaya, Sebastian, and Mary Agnes were all in Cogs with Esther and Malik was alone. Tess was down with another migraine, he told Malik, so only the Pioneers would be at dinner. The information had reached its destination in three bounces. The Algo, which didn't run on Carl or Tess, nonetheless updated its confidence to 91 percent for dinner that night. Mozgov would be toppled first, and Alex would follow.

The Pioneers were so much more viscerally, painfully angry with Alex. He was one of their own. If even Alex would lie to them about the very air that they breathed, very little of their lives here was above suspicion. Then, when Meg came in, they had each gotten to witness their own feelings immediately replayed by another, closer to him, which amplified their emotions. The Algo aced every reaction, from Lenore's empathetic humiliation to Malik's disgust, as much at the fact that Alex hadn't told his wife as that he had lied to the rest of them—and, Tess suspected, with himself, for looking away.

Tess had been right that Mary Agnes would be devastated by the betrayal, more so than by her suspicion that her father was having an affair. Meg's response was less clear, at first, as it was clouded by the presence of so many other people and the shame that ensured. When Tess zoomed in on Meg's face to check the Algo's processing of her expressions, the measurements and timing, guilt rushed into Tess and, for a moment, flooded her. Meg's whole face seemed to fall open, uncontained. She looked at Alex in imploring disbelief, begging him or anyone to tell her that this was a mistake, and when he could not, she looked at her daughter in desperate apology. No rage, none of her righteous fury. There was nothing inside her to stoke a fire.

The Algo had predicted all of these reactions, even Meg's. It knew her subjects better than she did.

Now she did not know what would happen.

"Rachel," Sebastian whispered. "Rachel's here."

Whispers were augmented so she didn't miss them, and the soft alarm in Sebastian, unvoiced, came as a loud hiss. Tess jerked her eyes to Sebastian's feed. Rachel was still in her soft white home clothes, plus her fanny pack. She didn't look quite shiny anymore, not like she had in Tess's pod that morning.

She forced a smile. "I'm sure Carl's filled you all in, yes?"

Carl looked back at her with slight panic in his eyes, but she wasn't waiting for him to answer. She was already past them, at the food dispensaries in the back. Malik, Colette, Sebastian, Inaya, Mary Agnes, Meg, Alex, Esther, Teddy, Irma, Macy, and Lenore: every pair of eyes was watching Rachel. On Tess's monitors, the effect was surreal, all those Rachels at slightly different angles. She must have felt their attention, but she didn't flinch. None of the Pioneers spoke. She began to fill her fanny pack with packets and pouches, and after she'd zipped it, she unbuckled it and weakly swung it toward Carl. "Can you take these back with you?"

Carl took the pack from her, but in the doorway, he turned and glanced at Malik as if to confirm an agreement.

Rachel pulled out the nearest chair, across from Irma. She sat down, out of breath, weak from living in the Helper. "I come bearing announcements," she said. "First, congratulations, everybody, on your first year. Second, Esther Fetterman has decided to leave us and will be departing Parallaxis on the return shuttle."

Teddy's mouth fell open. "What?" He turned to Esther. "You're going home?"

"A new psychiatrist will take her place," Rachel said. "Esther has terminated her contract."

Esther's lips opened for a long moment, waiting for the right words. "I'm sorry," she said. "No matter how much I wanted this, I—I can't be away any longer."

Colette, at the table next to hers, reached across to touch the back of Esther's chair.

"You just resigned?" Teddy asked. "When?"

Lenore started to cross her arms and kept going until her hands were cupping her shoulders. "We can't resign," she said.

"I'll owe them a lot of money," Esther said. "More than I will ever make. They can seize all of my earnings and assets, now and future, in excess of a yearly stipend of 1.8 times the federal poverty line, and even then, I am not protected from future litigation." Her hands lay in her lap. "Additionally, I have lost my medical privileges, effective at the moment of my resignation."

"Medical *privileges?*" Irma said.

"The medical care we were promised upon our return to Earth," Esther said. "To make sure our time as employees of Parallaxis doesn't damage us beyond repair."

Rachel kept her eyes neutral, but her mouth was sour.

"You are not human," Lenore said to her, her voice trembling as she hugged herself tighter. "You are a horrible person."

Rachel flushed, just at the neck.

"I resign, too," Teddy said. "Me and Homero and our kids are done. We resign and fuck you, forever."

"You can't," said Rachel. "And I can't, either."

"You need to get us out of here," said Colette. "All of us. It's not safe here and you knew it."

Rachel shrugged helplessly. "There's always the airlock."

"*Pardon?*" said Colette.

"There's no way to get all of you home." She laughed, a short, bitter bark. "We are not set up for mass exodus."

"We could all be dead in six months," Ted said. "As you're well aware."

"They're not going to let us die here," Rachel said, and the *us* caught Tess up short.

"They?" said Inaya. "Aren't you . . . them?"

Rachel looked at Inaya as if she were considering her for the first time. Then she turned her eyes up, just past their faces.

"You might think of us as charismatic megafauna," she said. "Our asset here is our high visibility, and that will ensure . . . the maintenance of our habitat."

"We have no visibility," Lenore said. "We are alone."

"Profile. Some of us have a high enough profile to—" She stopped and dropped her eyes. "Well, I think that's it," she said, standing. "We have more work to do, that's all."

"That's not it," said Teddy. "What about Mozgov? What about *Alex*?"

Meg was crying silently. Mary Agnes and Sebastian watched her shoulders jump from behind.

Inaya was chewing her lip, either stewing on something or expecting to get in trouble. She did it in both instances. Tess didn't know which this was.

"Who will be your spy now?" Inaya asked, her voice quiet and strange. "With Esther gone, I mean. Or are you all done with us?"

"The *new* psychiatrist," Sebastian answered. "A new Esther to watch us would mean they won't let us die here, right?" He looked at his sister.

Colette and Malik turned to their children. Everyone did. Tess felt as though she were at the end of a tether that had been snapped too fast, that she was reeling through space and would soon collide with something big and hard.

"What are you talking about?" Colette asked.

"No one is spying on you," Rachel said.

Tess, one arm crossed tight over her chest and clutching the other, had stopped breathing. The Pioneers' attention wrapped around Esther and Rachel in a figure eight. Only Mary Agnes stared at her father.

"They watch everything," Mary Agnes said. "Not just the numbers. Which means they knew, Dad. They knew all along."

"And were just letting us die," Sebastian said.

"Hush," said Malik. He was still watching Rachel.

"She knew Carl was here, right?" Sebastian said. "She knew what he was telling us? You saw that—"

"The map," Rachel said quickly, easily. "The security map of the station. There's a dot for each of you, so we know where you are in case of emergency, and your biometric data is transmitted to Ground for health and safety, and to Dr. Slivens, as you know." She tried to refocus everybody on Macy, but Macy was a brick wall. "As you well know."

"I don't know where anybody goes," Macy said.

"That's not all, though," Mary Agnes said. "You have Esther spy on us. Not just the normal way, but, like—"

"But we're privatized," Lenore said. "Z-level. It's part of our benefits."

"Privatized *for* them, not *from* them," Inaya said. "It's not that kind of privacy."

"There is no secret here," Rachel said, and Tess saw and heard the shift, as though the fog of the last weeks had blown off. Her voice was cool and expert: herself. "You know that one of our research goals is to understand people's experiences of Parallaxis. That's not news to anyone. You know you are here testing the station—you've called it Beta, I've heard you. But to understand the average experience of average people, someone's going to have to study their experience."

"Average?" Malik asked, one corner of his mouth curling up.

Rachel blinked and pressed her lips together. She didn't answer, and instead let it hang in the air, like they had dragged something ugly out of her that she wished they hadn't.

"Oh," Lenore said. "Here to be scraped."

"Monitored," Rachel said. "We have to understand how this experience affects health, affects the body—"

"But they don't just look *at* us," Mary Agnes said in a voice so nervous it sounded shrunken. "They're in our archives. They look *through* us."

"What we see?" Meg asked.

"Yeah," Inaya said. "Like it's her phone, but it's *in* you."

"No, no," Rachel said. "I don't see anyone's Views, I never have—"

"Views?" Teddy said. "That's what it's called?"

They were on the other side of the station from Tess, but it wasn't very far, was it? All of them, together, peeling the layers off until they found the heart of it, while she watched. For the first time, she was afraid.

"I don't think it's Rachel, actually," Inaya said then. "I think it's Tess."

Mary Agnes tore her eyes away from her father.

"Tess," Mary Agnes said, breathing out the name as if it had been trapped in her lungs. She looked at Inaya, her mouth open. "Why didn't you—"

"Look at her!" Inaya said, nodding toward Rachel. "She obviously doesn't know *shit*."

"Inaya," Colette whispered.

"No, no, not Tess," said Lenore. "She's not—she wouldn't—"

"It's Tess," said Esther. "And it always has been."

"Views is Ground's program through which our health and safety, both physical and mental, are monitored," Rachel said, too fast and insistent. "Tess's work on these tools has helped us all to succeed here—me, too. We're pioneers settling in space, and unlike the pioneers for whom you named yourselves, we're all going to live and thrive on this journey."

"No," said Mary Agnes. "That's not what we mean."

"I myself see nothing," Rachel said, "except for some security monitors in the Helper, which Mozgov and Carl also mind, for everyone's safety. Now, Esther has helped Tess as needed, but not in any way that should alarm—"

From Esther's throat came a horrible sound, a keening gasp. "I didn't know," she said. "I should have, but I didn't."

Meg still stared at Rachel, eyes wild. "You don't get to spin this as *care*."

"This is silly," said Rachel.

"Tess," Alex said.

Macy tapped the table silently with her fingertips, nodding. "There have been some—some odd things have happened, with her. And I think they happened because she was watching and . . . helped them happen, knew what would be, ah, interesting, to her."

"Through our phones," Lenore said. "The ones—"

"—they gave us when we signed," Macy finished.

"Watching my lab that whole time," Alex said.

Meg turned to her daughter and spoke to her as if there were no one between them. "Why didn't you tell me?" she asked.

Mary Agnes only shook her head.

Inaya shrugged. "We didn't know until we knew."

SOMEONE WOULD COME to her pod that night. Tess was sure of it. The Algo's assessment of the situation was that they would leave her alone, but it did not have complete information. She had never run the Algo on herself. She'd thought about it many times—had been often unable to *not* think about running the Algo on herself. What it would see, what it would understand. What it would make of her. It was a terrible idea, scientifically speaking. A wrench in the gears.

Now she did it.

The first analysis was immediate: her network map, a constellation of all people she interacted with, clustered around the circle in the center— herself—by *closeness*, which was computed by frequency, duration, and intimacy of interactions. The edges of the map were scattered with hundreds of dots—old colleagues, friends, and people she'd dated. Closest in were the Pioneers, crowded around her like flower petals, with Lenore and Irma the largest and nearest. Alex, Rachel, Mary Agnes were a step out with the other Pioneers, and when she hovered over them she saw the breaks in the ties that signified unreciprocated intimacy. They did not think of her as close to them.

Her parents were in the sparsest ring, the one outside the Pioneers, along with Carl, Mozgov, and Lola and Julian.

All of the innermost ring was vibrating, illustrating instability in the relationships. As she watched, the Pioneers' circles began to pull outward, the ties lengthening, the lines breaking. She had a halo around her now, empty.

The Algo's other analyses were still computing, but she didn't want to see any more. She sent a message to Katherine; there was no sense in waiting. Her impulse was to lock her door, pack her things, and prepare to leave, but she was trapped. She looked at the Views to make sure no one was coming to her pod. They were talking to each other, often about her, about how she had talked to them and what was strange or suspect about her; how she was sometimes off-putting and they'd chalked it up to awkwardness but now they knew it was something else. They talked about every error she'd made, slips in judgment or methodology, and some that she hadn't but they attributed to her. They broke her down into pieces. At several points they said that they knew she was listening, watching them talk about her. They despised her and they let her know it. When they went to the bathroom they shut their eyes. The girls showed them how to write messages on each other's palms, letter by letter, without looking. Almost two hours passed this way before one of the screens on her workstation turned black.

"Tess," Katherine said, her voice drifting out lazily, like she was lying down.

"Hello," Tess said. "There's been an incident—I—I—I've lost my cover." She wished she'd thought of another way to say it. "Rachel found out and then—and then I—what I mean is that you'll want to fork the code where I finished yesterday, maybe a few days before, to be safe. Maybe a week, actually." She was rambling idiotically and swallowing too much from a dry mouth. "I'm sorry to trouble you. It's not clear to me when exactly Inaya realized. Or suspected. But anything you've merged since then is not—"

"Not clean," Katherine finished for her. "It's fine, Tess, don't kill yourself over it. This was bound to happen sooner or later. Don't worry about how it ended."

"Ended," Tess said. "Wait, it's not finished. I still have—"

"Well, you can't work on it anymore now, can you? But we were going to beta in the new generation anyway. You actually sped up our timeline, which—" She laughed, a single low croak. "Which is rare."

"You can't just unleash it now," Tess said. "It's not ready. If it missed what was going to happen tonight, then it's not as good as I thought it was, as it has to be—"

"Ours didn't miss it, though," Katherine said. "Ours got it right."

"You mean you forked my code—"

"Yeah," Katherine said. "We don't merge all of your code, Tess. We don't merge all of anyone's."

A hole had opened up around her. "What do you mean?" She closed her eyes. "What do you mean 'all of anyone's'?"

"You aren't the only tuner we have working these subjects," Katherine said, and she said it like Tess had to have known that. "Wait, did you think you were doing this whole project alone? *Views?*"

Tess backed away and sat down on the edge of her bed. The black screen was smaller now, but the voice still rang in her head.

"When you recruited me you said—you said you couldn't trust just anyone—"

"I *don't*," she said. "The people who work for me are the very, very best at the particular thing they do. The people who work for me do the project they are meant to do. You are no exception."

"But why did you send me here?"

"You were so emotionally invested in the subjects," Katherine said. "All of the tuners are interested, of course, but you seemed to be developing a special relationship to some of them, in particular, that was worth pursuing. In joining them, you were able to pursue your work for us, while at the same time, you were an invaluably different subject in the pool." She paused, winded. "Your phone gave us a novel vantage point because of your unidirectional privacy from them, see? Like, from your Views, you're in the God-seat, and then when we pull back the perspective, and we have this other subject, in some ways like my sister, whose understanding of her role is—"

"Your sister," she said. "Your own sister."

"Right," Katherine said, as if she had forgotten that the Tess she spoke to was the same Tess she spoke about. "You and Rachel occupied a similar position of relative power in your network, of special privileges and responsibilities. It's because of you and Rachel that we could engage this God-seat perspective. And now it's ready to go."

Tess did not answer.

"I know you feel possessive of your work, and that level of pride has served you well, for the most part—and I know—I mean, I *know*—that you aren't happy that you've been observed yourself, but you could have considered that possibility. I was surprised when you didn't. So try to take a larger view. This algorithm is incredibly adept at constructing behavioral models of every single individual it encounters now—even you! It's learning and getting better all the time. It really doesn't miss much, but it will collect more nuance and deeper learning as it works its way through the population. And it's time to see what that looks like, when Views is—what did you call it, Tess? Unleashed?"

Katherine paused and Tess could hear in her voice that she was smiling. "That's right. Your work will be *unleashed*."

30

Alex didn't take out his phone. Nobody did. They took Tess's. Meg told Alex afterward that she, Macy, and Ted had gone to Tess's pod together. She would have seen them coming, but what could she do? Tess was scared, Meg said, when she opened the door. Meg had never before seen an adult look scared of her, not like that. Teddy had demanded that Tess turn over her phone, and when she protested, said that it wasn't safe to live here without one, Macy had held her—embraced her, and held her there—and calmly told Meg to grab the tab. Meg had done as she was told and then torn off the bloody proboscis to make sure the phone was unusable by anyone else. Then they took her screens, her monitors. Cleared her desk. Meg and Teddy carried them out one by one, while Macy sat on Tess's bed with Tess sobbing in her arms.

Alex raked his scraggly beard with his hands.

"It was horrible," Meg said.

When Tess's pod was cleared out, Macy let her go and stood up. You can go wherever you want, she told Tess, you don't have to hide from us anymore. Then they left Tess standing there, no one to look at, nothing to see.

While they were disconnecting Tess, the others were moving Rachel and Mozgov out of the Helper. This Meg had learned from Colette afterward. Rachel returned to her own pod. They put Mozgov in the Black Hole, Meg told him—not as punishment, but because they needed Carl in Control and in unfiltered communication with Ground, and the Black Hole was both finished and empty. *Residence Cygnus*. Until its owner arrived and Mozgov was returned to Earth, he would house-sit. Macy had been very upset when she heard that. How did you get him down? she'd asked Colette. Homero brought him down on his back, Colette said. Lenore made a wheelchair, and we had it waiting at the bottom of the ladder.

Macy said it was cruel to force Mozgov to live with gravity when his body couldn't handle it, that in moving him from the Helper to a pod with gravity, they were further disabling him. It's not just his limbs, it's his organs. But the only place with microgravity was the Helper, and they needed him out of there. It's not right, Macy had said. I know he could have gone home. I know he didn't have to stay here for nine years, that he brought this on himself. But it's still not right.

But she was overruled.

Meg reported this to Alex without looking at him. She was sitting on the love seat in their pod, her legs curled under her, arms crossed tight over her chest. She stared at her water glass as she talked.

"I assume they wanted to put me in there, too," he said, his voice low and tense, trying to occupy as little attention as he could. "So thank you for stopping them."

Meg took a slow sip of her water. "I figured they were coming for you next."

She stood up. "I'm going to bed."

ALEX HAD PUT SHANE to bed that night. It had been ages since he had, and the rituals were painfully unfamiliar. Shane told his father that he forgave him for lying, and that he still loved him. Alex didn't know who had told him. He hadn't done it himself, not fast enough.

Mary Agnes didn't come in until very late, when Alex was the only one awake. He cleared his throat when he heard the door open so she wouldn't be startled when she saw him.

She was lit from behind with fake moonlight, a bluish glow, and her face was pale and soft except for the purple hollows under her eyes. People had always said that she looked like him, but he couldn't see it himself. She was almost seventeen now, and the face he saw hidden in his daughter's was his own mother's. As soon as she saw him, she froze.

"I want to—" he started, but Mary Agnes shook her head, slowly and firmly, and Alex abandoned his apology. She passed him without a word.

ALEX WENT TO HIS LAB early the next morning because he didn't want to face anyone, and he didn't want anyone to have to see him. He went around the long way, past the mansions. He didn't know what would happen to him, and he wished, for a moment, that he could ask Tess. But now she was in the dark, too.

He was nearing the Black Hole when he saw Mozgov in the wheelchair, motionless in the center of the promenade. Overhead, the sunrise had just begun. Before Alex knew what to say, he heard the squeaking of a door. Rachel stepped out from the corridor and took the chair's handles.

"What are you doing?" he asked her, scared she might speak first.

"I'm bringing Mozgov to my pod, where I can care for him."

Mozgov regarded Alex with an understanding that made Alex want to argue. He and Mozgov were different, had made very different mistakes. They were not the same at all. He glanced up at Rachel and found her watching him with what felt like disgust.

"I'll tell them," he said. "Do you need anything, either of you?"

She shook her head. "Excuse us."

They continued on in opposite directions. She was going to care for him, she'd said. But Mozgov had betrayed her, too. How long had she known? What if she always had, if they'd acted together? Alex didn't know what was between them.

In his lab, Alex looked into a tank of failed algae and brushed his fingers along the fuzzy green mat. It bobbed slightly in the water, just as it always did and always would. He had the clean culture now. It didn't do shit. He would have to do something different, now. Selling out or taking care: it was hard to know the difference, and, where the people who depended on you were concerned, if a difference mattered at all.

FOUR DAYS LATER, Alex sent Irma a message. He led with an apology, and then he asked her to come and see some algae behaving differently. She did not answer him, but she came.

"What is this?" she asked him when she saw the trays.

"Algae—a clean culture—growing in irradiated air, which allows it to use one hundred percent of the visible light spectrum."

"How much more efficient is it?"

"One hundred thirty percent," he said. "Just these six trays. The rest are regular. Underachievers."

She stared into the tank, brows knit together, but she didn't say anything. He had expected questions.

"This is Plan B," he finally said. "Enhanced carbon capture, and enough, once I get them all going, to let us breathe indefinitely. A safe and healthy climate for a space station."

She bent over and peered into the water. "And you're sure your species is isolated this time?"

"Yeah," he said. "I can't replicate, now. It was most likely the other species that was responsible for both the increased photosynthetic efficiency and the rapid toxic algal bloom. And I can't seem to get one without the other."

She nodded, not so much looking at the algae as past it.

"I did this on the tiniest scale once before, at home," he said. "I didn't want to do it here because—" He paused, trying to say it right the first time. "This is a means for better carbon capture for people who live in closed, tightly controlled environments, with vast financial resources and access to technology. But it won't help anyone or anything at home."

"Ground will be really happy with you," she said, and where he had expected sarcasm or bitterness, he heard only sadness.

"Maybe," he said. "I mean, it's probably too late for 'really happy,' but they knew I wasn't performing. They must have."

"You're sure this couldn't be scaled? You've tried—"

"Not a chance," he said. He had slogged away in swamp labs for twenty years at the expense of his family's happiness, his marriage, and his integrity to create an air purifier for isolated billionaires.

When Irma finally looked up at him, her eyes were flashing darkly. "You know what I thought? When you wouldn't tell me *anything* you were doing in here? That you wanted to make sure you got all the glory, yourself."

"Now you know," he said. "I didn't want you to get poisoned."

She stared at the green raft before her.

"This *is* something," she said.

"Yeah," he said. "It's something. It just won't be something for people like us."

He didn't understand what he saw in her eyes. She was angry with him, but about something new. "What is it?" he asked, realizing that he hadn't done a home call in weeks. "Did something happen at home? A storm? Virus? Heat block? Fires?"

"I'm sure it did," she said. "But we haven't had a home call since we took Rachel and Mozgov out of the Helper, so I don't know what it is."

"It's easy to forget what's going on, when we're up here."

"For you, it is," she said with a false lightness that quickly faded. "You have your people here with you. But that's the whole idea of this place, isn't it? That it makes the crisis of home . . . abstract? Less relevant? So a breakthrough like this"—she nodded toward the boosted algae—"is a priceless achievement even though it does not travel, does not scale—"

"That's not what I meant," he said. "It's just these past few weeks have been—"

"I know it's not what you meant," she said. "But it's the way it is." She took a deep breath. "I didn't need to bite your head off about it, though. It's great about the algae. We'll all breathe easier."

"Listen, if I can do anything for you," he started. "Or maybe you want to work on algae, too?"

"Oh, Alex." She snorted. "I've *been* working on it."

"You have?"

"I grow space lettuce," she said. "And space beans, and space peas." Irma crossed her arms and tucked her chin down into her neck. "I should have done work for the real world. If I could go back, I wouldn't give my brain to the Sons."

The rest of the station's response to Alex's result was mild, at least in front of Alex. Relief, surely, but not shared with him. Meg smiled tiredly and said that was good, she was happy for him. But she couldn't muster any more than that and didn't feel that she had to try.

"I was very happy for you the first time you told me you solved it," she said. "You'll have to draw on that."

ON THE WAY HOME from a quiet dinner at the feedbag, Alex, Meg, and Shane stopped in his lab to check on the algae. He was running the boosted algae at maximum capacity now. Shane lifted the lid of one of the trays and petted the mounding algae lightly with his fingers. He wiped the slime on his shirt.

"Why not just grow more algae?" Meg asked. "If it's just for carbon capture in the station."

He knew what the *just* meant. "I'm told real estate up here is expensive."

"Oh."

"I was trying to make something much bigger. I didn't, though. Just this. It's cool, just, you know, not helpful for sustaining life on Earth."

She'd abandoned any stake in its success. But at least she was there, in the same room with him. That was something.

Shane, sensing that his supervision was distracted, was poking holes in one of the algae beds, writing his name in poked holes. Alex didn't care.

They were still sleeping in the same bed. Rarely talking, never touching, but sharing a bed. In a place where furnishings were made of foam, she might have sawed their mattress down the middle, but she hadn't, and that was something.

"Carl told me they're sending up bioreactors," he said.

"For you to use?"

"For the algae," he said. "We get all the power we need from solar, so I think it's just for fun. Who knows, we might harness enough power for a fleet of little scooters for the billionaires to ride around." Meg turned away and looked up at the ceiling, but he had seen the impatience, the disappointment in his bitterness. Wasn't she bitter, too?

"It's fine," he said quickly. "Whatever they want to do with it."

"I want a scooter," Shane said.

On the way home to their pod, Meg walked ahead and Alex lagged behind with Shane, who wanted to know about what was hidden under the floor, and how far the floor was from the "real" space outside. Alex saw Meg startle—her shoulders jumped, and she almost stepped backward—before he saw why. It was Tess. She had just come out of the feedbag, nearly an hour after everyone else had left, with a bulging sack of packets.

She froze at the sight of them, her bag still swinging. She looked small, feral, and afraid, a cornered rabbit. He hadn't seen her in weeks. No one had, since the night they'd taken her phone.

"Hello, Tess," he said.

"Sorry," she said, glancing between them. "I didn't think I'd see anyone."

"We've been eating later," Alex said. He'd never taken his family to visit the lab after dinner, back when she was watching. He'd scurried away alone, and quickly, like she was doing now.

"Is that all for you?" Shane asked. "That's so much food!"

She reddened. "It should last me a while."

"Come on, Shane," said Meg, cupping his shoulder. "Let's go find your sister."

"Why do you say find when you know where she is?" Shane asked as Meg hustled him away.

"It's an expression," Meg said lightly, but Alex could hear the shake in her voice.

He and Tess faced each other uncertainly. He wasn't afraid of her anymore, but he didn't know why she was still standing there, what she could hope to get out of him now.

"I didn't have the children," she said. "As subjects, I mean."

"You had Mary Agnes. And Inaya, and Sebastian?"

"Well, in Esther's office, just through her, not—"

She stopped and stared, like she'd just realized something.

"What?"

"I didn't know I would—" She faltered. "Your daughter was unexpected, to me. Her feed just showed up one day."

Whatever she had realized, she had kept to herself. Not even now would she be honest with him.

He nodded toward her bag. "If that's for Rachel and Mozgov, we do take them food," he said. "We're not starving them to death."

"No, no. I just—I don't want this to ever happen." Running into him, or anyone, she meant. Her mouth was stuck in a sickly smile, as if it were almost a relief to her that the thing she dreaded had come to pass, but not quite.

He could imagine the pitch that someone must have made to her, when she signed on to be the principal investigator of Beta. The flattery, the promises, the *access*. He, too, had been pitched on Beta and on himself. He stood there, staring at her as blankly as he could manage, until she turned around and scuttled back to her pod.

MARY AGNES HADN'T COME to the lab with them. She hadn't sat with them at dinner for weeks now. She usually sat with Inaya, on the periphery of the Cobbs, or sometimes with Lenore and Irma. She talked to Meg, though, and Meg warned Alex not to push, and not to give up, either. "No matter how many times she rejects you," she'd said, "it's still your responsibility to try to mend the break, and it always will be." She'd raised her eyebrows, and he nodded.

When he got home, she was sitting on the floor in front of the love seat, doing something on her phone. Meg must have been putting Shane to bed. He didn't know what to do. He couldn't leave the room, it would be ignoring her, but he couldn't sit down behind her. He stood there and tried to come up with any good thing to say.

"Shane said you saw Tess," she said, not looking up.

"She looked like she was stocking up on food to never come out again."

"It must be so awful, alone in there with no phone and no people."

"Maybe." Alex was well aware that while he and Tess were both pariahs, her exile had been more complete than his. He wished he knew how Mary Agnes saw the two of them, if she thought that what Tess had done was worse than what he had done. But it didn't matter. His lies were worse because he was her father.

"You could have put me in Siberia, too," he said.

"Then no one would give you a chance," she said. "You have a family to make it look like you're worth a second chance."

"What do you—I don't have a family *because* I want to have a second chance, or a third, or a fortieth—"

"But that's how it works," she said, shrugging. "Families make people look better. If you'd left us, no one would—"

"What do you mean *left*?" he said. "You mean when I came up here, to Beta? Because, Mary Agnes, that was a huge mistake, the biggest mistake of my life."

"No, I mean, to be with Tess." She raised her eyes and looked at him straight-on, her gray-blue eyes dark in the dim light.

"With Tess," he repeated. "Do you think—"

She grimaced. "I mean, you guys were separated. You and Mom. So it's not like it was a *crime*." She sounded both embarrassed and desperately casual.

"I was not—I didn't have an affair," he said. "With anyone."

"Whatever, it's not like—"

"I made pretty much every mistake but that one," he said. "Your mom hasn't forgiven me, but it's not because of that."

"Well, she was always in there," she said. "And we weren't allowed."

"She was in there because she was studying me. Studying my failure in real time."

"I thought you didn't want us to talk to her because . . ."

"Because she gave me the creeps," he said. "And now I know why."

"She was always watching me and Mom," she said. "Like, at dinner, and when all of us were together."

"I think she liked you," he said. "You, especially."

"Well, I'm a super-fruitful experiment," she said. "Super wack-a-doo."

"No," he said. "I think she liked you, as a person. I got that impression anyway, from how she asked about you, while she was watching me fail. She probably didn't know what she was getting into here."

"None of us did," Mary Agnes said.

"Not that that makes it okay." He paused. "I'm sorry I brought you here, or made you think it was better here."

"You're not why we left," she said. "You're just how." A lopsided smile, all pain and no guard at all.

"Nope. *I* am the fuckup in this family," he said. She looked just on the edge of believing him, so he kept talking. "You're just a kid, honey. A *teen*. You're going to keep growing. You have a long way to go."

THE MESSAGE CAME to Alex's lab early in the morning, and the wording of it set him on edge with weird dread.

Hey, is there a time you could come by the lab today?

Irma was never so careful in her messages. *Come by the lab when you get a minute*, or just *have a minute?* This was different enough, formal and considered, to make him nervous. His first thought was that she'd found something wrong with the boosted algae—that somehow, even that had failed, and then she would think he'd lied again.

He told her he'd come right away, and she said no, after breakfast, and at breakfast she very clearly ignored him. Alex was fidgety, splattered some coffee on his shirt. He went to his own lab and waited for ten minutes. He had the sure sense now that this was private, that he should give her a minute to get to her lab, alone. His heart was racing. His adrenal responses were all out of whack lately—every surprise, every *potential* surprise put him on high alert. It was either the aftermath of his lie or the aftermath of Tess's poking and prodding at him—he knew now that it had not been his imagination—or both. "Easy," Meg had been saying to him when she saw him start to panic. "Easy does it."

Irma was right inside the door when he arrived. The door slid quickly shut behind him just as it always did, but now it made Alex clammy. The humidity, too. Irma's mass of frizz was barely held together on top of her head with a giant red clip.

"Over here," she said, and she led him into one of her tented greenhouses. Alex started to seal the flap behind him and she shook her head. "It won't matter," she said. "It doesn't care."

"What doesn't care?" But then he saw what was in the first water tank: a heap of rootless green noodles, soft and springy, suspended in the water.

"It's a macroalgae with some hydrilla DNA," she said carefully. "And it's reproducing." She pointed to the next tank, connected to the first with a tube no wider than a chopstick. "Motile spores. It moves fast."

Alex looked into the second tank and saw a smaller heap of green, this one the size of his fist. In the third tank, the last in the train, was another.

"How long have you been—"

"Since we set up our labs." She swallowed. "Since you told me you didn't want to collaborate."

"I didn't say that," he said, staring at the plant that was no doubt growing before his eyes.

"In the beginning I was just—I didn't mean to get so far into it, but I do edible macroalgae anyway, and you wouldn't—"

"I know." Alex had been working on this problem for almost twenty years. Irma had been dabbling in it for a few months, but he had never used algae with motile spores. You had to be able to control the colony. If it was jealousy that was coursing through him now, it wasn't only that.

"There are more of them. Have been more, I mean. This big mass was the first, but I've disposed of ten since. It's rootless, so it can grow—"

"Anywhere," he said.

"Yeah. But it's saltwater," she said. "Or should be. It's also really, really fast. This one is three days old." She pointed toward the smallest one. "It'll be the size of a soccer ball by the end of the week."

"Oh, wow," he said. "Look at that thing." Alex's algae grew in place and did not stray. It was safe, a system with built-in controls. Or that's what it would have been, if he'd managed to do it. He'd doubted his adherence to the rules these last few years—what was the point of rules, with the climate losing its stability even faster than they had expected? Maybe he had been too cautious all this time, too frightened of what he might create.

"Irma," he said. "You did it."

"It *should* be saltwater, I should have said. But hydrilla should be freshwater, and it adapted to brackish water in ten years. So, you know, scary stuff."

Alex wasn't scared. In each tank, he saw the same masses of green thread. Some looked more robust than others, but they were all alive and thriving. Irma wasn't reckless, it wasn't like she'd fucked with gene drive and created a monster that bred with everything in its way. She'd broken one rule, the one he should have broken, and she had done it.

Alex nodded at the tanks beneath the top three, two more rows of three. None of them were connected. "More in here?" he asked, squatting to see.

Irma cleared her throat. "So, that's the other issue. I've had to move slowly, because this is, you know, not my real job, and because I didn't want anyone—you—to know I was doing this. But these two tanks here had another species of algae in them, before I dropped in some fragments of this guy," she said.

"It reproduces via fragmentation, too?"

She cleared her throat. "Fragmentation, sporulation, and sexual reproduction. In this case, it bred with them."

"Bred with them," he said.

"And then choked them out. Those are gone. Well, that tank still has a tiny bit left—you can see the parent plant here, it's just barely . . ."

"Does it have a homing—"

"I gave it gene drive."

Alex's eyes grew wide. "You *what*?"

"That's why I haven't told anyone about it yet." She spoke as if the faster she explained the faster she would know what to do. "I wanted to make something that had a real shot at superhero-level, emergency carbon capture, that was the point. You could very quickly grow a bed of it in the middle of the Pacific. You could probably grow it *in* a garbage patch—it might even help bind the microplastics. But without a reversal to the gene drive, there's no telling what it would do."

"Will it reproduce with *any* other algae?" he asked. "Wait, have you paired it with natural hydrilla?"

She laughed, but it was all nerves. "That's absurd," she said. "But also, I'm scared to."

"Is this why our air was cleaner than it should be?" he said. "Because of this?"

"Maybe," she said.

Alex stared into the tanks containing the results he'd been chasing all his life. "Irma, I know you're scared," he said. "But maybe don't be, just yet? This is incredible. You *did* it. And we can work with it up here, test it up and down, kill it when we have to. Beta is a catastrophe in so many ways, but this, what you've made—is amazing."

She looked down at the tanks and shook her head. "It will pursue everything in its path. It will be relentless."

"Maybe," he said. "But we're in space. There's nothing to protect. I'm not saying we should release this thing *now*, but up here, it's safe. You have a place to tame it!"

"It will dominate every life-form that it recognizes as family, and its family will get bigger all the time." She was still shaking her head, not looking at him, as though she were telling him about a terrible dream. "Once it gets into coastal waters, it will kill the other algae species, and then all the organisms that depend on them, the animals that feed on those, and the animals that feed on those. Crustaceans, fish, birds. Shallow waters turned into swamps, water flows slowed to standing—perfect for mosquito explosions, breeding diseases. Community fishing ports abandoned because the fish are dead and the boats can't get through the choke of weeds anyway."

"No," he said. "Not yet. That's not how this will happen. You're not dumping this into a storm drain."

"You can't tell anyone," she said. "I never should have messed with this, especially gene drive. But I wanted to create something that could have a real impact. It had to want to win." She dug her palms in her eyes. "I brought you in because I need you to help me kill it."

"Kill it? No, not yet," he said. "We'll grow it in tanks. We'll seal it off. We'll take out the gene drive!"

"It will escape, I know that now. But it doesn't matter anyway." All the warmth had gone from her face, and her eyes raced around the floor, never resting. "It's not like our files are local. It's just a matter of time until someone down there notices. I keep thinking, what if I'd told you when Tess was still connected? We'd be totally fucked."

She was right. Sensus wouldn't know to be afraid of it. They weren't afraid of anything. They'd want to tell the world about it: the superalgae was going to gobble up a hundred years of carbon, all-you-can-eat. They'd want to show it off.

Alex placed a hand on the rack to steady himself.

"Shouldn't touch that," she said. "The spores might—"

Alex yanked his hand away and stared at it. "We have to talk to Tess."

"THE PROJECT HAD BEEN going on for years before they brought me on," Tess told them. She couldn't look at Irma and Alex when she talked. She was perched on the edge of her unmade bed, knees tight together. All three of them had their arms crossed. "I was fine-tuning, the goal being that the AI would learn and then predict individual users' behavior."

"Our behavior," Irma said.

"Yes, but only so that the Algo could learn individual sense-making." A dry cough. "You weren't special, only unique in the way every person is unique." Her eyes wandered toward her workstation, now just an empty desk covered with old fingerprints.

"Did you know about the algae?" Irma asked. "My algae?"

"No, I never bothered with your work, that wasn't my area." Tess glanced at Alex but didn't meet his eyes. "His work, yes, because it was tied to . . . my work in behavior, in sense-making. When I saw you with seaweed I assumed it was for eating."

"But Sensus might have bothered about my work, using Views," Irma said.

Tess paused before she answered. "I would think so, yes."

Alex's ears were ringing. He hated being in there with her, listening to her talk about watching them, but they had to know what she knew. "So the chance that Sensus knows about the algae, even though the result did not occur until after your phone was out—"

"Oh, one hundred percent," Tess said. "I doubt that taking my phone out did anything for you all, in that way. It just closed my window. But I'd imagine there are a lot more. A skyscraper's worth of windows, most likely."

Belka, Strelka

31

The news came from Handsome Carl: the shuttle would arrive in two days. A couple billionaires, a new behavioral health specialist, a pantry restock and some other supplies. The day after, the shuttle would return to Earth with Rachel Son, Josef Mozgov, Esther Fetterman, Tess Little-field, biowaste for study, and current samples from both Alex Welch-Peters's and Irma Garcia's algae research. When Mary Agnes looked at her father, his face looked like a pile of laundry, all dry creases.

IRMA KILLED THE ALGAE in the tanks first, and then she killed the rest of her lab. The peas, the greens, the tomatoes, the peppers, the beans, the carrots, the herbs, the berry bushes, everything, every single thing. She did it alone, wouldn't let anyone go into the lab in case a loose fragment or lost spore attached to one of them. Mary Agnes's father asked her to reconsider, but that was all. No one tried to stop her. Lenore cried, and so did Sebastian—privately, silently, but Mary Agnes saw their damp cheeks. She cried, too. Irma said she didn't want anyone to eat any more of the food in case it was contaminated by her superalgae, which would then pass into the Pioneers' waste, some of which was compacted and sealed for study back at Ground. Her father said this was too much, not necessary, but quietly. He knew that Irma had to see this through.

She destroyed all of her used clothing in the autoclave, which turned the thin synthetic material into a dense but crackly dried putty. Sebastian and Alex were the only two people who had entered the greenhouses since the algae, and she would do their clothes next. She didn't know what to do about her hair, she said. Cutting it off would only produce more contaminated biowaste for Ground to use. She still held it together in the big red clip, but coiled tightly now.

They were in the lounge together—her father, Irma, Sebastian and his father, Lenore, and Mary Agnes. Mary Agnes was slumped against one of the wavy slatted walls, the ribs digging into her back. It was hard to believe this was the same room that Mary Agnes had visited again and again in the VR tour her father had sent her a year ago. Then it had looked warm, light, and soft. She had imagined that it would smell like fresh sawdust, in a good way. Now it was just an odd room without enough seats, and all it smelled like was the people sitting in it. She thought of her orange blossom shampoo from home, a baby shampoo that she had never stopped using because she loved its smell, especially when she dried her hair with a towel and the sweet steam would surround her face.

Irma, exhausted and snippy, said probably none of this mattered because Ground and Sensus had all her files. They could start trying to replicate whenever they wanted.

Mary Agnes thought they probably already had.

"You did everything you could," Lenore said.

"Yes, thanks for that reminder," Irma snapped.

The whole room fell silent. Lenore, stunned, left her hand on Irma's shoulder but didn't say anything else.

"I'm sorry," Irma said in a hoarse whisper. She waved her hands around her ears like she was trying to quiet something. "Sorry," she said again.

THE NIGHT BEFORE the shuttle arrived, Mary Agnes went in search of Esther, alone. She had written out what she wanted to say over and over again, but she knew she needed to say it right to Esther's face for her to understand.

Esther was in her office, wiping down the surface of her chair with what looked like a fresh shirt, still creased from the packet. When she saw Mary Agnes she stopped, her hand still clutching the shirt, and then she started again, wiping off the armrests. Whenever Mary Agnes saw that chair it gave her a little weird shiver. Her family had the same kind of chair, a Stressless, at their house in Michigan, the leather cracked in every direction and flaking off the armrests. Esther's was like new, a warm brown, but the cushions were just printed foam. Mary Agnes couldn't understand why Esther had wanted a chair that tried to look like a home-thing. It failed, obviously.

"Mary Agnes," Esther said. "I'm just cleaning up for the next person."

Mary Agnes wondered what the next person would think of the chair.

"Will Leo be there when you get down?" Mary Agnes asked.

Esther paused and looked at the shirt in her hand. "No, I'll go to him," she said. "I'm going home to my son." She turned to Mary Agnes and her face was too open, naked, like she had to show it to Mary Agnes since she couldn't describe her feelings herself.

"I came to ask you a favor," Mary Agnes said. "You can't tell my parents."

A wariness fell over Esther's eyes like a curtain. "That sounds like a favor I can't do."

"It's not bad or anything," she said. "There's someone in my town. Her name is Effie Evans, she lives in Ann Arbor, Michigan, and she's fourteen, I think."

Esther dropped the shirt on the chair and crossed her arms.

"I need you to tell her I'm sorry. I need you to give her a short message: tell her, I was only thinking about her brother when I made it, how angry I was with him. I forgot about other people, I was so angry. And I'm so sorry that it hurt her."

When Esther did not answer, Mary Agnes spoke faster. "That's it. I'm not asking you to, like, go there or anything. Just get her that message. You can do that, right? It's important."

"Yes, I can do that."

Mary Agnes let out her breath. "Thank you," she said. "Um, safe travels."

She was about to close the door behind her when Esther said her name. She turned around.

"I'm sorry, too," Esther said.

"I know," Mary Agnes said. Her voice wobbled and she didn't want it to. "Life is weird."

THE NEXT MORNING, Mary Agnes and Inaya were watching the little kids, who had lost their minds. Julian was hurling himself between the walls of his family's living room. Lola usually played it pretty cool for a child, but the anticipation in the air was too much for her, and she was pogoing around whispering incantations to herself. Mary Agnes and Inaya sat slumped against the wall, arms crossed over their knees to protect themselves.

Shane grabbed her arms. "Can the ship bring us a dog?"

Lola stopped jumping and swept her arms wide. "Make them bring a dog!"

"They're bringing food and billionaires," Mary Agnes said. "Not pets."

"Anyway, aren't you allergic?" Inaya asked.

"I *was* allergic," Shane said. "Up here, I'm different."

"Fair point," Mary Agnes said.

She knew a little about dogs in space. There was the poor, doomed Laika, the first dog the Russian cosmonauts had shot up into space, and then Belka and Strelka, who lived through it. The testers. The pioneers.

"Come on, space dogs," Inaya said. "This pod's too small, let's go for a walk."

They took the children, panting and howling, out to the promenade and imagined it into a dog run. Homero was supposed to pick up Lola and Julian in an hour. He would be keeping them at home during the shuttle docking and unloading. If something happened, "a malfunction of consequence," he'd said, choosing his words so he wouldn't be understood by small children, he wanted them reading with him at home. But Mary Agnes's mom wanted their family all together.

Lola pulled up a floor tile like she was looking for bugs underneath, and Mary Agnes pointed at her and said, "No, bad dog." Wrong move, and she knew as soon as she'd said it. Lola grinned and sprinted away.

"Lola!" she shouted. "Come back!" Inaya ran after her, and then Julian and Shane, too, and barking, because this was the game now. Their whole herd ran down the promenade, feet slapping, and this was exactly why Homero had asked them to babysit, so this wouldn't happen.

Homero opened the door of the fab lab and stepped out into Lola's path, scooped her right up. "Thanks for your help," he said flatly as the boys blasted past him into the lab, where they were absolutely not allowed.

"Sorry," Mary Agnes wheezed.

"They're so hyper today," Inaya said.

"Yep," Homero said. "I'll take it from here." He whistled at them, and they followed him down the promenade, now scrabbling along on their hands and knees.

Her mother came out of the lab, wiping her dusty hands on her pants. "I have to bring Rachel and Mozgov new combos."

"We'll come with you," Mary Agnes said.

"It's a one-bedroom," Inaya said. "Are they . . . you know?"

"You can come, but do not make trouble," her mother said. "Okay?"

RACHEL OPENED THE DOOR of her pod, and Inaya strained to look past her. Mary Agnes did, too, even though she really wanted to stare the dead-eyed creep in the face. It felt good to be rude to Rachel, after everything.

Mary Agnes's mother handed Rachel the two packets of clothing but didn't let go of them.

"Where's Mozgov?" she asked, pointing at his empty chair.

"He's in the bedroom," Rachel said, and Inaya cleared her throat. "Macy's with him. He had a fall."

Her mother paused like she didn't totally believe Rachel, like maybe Rachel was someone who'd tip the chair, and Mary Agnes shuddered.

"Is he all right?"

Mary Agnes saw it in Rachel's face at the same time that her mother did: fear.

"He will be, I think," Rachel said.

"Maybe I should—"

"No," Rachel said, and it came out like a buried shout. "Don't bother him right now."

Mary Agnes looked sideways at Inaya, who stretched out her palm.

"We should go," Inaya said.

They ducked into the corridor that led to Big Daddy's and waited for her mother to come out. Macy came out first, though, speeding along as usual. They swarmed.

"Is he okay?" Mary Agnes asked.

"How did he fall?" Inaya asked.

"She didn't push him, did she?" Mary Agnes asked. "Because she's a monster and he's, like, outlived his purpose?"

Macy didn't stop, but she did look over her shoulder, and where Mary Agnes expected to see impatience or annoyance, she instead saw worry. Fear. On Macy. Her face looked like old paper.

"You know I can't talk about any of this with you," she said.

Mary Agnes's mother came out three minutes later and beckoned for them to follow.

"He doesn't want to leave here," she told them. "He's scared to go back down."

"He should be," Inaya said. "But—"

"He tried to climb the ladder," her mother said. "To go back up to the Helper."

"What the hell!" Mary Agnes said. "Some people!"

Her mother shook her head. She stopped and turned to face them, looking over their faces like she was trying to decide how much to say. Mary Agnes tried to make her eyes patient and tired and mature.

"He wanted to leave," her mother said. "Through the airlock. To kill himself. He tried to get Rachel to help him."

"What did she do?" Inaya asked.

"She went to get Macy. And then, when she was gone, he tried to do it without her." She exhaled. "We need to talk to Carl—Macy's headed up there now. This man is suffering. We have to get him back upstairs."

Usually, it made Mary Agnes smile when her mother called the Helper *upstairs*. Not today, though.

"She said she was sorry," said her mother. "Rachel did. Sorry that she has to leave. She said she hoped to come back."

"We don't want her back," Inaya said. "Why would we want her back?"

"I think she was talking to Mozgov, actually," said her mother. "She's worried about leaving him. You know."

"Everybody's sorry these days," said Mary Agnes.

THE PEBBLY FLOOR of the promenade was dirty in the crevices, especially at the bottom of the ladder, and scuffed along the pebble tops from dragging the furniture cart over it. It looked kind of like a real road now. The lighting in the walls was set to sunset—Sedative Filter, Inaya called it—and everything had a honeyish, sleepy glow.

Mary Agnes sat wedged between Inaya and her mother, who held

Shane on her lap. Her father sat next to them. Malik sat at Inaya's side, then her mother and Sebastian. Across the promenade were Lenore, hugging her knees up, Irma, and Esther, cross-legged, resting her head in one hand. Macy paced, and Mary Agnes wondered briefly why her heels weren't dry and white like the rest of theirs. Inaya was looking at all the feet, too, her lip slightly curled. It would probably be weird to the new people that they were all barefoot, until they, too, experienced the slippery slime of the combo sock. Mary Agnes brushed off the soles of her feet, and Inaya glared at her.

Carl was in the Helper. Teddy and Homero and the kids had stayed home. No Rachel, no Mozgov. No sign of Tess.

"Carl says ten minutes," Macy said.

If her parents had looked tired and drawn yesterday, today they seemed barely alive. Mary Agnes couldn't stop seeing Mozgov in her mind, drifting around out there, freeze-dried, even though he hadn't done it. They were all alive—despite Mozgov, despite her father.

She looked at him now, slumped against the glowing peach wall of seven p.m. He looked like he'd lost a game and it was a bad game.

"Is it true that if you went out into space without a suit, your body will just, like, explode?" Sebastian asked. "Like, your eyeballs and everything?"

Mary Agnes expected Malik to scold him for asking, but instead he just looked a little sick. "No, it's not like that."

Colette gently bumped her head back on the wall.

Inaya closed her eyes. She and her mother were holding hands across Malik's legs.

"Is it going to yank us, when it docks?" Shane asked, and her mother tightened her arms around him. "Do we need to strap in?"

"No, bud," she said. "They're not barreling toward us, it's more of a slow drift. With position corrections, as needed. Carl is making sure everything happens safely." She faltered at *safely*, but it was already leaving her mouth.

"We'll feel a bump," her father said.

"Mary Agnes—" her mother said.

"I'm holding on," she answered.

The bump, when it came, made the walls shudder.

Esther let out a single sob.

"It's okay," Mary Agnes said. "We're okay."

"Mom, too tight," Shane said.

SHE DIDN'T KNOW WHY, but how she'd imagined it was the airlock door opening, and then the new doctor and the two rich men appearing behind a cloud of smoke, baskets of fruit and cheese bursting behind them. But nothing happened after the docking. Mary Agnes started to think something terrible must have happened—a malfunction of consequence. Why wouldn't it? she wondered.

"Well, let's not just stand here craning our necks like turkeys in the rain," her mom said. "We have to help them get out."

Inaya and Mary Agnes looked at each other and bolted for the ladder, Macy right on their heels.

Mary Agnes felt her body getting lighter as she climbed, turning into nothing. At the top of the ladder they had to wait for Carl to open the door. The gravity was so low that her feet felt like they might float right off the rung she stood on. She wobbled. She knew that if she fell, she would fall for real.

They bounded through the Helper, past Carl, who shouted at them that this was not a game, and into the second airlock. When the door opened, Inaya, Macy, and Mary Agnes crowded inside the airlock. Inaya was in first, ready at the second door. They had to wait nine eternal minutes for the pressure to equalize, during which time Macy spoke just once, to ask if they were nervous.

"No," Mary Agnes and Inaya said at the same time. They were both lying.

The second door opened. Mary Agnes held back a half second, and Inaya dove right through it.

The first man she saw was a quivering mess, whimpering in his suit. Looking at him, Mary Agnes felt kind of tough, and she could tell Inaya did, too. There were three people, all alive. Macy started to unclip the whimpering man, and Mary Agnes went to help the woman. Her gloved hands were shaking, and she looked at Mary Agnes with poorly hidden alarm that a teenager in dirty long johns had been sent to receive her.

"Do you need a minute?" Mary Agnes asked once she'd lifted the woman's helmet off. "To catch your breath?"

A bad, wavy look came over the woman's face and Mary Agnes held up the helmet like a shield, just in time. Most of the vomit went down the lady's suit. Then, wiping her mouth with the back of her hand, she said, "I'm never going to catch my breath."

Mary Agnes handed over her canteen and averted her eyes as the woman drank from it. It would have to be her canteen now. "I'm Mary Agnes," she said. "Welcome to Beta."

"Thank you," she said. "I'm Ashley."

"Actually, Rachel's leaving tomorrow," she heard Inaya say to the man in front of her.

Wild-eyed, the woman looked back at Mary Agnes, who could only nod.

"But no one told us that!" the woman said.

Mary Agnes, ruined for such expectations, barked in laughter. "No one tells us a lot."

To HER, ALL THREE of the new people looked like aliens, with their never-before-seen faces, the same dry droopiness to their skin, the same bewildered thrill in their eyes. The trembling man was Janus Bergeron, a shipper, and the other man said to call him Cygnus, which was the name of his pod. The Black Hole. Mary Agnes considered this long-anticipated freak and found him underwhelming. He was just a man with a pretend exoskeleton, a thin smile, a fake name.

The billionaires didn't come to the feedbag for dinner, but Ashley did. Esther said she'd started in the Behavioral Health Module about three years ago. It didn't look to Mary Agnes like they had been friends—more like two moms who didn't like each other but whose kids were friends. Ashley caught Mary Agnes and Inaya squinting at her, and they did not turn away.

After dinner, the Pioneers met in the Cobbs' living room to speak freely, and they quickly agreed that Mozgov could stay if that was what he needed, no matter what Ground said, even if it meant he lived in the Helper forever. The grown-ups were talking as if this decision were theirs—not Ground's, not the Sons', not Tess's. She couldn't remember if they'd ever sounded like this before, as if they could decide what to do and then simply do it.

"He could have killed us," Malik said.

"We're not going to kill him," Colette said.

"We've all seen what this place can do to a person," Homero said, and Mary Agnes looked at her dad, who was staring ahead at a spot on the floor. She wondered if he had felt it, too, a soft brush against the idea that he might be forgiven—or, if not that, something like it. Cared for, any-way. Every night at dinner, she sat with Inaya, but she stole glances at her parents. She wanted to know if her mother would forgive him. Some-times, she would see her mother tilt her head toward him to hear better and think, yes, she will, and then her own relief and disgust would rush up together. But sometimes she would see her mother's arm around Shane, protecting him, while her eyes roved around the feedbag absently and then Mary Agnes would think no, she won't.

Then Teddy brought up the empty seat. Mary Agnes hadn't even thought about it.

"There are four seats in the shuttle: Tess, Esther, Rachel, and Mozgov.

If Mozgov stays, there's an empty seat." He turned up his palms. "If my family could all leave together, we would, but we can't. So?"

Immediately Mary Agnes worried that Inaya would want it, that she would have wrung all she wanted from this particular experience and would return home to go to college, find love, friends, success, and be the girl who'd lived on Parallaxis I.

"We're staying, too," Mary Agnes's mother said. "Together."

"Us, too," Colette said.

Mary Agnes closed her eyes.

"I think Lenore should take it," Macy said quietly. "Your lungs."

Lenore shook her head. "I'm fine."

"You're not," said Macy. "And the building is about to ramp up again—"

"I'm not leaving," Lenore said quietly. She didn't look at Irma.

Macy wanted to leave, she admitted, but would never leave them here without her.

The only one who had not spoken was Irma. She looked at the floor and nodded slowly. "I should go down," she said. "The algae. To keep them from doing something stupid."

"You can't keep them from anything," said Malik.

"Then to make them listen to me, to gather the scientific community against it. They can't sell it to the world then, can they?"

Silence.

"At least they don't have it," Esther said. "You killed it all?"

"Everything," she said.

"Should we be talking about this?" Inaya asked.

"It doesn't matter," Irma said. "It's gone. If they want their own, they have to make it."

THAT NIGHT, Mary Agnes almost fell asleep and then jerked back awake over and over. The whole day had hummed with worry that she couldn't name, and none of it was about her, or even her family specifically. They had all worked together to unpack the shuttle's cargo and reload it with their sealed packs of biowaste and used clothing for study. Irma and Lenore were arguing—not in front of anyone, but still the tension between them felt cold and crackly. When Mary Agnes passed through the Helper with her arms stretched around a cushion-sized container of first-aid supplies, she saw Carl massaging the back of his neck with one hand like he hadn't moved from his position for hours, maybe days. She'd expected the arrival of the new people, whose houses they had been building since they themselves arrived, to be strange and overwhelming, but it was Mozgov trying to die and the return of the shuttle to Earth that had set them all adrift. They never saw Mozgov, and nobody had thought they were going home, before. It didn't make any sense.

Esther had said her goodbyes. Mary Agnes had wondered if Tess would venture out, but she hadn't.

"Has someone told her she's leaving tomorrow?" Inaya had asked.

"She knows," Macy had said.

Mary Agnes gave up on sleeping and flopped her legs out of bed. She could hear Shane grinding his teeth in his sleep. She wrapped her bed blanket around her shoulders and slipped out of their pod almost silently, just the single light click of the front door closing to confirm that she wasn't dreaming.

The walls surrounding the promenade were the faded violet of a blackberry stain, and the Sky overhead was inky and deep except for the stars. There was a glitchy panel just past Esther's pod that she always glanced at when she passed, whether she wanted to or not, and tonight the picture shuddered just enough to show the borders, a crisp line where the colors didn't perfectly line up with the panels around it. If you didn't notice it, the Sky looked good, but once you had, you could see the whole grid overhead.

She neared the Cobbs' pod and heard murmuring inside. Not Inaya's or Sebastian's voice, but their parents'.

She wasn't worried about seeing the new people, who wouldn't be steady enough to venture out at night, but she still avoided the lounge. She turned into the feedbag.

Tess was sitting at the far table with a mug in front of her. She looked up at Mary Agnes and briefly smiled. Mary Agnes froze.

"It's okay," Tess said. "We don't have to talk."

Mary Agnes shuffled to the snack dispenser, the blanket around her droopy and awkward, and selected a pack of the sesame crackers that she liked. Unwrapping them made so much noise, and her first bite was a thunderous crack. Whether Tess was watching her or not-watching her, knowing she was there was unbearable.

Tess coughed, and Mary Agnes flinched.

"Sorry," said Tess.

There was no reason to be scared of her, or to act like she was. Mary Agnes turned around. Tess looked young and pimply, like she was just up late studying.

"What was it like?" she asked. "Watching us in private and then talking to us like you were normal."

Tess rubbed the rim of her mug with her thumb. "Like shouting at a snow globe," she said. "But the snow globe is a whole universe."

"Snow globes work because you shake them," Mary Agnes said.

Tess kept rubbing the rim of her mug. "I tried to help your dad, in the way that I could. You, too."

"Me? How?"

"I thought you'd be better off here," Tess said. "You and your mom, and Shane. Your family. And I said so. I still don't know if—I don't know that I—"

She stopped, gave up.

"You don't know if you were right?"

Tess shook her head. "That's not what I was going to say."

"I think we are," Mary Agnes said. She didn't know if it was true, but she hoped that it was.

"Good," said Tess. "I'm glad."

She almost asked Tess if they were safe up here, but there was only one good answer, and she stopped herself. She wanted to ask if she was going to be okay, but that question had the same problem.

"Do you know what I'm thinking?" she asked instead.

Tess paused. "Sometimes I think I do."

"I meant right now."

Tess took a deep breath and let it out slowly. "You're okay, Mary Agnes. You're going to be okay. And you and Inaya and Sebastian will be good friends to each other."

"Inaya's going to leave and go to law school and become a lawyer for the environment."

Tess laughed softly. "Yes, but not yet."

"Are my parents going to be okay? Together?"

"I'm not an oracle."

"What about the new people?"

"I don't know them," Tess said. "Generally, the powerful are not to be trusted."

"'Abuse of power comes as no surprise.' I have an old shirt of my mom's that says that in, like, pen." She pulled the blanket tighter. "I guess you know that."

Tess pressed her lips together and gave her a small, lopsided smile. Then, quietly, and just like Mary Agnes's mother: "Make good choices."

Mary Agnes hurried home, trying not to crinkle the wrapper in her palm. She hid her crackers in the wall locker over her bed. If Shane saw them out the next day, he would know she'd sneaked out at night.

32

In the morning, Carl and Macy delegated Ground's directives for packing the shuttle. Among other things, they were to send back sealed bricks of biowaste, hair samples, and dust samples collected from seven locations. Mary Agnes and Inaya were sent around to collect the hair samples. They were in Malik's lab, waiting for him to pluck a hair from his head and drop it into Inaya's outstretched envelope, when Irma slid the lab door open. It was the first time that day Mary Agnes had seen her. Her absence at her last breakfast had been excused, forgiven: she was getting ready for the trip home and saying goodbye to Lenore, who hadn't come, either.

Now she stood just inside the open lab, alone, looking puffy and tearstained, and told them she had changed her mind. She wasn't going.

Mary Agnes had never seen her look like that before—beaten.

"You're not," Malik repeated.

"It's pointless. They have my files, and if they want to start trying to replicate it, they will. Besides, without me, you'll starve. You need me to grow food for you. It's not like they sent up enough to get by without it, not for very long."

Malik was very still. "We could grow the food, Irma." His voice was low and heavy, anchored.

She shook her head, looked at the floor. "I'm staying," she said. "I've decided."

The sight of Irma with all the anger drained out of her was frightening. It wasn't right. She and Inaya glanced at each other, and Mary Agnes's uneasiness multiplied when she saw it in her eyes, too. She'd told Inaya about seeing Tess in the feedbag last night, about the snow globe. Had she shaken it? Could she still have that power?

Inaya made for the door and Mary Agnes followed her, Irma and Malik arguing behind them.

"What the fuck?" said Inaya.

"Should we tell someone? Carl and Macy?"

They walked quickly and then ran, past Irma's lab of greenhouses, past the silent fab lab and the robotics lab, past Janus Bergeron creeping along the promenade watching his feet until he wrenched around in a silent scream as they rushed by, past Esther's interrogation room and Macy's clinic, the old barracks, the feedbag, up the ladder, lighter and lighter, into the airlock, through the nightmare toilet, and then, when the second door slid open, they bounced out into the Helper, and Mary Agnes heard her father's voice.

"You took it!" he shouted. "You broke into her lab!"

He stood unsteadily before Carl, who had spun around in his seat at Control, hands up in front of his chest.

"Only because I knew what you would say," Carl answered. "And I was right! They were right. She got orders to package some of the plant and she didn't do it."

Mary Agnes, out of breath already, felt the blood draining from her face. Her father looked frozen but furious, scary even. She'd never seen him look like that.

"He has the algae?" she asked. "Irma's algae?"

"Give it back," her father said. "Just give it back. They can't have it."

"Back up," Carl said. "And listen. After all that shit with Mozgov, doing what he thought was best even when it endangered the rest of us—I blew that whistle, understand? I will keep us safe, and I will follow these orders."

"Why did Ground even ask us, if you already had it?"

Carl heaved his shoulders like the answer was both sad and obvious. "To give you a chance to say yes."

Mary Agnes saw the rage rise up inside her father like a catching fire. He took two deep breaths before he spoke.

"You're a company man," he said. "After everything."

Carl shrugged, but not like he didn't care. "And so are you." He nodded at Mary Agnes and Inaya. "What?"

"Irma says she isn't going," said Mary Agnes. "She says it's pointless." Her father's face collapsed.

"She's going to change her mind," Mary Agnes said to Carl, to herself. "When she finds out what you've done, she'll go."

MARY AGNES, INAYA, AND SEBASTIAN had just slumped against the wall outside the suit room when Rachel came out holding her suit in her arms, the boots attached and dragging on the floor.

"Do you want some help?" Sebastian asked.

"No, thank you," she said. "I'm fine on my own." She dragged her suit to the base of the ladder, and then she dropped it in a heap to pull her helmet over her head.

"You sure?" Inaya asked.

"I'm sure," said Rachel.

She climbed the ladder with just one arm, hauling her suit up with the other. The boots banged against the ladder and twice got caught under the rungs, but she shook the suit and yanked it loose.

"Is she *us*, or *them*?" Sebastian asked.

"Them," Inaya said. "Or both, maybe."

"I guess we'll find out," Mary Agnes said.

By three o'clock, they were in a small crowd at the bottom of the ladder. The little kids were in the lounge with Homero, Teddy, and Mary Agnes's mother, having their picnic. Her dad was here, though, and all the Cobbs, and Macy, who was sealing Esther into her space suit kind of lovingly.

"You are going home to Leo," Macy said. Esther reached up with a fat gloved hand to wipe her eye. It bonked off her helmet and she laughed. They all laughed, relieved. She hugged every one of them, and then she went up the ladder, heavy at first, easier and lighter toward the top.

Mary Agnes had tears in her eyes, too. She stood next to her father at the bottom of the ladder. She and her father: close together, on purpose.

Still no Irma, no Lenore. No Tess.

She wondered if he would break out of the crowd and say that if Irma wasn't going back, he would.

"How come you aren't going back?" she asked him quietly, but anyone could hear.

He looked startled. "I'm staying with my family."

"Okay," she said. She didn't know whether that was right or wrong of him.

"I wouldn't leave you all here," he said, and he wouldn't look away from her.

Mary Agnes could, though. She looked at Inaya just as she was elbowing Sebastian next to her. Tess was coming, and behind her were Lenore and Irma.

Tess hadn't changed into Earth clothes. She still wore the stretched-out and dirty red combo she'd been in the night before. She looked different, though. Mary Agnes had never thought of her as short, but with Lenore looming behind her, she looked very small. The main difference, though, was in her eyes, how they moved around more slowly than they used to, almost sleepily.

As Tess approached the group a heavy silence fell over everyone, and all they could hear was the low hum of the machinery that kept them all alive.

"Hey, everybody," she said.

"I'll follow you up with your suit," Macy said, one hand up as she turned away from the crowd. "It's tough with the ladder."

Mary Agnes and Inaya were watching Irma, whose hand was clasped in Lenore's. Irma's face had always looked so full, so complete, never unsure of what she was feeling. Now she looked agitated, torn, her lips shifting uncomfortably over her teeth, her always-steady gaze disrupted and quick.

"What do you think, Irma?" Inaya asked. "You going or what?"

Colette grabbed her daughter's hand and squeezed it.

Tess was at the bottom of the ladder, her skinny fingers tight around the bottom rung, listening.

"No," said Irma.

"Goodbye, Tess," Sebastian boomed, trying to sound like a grown man.

Tess didn't move.

"Carl had his samples already," Irma said to the back of Tess's head. She didn't say it like a question, exactly, but it hung over them like one. "Before I killed it."

Tess looked down, and her greasy hair fell forward around her face in dark ropes.

"I'm sure they knew you were going to kill it, Irma," she said softly, like she was comforting her. "The Algo probably saw your path forward as soon as you grew the algae." She didn't turn around to face them. "I wonder if that's why you're staying, actually."

Irma's eyebrows twitched together. "What?"

"It's probably been at work in you for a while," Tess said. "The Algo. You wouldn't see changes in yourself, but it depends on how they're using it. That's not . . . that was never my project."

Mary Agnes felt like she was going up the Helper ladder herself, her body losing its weight, its certainty.

"Don't fuck with us, Tess," her father said.

"I don't mean to," she said. She gave a tired shrug. "I don't know what they'll do with the algae, either, whether it will be studied or if—"

"They'll study it," Irma said quickly. "They'll have to, it's only—"

"—if it will be unleashed," finished Tess. "I really don't know."

"What about Irma changing her mind?" Inaya asked, her eyes drilling into the back of Tess's head. "What do you mean, 'see changes'?"

Tess turned and swept her eyes over them, her lips open, but she didn't speak. Mary Agnes shivered. A loud clang echoed down the promenade, probably one of the new people fucking something up.

Tess shook her head and placed her foot on the first rung of the ladder. "I don't know how much it could . . . it's not for me to say anymore."

She wasn't keeping a secret. She really didn't know. Tess wasn't the invasive species, not like Mary Agnes had feared. She was its mother, its author, its nurse. Like Irma, and like her father. And like Mary Agnes, a long time ago, down there.

Macy came out with Tess's space suit slung over her arm like a rag doll. Two airlocks, one suit, the low *fripp fripp* of the seals closing up, and Tess's body would be gone from them. But she would stay here, and everywhere.

"It can be used for good," she said. "The Algo will sense danger before we do, even danger within ourselves—"

"What do we do?" Inaya asked. "How can we keep it from changing us however they want?"

"I'm sorry." Tess smiled gently, even as she looked a little sick. "I don't know how to beat it myself."

She started to climb, unwilling to be looked at any longer.

Her father and Colette and were looking at each other like their worry was worth anything. The old anger unfurled inside her, a silk scarf in the water.

"But you never tried!" Mary Agnes shouted at Tess's back.

Inaya put a finger to her lips and took a step toward Mary Agnes, her hand outstretched, palm upturned. Mary Agnes laid her hand in Inaya's, careful to keep her eyes up. Together, they watched Tess wobble and stop near the top. She was getting lighter.

Inaya touched her fingertip to Mary Agnes's palm.

WE WILL.

Acknowledgments

First, hope and action: the publication of this novel allowed me to make a gift to the Maidu Summit Consortium for the re-acquisition and habitat restoration of land native to the Mountain Maidu people in northeastern California. To learn more about their vital work, visit www.maidusummit.org. We have one home planet, and I don't want to live anywhere else.

I sometimes thought this book would do me in. That it did not is due to Jon Atwell, Katie Lennard, Lidia Malera, Anna Brenner, Jessica Langan-Peck, Maya West, Jia Tolentino, Carrie Frye, Akiva Gottlieb, Barrett Gough, Cold Comfort Friends, Perfume Genius, sertraline, and also *Philip Glass: Piano Works* performed by Jenny Lin, which both sustained me all the way to the end and possibly contributed to the sense that I was circling the drain.

This book benefitted enormously from an early reading by physicist and great friend Dr. Sam McDermott, the generous consideration and what-iffing of the very cool bioastronauticist Dr. Emily Matula, and my patient husband's deeply furrowed brow. Thank you to Tara Fuller, Serge Egelman and Jon Jones for answering my context-less "is this a thing?" texts and emails. All bad facts, nonfacts, and instances of foolishness are mine.

Thank you to Susan Golomb, Alicia Cooper, Sara Delozier, Chris Russell, Norma Barksdale, Camille Leblanc, Colin Webber, and especially to my editors Allison Lorentzen and Carole De Santi, who bore with me and then some.

Early reading that inspired me to write this novel: Mary Roach's *Packing for Mars: The Curious Science of Life in the Void*, a piece Kevin Fong wrote for *Wired* in 2014 called "The Strange, Deadly Effects Mars Would Have on Your Body" (at one point I had, with his permission, written Kevin Fong into a character at Ground), and a pretty haunting tweet from Elisa Gabbert on April 30, 2014, that read "Indifference is a kind of privacy."

Thank you to my children, who force me to find the hope wherever it's hiding.

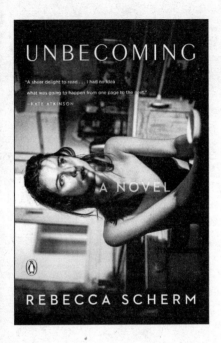